THE HONORABLE
PETER STIRLING

AND

WHAT PEOPLE THOUGHT
OF HIM

BY

PAUL LEICESTER FORD

NEW YORK

HENRY HOLT AND COMPANY

PRINTED IN THE
UNITED STATES OF AMERICA

THE HONORABLE PETER STIRLING

CHAPTER I

ROMANCE AND REALITY

Mr. Pierce was talking. Mr. Pierce was generally talking. From the day that his proud mamma had given him a sweetmeat for a very inarticulate "goo" which she translated into "papa," Mr. Pierce had found speech profitable. He had been able to talk his nurse into granting him every indulgence. He had talked his way through school and college. He had talked his wife into marrying him. He had talked himself to the head of a large financial institution. He had talked his admission into society. Conversationally, Mr. Pierce was a success. He could discuss Schopenhauer or cotillion favors; St. Paul, the apostle, or St. Paul, the railroad. He had cultivated the art as painstakingly as a professional musician. He had countless anecdotes, which he introduced to his auditors by a "that reminds me of." He had endless quotations, with the quotation marks omitted. Finally he had an idea on every subject, and generally a theory as well. Carlyle speaks somewhere of an "inarticulate genius." He was not alluding to Mr. Pierce.

Like most good talkers, Mr. Pierce was a tongue despot. Conversation must take his course, or he would none of it. Generally he controlled. If an upstart endeavored to turn the subject, Mr. Pierce waited till the intruder had done speaking, and then quietly, but firmly, would remark: "Relative to the subject we were discussing a moment ago——" If any one ventured to speak, even *sotto voce*, before Mr. Pierce had finished all he had to say, he would

1

at once cease his monologue, wait till the interloper had finished, and then resume his lecture just where he had been interrupted. Only once had Mr. Pierce found this method to fail in quelling even the sturdiest of rivals. The recollection of that day is still a mortification to him. It had happened on the deck of an ocean steamer. For thirty minutes he had fought his antagonist bravely. Then, humbled and vanquished, he had sought the smoking-room, to moisten his parched throat, and solace his wounded spirit, with a star cocktail. He had at last met his superior. He yielded the deck to the fog-horn.

At the present moment Mr. Pierce was having things very much his own way. Seated in the standing-room of a small yacht were some eight people. With a leaden sky overhead, and a leaden sea about it, the boat gently rose and fell with the ground swell. Three miles away could be seen the flash-light marking the entrance to the harbor. But though slowly gathering clouds told that wind was coming, the yacht now lay becalmed, drifting with the ebb tide. The pleasure-seekers had been together all day, and were decidedly talked out. For the last hour they had been singing songs—always omitting Mr. Pierce, who never so trifled with his vocal organs. During this time he had been restless. At one point he had attempted to deliver his opinion on the relation of verse to music, but an unfeeling member of the party had struck up "John Brown's Body," and his lecture had ended, in the usual serial style, at the most interesting point, without even the promise of a "continuation in our next." Finally, however, the singers had sung themselves hoarse in the damp night air, the last "Spanish Cavalier" had been safely restored to his inevitable true-love, and the sound of voices and banjo floated away over the water. Mr. Pierce's moment had come.

Some one, and it is unnecessary to mention the sex, had given a sigh, and regretted that nineteenth century life was so prosaic and unromantic. Clearing his throat, quite as much to pre-empt the pause as to articulate the better, Mr. Pierce spoke:

"That modern times are less romantic and interesting than bygone centuries is a fallacy. From time immemo-

rial, love and the battle between evil and good are the
two things which have given the world romance and interest. Every story, whether we find it in the myths of
the East, the folklore of Europe, the poems of the
Troubadours, or in our newspaper of this morning, is
based on one or the other of these factors, or on both
combined. Now it is a truism that love never played so
important a part as now in shaping the destinies of
men and women, for this is the only century in which it
has obtained even a partial divorce from worldly and
parental influences. Moreover the great battle of society,
to crush wrong and elevate right, was never before so
bravely fought, on so many fields, by so many people as
to-day. But because our lovers and heroes no longer
brag to the world of their doings; no longer stand in the
moonlight, and sing of their 'derring does,' the world
assumes that the days of tourneys and guitars were the
only days of true love and noble deeds. Even our pro-
fessed writers of romance join in the cry. 'Draw life as it
is,' they say. 'We find nothing in it but mediocrity,
selfishness, and money-loving.' By all means let us have
truth in our novels, but there is truth and truth. Most of
New York's firemen presumably sat down at noon to-day
to a dinner of corned-beef and cabbage. But perhaps one
of them at the same moment was fighting his way through
smoke and flame, to save life at the risk of his own.
Boiled dinner and burned firemen are equally true. Are
they equally worthy of description? What would the
age of chivalry be, if the chronicles had recorded only the
brutality, filthiness and coarseness of their contemporaries?
The wearing of underclothing unwashed till it fell to
pieces; the utter lack of soap; the eating with fingers; the
drunkenness and foul-mouthedness that drove women
from the table at a certain point, and so inaugurated the
custom, now continued merely as an excuse for a cigar?
Some one said once that a man finds in a great city just
the qualities he takes to it. That's true of romance as
well. Modern novelists don't find beauty and nobility in
life, because they don't look for them. They predicate
from their inner souls that the world is 'cheap and nasty'
and that is what they find it to be. There is more true

romance in a New York tenement than there ever was in a baron's tower—braver battles, truer love, nobler sacrifices. Romance is all about us, but we must have eyes for it. You are young people, with your lives before you. Let me give you a little advice. As you go through life look for the fine things—not for the despicable. It won't make you any richer. It won't make you famous. It won't better you in a worldly way. But it will make your lives happier, for by the time you are my age, you'll love humanity, and look upon the world and call it good. And you will have found romance enough to satisfy all longings for mediæval times."

"But, dear, one cannot imagine some people ever finding anything romantic in life," said a voice, which, had it been translated into words would have said, "I know you are right, of course, and you will convince me at once, but in my present state of unenlightenment it seems to me that——" The voice, already low, became lower. "Now" —a moment's hesitation—"there is—Peter Stirling."

"Exactly," said Mr. Pierce. "That is a very case in point, and proves just what I've been saying. Peter is like the novelists of whom I've been talking. I don't suppose we ought to blame him for it. What can you expect of a son of a mill-foreman, who lives the first sixteen years of his life in a mill-village? If his hereditary tendencies gave him a chance, such an experience would end it. If one lives in the country, one may get fine thoughts by contact with Nature. In great cities one is developed and stimulated by art, music, literature, and contact with clever people. But a mill-village is one vast expanse of mediocrity and prosaicness, and it would take a bigger nature than Peter's to recognize the beautiful in such a life. In truth, he is as limited, as exact, and as unimaginative as the machines of his own village. Peter has no romance in him; hence he will never find it, nor increase it in this world. This very case only proves my point; that to meet romance one must have it. Boccaccio said he did not write novels, but lived them. Try to imagine Peter living a romance! He could be concerned in a dozen and never dream it. They would not interest him even if he did notice them. And I'll prove it to you." Mr. Pierce raised his voice. "We are discussing romance, Peter. Won't you stop that unsocial tramp of yours long enough to give us your opinion on the subject?"

A moment's silence followed, and then a singularly clear voice, coming from the forward part of the yacht, replied: "I never read them, Mr. Pierce."

Mr. Pierce laughed quietly. "See," he said, "that fellow never dreams of there being romance outside of novels. He is so prosaic that he is unconscious of anything bigger than his own little sphere of life. Peter may obtain what he wants in this world, for his desires will be of the kind to be won by work and money. But he will never be controlled by a great idea, nor be the hero of a true romance."

Steele once wrote that the only difference between the Catholic Church and the Church of England was, that the former was infallible and the latter never wrong. Mr. Pierce would hardly have claimed for himself either of these qualities. He was too accustomed in his business to writing, "E. and O. E." above his initials, to put much faith in human dicta. But in the present instance he felt sure of what he said, and the little group clearly agreed. If they were right, this story is like that recounted in Mother Goose, which was ended before it was begun. But Mr. Pierce had said that romance is everywhere to those who have the spirit of it in them. Perhaps in this case the spirit was lacking in his judges—not in Peter Stirling.

CHAPTER II

APPEARANCES

THE unconscious illustration of Mr. Pierce's theory was pacing backwards and forwards on the narrow space between the cuddy-roof and the gunwale, which custom dignifies with the name of deck. Six strides forward and turn. Six strides aft and turn. That was the extent of the beat. Yet had Peter been on sentry duty, he could not have continued it more regularly or persistently. If he were walking off his supper, as most of those seated aft would have suggested, the performance was not particularly interesting. The limit and rapidity of the walk resembled the tramp of a confined animal, exercising its last meal. But when one stands in front of the lion's cage, and sees that restless and tireless stride, one cannot but wonder how much of it is due to the last shin-bone, and how much to the wild and powerful nature under the tawny skin. The question occurs because the nature and antecedents of the lion are known. For this same reason the yachters were a unit in agreeing that Stirling's unceasing walk was merely a digestive promenade. The problem was, whether they were right? Or whether, to apply Mr. Pierce's formula, they merely imposed their own frame of mind in place of Stirling's, and decided, since their sole reason for walking at the moment would be entirely hygienic, that he too must be striding from the same cause?

Dr. Holmes tells us that when James and Thomas converse there are really six talkers. First, James as James thinks he is, and Thomas as Thomas thinks he is. Second, James as Thomas thinks him, and Thomas as James thinks him. Finally, there are James and Thomas as they really are. Since this is neither an autobiography nor an inspired story, the world's view of Peter Stirling must be adopted without regard to its accuracy. And because this view was the sum of his past and personal, these elements must be computed before we can know on what the world based its conclusions concerning him.

His story was as ordinary and prosaic as Mr. and Mrs. Pierce seemed to think his character. Neither riches nor poverty had put a shaping hand to it. The only child of his widowed mother, he had lived in one of the smaller manufacturing cities of New England a life such as falls to most lads. Unquestionably he had been rather more shielded from several forms of temptation than had most of his playmates, for his mother's isolation had made him not merely her son, but very largely her companion. In certain ways this had tended to make him more manly than the average fellow of his age, but in others it had retarded his development; and this backwardness had been further accentuated by a deliberate mind, which hardly kept pace with his physical growth. His school record was fair: "Painstaking, but slow," was the report in studies. "Exemplary," in conduct. He was not a leader among the boys, but he was very generally liked. A characteristic fact, for good or bad, was that he had no enemies. From the clergyman to the "hired help," everybody had a kind word for him, but tinctured by no enthusiasm. All spoke of him as "a good boy," and when this was said, they had nothing more to say.

One important exception to this statement is worthy of note. The girls of the High School never liked him. If they had been called upon for reasons, few could have given a tangible one. At their age, everything this world contains, be it the Falls of Niagara, or a stick of chewing gum, is positively or negatively "nice." For some crime of commission or omission, Peter had been weighed and found wanting. "He isn't nice," was the universal verdict of the scholars who daily filed through the door, which the town selectmen, with the fine contempt of the narrow man for his unpaid "help," had labelled, "For Females." If they had said that he was "perfectly horrid," there might have been a chance for him. But the subject was begun and ended with these three words. Such terseness in the sex was remarkable and would have deserved a psychological investigation had it been based on any apparent data. But women's opinions are so largely a matter of instinct and feeling, and so little of judgment and induction, that an analysis of the mental processes of the hundred girls who had reached this one conclusion, would probably have revealed in each a different method of obtaining this product. The important point is to recognize this consensus of opinion, and to note its bearing on the development of the lad.

That Peter could remain ignorant of this feeling was not conceivable. It puzzled him not a little when he first began to realize the prejudice, and he did his best to reverse it. Unfortunately he took the very worst way. Had he avoided the girls persistently and obviously, he might have interested them intensely, for nothing is more difficult for a woman to understand than a woman-hater; and from the days of mother Eve the unknown is rumored to

have had for her sex a powerful fascination. But he tried
to win their friendship by humbleness and kindness, and
so only made himself the more cheap in their eyes. "Fatty
Peter," as they jokingly called him, epitomized in two
words their contempt of him.

Nor did things mend when he went to Harvard.
Neither his mother's abilities nor his choice were able to
secure for him an *entrée* to the society which Cambridge
and Boston dole out stintedly to certain privileged collegians. Every Friday afternoon he went home, to return
by an early train Monday morning. In his first year it
is to be questioned if he exchanged ten words with women
whose names were known to him, except during these
home-visits. That this could long continue, was impossible. In his second year he was several times taken by
his chum, Watts D'Alloi, to call. But always with one
result. Invariably Peter would be found talking to
Mamma, or, better still, from his point of view, with
Pater-familias, while Watts chatted with the presumptive
attractions. Watts laughed at him always. Laughed still
more when one of these calls resulted in a note, "request-
ing the pleasure" of Mr. Peter Stirling's company to dinner. It was Watts who dictated the acceptance, helped
Peter put the finishing touches to his toilet, and eventually
landed him safely in Mrs. Purdie's parlor. His description to the boys that night of what followed is worthy of
quotation:

"The old fellow shook hands with Mrs. P., O. K.
Something was said about the weather, and then Mrs. P.
said, 'I'll introduce you to the lady you are to take down,
Mr. Stirling, but I shan't let you talk to her before dinner.
Look about you and take your choice of whom you would
like to meet?' Chum gave one agonized look round the
room. There wasn't a woman over twenty-five in sight!
And what do you think the wily old fox said? Call him
simple! Not by a circumstance! A society beau couldn't
have done it better. Can't guess! Well, he said, 'I'd
like to talk to you, Mrs. Purdie.' Fact! Of course she
took it as a compliment, and was as pleased as could be.
Well, I don't know how on earth he ever got through
his introduction or how he ever reached the dining-

room, for my inamorata was so pretty that I thought of nothing till we were seated, and the host took her attention for a moment. Then I looked across at chum, who was directly opposite, to see how he was getting on. Oh, you fellows would have died to see it! There he sat, looking straight out into vacancy, so plainly laboring for something to say that I nearly exploded. Twice he opened his lips to speak, and each time closed them again. The girl of course looked surprised, but she caught my eye, and entered into the joke, and we both waited for developments. Then she suddenly said to him, 'Now let's talk about something else.' It was too much for me. I nearly choked. I don't know what followed. Miss Jevons turned and asked me something. But when I looked again, I could see the perspiration standing on Peter's forehead, while the conversation went by jerks and starts as if it was riding over a ploughed field. Miss Callender, whom he took in, told me afterwards that she had never had a harder evening's work in her life. Nothing but 'yeses' and 'noes' to be got from him. She wouldn't believe what I said of the old fellow."

Three or four such experiences ended Peter's dining out. He was recognized as unavailable material. He received an occasional card to a reception or a dance, for anything in trousers passes muster for such functions. He always went when invited, and was most dutiful in the counter-calls. In fact, society was to him a duty which he discharged with the same plodding determination with which he did his day's studies. He never dreamed of taking his social moments frivolously. He did not recognize that society is very much like a bee colony—stinging those who approached it shyly and quietly, but to be mastered by a bold beating of tin pans. He neither danced nor talked, and so he was shunted by the really pleasant girls and clever women, and passed his time with wall-flowers and unbearables, who, in their normal sourness, regarded and, perhaps, unconsciously made him feel, hardly to his encouragement, that his companionship was a sort of penance. If he had been asked, at the end of his senior year, what he thought of young women and society, he would probably have stigmatized them, as he himself had been formerly: "not nice." All of which, again to apply Mr. Pierce's theory, merely meant that the phases which his own characteristics had shown him, had re-acted on his own mind, and had led him to conclude that girls and society were equally unendurable.

The condition was a dangerous one, and if psychology had its doctors they would have predicted a serious heart illness in store for him. How serious, would depend largely on whether the fever ran its natural course, or whether it was driven inwards by disappointment. If these doctors had ceased studying his mental condition and glanced at his physical appearance, they would have had double cause to shake their heads doubtingly.

Peter was not good-looking. He was not even, in a sense, attractive. In spite of his taking work so hardly and life so seriously, he was entirely too stout. This gave a heaviness to his face that neutralized his really pleasant brown eyes and thick brown hair, which were his best features. Manly the face was, but, except when speaking in unconscious moments, dull and unstriking. A fellow three inches shorter, and two-thirds his weight would have been called tall. "Big" was the favorite adjective used in describing Peter, and big he was. Had he gone through college ten years later, he might have won unstinted fame and admiration as the full-back on the team, or stroke on the crew. In his time, athletics were but just obtaining, and were not yet approved of either by faculties or families. Shakespeare speaks of a tide in the affairs of men. Had Peter been born ten years later the probabilities are that his name would have been in all the papers, that he would have weighed fifty pounds less, have been cheered by thousands, have been the idol of his class, have been a hero, have married the first girl he loved (for heroes, curiously, either marry or die, but never remain bachelors) and would have—but as this is a tale of fact, we must not give rein to imagination. To come back to realism, Peter was a hero to nobody but his mother.

Such was the man, who, two weeks after graduation from Harvard, was pacing up and down the deck of Mr. Pierce's yacht, the "Sunrise," as she drifted with the tide in Long Island Sound. Yet if his expression, as he walked, could for a moment have been revealed to those seated aft, the face that all thought dull and uninteresting would have riveted their attention, and set each one questioning whether there might not be something both heroic and romantic underneath. The set determination of his look can best be explained by telling what had given his face such rigid lines.

—————

CHAPTER III

A CRAB CHAPTER

Mr. PIERCE and those about him had clearly indicated by the conversation, or rather monologue, already recorded, that Peter was in a sense an odd number in the "Sunrise's" complement of pl ... re-seekers. Whether or no Mr. Pierce's monologu ... o indicated that he was not a man who dealt in od ... bers, or showered hospitality on sons of mill-overs ... s, the fact was nevertheless true. "For value rece ... ," or "I hereby promise to pay," were favorite f ... ulas of Mr. Pierce, and if not actually written in such invitations as he permitted his wife to write at his dictation to people whom he decided should be bidden to the Shrubberies, a longer or a shorter time would develop the words, as if written in sympathetic ink. Yet Peter had had as pressing an invitation and as warm a welcome at Mr. Pierce's country place as had any of the house-party ingathered during the first week of July. Clearly something made him of value to the owner of the Shrubberies. That something was his chum, Watts D'Alloi.

Peter and Watts were such absolute contrasts that it seemed impossible that they could have an interest or sympathy, in common. Therefore they had become chums. A chance in their freshman year had brought them together. Watts, with the refined and delicate sense of humor abounding in collegians, had been concerned with sundry freshmen in an attempt to steal (or, in collegiate terms, "rag") the chapel Bible, with a view to presenting it to some equally subtle humorists at Yale, expecting a similar courtesy in return from that college. Unfortunately for the joke, the college authorities had had the bad taste to guard against the annually attempted substitution. Two of the marauders were caught, while Watts only escaped by leaving his coat in the hands of the watchers. Even then he would have been captured had he not met Peter in his flight, and borrowed the latter's coat, in which he reached his room without detection. Peter was caught by the pursuers, and summoned before the faculty, but he easily proved that the captured coat was not his, and that he had but just parted from one of the tutors, making it certain that he could not have been an offender. There was some talk of expelling him for aiding and abetting in the true culprit's escape, and for refusing to tell who it was. Respect for his motives, however, and his unimpeachable record saved him from everything but an admonition from the president, which changed into a discussion of cotton printing before that august official had delivered half of his intended rebuke. People might not enthuse over Peter, but no one ever quarrelled with him. So the interview, after travelling from cotton prints to spring radishes, ended with a warm handshake, and a courteous suggestion that he come again when there should be no charges nor admonitions to go through with. Watts told him that he was a "devilish lucky" fellow to have been on hand to help, for Peter had proved his pluck to his class, had made a friend of the president and, as Watts considerately put it: "but for your being on the corner at 11:10 that evening, old chap, you'd never have known me." Truly on such small chances do the greatest events of our life turn. Perhaps, could Peter have looked into the future, he would have avoided that corner. Perhaps, could he have looked even further, he would have found that in that chance lay the greatest happiness of his life. Who can tell, when the bitter comes, and we later see how we could have avoided it, what we should have encountered in its place? Who can tell, when sweet comes, how far it is sweetened by the bitterness that went before? Dodging the future in this world is a success equal to that of the old woman who triumphantly announced that she had borrowed money enough to pay all her debts.

As a matter of course Watts was grateful for the timely assistance, and was not slow either to say or show it. He told his own set of fellows that he was "going to take that Stirling up and make him one of us," and Watts had a remarkable way of doing what he chose. At first Peter did not respond to the overtures and insistence of the handsome, well-dressed, free-spending, New York swell. He was too conscious of the difference between himself and Watts's set, to wish or seek identification with them. But no one who ever came under Watts's influence could long stand out against his sunny face and frank manner, and so Peter eventually allowed himself to be "taken up." Perhaps the resistance encountered only whetted Watts's intention. He was certainly aided by Peter's isolation. Whether the cause was single or multiple, Peter was soon in a set from which many a seemingly far more eligible fellow was debarred.

Strangely enough, it did not change him perceptibly. He still plodded on conscientiously at his studies, despite laughter and attempts to drag him away from them. He still lived absolutely within the comfortable allowance that his mother gave him. He still remained the quiet, serious looking fellow of yore. The "gang," as they styled themselves, called him "kill-joy," "graveyard," or "death's head," in their evening festivities, but Peter only puffed at his pipe good-naturedly, making no retort, and if the truth had really been spoken, not a man would have changed him a particle. His silence and seriousness added the dash of contrast needed to make the evening perfect. All joked him. The most popular verse in a class-song Watts wrote, was devoted to burlesquing his soberness, the gang never tired of singing at all hours and places:

"Goodness gracious! Who's that in the 'yard' a yelling in the rain?
  That's the boy who never gave his mother any pain,
        But now his moral character is sadly on the wane,
      'Tis little Peter Stirling, bilin' drunk again.
            Oh, the Sunday-school boy,
            His mamma's only joy,
      Is shouting drunk as usual, and raising Cain!"

Yet joke Peter as they would, in every lark, be it drive, sail, feed, drink, or smoke, whoever's else absence was commented upon, his never passed unnoticed.

In Sophomore year, Watts, without quite knowing why, proposed that they should share rooms. Nor would he take Peter's refusal, and eventually succeeded in reversing it.

"I can't afford your style of living," Peter had said quietly, as his principal objection.

"Oh, I'll foot the bills for the fixings, so it shan't cost you a cent more," said Watts, and when Peter had finally been won over to give his assent, Watts had supposed it was on this uneven basis. But in the end, the joint chambers were more simply furnished than those of the rest of the gang, who promptly christened them "the hermitage," and Peter had paid his half of the expense. And though he rarely had visitors of his own asking at the chambers, all cost of wine and tobacco was equally borne by him.

The three succeeding years welded very strong bands round these two. It was natural that they should modify each other strongly, but in truth, as in most cases, when markedly different characteristics are brought in contact, the only effect was to accentuate each in his peculiarities. Peter dug at his books all the harder, by reason of Watts's neglect of them. Watts became the more free-handed with his money because of Peter's prudence. Watts talked more because of Peter's silence, and Peter listened more because of Watts's talk. Watts, it is true, tried to drag Peter into society, yet in truth, Peter was really left more alone than if he had been rooming with a less social fellow. Each had in truth become the complement of the other, and seemed as mutually necessary as the positive and negative wires in electricity. Peter, who had been taking the law lectures in addition to the regular academic course, and had spent his last two summers reading law in an attorney's office, in his native town, taking the New York examination in the previous January, had striven to get Watts to do the same, with the ultimate intention of their hanging out a joint legal shingle in New York.

"I'll see the clients, and work up the cases, Watts, and

you'll make the speeches and do the social end," said Peter, making a rather long speech in the ardor of his wishes.

Watts laughed. "I don't know, old man. I rather fancy I shan't do anything. To do something requires that one shall make up one's mind what to do, and that's such devilish hard work. I'll wait till I've graduated, and had a chin with my governor about it. Perhaps he'll make up my mind for me, and so save my brain tissue. But anyway, you'll come to New York, and start in, for you must be within reach of me. Besides, New York's the only place in this country worth living in."

Such were the relations between the two at graduation time. Watts, who had always prepared his lessons in a tenth part of the time it had taken Peter, buckled down in the last few weeks, and easily won an honorable mention. Peter had tried hard to win honors, but failed.

"You did too much outside work, old man," said Watts, who would cheerfully have given his own triumph to his friend. "If you want success in anything, you've got to sacrifice other things and concentrate on the object. The Mention's really not worth the ink it's written with, in my case, but I knew it would please mammy and pappy, so I put on steam, and got it. If I'd hitched on a lot of freight cars loaded with stuff that wouldn't have told in Exams, I never could have been in on time."

Peter shook his head rather sadly. "You outclass me in brains, Watts, as much as you do in other things."

"Nonsense," said Watts. "I haven't one quarter of your head. But my ancestors—here's to the old coves—have been brain-culturing for three hundred years, while yours have been land-culturing; and of course my brain moves quicker and easier than yours. I take to a book, by hereditary instinct, as a duck to water, while you are like a yacht, which needs a heap of building and fitting before she can do the same. But you'll beat me in the long run, as easily as the boat does the duck. And the Honor's nothing."

"Except, as you said, to one's"—Peter hesitated for a moment, divided in mind by his wish to quote accurately, and his dislike of anything disrespectful, and then finished "to one's mother."

"That's the last person it's needed for, chum," replied Watts. "If there's one person that doesn't need the world's or faculty's opinion to prove one's merit, it's one's dear, darling, doting, self-deluded and undisillusioned mamma. Heigh-ho. I'll be with mine two weeks from now, after we've had our visit at the Pierces'. I'm jolly glad you are going, old man. It will be a sort of tapering-off time for the summer's separation. I don't see why you insist on starting in at once in New York? No one does any law business in the summer time. Why, I even think the courts are closed. Come, you'd better go on to Grey-Court with me, and try it, at least. My mammy will kill the fatted calf for you in great style."

"We've settled that once," said Peter, who was evidently speaking journalistically, for he had done the settling.

Watts said something in a half-articulate way, which certainly would have fired the blood of every dime museum-keeper in the country, had they been there to hear the conversation, for, as well as could be gathered from the mumbling, it related to a "pig-headed donkey" known of to the speaker. "I suppose you'll be backing out of the Pierce affair yet," he added, discontentedly.

"No," said Peter.

"An invitation to Grey-Court is worth two of the Shrubberies. My mother knows only the right kind of people, while Mr. Pierce——"

"Is to be our host," interrupted Peter, but with no shade of correction in his voice.

"Yes," laughed Watts, "and he is a host. He'll not let any one else get a word in edgewise. You are just the kind of talker he'll like. Mark my word, he'll be telling every one, before you've been two hours in the house, that you are a remarkably brilliant conversationalist."

"What will he say of you?" said Peter, in a sentence which he broke up into reasonable lengths by a couple of pulls at his pipe in the midde of it.

"Mr. Pierce, chum," replied Watts, with a look in his eyes which Peter had learned to associate with mischief on Watts's part, "has too great an affection for yours truly to object to anything I do. Do you suppose, if I hadn't been sure of my footing at the Shrubberies, that I should have dared to ask an invitation for"—then Watts hesitated for a moment, seeing a half-surprised, half-anxious look come into Peter's face, "for myself?" he continued.

"Tell truth and shame the devil," said Peter.

Watts laughed. "Confound you! That's what comes of letting even such a stupid old beggar as you learn to read one's thoughts. It's mighty ungrateful of you to use them against me. Yes. I did ask to have you included in the party. But you needn't put your back up, Mr. Unbendable, and think you were forced on them. Mr. Pierce gave me *carte blanche,* and if it hadn't been you, it would have been some other donkey."

"But Mrs. Pierce?" queried Peter.

"Oh," explained Watts, "of course Mrs. Pierce wiote the letter. I couldn't do it in my name, and so Mr. Pierce told her to do it. They're very fond of me, old man, because my governor is the largest stockholder, and a director in Mr. P.'s bank, and I was told I could bring down some fellows next week for a few days' jollity. I didn't care to do that, but of course I wouldn't have omitted you for any amount of ducats."

Which explanation solves the mystery of Peter's presence at the Shrubberies. To understand his face we must trace the period between his arrival and the moment this story begins.

CHAPTER IV

BEGINNINGS

How far Watts was confining himself to facts in the foregoing dialogue is of no concern, for the only point of value was that Peter was invited, without regard to whether Watts first asked Mr. Pierce, or Mr. Pierce first asked Watts. A letter which the latter wrote to Miss Pierce, as soon as it was settled that Peter should go, is of more importance and deserves quotation in full:

June 7th.

My Dear Helen—

Between your Pater and my Peter, it has taken an amount of diplomacy to achieve the scheme we planned last summer, which would be creditable to Palmerston at his palmiest and have made Bismarck even more marked than he is. But the deed, the mighty deed is done, and June twenty-ninth will see chum and me at the Shrubberies "if it kills every cow in the barn," which is merely another way of saying that in the bright lexicon of youth, there's no such word as fail.

Now a word as to the fellow you are so anxious to meet. I have talked to you so much about him, that you will probably laugh at my attempting to tell you anything new. I'm not going to try, and you are to consider all I say as merely a sort of underlining to what you already know. Please remember that he will never take a prize for his beauty—nor even for his grace. He has a pleasing way with girls, not only of not talking himself, but of making it nearly impossible for them to talk. For instance, if a girl asks me if I play croquet, which by the way, is becoming very *passé* (three last lines verge on poetry) being replaced by a new game called tennis, I probably say, "No. Do you?" In this way I make croquet good for a ten minutes' chat, which in the end leads up to some other subject. Peter, however, doesn't. He says "No," and so the girl can't go on with croquet, but must begin a new subject. It is safest to take the subject-headings from an encyclopædia, and introduce them in alphabetical order. Allow about ninety to the hour, unless you are brave enough to bear an occasional silence. If you are, you can reduce this number considerably, and chum doesn't mind a a pause in the least, if the girl will only look contented. If she looks worried, however, Peter gets worried, too. Just put the old chap between you and your mamma at meals, and pull him over any rough spots that come along. You, I know, will be able to make it easy for him. Neglect me to any extent. I shan't be jealous, and shall use that apparent neglect as an excuse for staying on for a week after he goes, so as to have my innings. I want the dear old blunderbuss to see how nice a really nice girl can be, so do your prettiest to him, for the sake of

WATTS CLARKSON D'ALLOI.

When Watts and Peter saved the "cows in the barn" by stepping off the train on June 29th, the effect of this letter was manifest. Watts was promptly bestowed on the front seat of the trap with Mr. Pierce, while Peter was quickly sitting beside a girl on the back seat. Of course an introduction had been made, but Peter had acquired a habit of not looking at girls, and as a consequence had yet to discover how far Miss Pierce came up to the pleasant word-sketch Watts had drawn of her. Indeed, Peter had looked longingly at the seat beside Mr. Pierce, and had attempted, in a very obvious manner, though one which seemed to him the essence of tact and most unapparent, to have it assigned to him. But two people, far his superior in natural finesse and experience, had decided beforehand that he was to sit with Helen, and he could not resist their skilful manœuvres. So he climbed into place, hoping that she wouldn't talk, or if that was too much to expect, that at least Watts would half turn and help him through.

Neither of these fitted, however, with Miss Pierce's plans. She gave Peter a moment to fit comfortably into his seat, knowing that if she forced the running before he had done that, he would probably sit awry for the whole drive. Then "I can't tell you how pleased we all are over Watts's success. We knew, of course, he could do it if he cared to, but he seemed to think the attempt hardly worth the making, and so we did not know if he would try."

Peter breathed more easily. She had not asked a question, and the intonation of the last sentence was such as left him to infer that it was not his turn to say something; which, Peter had noticed, was the way in which girls generally ended their remarks.

"Oh, look at that absurd looking cow," was her next remark, made before Peter had begun to worry over the pause.

Peter looked at the cow and laughed. He would like to have laughed longer, for that would have used up time, but the moment he thought the laugh could be employed in place of conversation, the laugh failed. However, to be told to look at a cow required no rejoinder, so there was as yet no cause for anxiety.

"We are very proud of our roads about here," said Miss Pierce. "When we first bought they were very bad, but papa took the matter in hand and got them to build with a rock foundation, as they do in Europe."

Three subjects had been touched upon, and no answer or remark yet forced upon him. Peter thought of *rouge et noir,* and wondered what the odds were that he would be forced to say something by Miss Pierce's next speech.

"I like the New England roadside," continued Miss Pierce, with an apparent relativeness to the last subject that delighted Peter, who was used by this time to much disconnection of conversation, and found not a little difficulty in shifting quickly from one topic to another. "There is a tangled finish about it that is very pleasant. And in August, when the golden-rod comes, I think it is glorious. It seems to me as if all the hot sunbeams of the summer had been gathered up in—excuse the expression—it's a word of Watts's—into 'gobs' of sunshine, and scattered along the roads and fields."

Peter wondered if the request to be excused called for a response, but concluded that it didn't.

"Papa told me the other day," continued Miss Pierce, "that there were nineteen distinct varieties of golden-rod. I had never noticed that there were any differences."

Peter began to feel easy and comfortable. He made a mental note that Miss Pierce had a very sweet voice. It had never occurred to Peter before to notice if a girl had a pleasant voice. Now he distinctly remembered that several to whom he had talked—or rather who had talked to him—had not possessed that attraction.

"Last year," said Miss Pierce, "when Watts was here, we had a golden-rod party. We had the whole house decked with it, and yellow lamps on the lawn."

"He told me about it," said Peter.

"He really was the soul of it," said Miss Pierce. "He wove himself a belt and chaplet of it and wore it all through the evening. He was so good-looking!"

Peter, quite unconscious that he had said anything, actually continued: "He was voted the handsomest man of the class."

"Was he really? How nice!" said Miss Pierce.

"Yes," said Peter. "And it was true." Peter failed to notice that a question had been asked, or that he had answered it. He began to think that he would like to look at Miss Pierce for a moment. Miss Pierce, during this interval, remarked to herself: "Yes. That was the right way, Helen, my dear."

"We had quite a houseful for our party," Miss Pierce remarked, after this self-approval. "And that reminds me that I must tell you about whom you meet to-day." Then the next ten minutes were consumed in naming and describing the two fashionable New York girls and their brother, who made the party then assembled.

During this time Peter's eyes strayed from Watts's shapely back, and took a furtive glance at Miss Pierce. He found that she was looking at him as she talked, but for some reason it did not alarm him, as such observation usually did. Before the guests were properly catalogued, Peter was looking into her eyes as she rambled on, and forgot that he was doing so.

The face that he saw was not one of any great beauty, but it was sweet, and had a most attractive way of showing every change of mood or thought. It responded quickly too, to outside influence. Many a girl of more real beauty was less popular. People liked to talk to Miss Pierce, and many could not escape from saying more than they wished, impelled thereto by her ready sympathy. Then her eyes were really beautiful, and she had the trimmest, dearest little figure in the world; "squeezable" was the word Watts used to describe it, and most men thought the same. Finally, she had a pleasant way of looking into people's eyes as she talked to them, and for some reason people felt very well satisfied when she did.

It had this effect upon Peter. As he looked down into the large gray eyes, really slate-color in their natural darkness, made the darker by the shadows of the long lashes, he entirely forgot place and circumstances; ceased to think whose turn it was to speak; even forgot to think whether he was enjoying the moment. In short he forgot himself and, what was equally important, forgot that he was talking to a girl. He felt and behaved as he did with men. "Moly hoses!" said Watts to himself on the front seat, "the old fellow's getting loquacious. Garrulity must be contagious, and he's caught it from Mr. Pierce." Which, being reduced to actual facts, means that Peter had spoken eight times, and laughed twice, in the half hour that was passed between the station and the Shrubberies' gate.

CHAPTER V

MINES AND COUNTER-MINES

THE sight of the party on the veranda of the Shrubberies brought a return of self-consciousness to Peter, and he braced himself, as the trap slowed up, for the agony of formal greetings. If Miss Pierce had been a less sweet, sympathetic girl, she could hardly have kept from smiling at the way Peter's face and figure stiffened, as the group came in sight. But Miss Pierce had decided, before she met Peter, that she should like him, and moreover, that he was a man who needed help. Let any woman reach these conclusions about a man, and for some reason quite beyond logic or philosophy, he ceases to be ridiculous. So instead of smiling, she bridged over the awful greetings with feminine engineering skill quite equal to some great strategic movement in war. Peter was made to shake hands with Mrs. Pierce, but was called off to help Miss Pierce out of the carriage, before speech was necessary. Then a bundle was missing in the bottom of the carriage, and Mr. Pawling, the New York swell, was summoned to help Peter find it, the incident being seized upon to name the two to each other. Finally, he was introduced to the two girls, but, almost instantly, Watts and Peter were sent to their rooms; and Miss Pierce, nodding her head in a way which denoted satisfaction, remarked as she went to her own room, "Really, Helen, I don't think it will be so very hard, after all. He's very tractable."

As Peter came downstairs, before dinner, he speculated on whether he should be able to talk to Miss Pierce. He rather doubted from past experience, if such a result was attainable, seeing that there were two other men, who would of course endeavor to do the same. But strangely enough the two men were already seated by the New York girls, and a vacant chair was next that holding Miss Pierce. What was more, he was at once summoned to fill it, and in five minutes was again entirely unconscious of everything but the slate-colored eyes, looking so pleasantly into his. Then he took Miss Pierce in to dinner, and sat between her and her mother, again becoming absorbed in the slate-colored eyes, which seemed quite willing to be absorbed. After dinner, too, when the women had succeeded the weed, Peter in some way found it very easy to settle himself near Miss Pierce. Later that night Peter sat in his room, or rather, with half his body out of the window, puffing his pipe, and thinking how well he had gone through the day. He had not made a single slip. Nothing to groan over. "I'm getting more experienced," he thought, with the vanity noticeable in even the most diffident of collegians, never dreaming that everything that he had said or done in the last few hours had been made easy for him by a woman's tact.

The following week was practically a continuation of this first day. In truth Peter was out of his element with the fashionables; Mr. Pierce did not choose to waste his power on him; and Mrs. Pierce, like the yielding, devoted wife she was, took her coloring from her husband. Watts had intended to look after him, but Watts played well on the piano, and on the billiard table; he rowed well and rode well; he sang, he danced, he swam, he talked, he played all games, he read aloud capitally, and, what was more, was ready at any or all times for any or all things. No man who can do half these had better intend seriously to do some duty in a house-party in July. For, however good his intentions, he will merely add to the pavement of a warmer place than even a July temperature makes Long Island Sound. Instinctively, Peter turned to Miss Pierce at every opportunity. He should have asked himself if the girl was really enjoying his company more than she did that of the other young people. Had he been to the manner born he would have known better than to force himself on a hostess, or to make his monopoly of a young girl so marked. But he was entirely oblivious of whether he was doing as he ought, conscious only that, for causes which he made no attempt to analyze, he was very happy when with her. For reasons best known to Miss Pierce, she allowed herself to be monopolized. She was even almost as devoted to Peter as he was to her, and no comparison could be stronger. It is to be questioned if she enjoyed it very much, for Peter was not talkative, and the little he did say was neither brilliant nor witty. With the jollity and "high jinks" (to use a word of Watts's) going on about her, it is hardly possible that Peter's society shone by contrast. Yet in drawing-room or carriage, on the veranda, lawn, or yacht's deck, she was ever ready to give him as much of her attention and help as he seemed to need, and he needed a good deal. Watts jokingly said that "the moment Peter comes in sight, Helen puts out a sign 'vacant, to let,'" and this was only one of many jokes the house-party made over the dual devotion.

It was an experience full of danger to Peter. For the first time in his life he was seeing the really charming phases which a girl has at command. Attractive as these are to all men, they were trebly so to Peter, who had nothing to compare with them but the indifferent attitudes hitherto shown him by the maidens of his native town, and by the few Boston women who had been compelled to "endure" his society. If he had had more experience he would have merely thought Miss Pierce a girl with nice eyes, figure and manner. But as a single glass of wine is dangerous to the teetotaller, so this episode had an overbalancing influence on Peter, entirely out of proportion to its true value. Before the week was over he was seriously in love, and though his natural impassiveness and his entire lack of knowledge how to convey his feelings to Miss Pierce, prevented her from a suspicion of the fact the more experienced father and mother were not so blind.

"Really, Charles," said Mrs. Pierce, in the privacy of their own room, "I think it ought to be stopped."

"Exactly, my dear," replied her other half, with an apparent yielding to her views that amazed and rather frightened Mrs. Pierce, till he continued: "Beyond question *it* should be stopped, since you say so. *It* is neuter, and as neutral things are highly objectionable, stop *it* by all means."

"I mean Mr. Stirling——" began Mrs. Pierce.

"Yes?" interrupted Mr. Pierce, in an encouraging, inquiring tone. "Peter is certainly neuter. I think one might say negative, without gross exaggeration. Still, I should hardly stop him. He finds enough difficulty in getting out an occasional remark without putting a stopper in him. Perhaps, though, I mistake your meaning, and you want Peter merely to stop here a little longer."

"I mean, dear," replied Mrs. Pierce, with something like a tear in her voice, for she was sadly wanting in a sense of humor, and her husband's jokes always half frightened her, and invariably made her feel inferior to him, "I mean his spending so much time with Helen. I'm afraid he'll fall in love with her."

"My dear," said Mr. Pierce, "you really should be a professional mind-reader. Your suggestion comes as an awful revelation to me. Just supposing he should—aye —just supposing he has, fallen in love with Helen!"

"I really think he has," said Mrs. Pierce, "though he is so different from most men, that I am not sure."

"Then by all means we must stop him. By the way, how does one stop a man's falling in love?" asked Mr. Pierce.

"Charles!" said Mrs. Pierce.

This remark of Mrs. Pierce's generally meant a resort to a handkerchief, and Mr. Pierce did not care for any increase of atmospheric humidity just then. He therefore concluded that since his wit was taken seriously, he would try a bit of seriousness, as an antidote.

"I don't think there is any occasion to interfere. Whatever Peter does can make no difference, for it is perfectly evident that Helen is nice to him as a sort of duty, and, I rather suspect, to please Watts. So anything she may do will be a favor to him, while the fact that she is attractive to Peter will not lessen her value to—others."

"Then you don't think——?" asked Mrs. Pierce, and paused there.

"Don't insult my intelligence," laughed Mr. Pierce. "I do think. I think things can't be going better. I was a little afraid of Mr. Pawling, and should have preferred to have him and his sisters later, but since it is policy to invite them and they could not come at any other time, it was a godsend to have sensible, dull old Peter to keep her busy. If he had been in the least dangerous, I should not have interfered, but I should have made him very ridiculous. That's the way for parents to treat an ineligible man. Next week, when all are gone but Watts, he will

have his time, and shine the more by contrast with what
she has had this week."

"Then you think Helen and Watts care for each other?"
asked Mrs. Pierce, flushing with pleasure, to find her own
opinion of such a delightful possibility supported by her
husband's.

"I think," said Mr. Pierce, "that the less we parents concern ourselves with love the better. If I have made opportunities for Helen and Watts to see something of each
other, I have only done what was to their mutual interests.
Any courtesy I have shown him is well enough accounted
for on the ground of his father's interest in my institution,
without the assumption of any matrimonial intentions.
However, I am not opposed to a marriage. Watts is the
son of a very rich man of the best social position in New
York, besides being a nice fellow in himself. Helen will
make any man a good wife, and whoever wins her will
not be the poorer. If the two can fix it between themselves, I shall cry *nunc dimittis,* but further than this, the
deponent saith and doeth not."

"I am sure they love each other," said Mrs. Pierce.

"Well," said Mr. Pierce, "I think if most parents would
decide whom it was best for their child to marry, and see
that the young people saw just enough of each other, before they saw too much of the world, they could accomplish their purpose, provided they otherwise kept their
finger out of the pot of love. There is a certain period in
a man's life when he must love something feminine, even
if she's as old as his grandmother. There is a certain
period in a girl's life when it is well-nigh impossible for her
to say 'no' to a lover. He really only loves the sex, and
she really loves the love and not the lover; but it is just as
well, for the delusion lasts quite as long as the more personal love that comes later. And, being young, they need
less breaking for double harness."

Mrs. Pierce winced. Most women do wince when a
man really verges on his true conclusions concerning love
in the abstract, however satisfactory his love in the con-
crete may be to them. "I am sure they love each other,"
she affirmed.

"Yes, I think they do," replied Mr. Pierce. "But five

years in the world before meeting would have possibly brought quite a different conclusion. And now, my dear, if we are not going to have the young people eloping in the yacht by themselves, we had better leave both the subject and the room, for we have kept them fifteen minutes as it is."

CHAPTER VI

A MONOLOGUE AND A DIALOGUE

It was at the end of this day's yachting that Peter was having his "unsocial walk." Early on the morrow he would be taking the train for his native town, and the thought of this, in connection with other thoughts, drew stern lines on his face. His conclusions were something to this effect:

"I suspected before coming that Watts and Miss Pierce loved each other. I was evidently wrong, for if they did they could not endure seeing so little of each other. How could he know her and not love her? But it's very fortunate for me, for I should stand no chance against him, even supposing I should try to win the girl he loved. She can't care for me! As Watts says, 'I'm an old stupid naturally, and doubly so with girls.' Still, I can't go tomorrow without telling her. I shan't see her again till next winter. I can't wait till then. Some one else—I can't wait."

Then he strode up and down half a dozen times repeating the last three words over and over again. His thoughts took a new turn.

"It's simply folly, and you have no right to give in to it. You have your own way to make. You have no right to ask mother for more than the fifteen hundred she says you are to have as an allowance, for you know that even if she gave you more, it would be only by scrimping herself. What is fifteen hundred a year to such a girl? Why, her father would think I was joking!"

Then Peter looked out on the leaden waters and wished it was not cowardly to end the conflict by letting them close over him. The dark color made him think, however, of a pair of slate-colored eyes, so instead of jumping in, he repeated "I can't wait" a few times, and walked with redoubled energy. Having stimulated himself thereby, he went on thinking.

"She has been so kind to me that—no—she can't care for me. But if she—if by chance—if—supposing she does! Why, the money is nothing. We can wait."

Peter repeated this last remark several times, clearly showing that he made a great distinction between "I can wait" and "We can wait." Probably the same nice distinction has been made before, and lovers have good authority for the distinction, for many an editor's public "We think" is the exact opposite of his private "I think." Then Peter continued:

"Of course I shall have difficulty with Mr. Pierce. He's a worldly man. That's nothing, though, if she cares for me. If she cares for me."

Peter repeated this last sentence a number of times and seemed to enjoy the prospect it conjured up. He saw Peter Stirling taking a fond farewell of a certain lady. He saw him entering the arena and struggling with the wild beasts, and of course conquering them. He saw the day when his successes would enable him to set up his own fireside. He saw that fireside made perfect by a pair of slate-colored eyes, which breakfast opposite him, follow him as he starts for his work, and greet him on his return. A pair of eyes to love when present, and think of when absent. Heigho! How many firesides and homes have been built out of just such materials!

From all this the fact can be gathered that Peter was really, despite his calm, sober nature, no more sensible in love matters than are other boys verging on twenty-one. He could not see that success in this love would be his greatest misfortune. That he could not but be distracted from his work. That he would almost certainly marry before he could well afford it, and thus overweight himself in his battle for success. He forgot prudence and common-sense, and that being what a lover usually does, he can hardly be blamed for it.

Bump!

Down came the air-castle. Home, fireside, and the slate-colored eyes dissolved into a wooden wharf. The dream was over.

"Bear a hand here with these lunch-baskets, chum," called Watts. "Make yourself useful as well as ornamental."

And so Peter's solitary tramp ceased, and he was helping lunch-baskets and ladies to the wharf.

But the tramp had brought results which were quickly to manifest themselves. As the party paired off for the walk to the Shrubberies, both Watts and Peter joined Miss Pierce, which was not at all to Peter's liking.

"Go on with the rest, Watts," said Peter quietly.

Miss Pierce and Watts both stopped short in surprise.

"Eh?" said the latter.

"You join the rest of the party on ahead," said Peter.

"I don't understand," said Watts, who could hardly have been more surprised if Peter had told him to drown himself.

"I want to say something to Miss Pierce," explained Peter.

Watts caught his breath. If Peter had not requested his absence and given his reason for wishing it, in Miss Pierce's hearing, Watts would have formed an instant conclusion as to what it meant, not far from the truth. But that a man should deliberately order another away, in the girl's hearing, so that he might propose to her, was too great an absurdity for Watts to entertain for more than a second. He laughed, and said, "Go on yourself, if you don't like the company."

"No," said Peter. "I want you to go on." Peter spoke quietly, but there was an inflexion in his singularly clear voice, which had more command in it than a much louder tone in others. Watts had learned to recognize it, and from past experience knew that Peter was not to be moved when he used it. But here the case was different. Hitherto he had been trying to make Peter do something. Now the boot was on the other leg, and Watts saw therein a chance for some fun. He therefore continued to stand still, as they had all done since Peter had exploded his first speech, and began to whistle. Both men, with that selfishness common to the sex, failed entirely to consider whether Miss Pierce was enjoying the incident.

"I think," remarked Miss Pierce, "that I will leave you two to settle it, and run on with the rest."

"Don't," spoke Peter quickly. "I have something to say to you."

Watts stopped his whistling. "What the deuce is the old boy up to?" he thought to himself. Miss Pierce hesitated. She wanted to go, but something in Peter's voice made it very difficult. "I had no idea he could speak so decidedly. He's not so tractable as I thought. I think Watts ought to do what he asks. Though I don't see why Mr. Stirling wants to send him away," she said to herself.

"Watts," said Peter, "this is the last chance I shall really have to thank Miss Pierce, for I leave before breakfast to-morrow."

There was nothing appealing in the way it was said. It seemed a mere statement of fact. Yet something in the voice gave it the character of a command.

"'Nough said, chum," said Watts, feeling a little cheap at his smallness in having tried to rob Peter of his farewell. The next moment he was rapidly overtaking the advance-party.

By all conventions there should have been an embarrassing pause after this extraordinary colloquy, but there was not. When Peter decided to do a thing, he never faltered in the doing. If making love or declaring it had been a matter of directness and plain-speaking, Peter would have been a successful lover. But few girls are won by lovers who carry business methods and habits of speech into their courtship.

"Miss Pierce," said Peter, "I could not go without thanking you for your kindness to me. I shall never forget this week."

"I am so glad you have enjoyed it," almost sang Miss Pierce, in her pleasure at this reward for her week of self-sacrifice.

"And I couldn't go," said Peter, his clear voice suddenly husking, "without telling you how I love you."

"Love me!" exclaimed Miss Pierce, and she brought the walk again to a halt, in her surprise.

"Yes," replied Peter simply, but the monosyllable meant more than the strongest protestations, as he said it.

"Oh," almost cried his companion, "I am so sorry."

"Don't say that," said Peter; "I don't want it to be a sorrow to you."

"But it's so sudden," gasped Miss Pierce.

"I suppose it is," said Peter, "but I love you and can't help telling it. Why shouldn't one tell one's love as soon as one feels it? It's the finest thing a man can tell a woman."

"Oh, please don't," begged Miss Pierce, her eyes full of tears in sympathy for him. "You make it so hard for me to say that—that you mustn't."

"I really didn't think you could care for me—as I cared for you," replied Peter, rather more to the voice than to the words of the last speech. "Girls have never liked me "

Miss Pierce began to sob. "It's all a mistake. A dreadful mistake," she cried, "and it is my fault."

"Don't say that," said Peter. "It's nothing but my blundering."

They walked on in silence to the Shrubberies, but as they came near to the glare of the lighted doorway, Peter halted a moment.

"Do you think," he asked, "that it could ever be different?"

"No," replied Miss Pierce.

"Because, unless there is—is some one else," continued Peter, "I shall not——"

"There is," interrupted Miss Pierce, the determination in Peter's voice frightening her into disclosing her secret.

Peter said to himself, "It is Watts after all." He was tempted to say it aloud, and most men in the sting of the moment would have done so. But he thought it would not be the speech of a gentleman. Instead he said, "Thank you." Then he braced himself, and added: "Please don't let my love cause you any sorrow. It has been nothing but a joy to me. Good-night and good-bye."

He did not even offer to shake hands in parting. They went into the hallway together, and leaving the rest of the party, who were already raiding the larder for an impromptu supper, to their own devices, they passed up-

stairs, Miss Pierce to bathe her eyes and Peter to pack
his belongings.

"Where are Helen and Stirling?" inquired Mr. Pierce
when the time came to serve out the Welsh rarebit he was
tending.

"They'll be along presently," said Watts. "Helen forgot something, and they went back after it."

"They will be properly punished by the leathery condition of the rarebit, if they don't hurry. And as we are
all agreed that Stirling is somewhat lacking in romance,
he will not get a corresponding pleasure from the longer
stroll to reward him for that. There, ladies and gentlemen, that is a rarebit that will melt in your mouth, and
make the absent ones regret their foolishness. As the
gourmand says in 'Richelieu,' 'What's diplomacy compared to a delicious pâté?'"

CHAPTER VII

FACING THE WORLD

ARMY surgeons recognize three types of wounded. One
type so nervous, that it drops the moment it is struck,
whether the wound is disabling or not. Another so nerve-
less, that it fights on, unconscious that it has been hit. A
third, who, feeling the wound, goes on fighting, sustained
by its nerve. It is over the latter sort that the surgeons
shake their heads and look anxious.

Peter did his packing quietly and quickly, not pausing
for a moment in the task. Then he went downstairs, and
joined the party, just finishing the supper. He refused,
it is true, to eat anything, and was quiet, but this phase
was so normal in him, that it occasioned no remark. Asked
where Miss Pierce was, he explained briefly that he had
left her in the hall, in order to do his packing and had not
seen her since.

In a few moments the party broke up. Peter said a
good-bye to each, quite conscious of what he was doing, yet
really saying more and better things than he had said in

his whole visit, and quite surprising them all in the apparent ease with which he went through the duty.

"You must come and see us when you have put your shingle out in New York," said Mr. Pierce, not quite knowing why, having previously decided that they had had enough of Peter. "We shall be in the city early in September, and ready to see our friends."

"Thank you," replied Peter. He turned and went upstairs to his room. He ought to have spent the night pacing the floor, but he did not. He went to bed instead. Whether Peter slept, we cannot say. He certainly lay very still, till the first ray of daylight brightened the sky. Then he rose and dressed. He went to the stables and explained to the groom that he would walk to the station, and merely asked that his trunk should be there in time to be checked. Then he returned to the house and told the cook that he would breakfast on the way. Finally he started for the station, diverging on the way, so as to take a roundabout road, that gave him a twelve-mile tramp in the time he had before the train left.

Perhaps the hardest thing Peter encountered was answering his mother's questions about the visit. Yet he never flinched nor dodged from a true reply, and if his mother had chosen, she could have had the whole story. But something in the way Peter spoke of Miss Pierce made Mrs. Stirling careful, and whatever she surmised she kept to herself, merely kissing him good-night with a tenderness that was unusual, not merely in a New Englander, but even in her. During the rest of his stay, the Pierces were quite as much kept out of sight, as if they had never been known. Mrs. Stirling was not what we should call a "lady," yet few of those who rank as such, would have been as considerate or tender of Peter's trouble, if the power had been given them to lay it bare. Love, sympathy, unselfishness and forbearance are not bad equivalents for breeding and etiquette, and have the additional advantage of meeting new and unusual conditions which sometimes occur to even the most conventional.

One hope did come to her. "Perhaps, now that"—and Mrs. Stirling left "that" blank even in her thoughts; "now my boy, my Peter, will not be so set on going to New

York." In this, however, she was disappointed. On the second day of his stay, Peter spoke of his intention to start for New York the following week.

"Don't you think you could do as well here?" asked Mrs. Stirling.

"Up to a certain point, better. But New York has a big beyond," said Peter. "I'll try it there first, and if I don't make my way, I'll come back here."

Few mothers hope for a son's failure, yet Mrs. Stirling allowed herself a moment's happiness over this possibility. Then remembering that her Peter could not possibly fail, she became despondent. "They say New York's full of temptations," she said.

"I suppose it is, mother," replied Peter, "to those who want to be tempted."

"I know I can trust you, Peter," said his mother, proudly, "but I want you to promise me one thing."

"What?"

"That if you do yield, if you do what you oughtn't to, you'll write and tell me about it?" Mrs. Stirling put her arms about Peter's neck, and looked wistfully into his face.

Peter was not blind to what this world is. Perhaps, had his mother known it as he did, she might have seen how unfair her petition was. He did not like to say yes, and could not say no.

"I'll try to go straight, mother," he replied, "but that's a good deal to promise."

"It's all I'm going to ask of you, Peter," urged Mrs. Stirling.

"I have gone through four years of my life with nothing in it I couldn't tell her," thought Peter. "If that's possible, I guess another four is." Then he said aloud, "Well, mother, since you want it, I'll do it."

The reason of Peter's eagerness to get to New York, was chiefly to have something definite to do. He tried to obtain this distraction of occupation, at present, in a characteristic way, by taking excessively long walks, and by struggling with his mother's supply of wood. He thought that every long stride and every swing of the axe was working him free from the crushing lack of purpose that had settled upon him. He imagined it would be even easier when he reached New York. "There'll be plenty to keep me busy there," was his mental hope.

All his ambitions and plans seemed in a sense to have become meaningless, made so by the something which but ten days before had been unknown to him. Like Moses he had seen the promised land. But Moses died. He had seen it, and must live on without it. He saw nothing in the future worth striving for, except a struggle to forget, if possible, the sweetest and dearest memory he had ever known. He thought of the epigram: "Most men can die well, but few can live well." Three weeks before he had smiled over it and set it down as a bit of French cynicism. Now—on the verge of giving his mental assent to the theory, a pair of slate-colored eyes in some way came into his mind, and even French wit was discarded therefrom.

Peter was taking his disappointment very seriously, if quietly. Had he only known other girls, he might have made a safe recovery, for love's remedy is truly the homeopathic "similia similibus curantur," woman plural being the natural cure for woman singular. As the Russian in the "Last Word" says, "A woman can do anything with a man—provided there is no other woman." In Peter's case there was no other woman. What was worse, there seemed little prospect of there being one in the future.

CHAPTER VIII

SETTLING

THE middle of July found Peter in New York, eager to begin his grapple with the future. How many such stormers have dashed themselves against its high ramparts, from which float the flags of "worldly success"; how many have fallen at the first attack; how many have been borne away, stricken in the assault; how many have fought on bravely, till driven back by pressure, sickness, or hunger; how few have reached the top, and won their colors!

As already hinted, Peter had chosen the law as his

ladder to climb these ramparts. Like many another fellow
he had but a dim comprehension of the struggle before
him. His college mates had talked over professions, and
agreed that law was a good one in New York. The attorney in his native town, "had known of cases where men
without knowing a soul in a place, had started in and
by hard work and merit had built up a good practice, and
I don't see why it can't be done as well in New York as
in Lawrence or Lowell. If New York is bigger, then
there is more to be done." So Peter, whose New York
acquaintances were limited to Watts and four other collegians, the Pierces and their fashionables, and a civil engineer originally from his native town, had decided that
the way to go about it was to get an office, hang up a
sign, and wait for clients.

On the morning after his arrival, his first object was a
lodging. Selecting from the papers the advertisements of
several boarding-houses, he started in search of one.
Watts had told him about where to locate, "so as to live
in a decent part of the city," but after seeing and pricing
a few rooms near the "Avenue," about Thirtieth Street,
Peter saw that Watts had been thinking of his own purse,
rather than of his friend's.

"Can you tell me where the cheaper boarding-houses
are?" he asked the woman who had done the honors of
the last house.

"If it's cheapness you want, you'd better go to Bleecker
Street," said the woman with a certain contemptuousness.

Peter thanked her, and, walking away, accosted the first
policeman.

"It's Blaker Strate, is it? Take the Sixth Avenue cars,
there beyant," he was informed.

"Is it a respectable street?" asked Peter.

"Don't be afther takin' away a strate's character," said
the policeman, grinning good-naturedly.

"I mean," explained Peter, "do respectable people live
there?"

"Shure, it's mostly boarding-houses for young men,"
replied the unit of "the finest." "Ye know best what
they're loike."

Reassured, Peter sought and found board in Bleecker Street, not comprehending that he had gone to the opposite extreme. It was a dull season, and he had no difficulty in getting such a room as suited both his expectations and purse. By dinner-time he had settled his simple household goods to his satisfaction, and slightly moderated the dreariness of the third floor front, so far as the few pictures and other furnishings from his college rooms could modify the effect of well-worn carpet, cheap, painted furniture, and ugly wall-paper.

Descending to his dinner, in answer to a bell more suitable for a fire-alarm than for announcing such an ordinary occurrence as meals, he was introduced to the four young men who were all the boarders the summer season had left in the house. Two were retail dry-goods clerks, another filled some function in a butter and cheese store, and the fourth was the ticket-seller at one of the middle-grade theatres. They all looked at Peter's clothes before looking at his face, and though the greetings were civil enough, Peter's ready-made travelling suit, bought in his native town, and his quiet cravat, as well as his lack of jewelry, were proof positive to them that he did not merit any great consideration. It was very evident that the ticket-seller, not merely from his natural self-assertion but even more because of his enviable acquaintances with certain actresses and his occasional privileges in the way of free passes, was the acknowledged autocrat of the table. Under his guidance the conversation quickly turned to theatrical and "show" talk. Much of it was vulgar, and all of it was dull. It was made the worse by the fact that they all tried to show off a little before the newcomer, to prove their superiority and extreme knowingness to him. To make Peter the more conscious of this, they asked him various questions.

"Do you like ——?" a popular soubrette of the day.

"What, never seen her? Where on earth have you been living?"

"Oh! Well, she's got too good legs to waste herself on such a little place."

They would like to have asked him questions about

himself, but feared to seem to lower themselves from their
fancied superiority, by showing interest in Peter. One
indeed did ask him what business he was in.

"I haven't got to work yet," answered Peter.

"Looking for a place," was the mental comment of all,
for they could not conceive of any one entitled to practise
law not airing his advantage. So they went on patron-
izing Peter, and glorifying themselves. When time had
developed the facts that he was a lawyer, a college graduate, and a man who seemed to have plenty of money
(from the standpoint of dry-goods clerks) their respect for
him considerably increased. He could not, however, over-
come his instinctive dislike to them. After the manly
high-minded, cultivated Harvard classmates, every moment of their society was only endurable, and he neither
went to their rooms nor asked them to his. Peter had
nothing of the snob in him, but he found reading or writing, or a tramp about the city, much the pleasanter way
of passing his evenings.

The morning after this first day in New York, Peter
called on his friend, the civil engineer, to consult him about
an office; for Watts had been rather hazy in regard to
where he might best locate that. Mr. Converse shook his
head when Peter outlined his plan.

"Do you know any New York people," he asked, "who
will be likely to give you cases?"

"No," said Peter.

"Then it's absolutely foolish of you to begin that way,"
said Mr. Converse. "Get into a lawyer's office, and make
friends first before you think of starting by yourself.
You'll otherwise never get a client."

Peter shook his head. "I've thought it out," he added,
as if that settled it.

Mr. Converse looked at him, and, really liking the fellow, was about to explain the real facts to him, when a
client came in. So he only said, "If that's so, go ahead.
Locate on Broadway, anywhere between the Battery and
Canal Street." Later in the day, when he had time, he
shook his head, and said, "Poor devil! Like all the rest."

Anywhere between the Battery and Canal Street represented a fairly large range of territory, but Peter went at

the matter directly, and for the next three days passed his time climbing stairs, and inspecting rooms and dark cells. At the end of that time he took a moderate-sized office, far back in a building near Worth Street. Another day saw it fitted with a desk, two chairs (for Peter as yet dreamed only on single clients) and a shelf containing the few law books that were the monuments of his Harvard law course, and his summer reading. On the following Monday, when Peter faced his office door he felt a glow of satisfaction at seeing in very black letters on the very newly scrubbed glass the sign of:

PETER STIRLING

Attorney and Counsellor-at-Law

He had come to his office early, not merely because at his boarding place they breakfasted betimes, but because he believed that early hours were one way of winning success. He was a little puzzled what to do with himself. He sat down at his desk and thrummed it for a minute. Then he rose, and spread his books more along the shelf, so as to leave little spaces between them, thinking that he could make them look more imposing thereby. After that he took down a book—somebody "On Torts,"—and dug into it. In the Harvard course, he had had two hours a week of this book, but Peter worked over it for nearly three hours. Then he took paper, and in a very clear, beautifully neat hand, made an abstract of what he had read. Then he compared his abstract with the book. Returning the book to the shelf, very much pleased with the accuracy of his memory, he looked at his watch. It was but half-past eleven. Peter sat down at his desk. "Would all the days go like this?" he asked himself. He had got through the first week by his room and office-seeking and furnishing. But now? He could not read law for more than four hours a day, and get anything from it. What was to be done with the rest of the time? What could he do to keep himself from thinking of—from thinking? He looked out of his one window, over the dreary stretch of roofs and the drearier light shafts spoken of flatteringly as yards. He compressed his lips, and resorted once more to his book. But he found his mind wandering, and realized that he had done all he was equal to on a hot July morning. Again he looked out over the roofs. Then he rose and stood in the middle of his room, thinking. He looked at his watch again, to make sure that he was right. Then he opened his door and glanced about the hall. It was one blank, except for the doors. He went down the two flights of stairs to the street. Even that had the deserted look of summer. He turned and went back to his room. Sitting down once more at his desk, and opening somebody "On Torts" again, he took up his pen and began to copy the pages literally. He wrote steadily for a time, then with pauses. Finally, the hand ceased to follow the lines, and became straggly. Then he ceased to write. The words blurred, the paper faded from view, and all Peter saw was a pair of slate-colored eyes. He laid his head down on the blotter, and the erect, firm figure relaxed.

There is no more terrible ordeal of courage than passive waiting. Most of us can be brave with something to do, but to be brave for months, for years, with nothing to be done and without hope of the future! So it was in Peter's case. It was waiting—waiting—for what? If clients came, if fame came, if every form of success came,—for what?

There is nothing in loneliness to equal the loneliness of a big city. About him, so crowded and compressed together as to risk life and health, were a million people. Yet not a soul of that million knew that Peter sat at his desk, with his head on the blotter, immovable, from noon one day till daylight of the next.

CHAPTER IX

HAPPINESS BY PROXY

THE window of Peter's office faced east, and the rays of the morning sun shining dazzlingly in his eyes forced him back to a consciousness of things mundane. He rose, and went downstairs, to find the night watchman just opening the building. Fortunately he had already met the man, so that he was not suspected as an intruder; and giving him a pleasant "good-morning," Peter passed into the street. It was a good morning indeed, with all that freshness and coolness which even a great city cannot take from a summer dawn. For some reason Peter felt more encouraged. Perhaps it was the consciousness of having beaten his loneliness and misery by mere physical endurance. Perhaps it was only the natural spring of twenty years. At all events, he felt dimly, that miserable and unhopeful as the future looked, he was not conquered yet; that he was going to fight on, come what might.

He turned to the river front, and after bargaining with a passing cart for a pint of what the poorer people of the city buy as milk, he turned north, and quickening his pace, walked till he had left the city proper and had reached the new avenue or "drive," which, by the liberality of Mr. Tweed with other people's money, was then just approaching completion. After walking the length of it, he turned back to his boarding-place, and after a plunge, felt as if he could face and fight the future to any extent.

As a result of this he was for the first time late at breakfast. The presider over the box-office had ascertained that Peter had spent the night out, and had concluded he would have a gird or two at him. He failed, however, to carry out his intention. It was not the first time that both he and his companions had decided to "roast" Peter, absent, but had done otherwise with Peter, present. He had also decided to say to Peter, "Who's your dandy letter-writer?" But he also failed to do that. This last intention referred to a letter that lay at Peter's place, and which was examined by each of the four in turn. That letter had an air about it. It was written on linen paper of a grade which, if now common enough, was not so common at that time. Then it was postmarked from one of the most fashionable summer resorts of the country. Finally, it was sealed with wax, then very unusual, and the wax bore the impression of a crest. They were all rather disappointed when Peter put that letter in his pocket, without opening it.

Peter read the letter at his office that morning. It was as follows:

Grey-Court, July 21st.

Dear Old Man—

Like a fool I overslept myself on the morning you left, so did not get my talk with you. You know I never get up early, and never can, so you have only your refusal to let me in that night to blame for our not having a last chat. If I had had the news to tell you that I now have, I should not have let you keep me out, even if you had forced me to break my way in.

Chum, the nicest girl in the world has told me that she loves me, and we are both as happy as can be. I know you will not be in a moment's doubt as to who she is. I have only run here to break it to my family, and shall go back to the Shrubberies early next week—to talk to Mr. Pierce, you understand!

My governor has decided that a couple of years' travel will keep me out of mischief as well as anything else he can devise, and as the prospect is not unpleasant, I am not going to let my new plans interfere with it, merely making my journeyings a *solitude à deux,* instead of solus. So we shall be married in September, at the Shrubberies, and sail for Europe almost immediately.

Now, I want you to stand by me in this, as you have in other things, and help me through. I want you, in short, to be my "best man" as you have been my best friend. "Best man," I should inform you, is an English wedding institution, which our swell people have suddenly discovered is a necessity to make a marriage ceremony legal. He doesn't do much. Holding his principal's hat, I believe, is the most serious duty that falls to him, though perhaps not stepping on the bridal dresses is more difficult.

My Mamma wants me to drive with her, so this must be continued in our next.

Aff.,   W.

Peter did not read law that morning. But after sitting in his chair for a couple of hours, looking at the opposite wall, and seeing something quite different, he took his pen, and without pause, or change of face, wrote two letters, as follows:

Dear Watts:

You hardly surprised me by your letter. I had suspected, both from your frequent visits to the Shrubberies, and from a way in which you occasionally spoke of Miss Pierce, that you loved her. After seeing her, I felt that it was not possible you did not. So I was quite prepared for your news. You have indeed been fortunate in winning such a girl. That I wish you every joy and happiness I need not say.

I think you could have found some other of the fellows better suited to stand with you, but if you think otherwise, I shall not fail you.

You will have to tell me about details, clothes, etc. Perhaps you can suggest a gift that will do? I remember Miss Pierce saying she was very fond of pearls. Would it be right to give something of that kind?

Faithfully yours, PETER.

DEAR MISS PIERCE:
A letter from Watts this morning tells me of his good fortune. Fearing lest my blunders may perhaps still give you pain, I write to say that your happiness is the most earnest wish of my life, and nothing which increases it can be other than good news to me. If I can ever serve you in any way, you will be doing me a great favor by telling me how.

Please give my regards to Mr. and Mrs. Pierce, and believe me,
Yours ever sincerely,
PETER STIRLING.

After these letters were written, Peter studied the wall again for a time. Studied it till long after the hour when he should have lunched. The wall had three cracks in it which approximated to an outline of Italy, but though Peter gazed at this particular wall a good many hours in the next few weeks, he did not discover this interesting fact till long after this time of wall-gazing.

In the early morning and after dinner, in spite of the summer heat, he took long walks. During the day he sat in his office doing nothing, with the exception of an occasional letter to his mother, and one or two to Watts in respect to the coming wedding. Two visits to the tailor's, and another to Tiffany's, which resulted in a pearl pin rather out of proportion to his purse, were almost the sole variations of this routine. It was really a relief to this terrible inactivity, when he found himself actually at the Shrubberies, the afternoon before the wedding.

Peter was rather surprised at the ease with which he went through the next twenty-four hours. It is true that the house was too full, and each person too busy, to trouble the silent groomsman with attention, so he might have done pretty much what he wished, without being noticed. He arrived late, thus having no chance for greetings till after a hurried dressing for dinner, when they were made in the presence of the whole party, who had waited his coming to go to the meal. He went through the ordeal well, even that with Miss Pierce, actually showing less embarrassment than she did. What was more astonishing, he calmly offered his arm to the bridesmaid who fell to his lot, and, after seating her, chatted without thinking that he was talking. Indeed, he hardly heeded what he did say, but spoke mechanically, as a kind of refuge from thought and feeling.

"I didn't find him a bit so," the girl said to Miss Pierce, later in the evening, with an indefiniteness which, if not merely feminine, must presuppose a previous conversation. "He isn't exactly talkative, but he is perfectly easy to get on with. I tried him on New York, and found he had gone into a good many odd places and can tell about them. He describes things very well, so that one sees them."

"It must be your tact, then, Miss Leroy," said Mrs. Pierce, "for we could get nothing out of him before."

"No! I had nothing to do with it, and, between ourselves, I think he disapproved of me. If Helen hadn't told me about him, I should have been very cool to him, his manner was so objectionable. He clearly talked to me because he felt it a duty, and not a pleasure."

"That's only that unfortunate manner of his," said Helen. "I really think at heart he's dreadfully afraid of us. At least that's what Watts says. But he only behaves as if—as if—well, you know what I mean, Alice!"

"Exactly," said Alice. "You can't describe it. He's so cool, and stolid, and silent, that you feel shoddy and cheap, and any simple little remark doesn't seem enough to say. You try to talk up to him, and yet feel small all the time." •

"Not at all," said Helen. "You talk down to him, as if he were—were—your old grandfather, or some one else you admired, but thought very dull and old-fashioned."

"But the worst is the way he looks at you. So gravely, even when you try to joke. Now I really think I'm passably pretty, but Mr. Stirling said as plainly as could be: 'I look at you occasionally because that's the proper thing to do when one talks, but I much prefer looking at that picture over your head.' I don't believe he noticed how my hair was dressed, or the color of my eyes. Such men are absolutely maddening. When they've finished their smoke, I'm going to make him notice me."

But Miss Leroy failed in her plan, try as she would. Peter did not notice girls any more. After worrying in his school and college days, over what women thought of him and how they treated him, he had suddenly ceased to trouble himself about them. It was as if a man, after long striving for something, had suddenly discovered that he did not wish it—that to him women's opinions had become worthless. Perhaps in this case it was only the Fox and the Grapes over again. At all events, from this time on Peter cared little what women did. Courteous he tried to be, for he understood this to be a duty. But that was all. They might laugh at him, snub him, avoid him. He cared not. He had struck women out of his plan of life. And this disregard, as we have already suggested, was sure to produce a strange change, not merely in Peter, but in women's view and treatment of him. Peter trying to please them, by dull, ordinary platitudes, was one thing. Peter avoiding them and talking to them when needs must, with that distant, uninterested look and voice, was quite another.

The next morning, Peter, after finding what a fifth wheel in a coach all men are at weddings, finally stood up with his friend. He had not been asked to stay on for another night, as had most of the bridal party, so he slipped away as soon as his duty was done, and took a train that put him into New York that evening. A week later he said good-bye to the young couple, on the deck of a steamship.

"Don't forget us, Peter," shouted Watts, after the fasts were cast off and the steamer was slowly moving into mid-stream.

Peter waved his hat, and turning, walked off the pier.

"Could he forget them?" was the question he asked himself.

CHAPTER X

WAITING

"MY friend," said an old and experienced philosopher to a young man, who with all the fire and impatience of his years wished to conquer the world quickly, "youth has many things to learn, but one of the most important is never to let another man beat you at waiting."

Peter went back to his desk, and waited. He gave up looking at the wall of his office, and took to somebody "On Torts" again. When that was finished he went through the other law books of his collection. Those done, he began to buy others, and studied them with great thoroughness and persistence. In one of his many walks, he stumbled upon the Apprentices' Library. Going in, he inquired about its privileges, and became a regular borrower of books. Peter had always been a reader, but now he gave from three or four hours a day to books, aside from his law study. Although he was slow, the number of volumes he not merely read but really mastered was marvellous. Books which he liked, without much regard to their popular reputation, he at once bought; for his simple life left him the ability to indulge himself in most respects within moderation. He was particularly careful to read a classic occasionally to keep up his Greek and Latin, and for the same reason he read French and German books aloud to himself. Before the year was out, he was a recognized quantity in certain book-stores, and was privileged to browse at will both among old and new books without interference or suggestion from the "stock" clerks. "There isn't any good trying to sell him anything," remarked one. "He makes up his mind for himself."

His reading was broadened out from the classic and belles-lettres grooves that were still almost a cult with the college graduate, by another recreation now become habitual with him. In his long tramps about the city, to vary the monotony, he would sometimes stop and chat with people—with a policeman, a fruit-vender, a long-

shore-man or a truckster. It mattered little who it was.
Then he often entered manufactories and "yards" and
asked if he could go through them, studying the methods,
and talking to the overseer or workers about the trade.
When he occasionally encountered some one who told him
"your kind ain't got no business here" he usually found
the statement "my father was a mill-overseer" a way to
break down the barrier. He had to use it seldom, for he
dressed plainly and met the men in a way which seldom
failed to make them feel that he was one of them. After
such inspection and chat, he would get books from the
library, and read up about the business or trade, finding
that in this way he could enjoy works otherwise too
technical, and really obtain a very good knowledge of
many subjects. Just how interesting he found such books
as "Our Fire-Laddies," which he read from cover to
cover, after an inspection of, and chat with, the men of
the nearest fire-engine station; or Latham's "The Sewage
Difficulty," which the piping of uptown New York induced
him to read; and others of diverse types is questionable.
Probably it was really due to his isolation, but it was
much healthier than gazing at blank walls.

When the courts opened, Peter kept track of the calen-
dars, and whenever a case or argument promised to be
interesting, or to call out the great lights of the profession, he attended and listened to them. He tried to write
out the arguments used, from notes, and finally this
practice induced him to give two evenings a week during
the winter mastering shorthand. It was really only a mental discipline, for any case of importance was obtainable
in print almost as soon as argued, but Peter was trying to
put a pair of slate-colored eyes out of his thoughts, and
employed this as one of the means.

When winter came, and his long walks became less
possible, he turned to other things. More from necessity
than choice, he visited the art and other exhibitions as they
occurred, he went to concerts, and to plays, all with due
regard to his means, and for this reason the latter were
the most seldom indulged in. Art and music did not come
easy to him, but he read up on both, not merely in standard books, but in the reviews of the daily press, and just

because there was so much in both that he failed to grasp, he studied the more carefully and patiently.

One trait of his New England training remained to him. He had brought a letter from his own Congregational church in his native town, to one of the large churches of the same sect in New York, and when admitted, hired a sitting and became a regular attendant at both morning and evening service. In time this produced a call from his new pastor. It was the first new friend he had gained in New York. "He seems a quiet, well-informed fellow," was the clergyman's comment: "I shall make a point of seeing something of him." But he was pastor of a very large and rich congregation, and was a hard-worked and hard-entertained man, so his intention was not realized.

Peter spent Christmastide with his mother, who worried not a little over his loss of flesh.

"You have been overworking," she said anxiously.

"Why, mother, I haven't had a client yet," laughed Peter.

"Then you've worried over not getting on," said his mother, knowing perfectly well that it was nothing of the sort. She had hoped that Peter would be satisfied with his six months' trial, but did not mention her wish. She marvelled to herself that New York had not yet discovered his greatness.

When Peter returned to the city, he made a change in his living arrangements. His boarding-place had filled up with the approach of winter, but with the class of men he already knew too well. Even though he met them only at meals, their atmosphere was intolerable to him. When a room next his office fell vacant, and went begging at a very cheap price, he decided to use it as a bedroom. So he moved his few belongings on his return from his visit to his mother's.

Although he had not been particularly friendly to the other boarders, nor made himself obtrusive in the least, not one of them failed to speak of his leaving. Two or three affected to be pleased, but "Butter-and-cheese" said he "was a first-rate chap" and this seemed to gain the assent of the table generally.

"I'm dreadfully sorry to lose him," his landlady in-

formed her other boarders, availing herself, perhaps, of the
chance to deliver a side hit at some of them. "He never
has complained once, since he came here, and he kept
his room as neat as if he had to take care of it himself."

"Well," said the box-office oracle, "I guess he's O. K.,
if he is a bit stiff; and a fellow who's best man to a big
New York swell, and gets his name in all the papers,
doesn't belong in a seven-dollar, hash-seven-days-a-week,
Bleecker Street boarding-house."

Peter fitted his room up simply, the sole indulgence (if
properly so called) being a bath, which is not a usual fitting of a New York business office, consciences not yet
being tubbable. He had made his mother show him how to
make coffee, and he adopted the Continental system of
meals, having rolls and butter sent in, and making a French
breakfast in his own rooms. Then he lunched regularly
not far from his office, and dined wherever his afternoon
walk, or evening plans carried him. He found that he
saved no money by the change, but he saved his feelings,
and was far freer to come and go as he chose.

He did not hear from the honeymoon party. Watts
had promised to write to him and send his address "as
soon as we decide whether we pass the winter in Italy
or on the Nile." But no letter came. Peter called on the
Pierces, only to find them out, and as no notice was taken
of his pasteboard, he drew his own inference, and did not
repeat the visit.

Such was the first year of Peter's New York life. He
studied, he read, he walked, and most of all, he waited.
But no client came, and he seemed no nearer one than the
day he had first seen his own name on his office door.
"How much longer will I have to wait? How long will
my patience hold out?" These were the questions he
asked himself, when for a moment he allowed himself to
lose courage. Then he would take to a bit of wall-gazing, while dreaming of a pair of slate-colored eyes.

CHAPTER XI

NEW FRIENDS

MR. CONVERSE had evidently thought that the only way for Peter to get on was to make friends. But in this first year Peter did not make a single one that could be really called such. His second summer broadened his acquaintance materially, though in a direction which promised him little law practice.

When the warm weather again closed the courts and galleries, and brought an end to the concerts and theatres, Peter found time harder to kill, the more, because he had pretty well explored the city. Still he walked much to help pass the time, and to get outside of his rooms into the air. For the same reason he often carried his book, after the heat of the day was over, to one of the parks, and did his reading there. Not far from his office, eastwardly, where two streets met at an angle, was a small open space too limited to be called a square, even if its shape had not been a triangle. Here, under the shade of two very sickly trees, surrounded by tall warehouses, were a couple of benches. Peter sat here many evenings smoking his pipe. Though these few square feet made perhaps the largest "open" within half a mile of his office, the angle was confined and dreary. Hence it is obvious there must have been some attraction to Peter, since he was such a walker, to make him prefer spending his time there rather than in the parks not far distant. The attraction was the children.

Only a few hundred feet away was one of the most densely crowded tenement districts of New York. It had no right to be there, for the land was wanted for business purposes, but the hollow on which it was built had been a swamp in the old days, and the soft land, and perhaps the unhealthiness, had prevented the erection of great warehouses and stores, which almost surrounded it. So it had been left to the storage of human souls instead of merchandise, for valuable goods need careful housing, while any place serves to pack humanity. It was not a nice district to go through, for there was a sense of heat, and dirt, and smell, and crowd, and toil, and sorrow throughout. It was probably no nicer to live in, and nothing proved it better than the overflow of the children therefrom into the little, hot, paved, airless angle. Here they could be found from five in the morning till twelve at night. Here, with guards set, to give notice of the approach of the children's joy-destroying Siva—otherwise the policeman—they played ball. Here "cat" and "one old cat" rendered bearable many a wilting hour for the little urchins. Here "Sally in our Alley" and "Skip-rope" made the little girls forget that the temperature was far above blood-heat. Here of an evening, Peter smoked and watched them.

At first he was an object of suspicion, and the sport visibly ceased when he put in an appearance. But he simply sat on one of the benches and puffed his pipe, and after a few evenings they lost all fear of him, and went on as if he were not there. In time, an intercourse sprang up between them. One evening Peter appeared with a stick of wood, and as he smoked, he whittled at it with a *real* jack-knife! He was scrutinized by the keen-eyed youngsters with interest at once, and before he had whittled long, he had fifty children sitting in the shape of a semicircle on the stone pavement, watching his doings with almost breathless interest. When the result of his work actually developed into a "cat" of marvellous form and finish, a sigh of intense joy passed through the boy part of his audience. When the "cat" was passed over to their mercies, words could not be found to express their emotions. Another evening, the old clothes-line that served for a jump-rope, after having bravely rubbed against the pavement many thousand times in its endeavor to lighten the joyless life of the little pack, finally succumbed, worn through the centre and quite beyond hope of further knotting. Then Peter rose, and going to one of the little shops that supplied the district soon returned with a *real* jump-rope, with *wooden handles!* So from time to time, *real* tops, *real* dolls, *real* marbles and various other *real,* if cheap, things, hitherto only enjoyed in dreams, or at most through home-made attempts, found their way into the angle, and were distributed among the little imps. They could not resist such subtle bribery, and soon Peter was on as familiar and friendly a footing as he could wish. He came to know each by name, and was made the umpire in all their disputes and the confidant in all their troubles. They were a dirty, noisy, lawless, and godless little community, but they were interesting to watch, and the lonely fellow grew to like them much, for with all their premature sharpness, they were really natural, and responded warmly to his friendly overtures.

After a time, Peter tried to help them a little more than by mere small gifts. A cheap box of carpenter's tools was bought, and under his superintendence, evenings were spent in the angle, in making various articles. A small wheelbarrow, a knife-and-fork basket, a clock-bracket and other easy things were made, one at a time. All boys and indeed some girls were allowed to help. One would saw off the end of a plank; another would rule a pencil line; the next would plane the plank down to that line; the next would bore the holes in it; the next would screw it into position; the next would sandpaper it. The work went very slowly, but every one who would, had his share in it, while the rest sat and watched. When the article was completed, lots were drawn for it, and happy was the fortunate one who drew the magnificent prize in life's lottery!

Occasionally too, Peter brought a book with him, and read it aloud to them. He was rather surprised to find that they did not take to Sunday-school stories or fairy tales. Wild adventures in foreign lands were the most effective; and together they explored the heart of Africa, climbed the Swiss mountains, fought the Western Indians, and attempted to discover the North Pole. They had a curious liking for torture, blood-letting, and death. Nor were they without discrimination.

"I guess that fellow is only working his jaw," was one little chap's criticism at a certain point of the narrative of a well-known African explorer, rather famous for his success in advertising himself. Again "that's bully," was the comment uttered by another, when Peter, rather than refuse their request to read aloud, had been compelled to choose something in Macaulay's Essays, and had read the description of the Black Hole of Calcutta. "Say, mister," said another, "I don't believe that fellow wasn't there, for he never could a told it like that, if he wasn't."

As soon as his influence was secure, Peter began to affect them in other ways. Every fight, every squabble, was investigated, and the blame put where it belonged. Then a mandate went forth that profanity was to cease; and, though contrary to every instinct and habit, cease it did after a time, except for an occasional unconscious slip. "Sporadic swearing," Peter called it, and explained what it meant to the children, and why he forgave that, while punishing the intentional swearer with exclusion from his favor. So, too, the girls were told that to "poke" tongues at each other, and make faces, was but another way of swearing; "for they all mean that there is hate in your hearts, and it is that which is wrong, and not the mere words or faces." He ran the risk of being laughed at, but they didn't laugh, for something in his way of talking to them, even when verging on what they called "goody-goody," inspired them with respect.

Before many weeks of this intercourse, Peter could not stroll east from his office without being greeted with yells of recognition. The elders, too, gave him "good-evening" pleasantly and smiled genially. The children had naturally told their parents about him, of his wonderful presents and great skill with knife and string.

"He can whittle anything you ask!"

"He knows how to make things you want!"

"He can tie a knot sixteen different kinds!"

"He can fold a newspaper into soldiers' and firemen's caps!"

"He's friends with the policeman!"

Such laudations, and a hundred more, the children sang of him to their elders.

"Oh," cried one little four-year-old girl, voicing the unanimous feeling of the children, "Mister Peter is just shplendid."

So the elders nodded and smiled when they met him,

and he was pretty well known to several hundred people whom he knew not.

But another year passed, and still no client came.

CHAPTER XII

HIS FIRST CLIENT

PETER sat in his office, one hot July day, two years after his arrival, writing to his mother. He had but just returned to New York, after a visit to her, which had left him rather discouraged, because for the first time, she had pleaded with him to abandon his attempt and return to his native town. He had only replied that he was not yet prepared to acknowledge himself beaten; but the request and his mother's disappointment had worried him. While he wrote came a knock at the door, and, in response to his "come in," a plain-looking laborer entered and stood awkwardly before him.

"What can I do for you?" asked Peter, seeing that he must assist the man to state his business.

"If you please, sir," said the man, humbly, "it's Missy. And I hope you'll pardon me for troubling you."

"Certainly," said Peter. "What about Missy?"

"She's—the doctor says she's dying," said the man, adding, with a slight suggestion of importance, blended with the evident grief he felt: "Sally, and Bridget Milligan are dead already."

"And what can I do?" said Peter, sympathetically, if very much at sea.

"Missy wants to see you before she goes. It's only a child's wish, sir, and you needn't trouble about it. But I had to promise her I'd come and ask you. I hope it's no offence?"

"No." Peter rose, and, passing to the next room, took his hat, and the two went into the street together.

"What is the trouble?" asked Peter, as they walked.

"We don't know, sir. They were all took yesterday, and two are dead already." The man wiped the tears from his eyes with his shirt-sleeve, smearing the red brick-dust with which it was powdered, over his face.

"You've had a doctor?"

"Not till this morning. We didn't think it was bad at first."

"What is your name?"

"Blackett, sir—Jim Blackett."

Peter began to see daylight. He remembered both a Sally and Matilda Blackett. That was probably "Missy."

A walk of six blocks transferred them to the centre of the tenement district. Two flights of stairs brought them to the Blacketts' rooms. On the table of the first, which was evidently used both as a kitchen and sitting-room, already lay a coffin containing a seven-year-old girl. Candles burned at the four corners, adding to the bad air and heat. In the room beyond, in bed, with a tired-looking woman tending her, lay a child of five. Wan and pale as well could be, with perspiration standing in great drops on the poor little hot forehead, the hand of death, as it so often does, had put something into the face never there before.

"Oh, Mister Peter," the child said, on catching sight of him, "I said you'd come."

Peter took his handkerchief and wiped the little head. Then he took a newspaper, lying on a chair, twisted it into a rude fan, and began fanning the child as he sat on the bed.

"What did you want me for?" he asked.

"Won't you tell me the story you read from the book? The one about the little girl who went to the country, and was given a live dove and real flowers."

Peter began telling the story as well as he could remember it, but it was never finished. For while he talked another little girl went to the country, a far country, from which there is no return—and a very ordinary little story ended abruptly.

The father and mother took the death very calmly. Peter asked them a few questions, and found that there were three other children, the eldest of whom was an errand boy, and therefore away. The others, twin babies, had been cared for by a woman on the next floor. He asked about money, and found that they had not enough to pay the whole expenses of the double funeral.

"But the undertaker says he'll do it handsome, and will let the part I haven't money for, run, me paying it off in weekly payments," the man explained, when Peter expressed some surprise at the evident needless expense they were entailing on themselves.

While he talked, the doctor came in.

"I knew there was no chance," he said, when told of the death. "And you remember I said so," he added, appealing to the parents.

"Yes, that's what he said," responded the father.

"Well," said the doctor, speaking in a brisk, lively way peculiar to him, "I've found what the matter was."

"No?" said the mother, becoming interested at once.

"It was the milk," the doctor continued. "I thought there was something wrong with it, the moment I smelt it, but I took some home to make sure." He pulled a paper out of his pocket. "That's the test, and Dr. Plumb, who has two cases next door, found it was just the same there."

The Blacketts gazed at the written analysis, with wonder, not understanding a word of it. Peter looked too, when they had satisfied their curiosity. As he read it, a curious expression came into his face. A look not unlike that which his face had worn on the deck of the "Sunrise." It could hardly be called a change of expression, but rather a strengthening and deepening of his ordinary look.

"That was in the milk drunk by the children?" he asked, placing his finger on a particular line.

"Yes," replied the doctor. "The milk was bad to start with, and was drugged to conceal the fact. These carbonates sometimes work very unevenly, and I presume this particular can of milk got more than its share of the doctoring."

"There are almost no glycerides," remarked Peter, wishing to hold the doctor till he should have had time to think.

"No," said the doctor. "It was skim milk."

"You will report it to the Health Board?" asked Peter.

"When I'm up there," said the doctor. "Not that it will do any good. But the law requires it."

"Won't they investigate?"

"They'll investigate too much. The trouble with them is, they investigate, but don't prosecute."

"Thank you," said Peter. He shook hands with the parents, and went upstairs to the fourth floor. The crape on a door guided him to where Bridget Milligan lay. Here preparations had gone farther. Not merely were the candles burning, but four bottles, with the corks partly drawn, were on the cold cooking stove, while a wooden pail filled with beer, reposed in the embrace of a washtub, filled otherwise with ice. Peter asked a few questions. There was only an elder brother and sister. Patrick worked as a porter. Ellen rolled cigars. They had a little money laid up. Enough to pay for the funeral. "Mr. Moriarty gave us the whisky and beer at half price," the girl explained incidentally. "Thank you, sir. We don't need anything." Peter rose to go. "Bridget was often speaking of you to us. And I thank you for what you did for her."

Peter went down, and called next door, to see Dr. Plumb's patients. These were in a fair way for recovery. "They didn't get any of the milk till last night," the gray-haired, rather sad-looking doctor told him, "and I got at them early this morning. Then I suspected the milk at once, and treated them accordingly. I've been forty years doing this sort of thing, and it's generally the milk. Dr. Sawyer, next door, is a new man, and doesn't get hold quite as quick. But he knows more of the science of the thing, and can make a good analysis."

"You think they have a chance?"

"If this heat will let up a bit," said the doctor, mopping his forehead. "It's ninety-eight in here; that's enough to kill a sound child."

"Could they be moved?"

"To-morrow, perhaps."

"Mrs. Dooley, could you take your children away to the country to-morrow, if I find a place for you?"

"It's very little money I have, sir."

"It won't cost you anything. Can you leave your family?"

"There's only Moike. And he'll do very well by himself," he was told.

"Then if the children can go, be ready at 10:15 tomorrow, and you shall all go up for a couple of weeks to my mother's in Massachusetts. They'll have plenty of good food there," he explained to the doctor, "grass and flowers close to the house and woods not far away."

"That will fix them," said the doctor.

"About this milk. Won't the Health Board punish the sellers?" Peter asked.

"Probably not," he was told. "It's difficult to get them to do anything, and at this season so many of them are on vacations, it is doubly hard to make them stir."

Peter went to the nearest telegraph, and sent a dispatch to his mother. Then he went back to his office, and sitting down, began to study his wall. But he was not thinking of a pair of slate-colored eyes. He was thinking of his first case. He had found a client.

CHAPTER XIII

THE CASE

PETER went to work the next morning at an hour which most of us, if we are indiscreet enough to wake, prefer to use as the preface to a further two to four hours' nap. He had spent his evening in a freshening of his knowledge in certain municipal laws, and other details which he thought he might need, and as early as five o'clock he was at work in the tenement district, asking questions and taking notes. The inquiry took little skill. The milk had come from the cart of a certain company, which passed daily through the locality, not to supply orders, but to peddle milk to whoever cared to buy. Peter had the cart pointed out that morning, but, beyond making a note of the exact name of the company, he paid no attention to it. He was aiming at bigger game than a milk cart or its driver.

His work was interrupted only by his taking Mrs. Dooley and the two children to the train. That done, Peter walked northwardly and westwardly, till he had nearly reached the river front. It took some little inquiry, but after a while he stumbled on a small shanty which had a sign:

NATIONAL MILK COMPANY

OFFICE

The place, however, was closed and no one around seemed connected with it, though a number of milk carts were standing about. Close to these was a long line of sheds, which in turn backed up against a great brewery. A couple of men lounged at the door of the sheds. Peter walked up to them, and asked if they could tell him where he could find any one connected with the milk company.

"The boss is off for lunch," said one. "I can take an order, if that's what you want."

Peter said it was not an order, and began chatting with the men. Before he had started to question them, a third man, from inside the sheds, joined the group at the door. "That cow's dead," he remarked as he came up.

"Is it?" said the one called Bill. Both rose, and went into the shed. Peter started to go with them.

"You can't come in," said the new-comer.

But Peter passed in, without paying the least attention to him.

"Come back," called the man, following Peter.

Peter turned to him: "You are one of the employees of the National Milk Company?" he asked.

"Yes," said the man, "and we have orders——"

Peter usually let a little pause occur after a remark to him, but in this case he spoke before the man completed his speech. He spoke, too, with the air of decision and command that quieted the man.

"Go back to your work," he said, "and don't order me round. I know what I'm about." Then he walked after the other two men as rapidly as the dimness permitted. The employee scratched his head, and then followed.

Dim as the light was, Peter could discern that he was passing between two rows of cows, with not more than space enough for men to pass each other between the rows. It was filthy, and very warm, and there was a peculiar smell in the air which Peter did not associate with a cow stable. It was a kind of vapor which brought some suggestion to his mind, yet one he could not identify. Presently he came upon the two men. One had lighted a lantern and was examining a cow that lay on the ground. That it was dead was plain. But what most interested Peter, although he felt a shudder of horror at the sight, were the rotted tail and two great sores on the flank that lay uppermost.

"That's a bad-looking cow," he said.

"Ain't it?" replied the one with the lantern. "But you can't help their havin' them, if you feed them on mash."

"Hold your tongue, Bill," said the man who had followed Peter.

"Take some of your own advice," said Peter, turning quickly, and speaking in a voice that made the man step back. A terrible feeling was welling up in Peter's heart. He thought of the poor little fever-stricken children. He saw the poor fever-stricken cow. He would like to—to——

He dropped the arm he had unconsciously raised. "Give me that lantern," he demanded.

The man hesitated and looked at the others.

"Give me that lantern," said Peter, speaking low, but his voice ringing very clear.

The lantern was passed to him, and taking it, he walked along the line of cows. He saw several with sores more or less developed. One or two he saw in the advanced stages of the disease, where the tail had begun to rot away. The other men followed him on his tour of inspection, and whispered together nervously. It did not take Peter long to examine all he wanted to see. Handing back the lantern at the door, he said: "Give me your names."

The men looked nonplussed, and shifted their weights uneasily from leg to leg.

"You," said Peter, looking at the man who had interfered with him.

"Wot do yer want with it?" he was asked.

"That's my business. What's your name?"

"John Tingley."

"Where do you live?"

"310 West 61st Street."

Peter obtained and wrote down the names and addresses of the trio. He then went to the "office" of the company, which was now opened.

"Is this an incorporated company?" he asked of the man tilted back in a chair.

"No," said the man, adding two chair legs to terra firma, and looking at Peter suspiciously.

"Who owns it?" Peter queried.

"I'm the boss."

"That isn't what I asked."

"That's what I answered."

"And your name is?"

"James Coldman."

"Do you intend to answer my question?"

"Not till I know your business."

"I'm here to find out against whom to get warrants for a criminal prosecution."

"For what?"

"The warrant will say."

The man squirmed in his chair. "Will you give me till to-morrow?"

"No. The warrant is to be issued to-day. Decide at once, whether you or your principal, shall be the man to whom it shall be served."

"I guess you'd better make it against me," said the man.

"Very well," said Peter. "Of course you know your employer will be run down, and as I'm not after the rest of you, you will only get him a few days' safety at the price of a term in prison."

"Well, I've got to risk it," said the man.

Peter turned and walked away. He went down town to the Blacketts.

"I want you to carry the matter to the courts," he told the father. "These men deserve punishment and if you'll let me go on with it, it shan't cost you anything; and by bringing a civil suit as well, you'll probably get some money out of it."

Blackett gave his assent. So too did Patrick Milligan, and "Moike" Dooley. They had won fame already by the deaths and wakes, but a "coort case" promised to give them prestige far beyond what even these distinctions conferred. So the three walked away proudly with Peter, and warrants were sworn to and issued against the "boss" as principal, and the driver and the three others as witnesses, made returnable on the following morning. On many a doorstep of the district, that night, nothing else was talked of, and the trio were the most envied men in the neighborhood. Even Mrs. Blackett and Ellen Milligan forgot their grief, and held a joint *soirée* on their front stoop.

"Shure, it's mighty hard for Mrs. Dooley, that she's away!" said one. "She'll be feeling bad when she knows what she's missed."

The next morning, Peter, the two doctors, the Blacketts, the Milligans, Dooley, the milk quintet, and as many inhabitants of the "district" as could crush their way in, were in court by nine o'clock. The plaintiffs and their friends were rather disappointed at the quietness of the proceedings. The examinations were purely formal except in one instance, when Peter asked for the "name or names of the owner or owners" of the National Milk Company. Here the defendant's attorney, a shrewd criminal lawyer, interfered, and there was a sharp passage at arms, in which an attempt was made to anger Peter. But he kept his head, and in the end carried his point. The owner turned out to be the proprietor of the brewery, as Peter had surmised, who thus utilized the mash from his vats in feeding cattle. But on Peter's asking for an additional warrant against him, the defendant's lawyer succeeded in proving, if the statement of the overseer proved it, that the brewer was quite ignorant that the milk sold in the "district" was what had been unsalable the day before to better customers, and that the skimming and doctoring of it was unknown to him. So an attempt to punish the rich man as a criminal was futile. He could afford to pay for straw men.

"Arrah!" said Dooley to Peter as they passed out of the court, "Oi think ye moight have given them a bit av yer moind."

"Wait till the trial," said Peter. "We mustn't use up our powder on the skirmish line."

So the word was passed through the district that "theer'd be fun at the rale trial," and it was awaited with intense interest by five thousand people.

CHAPTER XIV

NEW YORK JUSTICE

PETER saw the District Attorney the next morning for a few moments, and handed over to him certain memoranda of details that had not appeared in the committing court's record.

"It shall go before the grand jury day after to-morrow," that official told him, without much apparent interest in the matter.

"How soon can it be tried, if they find a true bill?" asked Peter.

"Can't say," replied the official.

"I merely wished to know," said Peter, "because three of the witnesses are away, and I want to have them back in time."

"Probably a couple of weeks," yawned the man, and Peter, taking the hint, departed.

The rest of the morning was spent in drawing up the papers in three civil suits against the rich brewer. Peter filed them as soon as completed, and took the necessary steps for their prompt service.

These produced an almost immediate result, in the shape of a call the next morning from the same lawyer who had defended the milkmen in the preliminary examination. Peter, as he returned from his midday meal, met the lawyer on the stairs.

"Ah, Mr. Stirling. Good-morning," said the man,

whose name was Dummer. "I've just left your office, finding it closed."

"Come in," said Peter.

The lawyer glanced around the plain room, and a quiet look of satisfaction came over his face. The two sat down.

"About those cases, Mr. Stirling?"

"Well?"

"For reasons you can easily understand, we don't wish them to come to trial."

"Well?"

"And we take it for granted that your clients will be quite willing to settle them."

"We will talk about that, after the criminal trial is over."

"Why not now?"

"Because we hope to make Coldman speak the truth in the trial, and thus be able to reach Bohlmann."

"You're wasting your time."

"Not if there's the smallest chance of sending the brewer to prison."

"There isn't. Coldman will stick to what he said if the thing is ever tried, which it won't be."

Peter eyed Dummer without changing a muscle. "The District Attorney told me that it ought to be in the courts in a couple of weeks."

Dummer smiled blandly, and slowly closed one eye. "The District Attorney tries to tell the truth," he said, "and I have no doubt he thought that was what he was telling you. Now name your figure?"

"The civil suits will not be compromised till the criminal one is finished."

"But I tell you the criminal one is dead. Squashed. Bohlmann and I have seen the right people, and they've seen the District Attorney. That case won't even go to the grand jury. So now, drop it, and say what you'll settle the civil suits for?"

"James Coldman shall go to prison for killing those children," said Peter, "and till he does, it is waste time to talk of dropping or settling anything."

"Humph," half laughed the lawyer, though with obvious disgust at the mulishness in Peter's face and voice. "You think you know it all. But you don't. You can work for ten years, and that case will be no nearer trial than it is to-day. I tell you, young man, you don't know New York."

"I don't know New York," said Peter, "but——"

"Exactly," interrupted Dummer. "And I do."

"Probably," replied Peter quietly. "You may know New York, Mr. Dummer, but you don't know me. That case shall be tried."

"Well," laughed Dummer, "if you'll agree not to press the civil suits, till that's out of the way, we shall have no need to compromise. Good-day."

The next morning Peter went to the District Attorney's office, and inquired for him.

"He's gone to Bar Harbor for a couple of weeks' vacation," he was told.

"Whom must I see in his stead?" And after some time Peter was brought face to face with the acting official.

"Mr. Nelson told me he should present the Coldman case to the grand jury to-day, and finding he has left the city, I wish to know who has it in charge?" asked Peter.

"He left all the presentments with me," the deputy replied, "but there was no such case as that."

"Could he have left it with some one else to attend to?"

"No."

Peter went back to his office, took down the Code and went over certain sections. His eyes had rather a sad look as they gazed at his wall, after his study, as if what he had read had not pleased him. But if the eyes were sad, the heavy jaw had a rigidity and setness which gave no indication of weakness or yielding.

For two weeks Peter waited, and then once more invaded officialdom.

"The District Attorney's engaged, and can't see you," he was told. Peter came again in the afternoon, with the same result. The next morning, brought only a like answer, and this was duplicated in the afternoon. The third day he said he would wait, and sat for hours in the anteroom, hoping to be called, or to intercept the officer. But it was only to see man after man ushered into the private office, and finally to be told that the District Attorney had gone to lunch, and would not return that day. The man who told him this grinned, and evidently considered it a good joke, nor had Peter been unconscious that all the morning the clerks and underlings had been laughing, and guying him as he waited. Yet his jaw was only set the more rigidly, as he left the office.

He looked up the private address of the officer in the directory, and went to see him that evening. He was wise enough not to send in his name, and Mr. Nelson actually came into the hall to see him.

The moment he saw Peter, however, he said: "Oh, it's you. Well, I never talk business except in business hours."

"I have tried to see you——" began Peter.

"Try some more," interrupted the man, smiling, and going toward the parlor.

Peter followed him, calmly. "Mr. Nelson," he said, "do you intend to push that case?"

"Of course," smiled Nelson. "After I've finished four hundred indictments that precede it."

"Not till then?"

"No."

"Mr. Nelson, can't you overlook politics for a moment, and think of——"

"Who said anything of politics?" interrupted Nelson. "I merely tell you there are indictments which have been in my office for five years and are yet to be tried, and that your case is going to take its turn." Nelson passed into the back room, leaving his caller alone.

Peter left the room, and passed out of the front door, just as a man was about to ring the bell.

"Is Mr. Nelson in?" asked the man.

"I have just left him, Mr. Dummer," said Peter.

"Ah! Good-evening, Mr. Stirling. I think I can guess your business. Well. How do you come on?" Dummer was obviously laughing internally.

Peter started down the steps without answering.

"Perhaps I can help you?" said Dummer. "I know Mr. Nelson very well in politics, and so does Mr. Bohlmann. If you'll tell me what you are after, I'll try to say a good word for you?"

"I don't need your help, thank you," said Peter calmly.

"Good," said Dummer. "You think a briefless lawyer of thirty can go it alone, do you, even against the whole city government?"

"I know I have not influence enough to get that case pushed, Mr. Dummer, but the law is on my side, and I'm not going to give up yet."

"Well, what are you going to do about it?" said Dummer, sneeringly.

"Fight," said Peter, walking away.

He went back to his office, and sitting at his desk, wrote a formal letter to the District Attorney, calling his attention to the case, and asking information as to when it would be brought to trial. Then he copied this and mailed the original. Then he read the Code again. After that he went over the New York reports, making notes. For a second time the morning sun found Peter still at his desk. But this time his head was not bowed upon his blotter, as if he were beaten or dead. His whole figure was stiff with purpose, and his jaw was as rigid as a mastiff's.

- - - - - -

CHAPTER XV

THE FIGHT

THE only reply which Peter received to his letter to the District Attorney, was a mere formal reiteration of that officer's verbal statement, that the case would be taken up in its due order, after those which preceded it had been dealt with. Peter knew enough of the numberless cases which never reach trial to understand that this meant in truth the laying aside of the case, till it was killed by the statute of limitations.

On receiving this reply, Peter made another move, by going to three newspapers, and trying to see their managing editors. One declined to see him. A second merely told Peter, after his statement, which the editor only allowed him partly to explain, that he was very busy and could not take time to look into it, but that Peter might come again in about a month. The third let Peter tell his story, and then shook his head:

"I have no doubt you are right, but it isn't in shape for us to use. Such a case rarely goes to trial for six months or a year, and so, if we begin an attack now, it will simply fall flat. If you can get us a written statement from the District Attorney that he doesn't intend to push the case, we can do something, but I suppose he's far too shrewd to commit himself."

"Yes."

"Then there's no use in beginning an attack, for you really have no powder. Come in again a year from now, and then we may be able to say something, if he hasn't acted in the meantime."

Peter left the office, knowing that that chance of pressure was gone. If the papers of the Republican party would not use it, it was idle spending time in seeing or trying to see the editors of the Democratic papers. He wasted therefore no more efforts on newspapers.

The next three days Peter passed in the New York Law Institute Library, deep in many books. Then he packed his bag, and took an afternoon train for Albany. He was going to play his last card, with the odds of a thousand to one against his winning. But that very fact only nerved him the more.

Promptly at ten o'clock, the morning after his arrival at the state capital, he sent in his card to the Governor. Fortunately for him, the middle of August is not a busy time with that official, and after a slight delay, he was ushered into the executive chamber.

Peter had been planning this interview for hours, and without explanation or preamble, he commenced his statement. He knew that he must interest the Governor promptly, or there would be a good chance of his being bowed out. So he began with a description of the cow-stables. Then he passed to the death of the little child. He sketched both rapidly, not taking three minutes to do it, but had he been pleading for his own life, he could not have spoken more earnestly nor feelingly.

The Governor first looked surprised at Peter's abruptness; then weary: then interested; and finally turned his revolving chair so as to put his back to Peter. And after Peter had ended his account, he remained so for a moment. That back was very expressive to Peter. For the first time he felt vanquished.

But suddenly the Governor turned, and Peter saw tears on his cheek. And he said, after a big swallow, "What do you want of me?" in a voice that meant everything to Peter.

"Will you listen to me for five minutes?" asked Peter, eagerly.

"Yes."

Then Peter read aloud a statement of the legal proceedings, and of his interviews with the District Attorney and with Dummer, in the clearest and most compact sentences he had been able to frame.

"You want me to interfere?" asked the Governor.

"Yes."

"I'm afraid it's not possible. I can of course remove the District Attorney, but it must be for cause, and I do not see that you can absolutely prove his non-intention to prosecute those scoundrels."

"That is true. After study, I did not see that you could remove him. But there's another remedy."

"What is that?"

"Through the State Attorney you can appoint a special counsel for this case."

"Are you sure?"

Peter laid one of the papers in his hands before the Governor. After reading it, the Governor rang a bell.

"Send for Mr. Miller," he said to the boy. Then he turned, and with Peter went over the court papers, till Mr. Miller put in an appearance.

"State the matter to Mr. Miller," said the Governor, and Peter read his paper again and told what he wished. "The power unquestionably exists," said the Attorney-General. "But it has not been used in many years. Perhaps I had better look into it a bit."

"Go with Mr. Miller, Mr. Stirling, and work over your papers with him," said the Governor.

"Thank you," said Peter simply, but his hand and face and voice said far more, as he shook hands. He went out with the first look of hope his face had worn for two years.

The ground which the Attorney-General and his subordinates had to traverse was that over which Peter had so well travelled already, that he felt very much at home, while his notes indeed aided the study, and were doubly welcomed, because the summer season had drained the office of its underlings. Half as assistant, and half as principal, he worked till three o'clock, with pleasure that grew, as he saw that the opinion of the Attorney-General seemed to agree more and more with his own. Then they returned to the Governor, to whom the Attorney-General gave his opinion that his present conclusion was that the Governor could empower him, or some appointee, to prosecute the case.

"Well," said the Governor, "I'm glad you think so. But if we find that it isn't possible, Mr. Stirling, I'll have a letter written to the District Attorney that may scare him into proceeding with the case."

Peter thanked him, and rose to go.

"Are you going to New York at once?" asked the Governor.

"Yes. Unless I can be of use here."

"Suppose you dine with me, and take a late train?"

"It will be a great pleasure," said Peter.

"Very well. Six sharp." Then after Peter had left the room, the Governor asked, "How is he on law?"

"Very good. Clear-headed and balanced."

"He knows how to talk," said the Governor. "He brought my heart up in my mouth as no one has done in years. Now, I must get word to some of the people in New York to find out who he is, and if this case has any concealed boomerang in it."

The dinner was a very quiet one with only the Governor and his wife. The former must have told his better-half something about Peter, for she studied him with a very kind look in her face, and prosaic and silent as Peter was, she did not seem bored. After the dinner was eaten, and some one called to talk politics with the Governor, she took Peter off to another room, and made him tell her about the whole case, and how he came to take it up, and why he had come to the Governor for help. She cried over it, and after Peter had gone, she went upstairs and looked at her own two sleeping boys, quite large enough to fight the world on their own account, but still little children to the mother's heart, and had another cry over them. She went downstairs later to the Governor's study, and interrupting him in the work to which he had settled down, put her arms about his neck, and kissed him. "You must help him, William," she said. "Do everything you can to have those scoundrels punished, and let him do it."

The Governor only laughed; but he pushed back his work, and his wife sat down, and told of her admiration and sympathy for Peter's fight. There was a bad time ahead for the criminal and his backers. They might have political influence of the strongest character, fighting their battle, but there was a bigger and more secret one at work. Say what we please, the strongest and most subtle "pull" this world as yet contains is the undercurrent of a woman's influence.

Peter went back to New York that night, feeling hopeful, yet doubtful. It almost seemed impossible that he had succeeded, yet at twenty-three, failure is hard to believe in. So he waited, hoping to see some move on the part of the State, and dreaming of nothing better. But better came, for only five days after his return his mail brought him a large envelope, and inside that envelope was a special commission, which made Peter a deputy of the Attorney-General, to prosecute in the Court of Sessions, the case of "The People of the State of New York *versus* James Coldman." If any one could have seen Peter's face, as he read the purely formal instrument, he would not have called it dull or heavy. For Peter knew that he had won; that in place of justice blocking and hindering him, every barrier was crushed down; that this prosecution rested with no officials, but was for him to push; that that little piece of parchment bound every court to support him; that if necessary fifty thousand troops would enforce the power which granted it. Within three hours, the first formal steps to place the case in the courts had been taken, and Peter was working at the evidence and law in the matter.

These steps produced a prompt call from Dummer, who showed considerably less assurance than hitherto, even though he tried to take Peter's success jauntily. He wanted Peter to drop the whole thing, and hinted at large sums of money, but Peter at first did not notice his hints, and finally told him that the case should be tried. Then Dummer pleaded for delay. Peter was equally obdurate. Later they had a contest in the court over this. But Peter argued in a quiet way, which nevertheless caught the attention of the judge, who ended the dispute by refusing to postpone. The judge hadn't intended to act in this way, and was rather surprised at his own conduct. The defendant's lawyer was furious.

No stone was left unturned, however, to prevent the case going to trial. Pressure of the sharpest and closest kind was brought to bear on the Governor himself—pressure which required backbone to resist. But he stood by his act: perhaps because he belonged to a different party than that in control of the city government; perhaps because of Peter's account, and the truthfulness in his face as he told it; perhaps because the Attorney-General had found it legal; perhaps because of his wife; perhaps it was a blending of all these. Certain it is, that all attempts to block failed, and in the last week in August it came before the court.

Peter had kept his clients informed as to his struggles, and they were tremendously proud of the big battle and ultimate success, as indeed were the residents of the whole district, who felt that it was really their own case. Then the politicians were furious and excited over it, while the almost unexampled act of the Governor had created a good deal of public interest in the case. So the court was packed and the press had reporters in attendance. Since the trial was fully reported, it is needless to go over the testimony here. What Peter could bring out, is already known. The defence, by "experts" endeavored to prove that the cowsheds were not in a really unhygienic condition; that feeding cows on "mash" did not affect their milk, nor did mere "skin sores;" that the milk had been sold by mistake, in ignorance that it was thirty-six hours old, and skimmed; and that the proof of this particular milk being the cause of the deaths was extremely inadequate and doubtful. The only dramatic incident in the testimony was the putting the two little Dooleys (who had returned in fat and rosy condition, the day before) on the stand.

"Did you find country milk different from what you have here?" Peter asked the youngest.

"Oh, yes," she said. "Here it comes from a cart, but in the country it squirts from a cow."

"Order," said the judge to the gallery.

"Does it taste differently?"

"Yes. It's sweet, as if they put sugar in it. It's lovely! I like cow milk better than cart milk."

"Damn those children!" said Dummer, to the man next him.

The event of the trial came, however, when Peter summed up. He spoke quietly, in the simplest language, using few adjectives and no invective. But as the girl at the Pierces' dinner had said, "He describes things so that one sees them." He told of the fever-stricken cows, and he told of the little fever-stricken children in such a way that the audience sobbed; his clients almost had to be ordered out of court; the man next Dummer mopped his eyes with his handkerchief; the judge and jury thoughtfully covered their eyes (so as to think the better); the reporters found difficulty (owing to the glary light), in writing the words despite their determination not to miss one; and even the prisoner wiped his eyes on his sleeve. Peter was unconscious that he was making a great speech; great in its simplicity, and great in its pathos. He afterwards said he had not given it a moment's thought and had merely said what he felt. Perhaps his conclusion indicated why he was able to speak with the feeling he did. For he said:

"This is not merely the case of the State *versus* James Coldman. It is the case of the tenement-house children, against the inhumanity of man's greed."

Dummer whispered to the man next him, "There's no

good. He's done for us." Then he rose, and made a clever defence. He knew it was wasting his time. The judge charged against him, and the jury gave the full verdict: "Man-slaughter in the first degree." Except for the desire for it, the sentence created little stir. Every one was still feeling and thinking of Peter's speech.

And to this day that speech is talked of in "the district."

————

CHAPTER XVI

THE CONSEQUENCES

Nor was it the district alone which talked of the speech. Perhaps the residents of it made their feelings most manifest, for they organized a torch-light procession that night, and went round and made Peter an address of thanks, Mr. Dennis Moriarty being the spokesman. The judge shook hands with him after the trial, and said that he had handled his case well. The defendant's lawyer told him he "knew his business." A number of the reporters sought a few words with him, and blended praise with questions.

The reporters did far more than this, however. It was the dull newspaper season, and the case had turned out to be a thoroughly "journalistic" one. So they questioned and interviewed every one concerned, and after cleverly winnowing the chaff, which in this case meant the dull, from the gleanings, most of them gave several columns the next morning to the story. Peter's speech was printed in full, and proved to read almost as well as it had sounded. The reporters were told, and repeated the tales without much attempt at verification, that Peter had taken the matter up without hope of profit; had paid the costs out of his own pocket; had refused to settle, "though offered nine thousand dollars;" had "saved the Dooley children's lives by sending them into the country;" and "had paid for the burials of the little victims." So all gave him a puff, and two of the better sort wrote really fine editorials about him. At election time, or any other than a dull season, the case would have had small attention, but August is the month, to reverse an old adage, when "any news is good news."

The press began, too, a crusade against the swill-milk dealers, and the men who had allowed all this to be possible. "What is the Health Board about, that poison for children can be sold in the public streets?" "Where is the District Attorney, that prosecutions for the public good have to be brought by public-spirited citizens?" they demanded. Lynx-eyed reporters tracked the milk-supplies of the city, and though the alarm had been given, and many cows had been hastily sent to the country, they were able to show up certain companies, and print details which were quite lurid enough, when sufficiently "colored" by their skilful pens. Most residents of New York can remember the "swill-milk" or "stump-tail milk" exposures and prosecutions of that summer, and of the reformation brought about thereby in the Board of Health. As the details are not pleasant reading, any one who does not remember is referred to the daily press, and, if they want horrible pictures, to Frank Leslie's Illustrated Weekly. Except for the papers, it is to be questioned if Peter's case would have resulted in much more than the punishment of the man actually convicted; but by the press taking the matter up, the moment's indignation was deepened and intensified to a degree which well-nigh swept every cow-stable off the island, and drove the proper officials into an activity leading to great reforms.

No one was more surprised than Peter, at the sudden notoriety, or at the far-reaching results. He collected the articles, and sent them to his mother. He wrote:

"Don't think that this means any great start. In truth, I am a hundred dollars the poorer for the case, and shall have to cut off a few expenses for the rest of the year. I tell you this, because I know you will not think for a moment that I grudge the money, and you are not to spoil my trifling self-denial by any offer of assistance. You did quite enough in taking in those two little imps. Were they very bad? Did they tramp on your flowers, and frighten poor old Russet [Russet was the cat] out of his fast waning lives? It was a great pleasure to me to see them so plump and brown, and I thank you for it. Their testimony in court was really amusing, though at the same time pathetic. People tell me that my speech was a good one. What is more surprising, they tell me that I made the prisoner, and Mr. Bohlmann, the brewer, who sat next to Dummer, both cry. I confess I grieve over the fact that I was not prosecuting Bohlmann. He is the real criminal, yet goes scot free. But the moral effect is, I suppose, the important thing, and any one to whom responsibility could be traced (and convicted) gives us that. I find that Mr. Bohlmann goes to the same church I attend!"

His mother was not surprised. She had always known her Peter was a hero, and needed no "New York papers" to teach her the fact. Still she read every line of the case, and of the subsequent crusade. She read Peter's speech, again and again, stopping to sob at intervals, and hugging the clipping to her bosom from time to time, as the best equivalent for Peter, while sobbing: "My boy, my darling boy." Every one in the mill-town knew of it, and the clippings were passed round among Peter's friends, beginning with the clergyman and ending with his schoolboy companions. They all wondered why Peter had spoken so briefly. "If I could talk like that," said a lawyer to the proud mother, "I'd have spoken for a couple of hours." Mrs. Stirling herself wished it had been longer. Four columns of evidence, and only a little over a half column of speech! It couldn't have taken him twenty minutes at the most. "Even the other lawyer, who had nothing to say but lies, took over a column to his speech. And his was printed close together, while that of Peter's was spread out (*e.g.* solid and leaded) making the difference in length all the greater." Mrs. Stirling wondered if there could be a conspiracy against her Peter, on the part of the Metropolitan press. She had promptly subscribed for a year to the New York paper which glorified Peter the most, supposing that from this time on his name would appear on the front page. When she found it did not and that it was not mentioned in the press and Health Board crusade against the other "swill-milk" dealers, she became convinced that there was some definite attempt to rob Peter of his due fame. "Why, Peter began it all," she explained, "and now the papers and Health Board pretend it's all their doings." She wrote a letter to the editor of the paper—a letter which was passed round the office, and laughed over not a little by the staff. She never received an answer, nor did the paper give Peter the more attention because of it.

Two days after the trial, Peter had another call from Dummer.

"You handled that case in great style, Mr. Stirling," he told Peter. "You know the ropes as well as far older men. You got just the right evidence out of your witnesses, and not a bit of superfluous rubbish. That's the mistake most young men make. They bury their testimony in unessential details. I tell you, those two children were worth all the rest put together. Did you send them to the country on purpose to get that kind of evidence?"

"No," said Peter.

"Well, every man in that jury was probably a father, and that child's talk took right hold of them. Not but that your speech would have done the business. You were mighty clever in just telling what you saw, and not going into the testimony. You could safely trust the judge to do that. It was a great speech."

"Thank you," said Peter.

"He's not to be taffied," thought the lawyer. "Plain talking's the way to deal with him." He ended his allusions to the trial, and said: "Now, Mr. Stirling, Mr. Bohlmann doesn't want to have these civil suits go any further. Mr. Bohlmann's a man of respectability, with a nice wife and some daughters. The newspapers are giving him quite enough music without your dragging him into court."

"It's the only way I can reach him," said Peter.

"But you mustn't want to reach him. He's really a well-meaning man, and if you ask your clergyman—for I believe you go to Dr. Purple's church?—you'll find he's very charitable and generous with his money."

Peter smiled curiously. "Distributing money made that way is not much of a charity."

"He didn't know," said the lawyer. Then catching a look which came into Peter's face, he instantly added, "At least, he had no idea it was that bad. He tells me that he hadn't been inside those cow-sheds for four years."

"Come and see me to-morrow," said Peter.

After Dummer had gone, Peter walked uptown, and saw his clergyman.

"Yes," he was told, "Mr. Bohlmann has always stood high in the church, and has been liberal and sensible with his money. I can't tell you how this whole thing has surprised and grieved me, Mr. Stirling. It must be terrible for his wife. His daughters, too, are such nice sweet girls. You've probably noticed them in church?"

"No." Peter had not noticed them. He did not add that he did not notice young girls—that for some reason they had not interested him since—since——

"Where does he live?" inquired Peter.

"Not ten blocks from here," replied Dr. Purple, and named the street and number.

Peter looked at his watch and, thanking the clergyman, took his leave. He did not go back to his office, but to the address, and asked for Mr. Bohlmann. A respectable butler showed him into a handsome parlor and carried his name to the brewer.

There were already two girls in the room. One was evidently a caller. The other, a girl with a sweet, kindly, German face, was obviously one of the "nice" daughters. His arrival checked the flow of conversation somewhat, but they went on comparing their summer experiences. When the butler came back and said aloud, "Mr. Bohlmann will see you in the library, Mr. Stirling," Peter noticed that both girls turned impulsively to look at him, and that the daughter flushed red.

He found Mr. Bohlmann standing uneasily on the rug by the fireplace, and a stout woman gazing out of the window, with her back to the room.

"I had a call from your lawyer this morning, Mr. Bohlmann," said Peter, "and I have taken the liberty of coming to see you about the cases."

"Sid down, sid down," said his host, nervously, though not sitting himself.

Peter sat down. "I want to do what is best about the matter," he said.

The woman turned quickly to look at him, and Peter saw that there were tears in her eyes.

"Vell," said the brewer, "what is dat?"

"I don't know," said Peter, "and that's why I've come to see you."

Mr. Bohlmann's face worked for a moment. Then suddenly he burst into tears. "I give you my word, Mr. Stirling," he said, "that I didn't know it was so. I haven't had a happy moment since you spoke that day in court." He had heretofore spoken in English with a slight German accent. But this he said in German. He sat down at the table and buried his face in his arms. His wife, who was also weeping, crossed to him, and tried to comfort him by patting him on the back.

"I think," said Peter, "we had best drop the suits."

Mr. Bohlmann looked up. "It is not the money, Mr. Stirling," he said, still speaking in German. "See." He drew from a drawer in his desk a check-book, and filling up a check, handed it to Peter. It was dated and signed, but the amount was left blank. "There," he said, "I leave it to you what is right."

"I think Mr. Dummer will feel we have not treated him fairly," said Peter, "if we settle it in this way."

"Do not think of him. I will see that he has no cause for complaint," the brewer said. "Only let me know it is ended, so that my wife and my daughters——" he choked, and ended the sentence thus.

"Very well," said Peter. "We'll drop the suits."

The husband and wife embraced each other in true German fashion.

Peter rose and came to the table. "Three of the cases were for five thousand each, and the other two were for two thousand each," he said, and then hesitated. He wished to be fair to both sides. "I will ask you to fill in the check for eight thousand dollars. That will be two each for three, and one each for two."

Mr. Bohlmann disengaged himself from his wife, and took his pen. "You do not add your fee," he said.

"I forgot it," laughed Peter, and the couple laughed with him in their happiness. "Make it for eight thousand, two hundred and fifty."

"Och," said the brewer once more resuming his English. "Dat is too leedle for vive cases."

"No," said Peter. "It was what I had decided to charge in case I got any damages."

So the check was filled in, and Peter, after a warm handshake from both, went back to his office.

"Dat iss a fine yoong mahn," said the brewer.

CHAPTER XVII

A NEW FRIEND

THE day after this episode, Peter had the very unusual experience of a note by his morning's mail. Except for his mother's weekly letter, it was the first he had received since Watts had sailed, two years before. For the moment he thought that it must be from him, and the color came into his face at the mere thought that he would have news of—of—Watts. But a moment's glance at the writing showed him he was wrong, and he tore the envelope with little interest in his face. Indeed after he had opened it, he looked at his wall for a moment before he fixed his mind on it.

It contained a brief note, to this effect:

"A recent trial indicates that Mr. Stirling needs neither praise nor reward as incentives for the doing of noble deeds.

"But one who prefers to remain unknown cannot restrain her grateful thanks to Mr. Stirling for what he did; and being debarred from such acts herself, asks that at least she may be permitted to aid him in them by enclosing a counsel fee for 'the case of the tenement children of New York against the inhumanity of men's greed.'

"September third."

Peter looked at the enclosure, and found it was a check for five hundred dollars. He laid it on his desk, and read the note over again. It was beyond question written by a lady. Every earmark showed that, from the delicate scent of the paper, to the fine, even handwriting. Peter wanted to know who she was. He looked at the check to see by whom it was signed; to find that it was drawn by the cashier of the bank at which it was payable.

Half an hour later, a rapid walk had brought him to the bank the name of which was on the check. It was an uptown one, which made a specialty of family and women's accounts. Peter asked for the cashier.

"I've called about this check," he said, when that official materialized, handing the slip of paper to him.

"Yes," said the cashier kindly, though with a touch of the resigned sorrow in his voice which cashiers of "family's" and women's banks acquire. "You must sign your name on the back, on the left-hand end, and present it to the paying-teller, over at that window. You'll have to be identified if the paying-teller doesn't know you."

"I don't want the money," said Peter. "I want to know who sent the check to me?"

The cashier looked at it more carefully. "Oh!" he said. Then he looked up quickly at Peter, with considerable interest. "Are you Mr. Stirling?"

"Yes."

"Well, I filled this up by order of the president, and you'll have to see him about it, if you want more than the money."

"Can I see him?"

"Come this way."

They went into a small office at the end of the bank.

"Mr. Dyer," said the cashier, "this is Mr. Stirling, and he's come to see about that check."

"Glad to see you, Mr. Stirling. Sit down."

"I wish to learn who sent the check."

"Very sorry we can't oblige you. We had positive instructions from the person for whom we drew it, that no name was to be given."

"Can you receive a letter?"

"That was forbidden too."

"A message?"

"Nothing was said about that."

"Then will you do me the favor to say to the lady that the check will not be cashed till Mr. Stirling has been able to explain something to her."

"Certainly. She can't object to that."

"Thank you."

"Not at all." The president rose and escorted him to

the door. "That was a splendid speech of yours, Mr. Stirling," he added. "I'm not a bit ashamed to say that it put salt water in my old eyes."

"I think," said Peter, "it was the deaths of the poor little children, more than anything I said, that made people feel it."

The next morning's mail brought Peter a second note, in the same handwriting as that of the day before. It read:

"Miss De Voe has received Mr. Stirling's message and will be pleased to see him in regard to the check, at half after eleven to-day (Wednesday) if he will call on her.

"Miss De Voe regrets the necessity of giving Mr. Stirling such brief notice, but she leaves New York on Thursday."

As Peter walked up town that morning, he was a little surprised that he was so cool over his intended call. In a few minutes he would be in the presence of a lady, the firmness of whose handwriting indicated that she was not yet decrepit. Three years ago such a prospect would have been replete with terror to him. Down to that—that week at the Pierces', he had never gone to a place where he expected to "encounter" (for that was the word he formerly used) women without dread. Since that week— except for the twenty-four hours of the wedding, he had not "encountered" a lady. Yet here he was, going to meet an entire stranger without any conscious embarrassment or suffering. He was even in a sense curious. Peter was not given to self-analysis, but the change was too marked a one for him to be unconscious of it. Was it merely the poise of added years? Was it that he had ceased to care what women thought of him? Or was it that his discovery that a girl was lovable had made the sex less terrible to him? Such were the questions he asked himself as he walked, and he had not answered them when he rang the bell of the old-fashioned, double house on Second Avenue.

He was shown into a large drawing-room, the fittings of which were still shrouded in summer coverings, preventing Peter from inferring much, even if he had had time to do so. But the butler had scarcely left him when, with a

well-bred promptness from which Peter might have drawn
an inference, the rustle of a woman's draperies was heard.
Rising, Peter found himself facing a tall, rather slender
woman of between thirty-five and forty. It did not need
a second glance from even Peter's untrained eye, to realize
the suggestion of breeding in the whole atmosphere about
her. The gown was of the simplest summer material, but
its very simplicity, and a certain lack of "latest fashion"
rather than "old-fashionedness" gave it a quality of
respectability. Every line of the face, the set of the head,
and even more the carriage of the figure, conveyed the
"look of race."

"I must thank you, Mr. Stirling," she said, speaking
deliberately, in a low, mellow voice, by no means so common then as our women's imitation of the English tone
and inflexion has since made it, "for suiting your time
to mine on such short notice."

"You were very kind," said Peter, "to comply with my
request. Any time was convenient to me."

"I am glad it suited you."

Peter had expected to be asked to sit down, but, nothing
being said, began his explanation.

"I am very grateful, Miss De Voe, for your note, and
for the check. I thank you for both. But I think you
probably sent me the latter through a mistake, and so I
did not feel justified in accepting it."

"A mistake?"

"Yes. The papers made many errors in their statements. I'm not a 'poor young lawyer,' as they said. My
mother is comfortably off, and gives me an ample allowance."

"Yes?"

"And what is more," continued Peter, "while they were
right in saying that I paid some of the expenses of the
case, yet I was more than repaid by my fees in some civil
suits I brought for the relatives of the children, which
we settled very advantageously."

"Won't you sit down, Mr. Stirling?" said Miss De Voe.
"I should like to hear about the cases."

Peter began a very simple narrative of the matter. But
Miss De Voe interjected questions or suppositions here

and there, which led to other explanations, and before Peter had finished, he had told not merely the history of the cases, but much else. His mention of the two Dooley children had brought out the fact of their visit to his mother, and this had explained incidentally her position in the world. The settlement of the cases involved the story of the visit to the brewer's home, and Peter, to justify his action, added his interview with his pastor. Peter's connection with the case compelled him to speak of his evenings in the "angle," and the solitary life that had sent him there. Afterwards, Peter was rather surprised at how much he had told. He did not realize that a woman with tact and experience can, without making it evident, lead a man to tell nearly anything and everything he knows, if she is so minded. If women ever really take to the bar seriously, may Providence protect the average being in trousers, when on the witness stand!

As Peter talked, a clock struck. Stopping short, he rose. "I must ask your pardon," he said. "I had no idea I had taken so much of your time." Then putting his hand in his pocket, he produced the check. "You see that I have made a very good thing out of the whole matter and do not need this."

"One moment, Mr. Stirling," said the lady, still sitting. "Can you spare the time to lunch with me? We will sit down at once, and you shall be free to go whenever you wish."

Peter hesitated. He knew that he had the time, and it did not seem easy to refuse without giving an excuse, which he did not have. Yet he did not feel that he had the right to accept an invitation which he had perhaps necessitated by his long call.

"Thank you," said his hostess, before he had been able to frame an answer. "May I trouble you to pull that bell?"

Peter pulled the bell, and coming back, tendered the check rather awkwardly to Miss De Voe. She, however, was looking towards a doorway, which the next moment was darkened by the butler.

"Morden," she said, "you may serve luncheon at once."

"Luncheon is served, madam," said Morden.

Miss De Voe rose. "Mr. Stirling, I do not think your

explanation has really affected the circumstances which led me to send that check. You acknowledge yourself that you are the poorer for that prosecution, and received no fees for trying it. As I wrote you, I merely was giving a retaining fee in that case, and as none other has been given, I still wish to do it. I cannot do such things myself, but I am weal—I—I can well afford to aid others to do them, and I hope you will let me have the happiness of feeling that I have done my little in this matter."

"Thank you," said Peter. "I was quite willing to take the money, but I was afraid you might have sent it under a misconception."

Miss De Voe smiled at Peter with a very nice look in her face. "I am the one to say 'thank you,' and I am most grateful. But we will consider this as ended, and discuss luncheon in its place."

Peter, despite his usual unconsciousness, could not but notice the beauty of the table service. The meal itself was the simplest of summer luncheons, but the silver and china and glass were such as he had never seen before.

"What wine will you have with your luncheon, Mr. Stirling?" he was asked by his hostess.

"I don't—none for me," replied Peter.

"You don't approve of wine?" asked his hostess.

"Personally I have no feeling about it."

"But?" And there was a very big question mark in Miss De Voe's voice.

"My mother is strongly prejudiced against it, so I do not take it. It is really no deprivation to me, while it would mean great anxiety to her if I drank."

This started the conversation on Peter's mother and his early years, and before it had ended, his hostess had succeeded in learning much more about his origin and his New York life. The clock finally cut him short again, for they lingered at the table long after the meal was finished, though Miss De Voe made the pretence of eating a grape occasionally. When three o'clock struck, Peter, without the least simulating any other cause for going, rose hastily.

"I have used up your whole afternoon," he said, apologetically.

"I think," smiled Miss De Voe, "that we are equal culprits in that. I leave town to-morrow, Mr. Stirling, but return to the city late in October, and if your work and inclination favor it, I hope you will come to see me again?"

Peter looked at the silver and the china. Then he looked at Miss De Voe, so obviously an aristocrat.

"I shall be happy to," he said, "if, when you return, you will send me word that you wish to see me."

Miss De Voe had slightly caught her breath while Peter hesitated. "I believe he is going to refuse!" she thought to herself, a sort of stunned amazement seizing her. She was scarcely less surprised at his reply.

"I never ask a man twice to call on me, Mr. Stirling," she said, with a slight hauteur in her voice.

"I'm sorry for that," said Peter quietly.

Miss De Voe caught her breath again. "Good-afternoon," she said, holding out her hand. "I shall hope to see you."

"Good-bye," said Peter, and the next moment was walking towards his office.

Miss De Voe stood for a moment thinking. "That was curious," she thought, "I wonder if he intends to come?"

The next evening she was dining with relatives in one of the fashionable summering places, and was telling them about her call "from Mr. Stirling, the lawyer who made that splendid speech."

"I thought," she said, "when I received the message, that I was going to be buried under a bathos of thanks, or else have my gift declined with the expectation that I would gush over the disinterestedness of the refusal. Since I couldn't well avoid seeing him, I was quite prepared to snub him, or to take back the money without a word. But he wasn't a bit that kind of creature. He isn't self-assured nor tonguey—rather the reverse. I liked him so that I forced him to stay to luncheon, and made him tell me a good deal about himself, without his knowing I was doing so. He leads a very unusual life, without seeming conscious that he does, and he tells about it very well. Uses just the right word every time, so that you know exactly what he means, without taxing your own brain to fill up blanks. He has such a nice voice too. One that makes you certain of the absolute truth underneath. No. He isn't good looking, though he has fine eyes, and hair. His face and figure are both too heavy."

"Is he a gentleman, cousin Anneke?" asked one of the party.

"He is a little awkward, and over-blunt at moments, but nothing to which one would give a second thought. I was so pleased with him that I asked him to call on me."

"It seems to me," said another, "that you are over-paying him."

"That was the most curious part," replied Miss De Voe. "I'm not at all sure that he means to come. It was really refreshing not to be truckled to, but it is rather startling to meet the first man who does not want to win his way to my visiting list. I don't think he even knows who Miss De Voe is."

"He will find out quick enough," laughed a girl, "and then he will do what they all do."

"No," said Miss De Voe. "I suspect it will make no difference. He isn't that kind, I think. I really am curious to see if I have to ask him a second time. It will be the only case I can remember. I'm afraid, my dears, your cousin is getting to be an old woman."

Peter had, in truth, met, and spent over four hours in the company of a woman whom every one wished to know. A woman equally famous for her lineage, her social position, her wealth and her philanthropy. It would not have made any difference, probably, had he known it, though it might have increased his awkwardness a little. That he was not quite as unconscious as Miss De Voe seemed to think, is shown by a passage in a letter he wrote to his mother:

"She was very much interested in the case, and asked a good many questions about it, and about myself. Some which I would rather not have answered, but since she asked them I could not bring myself to dodge them. She asked me to come and see her again. It is probably nothing but a passing interest, such as this class feel for the moment."—[Then Peter carefully inked out "such as this class feel for the moment," and reproved himself that his bitterness at—at—at one experience, should make him condemn a whole class]—"but if she asks me again I shall go, for there is something very sweet and noble about her. I think she is probably some great personage."

Later on in the letter he wrote:

"If you do not disapprove, I will put this money in the savings bank, in a special or trustee account, and use it for any good that I can do for the people about here. I gave the case my service, and do not think I am entitled to take pay when the money can be so much better employed for the benefit of the people I tried to help."

CHAPTER XVIII

ANOTHER CLIENT

PETER had seen his clients on the morning following the settlement of the cases, and told them of their good fortune. They each had a look at Bohlmann's check, and then were asked how they would like their shares.

"Sure," said Dooley, "Oi shan't know what to do wid that much money."

"I think," said Peter, "that your two thousand really belongs to the children."

"That it does," said Mrs. Dooley, quite willing to deprive her husband of it, for the benefit of her children.

"But what shall Oi do wid it?" asked Mr. Dooley.

"I'd like Mr. Stirling to take charge of mine," said Blackett.

"That's the idea," said Dooley.

And so it was settled by all. Peter said the best thing would be to put it in the savings bank. "Perhaps later we'll find something better." They all went around to a well-known institution on the Bowery, and Peter interviewed the cashier. It proved feasible to endorse over the check to the bank, and credit the proper share to each.

"I shall have to ask you to give me the odd two hundred and fifty," Peter said, "as that is my legal fee."

"You had better let me put that in your name, Mr. Stirling?" said the president, who had been called into the consultation.

"Very well," said Peter. "I shall want some of it before long, but the rest will be very well off here." So a book was handed him, and the president shook him by the hand with all the warmth that eight thousand two hundred and fifty dollars of increased assets and four new depositors implied.

Peter did not need to draw any of the two hundred and fifty dollars, however. In November he had another knock at his door.

It proved to be Mr. Dennis Moriarty, of whom we have incidentally spoken in connection with the half-price drinks for the Milligan wake, and as spokesman of the torchlight procession.

"Good-mornin' to yez, sir," said the visitor.

It was a peculiarity of Peter's that he never forgot faces. He did not know Mr. Moriarty's name, never having had it given him, but he placed him instantly.

"Thank you," said Peter, holding out his hand. Peter did not usually shake hands in meeting people, but he liked the man's face. It would never take a prize for beauty. The hair verged on a fiery red, the nose was a real sky-scraper and the upper lip was almost proboscidian in its length. But every one liked the face.

"It's proud Oi'm bein' shakin' the hand av Misther Stirling," said the Irishman.

"Sit down," said Peter.

"My name's Moriarty, sir, Dinnis Moriarty, an' Oi keeps a saloon near Centre Street, beyant."

"You were round here in the procession."

"Oi was, sir. Shure, Oi'm not much at a speech, compared to the likes av yez, but the b'ys would have me do it."

Peter said something appropriate, and then there was a pause.

"Misther Stirling," finally said Moriarty, "Oi was up before Justice Gallagher yesterday, an' he fined me bad. Oi want yez to go to him, an' get him to be easier wid me. It's yezself can do it."

"What were you fined for?" asked Peter.

"For bein' open on Sunday."

"Then you ought to be fined."

"Don't say that till Oi tell yez. Oi don't want to keep my place open, but it's in my lease, an' so Oi have to."

"In your lease?" enquired Peter.

"Yes." And the paper was handed over to him.

Peter ran over the three documents. "I see," he said, "you are only the caretaker really, the brewer having an assignment of the lease and a chattel mortgage on your fixtures and stock."

"That's it," said Dennis. "It's mighty quick yez got at it. It's caretaker Oi am, an' a divil of a care it is. Shure, who wants to work seven days a week, if he can do wid six?"

"You should have declined to agree to that condition."

"Then Oi'd have been turned out. Begobs, it's such poor beer that it's little enough Oi sell even in seven days."

"Why don't you get your beer elsewhere then?"

"Why, it's Edelhein put me in there to sell his stuff, an' he'd never let me sell anythin' else."

"Then Edelhein is really the principal, and you are only put in to keep him out of sight?"

"That's it."

"And you have put no money in yourself?"

"Divil of a cent."

"Then why doesn't he pay the fine?"

"He says Oi have no business to be after bein' fined. As if any one sellin' his bccr could help bein' fined!"

"How is that?" said Peter, inferring that selling poor beer was a finable offence, yet ignorant of the statute.

"Why, yez see, sir, the b'ys don't like that beer—an' sensible they are—so they go to other places, an' don't come to my place."

"But that doesn't explain your fines."

"Av course it does. Shure, if the boys don't come to my place, it's little Oi can do at the primary, an' so it's no pull Oi have in politics to get the perlice an' the joodges to be easy wid me, like they are to the rest."

Peter studied his blank wall a bit.

"Shure, if it's good beer Oi had," continued Moriarty, "Oi'd be after beatin' them all, for Oi was always

popular wid the b'ys, on account of my usin' my fists
so fine."

Peter smiled. "Why don't you go into something
else?" he asked.

"Well, there's mother and the three childers to be
supported, an' then Oi'd lose my influence at the primary."

"What kind of beer does Mr. Bohlmann make?" asked
Peter, somewhat irrelevantly.

"Ah," said Moriarty, "that's the fine honest beer!
There's never anythin' wrong wid his. An' he treats his
keepers fair. Lets them do as they want about keepin'
open Sundays, an' never squeezes a man when he's down
on his luck."

Peter looked at his wall again. Peter was learning
something.

"Supposing," he asked, "I was able to get your fine
remitted, and that clause struck out of the lease. Would
you open on Sunday?"

"Divil a bit."

"When must you pay the fine?"

"Oi'm out on bail till to-morrow, sir."

"Then leave these papers with me, and come in about
this time."

Peter studied his wall for a bit after his new client
was gone. He did not like either saloon-keepers or law-
breakers, but this case seemed to him to have—to have
—extenuating circumstances. His cogitations finally resulted in his going to Justice Gallagher's court. He found
the judge rather curt.

"He's been up here three times in as many months,
and I intend to make an example of him."

"But why is only he arrested, when every saloon keeper
in the neighborhood does the same thing?"

"Now, sir," said the judge, "don't waste any more of
my time. What's the next case?"

A look we have mentioned once or twice came into
Peter's face. He started to leave the court, but encountered at the door one of the policemen whom he was
"friends with," according to the children, which meant that
they had chatted sometimes in the "angle."

"What sort of a man is Dennis Moriarty?" he asked of him.

"A fine young fellow, supporting his mother and his younger brothers."

"Why is Justice Gallagher so down on him?"

The policeman looked about a moment. "It's politics, sir, and he's had orders."

"From whom?"

"That's more than we know. There was a row last spring in the primary, and we've had orders since then to lay for him."

Peter stood and thought for a moment. "What saloon-keeper round here has the biggest pull?" he asked.

"It's all of them, mostly, but Blunkers is a big man."

"Thank you," said Peter. He stood in the street thinking a little. Then he walked a couple of blocks and went into Blunkers's great gin palace.

"I want to see the proprietor," he said.

"Dat's me," said a man who was reading a paper behind the bar.

"Do you know Justice Gallagher?"

"Do I? Well, I guess," said the man.

"Will you do me the favor to go with me to his court, and get him to remit Dennis Moriarty's fine?"

"Will I? No. I will not. Der's too many saloons, and one less will be bully."

"In that case," said Peter quietly, "I suppose you won't mind my closing yours up?"

"Wot der yer mean?" angrily inquired the man.

"If it comes to closing saloons, two can play at that game."

"Who is yer, anyway?" The man came out from behind the bar, squaring his shoulders in an ugly manner.

"My name's Stirling. Peter Stirling."

The man looked at him with interest. "How'll yer close my place?"

"Get evidence against you, and prosecute you."

"Dat ain't de way."

"It will be my way."

"Wot yer got against me?"

"Nothing. But I intend to see Moriarty have fair play.

You want to fight on the square too. You're not a man
to hit a fellow in the dark."

Peter was not flattering the man. He had measured
him and was telling him the result of that measure. He
told it, too, in a way that made the other man realize the
opinion behind the words.

"Come on," said Blunkers, good-naturedly.

They went over to the court, and a whispered colloquy
took place between the justice and the bartender.

"That's all right, Mr. Stirling," presently said the judge.
"Clerk, strike Dennis Moriarty's fine off the list."

"Thank you," said Peter to the saloon keeper. "If I
can ever do a turn for you, let me know it."

"Dat's hunky," said the man, and they parted.

Peter went out and walked into the region of the
National Milk Company, but this time he went to the
brewery. He found Mr. Bohlmann, and told him the
story, asking his advice at the end.

"Dondt you vool von minute mit dod Edelhein. I
dells you vot I do. I harf choost a blace vacant down in
Zender Streed, and your frient he shall it haf."

So they chatted till all the details had been arranged.
Dennis was to go in as caretaker, bound to use only
Bohlmann's beer, with a percentage on that, and the profits
on all else. He was to pay the rent, receiving a sub-
lease from Bohlmann, who was only a lessee himself, and
to give a chattel mortgage on the stock supplied him.
Finally he was to have the right of redemption of stock,
lease, and good will at any time within five years, on making certain payments.

"You draw up der babers, Misder Stirling, and send
der bill to me. Ve vill give der yoonger a chance," the
brewer said.

When Dennis called the next day, he was "spache-
less" at the new developments. He wrung Peter's hand.

"Arrah, what can Oi say to yez?" he exclaimed finally.
Then having found something, he quickly continued:
"Now, Patsy Blunkers, look out for yezself. It's the
divil Oi'll give yez in the primary this year."

He begged Peter to come down the opening night, and
help to "celebrate the event."

"Thank you," said Peter, "but I don't think I will."

"Shure," said Dennis, "yez needn't be afraid it won't be orderly. It's myself can do the hittin', an' the b'ys know it."

"My mother brought me up," Peter explained, "not to go into saloons, and when I came to New York I promised her, if I ever did anything she had taught me not to, that I would write her about it. She would hardly understand this visit, and it might make her very unhappy."

Peter earned fifty dollars by drawing the papers, and at the end of the first month Dennis brought him fifty more.

"Trade's been fine, sir, an' Oi want to pay somethin' for what yez did."

So Peter left his two hundred and fifty dollars in the bank, having recouped the expenses of the first case out of his new client.

He wrote all about it to his mother:

"I am afraid you won't approve of what I did entirely, for I know your strong feeling against men who make and sell liquor. But I somehow have been made to feel in the last few days that more can be done in the world by kindness and help than by frowns and prosecutions. I had no thought of getting money out of the case, so I am sure I was not influenced by that. It seemed to me that a man was being unfairly treated, and that too, by laws which are meant for other purposes. I really tried to think it out, and do what seemed right to me. My last client has a look and way of speaking that makes me certain he's a fine fellow, and I shall try to see something of him, provided it will not worry you to think of me as friendly with a saloon-keeper. I know I can be of use to him."

Little did Peter know how useful his last client would be to him.

CHAPTER XIX

THE PRIMARY

AFTER this rush of work, Peter's life became as routine as of yore. The winter passed without an event worth noting, if we except a steadily growing acquaintance with the dwellers of the district. But in July a new phase was injected into it by a call from Dennis Moriarty.

"Good-mornin' to yez, sir, an' a fine day it is," said the latter, with his usually breezy way.

"Yes," said Peter.

"Misther Stirling. An' is it engaged yez are for this night?"

"No." Peter had nothing.

"Then," said Dennis, "maybe ye'll be afther goin' wid me to the primary?"

"What primary?"

"For the election of delegates to the convention, shure."

"No. What party?"

"What party is it?"

"Yes."

"Misther Stirling, do yez know my name?"

"Dennis Moriarty, isn't it?"

"Yes. An' what's my business?"

"You keep a saloon."

"Yes. An' what ward do Oi live in?"

"The sixth, don't you?"

"Then," said Dennis, his upper lip twisting into a smile of enormous proportions, "Oi suppose yez afther thinkin' Oi'm a dirty black Republican."

Peter laughed, as few could help doing, when Dennis led the way. "Look here, Dennis," he said, "don't you run down that party. My father was a Democrat, but he voted for Lincoln, and fought for the blacks when the time came, and though I'm a Democrat like him, the Republicans are only black in their sympathies, and not in their acts."

"An' what do yez say to the whisky frauds, an' black Friday, an' credit mobilier?" asked Dennis.

"Of course I don't like them," said Peter; "but that's the politicians, not the party."

"Shure," said Dennis, "what's the party but the men that run it?"

"You've seen something of Mr. Bohlmann lately, Dennis?"

"Yes."

"Well, he was the man who put Coldman in charge of that cow stable. Yet he's an honest man."

Dennis scratched his head. "It's a convincin' way yez have wid yez," he said; "but it's scoundrels the Republicans are, all the same. Look at them in the district; there's not one a decent man would invite to drink wid him."

"I think, Dennis," said Peter, "that when all the decent men get into one party, there'll be only one worth talking about."

"Av course," replied Dennis. "That's the reason there's only the Democratic party in New York City."

"Tell me about this primary," said Peter, concluding that abstract political philosophy was not the way to liberalize Dennis.

"It's most important, it is," he was told, "it's on top Patsy Blunkers an' his gang av dirty spalpeens (Dennis seemed to forget that he had just expressed the opinion that all the "decent" men were Democrats) have been this two years, but we've got orders for a new enrollment at last, an' if we don't knock them this time, my name isn't Dinnis Moriarty."

"What is the question before the meeting?"

"Afther the enrollment, it's to vote for delegates."

"Oh! Then it's just a struggle over who shall be elected?"

"That's it. But a fine, big fight it will be. The whole district's so excited, sir, that it's twice Oi've had to pound the b'ys a bit in my saloon to keep the peace."

"What do you want of me?"

"Shure, every vote counts on a night like this. An' ye'd be afther helpin' us big, for the district likes yez."

"But, Dennis, I can't vote without knowing something about the way things are. I shouldn't know whether I was voting rightly."

"Why, a man votes right when he votes for his friends!"

"No; a man votes right when he votes for his convictions."

"Convictions, is it?"

"Yes. That is, he votes as he thinks is best for the country."

"That, maybe, is the way yez do it where yez come from," said Dennis, "but it's no good it would be here. Convictions, whatever they be, are never nominated here. It's real things we're afther votin' for in New York."

Peter laughed. "I've got to take you in hand, Dennis, and you've got to take me in hand. I think we both need each other's help. Yes, I'll come to the primary. Will they let me vote?"

"The dirty spalpeens will never dare to stop yez! Thank yez, sir. Oi'll be along for yez about eight."

"Remember, though, Dennis—I don't say how I'll vote."

"Yez just listen, an' Oi'm not afraid av what ye'll do."

That evening, Peter was ushered into a large hot room, pretty well packed with men, and the interstices already filled in with dense tobacco smoke. He looked about him curiously, and was surprised to find how many of the faces he knew. Blackett, Dooley, and Milligan were there, and shook hands with him warmly. Judge Gallagher and Blunkers were in evidence. In plain clothes were two policemen, and three of the "fire-laddies," who formed part of the "crew" of the nearest engine, with all of whom he had often chatted. Mr. Dummer, his rival lawyer in the case, and one of the jurymen in it, likewise were visible. Also many faces which were familiar to Peter by a former occasional friendly word or nod exchanged in passing. Intense excitement evidently reigned, and every one was whispering in a sort of breathless way, which showed how deeply interested they were.

At Dennis's suggestion, made in walking to the room, Peter presented himself without guidance, at the desk. Some one behind him asked if he lived in the ward, and for how long, but this was the only apparent opposition made to the prompt entering of his name. Then Peter strolled round and talked to those whom he knew, and tried to find out, without much success, just what was the division. Every one knew that a fight was on, but in just what it consisted they seemed neither to know nor care. He noticed that hot words were constantly exchanged at the enrolling desk, over would-be members, but not understanding the exact nature of the qualifications needed, he could not follow the disputes. Finally these ceased, for want of applicants.

"Misther Stirling," said Dennis, coming up to him hurriedly. "Will yez be afther bein' chairman for us?"

"No. I don't know anything about the proceedings."

"It don't take any," said Dennis. "It's only fair play we're afther."

He was gone again before Peter could say anything. The next instant, the enrolling officer rose and spoke.

"Are there any more to be enrolled?" he called. No one came forward, so after a moment he said: "Will the meeting choose a presiding officer?"

"Mr. Chairman," rang two voices so quickly that they in truth cut the presiding officer off in his suggestion.

"Mr. Muldoon," said that officer.

"Oi spoke first," shouted Dennis, and Peter felt that he had, and that he was not having fair play.

Instantly a wave of protest, denials, charges, and counter-charges swept through the room. Peter thought there was going to be a fight, but the position was too critical to waste a moment on what Dennis styled "a diversion." It was business, not pleasure, just then.

"Mr. Muldoon," said the officer again, not heeding the tempest in the least.

"Mr. Chairman," shouted Muldoon, "I am proud to nominate Justice Gallagher, the pride of the bar, for chairman of this distinguished meeting, and I move to make his election unanimous."

"Misther Chairman," shouted Dennis.

"Mr. Moriarty," said the officer.

"Misther Chairman, Oi have the honor to nominate for chairman av this meetin' the people's an' the children's friend, Misther Peter Stirling, an' Oi don't have to move to make it unanimous, for such is the intelligence an' manhood av this meetin' that it will be that way for shure."

Peter saw a hurried consultation going on between Gallagher, Muldoon, and two others, during the latter part of this speech, and barely had Dennis finished his remarks when Justice Gallagher spoke up.

"Mr. Chairman."

"The Honorable Justice Gallagher," said that gentleman.

"I take pride in withdrawing in favor of Mr. Stirling, who so justly merits the honor of presiding on this important occasion. From recent events too well known to need mention, I am sure we can all look to him for justice and fairness."

"Bad cess to him!" groaned Dennis. "Oi hoped they'd be just fools enough to oppose yez, an' then we'd have won the first blood."

Peter was chosen without dissent, and was escorted to the seat behind the desk.

"What is the first business before the meeting?" he asked of Gallagher, aside, as he was taking his seat.

"Election of delegates to the State convention. That's all to-night," he was told.

Peter had presided at college in debates, and was not flurried. "Will you stay here so as to give me the names of those I don't know?" he said to the enrolling officer. "The meeting will please come to order," he continued aloud. "The nomination of delegates to the State convention is the business to be acted upon."

"Misther Chairman," yelled Dennis, evidently expecting to find another rival as before. But no one spoke.

"Mr. Moriarty," said Peter.

"Misther Chairman. It's my delight to nominate as delegates to the State convention, the Honorable Misther Schlurger, our distinguished representative in the Assembly, the Honorable Misther Kennedy, our noble Police Commissioner, an' Misther Caggs, whom it would be insult for me to praise in this company."

"Second the motion," said some one.

"Mr. Chairman," shouted a man.

"That's Caggs," said the enrolling officer.

"Mr. Caggs," said Peter.

"Mr. Chairman," said Caggs, "I must decline the honor offered me from such a source."

"What?" shrieked Dennis, amazement and rage contesting for first place in voice and expression.

"Mr. Chairman," said Dummer.

"Mr. Dummer," said Peter.

"I have the honor to nominate the Honorable Justice Gallagher, Mr. Peter Sweeney, and Mr. Caggs, to whom Mr. Moriarty has just paid so glowing a tribute, as delegates to the State convention."

"Second the——" shouted some one, but the rest was

drowned by another storm which swept through the room. Even above the tumult, Peter could hear Dennis challenging and beseeching Mr. Caggs to come "outside an' settle it like gentlemen." Caggs, from a secure retreat behind Blunkers's right arm, declined to let the siren's song tempt him forth. Finally Peter's pounding brought a degree of quiet again.

"Misther Chairman," said Dennis.

"Mr. Moriarty," said Peter.

"Misther Chairman. Oi'll not take the valuable time av this meetin' to speak av dirty, cowardly, black-hearted, treacherous snakes, wid souls blacker than the divil's own——"

"Order!" said Peter to the crowd.

"No," continued Dennis, in answer to the audible remarks of the opposition. "It's no names Oi'm callin'. If yez know such a beast, such a snake, fit it to him. Oi'm mentionin' no names. As Oi was sayin', Misther Chairman, Oi'll not waste the time av this meetin' wid discribin' the conduct av a beast so vile that he must be the contempt av every honest man. Who would have been driven out by St. Patrick, wid the rest av the reptiles, if he'd lived at that time. Oi only rise to widdraw the name av Caggs from the list Oi nominated for delegates to the state convention, an' to put in place av it that av a man who is as noble an' true, as some are false an' devilish. That of Misther Peter Stirling, God bless him!"

Once more chaos came. Peter pounded in vain. Both sides were at fever heat. Finally Peter rose.

"Gentlemen," he shouted, in a voice that rang through the hall above even the tumult, "if this meeting does not come to order, I shall declare it adjourned."

Instant quiet fell, for all had paused a moment to hear his words, and they concluded that he was in earnest.

"Was the last motion seconded?" asked the chairman calmly.

"I seconded it," shouted Blackett and Milligan together.

"You have heard the nominations, gentlemen. Has any one any remarks to make?"

A man next Justice Gallagher said, "Mr. Chairman,"

and being duly recognized, proceeded to talk for ten minutes in a very useless way. But during this time, Peter noticed first a good deal of whispering among Blunkers's friends, and then an interview between Gallagher and Dennis. The latter was apparently not reconcilable, and shook his head in a way that meant war. Then there was more consultation between the opposition, and another confab with Dennis, with more headshakes on his part. Finally a compromise having been evidently made impossible, the orator was "called down" and it was voted to proceed to an election. Peter named one of the firemen, Dooley, and Blunkers, tellers, who, after a ballot, announced that Dennis had carried his nominations, Peter heading the list with two hundred and twelve votes, and the others getting one hundred and seventy-two, and one hundred and fifty-eight respectively. The "snake" got but fifty-seven votes.

"Shure," said Dennis, later, "maybe we don't vote for convictions here, but we don't vote for the likes av him!"

"Then you are voting for convictions," said Peter.

"It's yezself is the convictions then," said Dennis.

Perhaps he was right.

CHAPTER XX

A POLITICAL DEBUT

PETER declared the meeting adjourned as soon as the results of the election had been read, and slipped away in the turmoil that immediately followed, without a word to any one. He was in truth not bewildered—because he had too much natural poise and phlegm—but he was surprised by the suddenness of it all, and wanted to think before talking with others. So he took advantage of the mutual bickerings and recriminations which seemed the order of the day, to get back to his office, and there he sat, studying his wall for a time. Then he went to bed, and slept as quickly and as calmly as if he had spent his evening in reading the "Modern Cottage Architecture" or "Questions de Sociologie," which were on his table, instead of presiding at a red-hot primary, and being elected a delegate.

The next morning Dennis came to see him as early as well could be.

"Misther Stirling," he said, his face expanding into the broadest of grins, "let me salute the delegate to the State convention."

"Look here, Dennis," said Peter, "you know you had no business to spring that on me."

"Ah, sir! Shure, when that dirty little spalpeen av a Caggs went back on us so, what could Oi do? Oi know it's speak to yez Oi ought, but wid de room yellin' like that it's devilish tryin' to do the right thing quick, barrin' it's not hittin' some one's head, which always comes natural."

"Well," said Peter, "of course I'm very much pleased to have been chosen, but I wish it could have been done with less hard feeling."

"Hard feelin', is it?"

"Yes."

"Shure, the b'ys are as pleased an' kindly this mornin' as can be. It's a fight like that makes them yieldin' an' friendly. Nothin' but a little head-punchin' could make them in a sweeter mood, an' we'd 'a' given them that if little Caggs had had any sense in him."

"You mean Gallagher and Blunkers and the rest of them?"

"Av course. That little time last night didn't mean much. No one feels bad over that. Shure, it's Gallagher was in my place later last night, an' we had a most friendly time, he treatin' the whole crowd twice. We've got to fight in the primary to keep the b'ys interested, but it's seldom that they're not just as friendly the next day."

Peter looked at his wall. He had not liked Gallagher at either time he had met him. "Still," he thought to himself, "I have no right to prevent him and Dennis being friends, from the little I've seen."

"Now, sir, about the convention?" said Dennis.

"I suppose Porter is the best man talked of for the nomination," remarked Peter.

"Begobs, sir, that he's not," said Dennis. "It's Justice Gallagher was tellin' me himself that he was a poor kind av creature, wid a strong objection to saloons."

Peter's eye lost its last suggestion of doubt. "Oh, Justice Gallagher told you that?" he asked. "When?"

"Last night."

"After the primary?"

"Av course."

"Whom does he favor?"

"Catlin."

"Well, Dennis, you've made me a delegate, but I've got to vote my own way."

"Shure, sir, Oi'd not have yez do anythin' else. It's yezself knows better than me. Oi was only tellin' yez what the Justice——"

A knock at the door interrupted him. It proved to be Gallagher, who greeted them both in a hearty, friendly way. Peter brought another chair from his bedroom.

"Well, Mr. Stirling, that was a fine contest we had last night," said his honor.

"It seemed to be earnest," said Peter.

"It's just as well our friend here sprang your nomination on us as a surprise, for if we had known, we should not have put up an opposition candidate. You are just the sort of man we want to represent us in the convention."

"I have never met my colleagues," said Peter. "What kind of men are they?"

So he got Gallagher's opinion, and Dennis's opinion. Then he wanted to know about the candidates, asking questions about them at considerable length. The intentions of the other city delegates were next introduced. Finally the probable planks of the platform were brought up. While they were still under discussion Gallagher said the sitting of his court compelled him to leave.

"I'll come in some time when I have more to spare."

Gallagher went to his court, and found a man waiting for him there.

"He's either very simple or very deep," said Gallagher. "He did nothing but ask questions; and try my best I could not get him to show his hand, nor commit himself.

It will be bad if there's a split in a solid delegation!"

"I hope it will be a lesson to you to have things better arranged."

"Blunkers would have it that way, and he's not the kind of man to offend. We all thought he would win."

"Oh, let them have their fights," said the man crossly; "but it's your business to see that the right men are put up, so that it doesn't make any difference which side wins."

"Well," said Gallagher, "I've done all I could to put things straight. I've made peace, and got Moriarty on our side, and I've talked to this Stirling, and made out a strong case for Catlin, without seeming to care which man gets the nomination."

"Is there any way of putting pressure on him?"

"Not that I can find out. He's a young lawyer, who has no business."

"Then he's a man we don't need to conciliate, if he won't behave?"

"No. I can't say that. He's made himself very popular round here by that case and by being friendly to people. I don't think, if he's going into politics, that it will do to fight him."

"He's such a green hand that we ought to be able to down him."

"He's new, but he's a pretty cool, knowing chap, I think. I had one experience with him, which showed me that any man who picked him up for a fool would drop him quick." Then he told how Dennis's fine had been remitted.

In the next few weeks Peter met a good many men who wanted to talk politics with him. Gallagher brought some; Dennis others; his fellow-ward delegates, more. But Peter could not be induced to commit himself. He would talk candidates and principles endlessly, but without expressing his own mind. Twice he was asked point blank, "Who's your man?" but he promptly answered that he had not yet decided. He had always read a Democratic paper, but now he read two, and a Republican organ as well. His other reading lessened markedly, and the time gained was spent in talking with men in the "district." He even went into the saloons and listened to the discussions.

"I don't drink," he had to explain several times, "because my mother doesn't like it." For some reason this explanation seemed to be perfectly satisfactory. One man alone sneered at him. "Does she feed yer still on milk, sonny?" he asked. "No," said Peter, "but everything I have comes from her, and that's the kind of a mother a fellow wants to please; don't you think so?" The sneerer hesitated, and finally said he "guessed it was." So Peter was made one of them, and smoked and listened. He said very little, but that little was sound, good sense, and, if he did not talk, he made others do so; and, after the men had argued over something, they often looked at Peter, rather than at their opponents, to see if he seemed to approve of their opinions.

"It's a fine way he has wid the b'ys," Dennis told his mother. "He makes them feel that he's just the likes av them, an' that he wants their minds an' opinions to help him. Shure, they'd rather smoke one pipe av his tobaccy than drink ten times at Gallagher's expense."

After Peter had listened carefully and lengthily, he wrote to "The Honorable Lemuel Porter, Hudson, N. Y.," asking him if he could give him an hour's talk some day. The reply was prompt, and told Peter that Porter would be glad to see him any time that should suit his convenience. So Peter took a day off and ran up to Hudson.

"I am trying to find out for whom I should vote," he explained to Porter. "I'm a new man at this sort of thing, and, not having met any of the men talked of, I preferred to see them before going to the convention."

Porter found that Peter had taken the trouble to go over a back file of papers, and read some of his speeches.

"Of course," Peter explained, "I want, as far as possible, to know what you think of questions likely to be matters for legislation."

"The difficulty in doing that, Mr. Stirling," he was told, "is that every nominee is bound to surrender his opinions in a certain degree to the party platform, while other opinions have to be modified to new conditions."

"I can see that," said Peter. "I do not for a moment

expect that what you say to-day is in any sense a pledge. If a man's honest, the poorest thing we can do to him is to tie him fast to one course of action, when the conditions are constantly changing. But, of course, you have opinions for the present state of things?"

Something in Peter's explanation or face pleased Mr. Porter. He demurred no more, and, for an hour before lunch, and during that meal, he talked with the utmost freedom.

"I'm not easily fooled on men," he told his secretary afterwards, "and you can say what you wish to that Stirling without danger of its being used unfairly or to injure one. And he's the kind of man to be won by square dealing."

Peter had spoken of his own district. "I think," he said, "that some good can be done in the way of non-partisan legislation. I've been studying the food supplies of the city, and, if I can, I shall try to get a bill introduced this winter to have official inspections systematized."

"That will receive my approval if it is properly drawn. But you'll probably find the Health Board fighting you. It's a nest of politicians."

"If they won't yield, I shall have to antagonize them, but I have had some talks with the men there, in connection with the 'swill-milk' investigations, and I think I can frame a bill that will do what I want, yet which they will not oppose. I shall try to make them help me in the drafting, for they can make it much better through their practical experience."

"If you do that, the opposition ought not to be troublesome. What else do you want?"

"I've been thinking of a general Tenement-house bill, but I don't think I shall try for that this winter. It's a big subject, which needs very careful study, in which a lot of harm may be done by ignorance. There's no doubt that anything which hurts the landlord, hurts the tenant, and if you make the former spend money, the tenant pays for it in the long run. Yet health must be protected. I shall try to find out what can be done."

"I wish you would get into the legislature yourself, Mr. Stirling."

"I shall not try for office. I want to go on with my profession. But I shall hope to work in politics in the future."

Peter took another day off, and spent a few minutes of it with the other most promising candidate. He did not see very much of him, for they were interrupted by another caller, and Peter had to leave before he could have a chance to continue the interview.

"I had a call to-day from that fellow Stirling, who's a delegate from the sixth ward," the candidate told a "visiting statesman" later. "I'm afraid he'll give us trouble. He asks too many questions. Fortunately Dewilliger came to see me, and though I shouldn't have seen him ordinarily, I found his call very opportune as a means of putting an end to Stirling's cross-examination."

"He's the one doubtful man on the city's delegation," said the statesman. "It happened through a mistake. It will be very unfortunate if we can't cast a solid city vote."

Peter talked more in the next few days. He gave the "b'ys" his impressions of the two candidates, in a way which made them trust his conclusions. He saw his two fellow delegates, and argued long and earnestly with them. He went to every saloon-keeper in the district, and discussed the change in the liquor law which was likely to be a prominent issue in the campaign, telling them what he had been able to draw from both candidates about the subject.

"Catlin seems to promise you the most," he told them, "and I don't want to say he isn't trying to help you. But if you get the law passed which he promises to sign, you won't be much better off. In the first place, it will cost you a lot of money, as you know, to pass it; and then it will tempt people to go into the business, so that it will cut your profits that way. Then, you may stir up a big public sentiment against you in the next election, and so lay yourselves open to unfriendly legislation. It is success, or trying to get too much, which has beaten every party, sooner or later, in this country. Look at slavery. If the Southerners had left things as they were under the Missouri Compromise, they never would have stirred up the popular outbreak that destroyed slavery.

Now, Porter is said to be unfriendly to you, because he wants a bill to limit the number of licenses, and to increase the fee to new saloons. Don't you see that is all in your favor, though apparently against you? In the first place, you are established, and the law will be drawn so as to give the old dealer precedence over a new one in granting fresh licenses. This limit will really give the established saloon more trade in the future, by reducing competition. While the increase in fee to new saloons will do the same."

"By ——, yer right," said Blunkers.

"That's too good a name to use that way," said Peter, but more as if he were stating a fact than reproving.

Blunkers laughed good-naturedly. "Yer'll be gettin' usen to close up yet, Mister Stirling. Ye're too good for us."

Peter looked at him. "Blunkers," he said warmly, "no man is too good not to tell the truth to any one whom he thinks it will help."

"Shake," said Blunkers. Then he turned to the men at the table. "Step up, boys," he called. "I sets it up dis time to drink der health of der feller dat don't drink."

The boys drank.

CHAPTER XXI

A POLITICAL DINNER

PETER had only a month for work after reaching his own conclusions, before the meeting of the convention, but in that month he worked hard. As the result, a rumor, carrying dismay to the party leaders, became current.

"What's this I hear?" said Gallagher's former interviewer to that gentleman. "They say Schlurger says he intends to vote for Porter, and Kennedy's getting cold?"

"If you'll go through the sixth you'll hear more than that."

"What do you mean?"

"There was a torchlight last night, of nearly every voter

in the ward, and nothing but Stirling prevented them from making the three delegates pledge themselves to vote for Porter. He said they must go unbound."

The interviewer's next remark is best represented by several "blank its," no allusion however being intended to bed-coverings. Then he cited the lower regions to know what it all meant.

"It means that that chap Stirling has got to be fixed, and fixed big. I thought I knew how to wire pull, and manage men, but he's taken hold and just runs it as he wants. It's he makes all the trouble."

The interviewer left the court, and five minutes later was in Stirling's office.

"My name's Green," he said. "I'm a delegate to the convention, and one of the committee who has the arranging of the special train and accommodations at Saratoga."

"I'm glad you came in," said Peter. "I bought my ticket yesterday, and the man at headquarters said he'd see that I was assigned a room at the United States."

"There'll be no trouble about the arrangements. What I want to see you for, is to ask if you won't dine with me this evening? There's to be several of the delegates and some big men there, to talk over the situation."

"I should like to," said Peter.

The man pulled out a card, and handed it to Peter. "Six o'clock sharp," he said. Then he went to headquarters, and told the result of his two interviews. "Now who had better be there?" he asked. After consultation, a dinner of six was arranged.

The meal proved to be an interesting one to Peter. First, he found that all the guests were well-known party men, whose names and opinions were matters of daily notice in the papers. What was more, they talked convention affairs, and Peter learned in the two hours' general conversation more of true "interests" and "influences" and "pulls" and "advantages" than all his reading and talking had hitherto gained him. He learned that in New York the great division of interest was between the city and country members, and that this divided interest played a part in nearly every measure. "Now," said one of the best known men at the table, "the men who represent the city, must look out for the city.   Porter's a fine man, but he has no great backing, and no matter how well he intends by us, he can't do more than agree to such bills as we can get passed.   But Catlin has the Monroe members of the legislature under his thumb, and his brother-in-law runs Onondaga.   He promises they shall vote for all we want.   With that aid, we can carry what New York City needs, in spite of the country members."

"Would the country members refuse to vote for really good and needed city legislation?" asked Peter.

"Every time, unless we agree to dicker with them on some country job.   The country members hold the interest of the biggest city in this country in their hands, and threaten or throttle those interests every time anything is wanted."

"And when it comes to taxation," added another, "the country members are always giving the cities the big end to carry."

"I had a talk with Catlin," said Peter.   "It seemed to me that he wasn't the right kind of man."

"Catlin's a timid man, who never likes to commit himself.   That's because he always wants to do what his backers tell him.   Of course when a man does that, he hasn't decided views of his own, and naturally doesn't wish to express what he may want to take back an hour later."

"I don't like straw men," said Peter.

"A man who takes other people's opinions is not a bad governor, Mr. Stirling.   It all depends on whose opinion he takes.   If we could find a man who was able to do what the majority wants every time, we could re-elect him for the next fifty years.   You must remember that in this country we elect a man to do what we want—not to do what he wants himself."

"Yes," said Peter.   "But who is to say what the majority wants?"

"Aren't we—the party leaders—who are meeting daily the ward leaders, and the big men in the different districts, better able to know what the people want than the man who sits in the governor's room, with a door-keeper to prevent the people from seeing him?"

"You may not choose to do what the people want."

"Of course. I've helped push things that I knew were unpopular. But this is very unusual, because it's risky. Remember, we can only do things when our party is in power, so it is our interest to do what will please the people, if we are to command majorities and remain in office. Individually we have got to do what the majority of our party wants done, or we are thrown out, and new men take our places. And it's just the same way with the parties."

"Well," said Peter, "I understand the condition better, and can see what I could not fathom before, why the city delegates want Catlin. But my own ward has come out strong for Porter. We've come to the conclusion that his views on the license question are those which are best for us, and besides, he's said that he will stand by us in some food and tenement legislation we want."

"I know about that change, and want to say, Mr. Stirling, that few men of your years and experience, were ever able to do as much so quickly. But there are other sides, even to these questions, which you may not have yet considered. Any proposed restriction on the license will not merely scare a lot of saloon-keepers, who will only understand that it sounds unfriendly, but it will alienate every brewer and distiller, for their interest is to see saloons multiplied. Then food and tenement legislation always stirs up bad feeling in the dealers and owners. If the opposite party would play fair, we could afford to laugh at it, but you see the party out of power can oppose about anything, knowing that a minority is never held responsible, and so by winning over the malcontents which every piece of legislation is sure to make, before long it goes to the polls with a majority, though it has really been opposing the best interests of the whole state. We can't sit still, and do nothing, yet everything we do will alienate some interest."

"It's as bad as the doctrine of fore-ordination," laughed another of the party:

> "You can't if you will,
> You can if you won't,
> You'll be damned if you do,
> You'll be damned if you don't."

"You just said," stated Peter, "that the man who could do what the majority wants done every time, would be re-elected. Doesn't it hold true as to a party?"

"No. A party is seldom retained in power for such reasons. If it has a long tenure of office it is generally due to popular distrust of the other party. The natural tendency otherwise is to make office-holding a sort of see-saw. Let alone change of opinion in older men, there are enough new voters every four years to reverse majorities in almost every state. Of course these young men care little for what either party has done in the past, and being young and ardent, they want to change things. The minority's ready to please them, naturally. Reform they call it, but it's quite as often 'Deform' when they've done it."

Peter smiled and said, "Then you think my views on license, and food-inspection, and tenement-house regulation are 'Deformities'?"

"We won't say that, but a good many older and shrewder heads have worked over those questions, and while I don't know what you hope to do, you'll not be the first to want to try a change, Mr. Stirling."

"I hope to do good. I may fail, but it's not right as it is, and I must try to better it." Peter spoke seriously, and his voice was very clear. "I'm glad to have had this talk, before the convention meets. You are all experienced men, and I value your opinions."

"But don't intend to act on them," said his host good-naturedly.

"No. I'm not ready to say that. I've got to think them over."

"If you do that, Mr. Stirling, you'll find we are right. We have not been twenty and thirty years in this business for nothing."

"I think you know how to run a party—but poisoned milk was peddled in my ward. I went to law to punish the men who sold it. Now I'm going into politics to try and get laws and administration which will prevent such evils. I've told my district what I want. I think it will support me. I know you can help me, and I hope you will. We may disagree on methods, but if we both wish the good of New York, we can't disagree on results." Peter stopped, rather amazed himself at the length of his speech.

"What do you want us to do?"

"You say that you want to remain in control. You say you can only do so by majorities. I want you to give this city such a government that you'll poll every honest vote on our side," said Peter warmly.

"That's only the generalization of a very young man," said the leader.

Peter liked him all the better for the snub. "I generalized, because it would make clear the object of my particular endeavors. I want to have the Health Board help me to draft a food-inspection bill, and I want the legislature to pass it, without letting it be torn to pieces for the benefit of special interests. I don't mind fair amendments, but they must be honest ones."

"And if the Health Board helps you, and the bill is made a law?"

Peter looked Mr. Costell in the face, and spoke quietly: "I shall tell my ward that you have done them a great service."

Two of the men moved uneasily in their seats, as if not comfortable, and a third scowled.

"And if we can give you some tenement-house legislation?"

"I shall tell my ward that you have done them a great service." Peter spoke in the same tone of voice, and still looked Mr. Costell in the face.

"And if we don't do either?"

"What I shall do then will depend on whether you refuse for a good reason or for none. In either case I shall tell them the facts."

"This is damned——" began one of the dinner-party, but the lifting of Mr. Costell's hand stopped the speech there.

"Mr. Stirling," said Mr. Costell, rising as he spoke, "I

hope when you come to think it over, that you will vote
with us for Catlin. But whether you do or not, we want
you to work with us. We can help you, and you can help
us. When you are ready to begin on your bills, come
and see me."

"Thank you," said Peter. "That is just what I want."
He said good-night to the company, and left the house.

"That fellow is going to be troublesome," said Green.

"There's no good trying to get anything out of him.
Better split with him at once," said the guest who had
used the expletive.

"He can't have any very big hold," said a third. "It's
only that trial which has given him a temporary popularity."

"Wait and see if he goes back on Catlin, and if he does,
lay for him," remarked Green.

A pause came, and they all looked at Costell, who was
smiling a certain deep smile that was almost habitual
with him, and which no one had ever yet been able to
read. "No," he said slowly. "You might beat him,
but he isn't the kind that stays beat. I'll agree to outwit
any man in politics, except the man who knows how to
fight and to tell the people the truth. I've never yet
seen a man beaten in the long run who can do both those,
unless he chose to think himself beaten. Gentlemen,
that Stirling is a fighter and a truth-teller, and you can't
beat him in his ward. There's no use having him against
us, so it's our business to see that we have him with us.
We may not be able to get him into line this time, but we
must do it in the long run. For he's not the kind that
lets go. He's beaten Nelson, and he's beaten Gallagher,
both of whom are old hands. Mark my words, in five
years he'll run the sixth ward. Drop all talk of fighting
him. He is in politics to stay, and we must make it worth
his while to stay with us."

CHAPTER XXII

POLITICS

PETER sat up later than was prudent that night, study-ing his blank wall. Yet when he rose to go to bed, he gave his head a puzzled shake. When he had gone through his papers, and drunk his coffee the next morning, he went back to wall-gazing again. He was working over two conundrums not very easy to answer, which were somewhat to this effect:

Does the best man always make the best official?

Is the honest judgment of a fellow verging on twenty-four better than the experienced opinion of many far older men?

Peter began to think life had not such clear and direct "right" and "wrong" roads as he had thought. He had said to himself long ago that it was easy to take the right one, but he had not then discovered that it is often diffi-cult to know which is the right, in order to follow it. He had started in to punish Bohlmann, and had compromised. He had disapproved of Dennis breaking the law, and had compromised his disapproval. He had said he should not go into saloons, and had ended by going. Now he was confronted with the problem whether the interests of his ward would be better served by the nomination of a man of good record, whom Peter personally liked, or by that of a colorless man, who would be ruled by the city's leaders. In the one case Peter feared no support for his measures from his own party. In the other case he saw aid that was tantamount to success. Finally he shook himself.

"I believe Dennis is right," he said aloud. "There are more 'real' things than 'convictions' in New York poli-tics, and a 'real' thing is much harder to decide about in voting than a 'conviction.'"

He went to his bedroom, packed his bag, and took his way to the station. There he found a dense crowd of delegates and "well-wishers," both surrounding and filling the special train which was to carry New York's contribution to the collected party wisdom, about to concentrate at Saratoga.

Peter felt like a stranger in the crowd, but on mingling in it he quickly found himself a marked man. He was seized upon by one of the diners of the evening before, and soon found himself forming part of a group, which constantly changed its components, but continued to talk convention affairs steadily. Nor did the starting of the train, with cheers, brass bands, flags, and other enthusing elements, make more than a temporary break. From the time the special started, till it rolled into Saratoga, six hours later, there was one long series of political debates and confabs. Peter listened much, and learned much, for the talk was very straight and plain. He had chats with Costell and Green. His two fellow-delegates from "de sixt" sought him and discussed intentions. He liked Schlurger, a simple, guileless German, who wanted only to do what his constituents wished him to do, both in convention and Assembly. Of Kennedy he was not so sure. Kennedy had sneered a little at Peter's talk about the "best man," and about "helping the ward," and had only found that Peter's ideas had value after he had been visited by various of the saloon-keepers, seen the vast torchlight meeting, and heard the cheers at Peter's arguments. Still, Peter was by no means sure that Kennedy was not a square man, and concluded he was right in not condemning him, when, passing through one of the cars, he overheard the following:

"What kind of man is that Stirling, who's raised such hell in the sixth?"

"I don't know him, but Kennedy told me, before he'd swung round, that he was a darned good sort of a cuss."

This was flattery, Peter understood, however questionable the form might seem, and he was pleased. Very few of us do not enjoy a real compliment. What makes a compliment uncomfortable is either a suspicion that the maker doesn't mean it, or a knowledge that it is not merited.

Peter went at once to his room on reaching the hotel in Saratoga, intending to make up the sleep of which his long "think" the night before had robbed him. But scarcely had the colored gentleman bowed himself out, after the usual "Can I get de gentleman a pitcher of ice water" (which translated means: "Has de gentleman any superfluous change?") when a knock came at the door. Peter opened it, to find a man outside.

"Is this Mr. Stirling's room?" inquired the individual.

"Yes."

"Can I see him?"

"Come in." Peter moved his bag off one of his chairs, and his hat and overcoat off the other.

"Mr. Stirling," said the stranger as he sat down, "I am Senator Maguire, and am, as perhaps you know, one of Porter's managers."

"Yes."

"We understand that you are friendly to us. Now, I needn't say that New York is otherwise a unit in opposing us."

"No," said Peter. "My fellow-delegates from the sixth, Schlurger and Kennedy, stand as I do!"

"Are you sure?"

"Yes."

"The change must have been very sudden. They were elected as Catlin men, we were told."

"Yes. But there's quite a different feeling in the ward now, and they have yielded to it."

"That's good news."

"We all three come here prepared to do what seems best."

The Senator's expression lost some of the satisfaction Peter's news had put into it. He gave a quick look at Peter's face, as if to try and find from it what lay behind the words. He hesitated, as if divided in mind over two courses of action. Finally he said:

"I needn't tell you that this opposition of practically the whole of the New York City delegation, is the most serious set-back to Porter's chance. Now, we have talked it over, and it seemed to us that it would be a great card for him if he could be nominated by a city delegate. Will you do it?"

"I don't know him well enough, do I? Doesn't the nominating delegate have to make a speech in his favor?"

"Yes. But I can give you the material to-night. Or if you prefer, we'll give it to you all written for delivery?"

"I don't make other men's speeches, Mr. Maguire."

"Suit yourself about that. It shall be just as you please."

"The difficulty is that I have not decided myself, yet, how I shall vote, and of course such an act is binding."

Mr. Maguire's countenance changed again. "I'm sorry to hear that. I hoped you were for Porter. He's far away the best man."

"So I think."

The Senator leaned back in his chair, and tucked his thumbs into the armholes of his waistcoat. He thought he had fathomed Peter, and felt that the rest was plain sailing. "This is not a chap to be tolled. I'll give him the gaff at once," was his mental conclusion. Then he asked aloud:

"What do you want?"

It was a question susceptible of many different constructions, but as Mr. Maguire asked it, it seemed to him to have but one, and that not very honest. Peter hesitated. The temptation was strong to lead the Senator on, but he did not like to do it. It seemed to savor of traps, and Peter had never liked traps. Still—he did want to know if the managers on Porter's side would stoop to buy his support by some bargain. As Peter hesitated, weighing the pros and cons, Maguire spoke again.

"What does the other side offer you?"

Peter spoke quickly. "They haven't offered me anything, but advice. That is, Costell said he'd try and help me on some legislation I want——"

"Special?" interrupted Maguire.

"No. General. I've talked about it with Porter as well."

"Oh! Indeed?"

"I'm really anxious to get that. Otherwise I want nothing."

"Whew," said the Senator to himself. "That was a narrow squeak. If he hadn't spoken so quickly, I should have shown my hand before the call. I wonder if he got any inkling?" He never dreamed that Peter had spoken quickly to save that very disclosure.

"I needn't say, Mr. Stirling, that if you can see your way to nominate Porter, we shall not forget it. Nor will he. He isn't the kind of man who forgets his friends. Many a man in to-morrow's convention would give anything for the privilege we offer you."

"Well," said Peter, "I realize the honor offered me, but I don't see my way to take it. It will please me better to see him nominated by some one who has really stood close to him, than to gain his favor by doing it myself."

"Think twice, Mr. Stirling."

"If you would rather, I will not give you my answer till to-morrow morning?"

"I would," said Maguire rising. "Try and make it favorable. It's a great chance to do good for yourself and for your side. Good-night."

Peter closed his door, and looked about for a bit of blank wall. But on second thought he sat down on his window-sill, and, filling his pipe, tried to draw conclusions as well as smoke from it.

"I wonder," he pondered to himself, "how much of that was Maguire, and how much Porter? Ought I, for the sake of doing my best for my ward, to have let him go on? Has an agent any right to refuse what will help his client, even if it comes by setting pitfalls?"

Rap, rap, rap.

"Come in," called Peter, forgetting he had turned down his light.

The door opened and Mr. Costell came in. "Having a quiet smoke?" he asked.

"Yes. I haven't a cigar to offer you. Can you join me in a pipe?"

"I haven't come to that yet. Suppose you try one of my cigars." Costell sat down on the window-ledge by Peter.

"Thank you," said Peter. "I like a cigar, but it must be a good one, and that kind I can't afford." He lit the cigar, and leaned back to luxuriate in it.

"You'll like that, I'm sure. Pretty sight, isn't it?"

Costell pointed to the broad veranda, three stories below them, gay with brilliant dresses.

"Yes. It's my first visit here, so it's new to me."

"It won't be your last. You'll be attending other conventions than this."

"I hope so."

"One of my scouts tells me you've had a call from Maguire?"

"Yes." Peter hesitated a moment. "He wants me to nominate Porter," he continued, as soon as he had decided that plain speaking was fair to Maguire.

"We shall be very sorry to see you do it."

"I don't think I shall. They only want me because it would give the impression that Porter has a city backing, and to try to give that amounts to a deception."

"Can they get Schlurger or Kennedy?"

"Schlurger is safe. I don't know about Kennedy."

"Can you find out for us?"

"Yes. When would you like to know?"

"Can you see him now? I'll wait here."

Peter rose, looking at his cigar with a suggestion of regret. But he rubbed out the light, and left the room. At the office, he learned the number of Kennedy's room, and went to it. On knocking, the door was opened only a narrow crack.

"Oh! it's you," said Kennedy. "Come in."

Peter entered, and found Maguire seated in an easy attitude on a lounge. He noticed that his thumbs were once more tucked into his waistcoat.

"Mr. Kennedy," said Peter without seating himself, "there is an attempt being made to get a city delegate to nominate Porter. It seems to me that is his particular friends' business."

Maguire spoke so quickly that Kennedy had no chance to reply: "Kennedy's promised to nominate him, Mr. Stirling, if you won't."

"Do you feel that you are bound to do it?" asked Peter.

Kennedy moved uneasily in his chair. "Yes, I suppose I have promised."

"Will you release Mr. Kennedy from his promise if he asks it?" Peter queried to Maguire.

"Why, Mr. Stirling, I don't think either he or you ought to ask it."

"That was not my question."

It was the Senator's turn to squirm. He did not want to say no, for fear of angering Peter, yet he did not like to surrender the advantage. Finally he said: "Yes, I'll release him, but Mr. Kennedy isn't the kind of a man that cries off from a promise. That's women's work."

"No," said Kennedy, stiffening suddenly in backbone, as he saw the outlet opened by Maguire, between antagonizing Peter, and retracting his consent. "I don't play baby. Not me."

Peter stood thinking for a longer time than the others found comfortable. Maguire whistled to prove that he was quite at ease, but he would not have whistled if he had been.

"I think, Mr. Kennedy, that I'll save you from the difficulty by nominating Mr. Porter myself," said Peter finally.

"Good!" said Maguire; and Kennedy, reaching down into his hip pocket, produced a version of the holy text not yet included in any bibliography. Evidently the atmosphere was easier. "About your speech, Mr. Stirling?" continued the Senator.

"I shall say what I think right."

Something in Peter's voice made Maguire say: "It will be of the usual kind, of course?"

"I don't know," said Peter, "I shall tell the facts."

"What sort of facts?"

"I shall tell how it is that a delegate of the sixth ward nominates Porter."

"And that is?"

"I don't see," said Peter, "why I need say it. You know it as well as I do."

"I know of many reasons why you should do it."

"No," said Peter. "There's only one, and that has been created in the last ten minutes. Mr. Maguire, if you insist on the sixth ward nominating Mr. Porter, the sixth ward is going to tell why it does so. I'm sorry, for I like Porter, but the sixth ward shan't lend itself to a fraud, if I can help it."

Kennedy had been combining things spiritual and aqueous at his wash-stand. But his interest in the blending seemed suddenly to cease. Maguire, too, took his thumbs from their havens of rest, and looked dissatisfied.

"Look here, Mr. Stirling," he said, "it's much simpler to leave it to Kennedy. You think you're doing what's right, but you'll only do harm to us, and to yourself. If you nominate Porter, the city gang won't forgive you, and unless you can say what we want said, we shall be down on you. So you'll break with both sides."

"I think that is so. That is why I want some real friend of Porter's to do it."

Maguire laughed rather a forced laugh. "I suppose we've got to satisfy you. We'll have Porter nominated by one of our own crowd."

"I think that's best. Good-evening." Peter went to the door.

"Mr. Stirling," called Kennedy. "Won't you stay and take some whisky and water with us?"

"Thank you," said Peter. "Mr. Costell's in my room and he must be tired of waiting." He closed the door, and walked away.

The couple looked at each other blankly for a moment.

"The —— cuss is playing a double game," Maguire gasped.

"I don't know what it means!" said Kennedy.

"Mean?" cried Maguire. "It can mean only one thing. He's acting under Costell's orders."

"But why should he give it away to us?"

"How the —— should I know? Look here, Kennedy, you must do it, after all."

"I don't want to."

"Tut, tut, man, you must."

"But my ward?"

"Come. We'll make it quarantine, as you want. That's six years, and you can —— your ward."

"I'll do it."

"That's the talk."

They sat and discussed plans and whisky for nearly an hour. Then Maguire said good-night.

"You shall have the speech the first thing in the morning," he said at parting. Then as he walked down the long corridor, he muttered, "Now then, Stirling, look out for the hind heel of the mule."

Peter found Costell still waiting for him.

"It took me longer than I thought, for Maguire was there."

"Indeed!" said Costell, making room for Peter on the window-ledge.

Peter re-lit his cigar. "Maguire promises me that Porter shall be nominated by one of his friends."

"He had been trying Kennedy?"

"I didn't ask."

Costell smiled. "I had no business to ask you that?"

"No," Peter said frankly.

Both puffed their cigars for a time in silence.

Then Costell began talking about Saratoga. He told Peter where the "Congress" Spring was, and what was worth seeing. Finally he rose to go. He held out his hand, and said:

"Mr. Stirling, you've been as true as steel with us, and with the other men. I don't want you to suppose we are not conscious of it. I think you've done us a great service to-night, although it might have been very profitable to you if you had done otherwise. I don't think that you'll lose by it in the long run, but I'm going to thank you now, for myself. Good-night."

Peter had a good night. Perhaps it was only because he was sleepy, but a pleasant speech is not a bad nightcap. At least it is better than a mental question-mark as to whether one has done wrong. Peter did not know how it was coming out, but he thought he had done right, and need not spend time on a blank wall that evening.

CHAPTER XXIII

THE CONVENTION

THOUGH Peter had not gone to bed so early as he hoped, he was up the next morning, and had tramped his eight miles through and around Saratoga, before the place gave many evidences of life. He ended his tramp at the Congress Spring, and tasted the famous water, with exceeding disgust at the result. As he set down his half-finished tumbler, and turned to leave, he found Miss De Voe at his elbow, about to take her morning glass.

"This is a very pleasant surprise," she said, holding out her hand. "When did you arrive?"

"I only came last night."

"And how long shall you be here?"

"I cannot say. I am attending the convention, and my stay will depend on that."

"Surely you are not a Democrat?" said Miss De Voe, a shade of horror showing itself in her face, in spite of her good breeding. In those days it was not, to put it mildly, a guarantee of respectability to belong to that party, and Miss De Voe had the strong prejudices of her social station, all the more because she was absolutely ignorant of political events.

Peter said he was.

"How can you be? When a man can ally himself with the best, why should he choose the worst?"

"I think," said Peter quietly, "that a Pharisee said the same thing, in different words, many hundred years ago."

Miss De Voe caught her breath and flushed. She also became suddenly conscious of the two girls who had come to the spring with her. They had been forgotten in the surprise over Peter, but now Miss De Voe wondered if they had heard his reply, and if they had enough Bible lore to enable them to understand the reproof.

"I am sure you don't mean that," she said, in the sting of the moment.

"I am very sorry," said Peter, "if I made an unkind speech. What I meant was that no one has a right to pick out the best for himself. I am sure, from your letter to me, that you think a man should help those not as well off as himself."

"Oh, but that is very different. Of course we should be charitable to those who need our help, but we need not mix in their low politics."

"If good laws, and good administration can give the poor good food, and good lodgings, don't you think the best charity is to 'mix' in politics, and try to obtain such results?"

"I want you to know my two cousins," Miss De Voe replied. "Dorothy, I wish to present Mr. Stirling. My cousin, Miss Ogden, and Miss Minna Ogden."

Peter saw two very pretty girls, and made a bow to them.

"Which way are you walking?" asked Miss De Voe.

"I have been tramping merely for exercise," said Peter, "and stopped here to try the spring, on my way to the United States."

"It is hardly worth while, but if you will get into our carriage, we will drop you there. Or if you can spare the time, we will drive to our cottage, and then send you back to the hotel."

"Thank you," said Peter, "but I shall only crowd you, I fear."

"No. There is plenty of room."

"Will the convention be interesting to watch, Mr. Stirling?" asked one of the girls, as soon as they were seated.

"I don't know," Peter told her. "It is my first experience at it. There is pretty strong feeling, and that of course makes it interesting to the delegates, but I am not sure that it would be so to others."

"Will there be speeches, and cheers, and all that sort of thing?"

"Yes."

"Cousin Anneke, won't you take us? It will be such fun!"

"Are spectators admitted, Mr. Stirling?"

"I believe so. I heard something about tickets last night. If you care to go, I'll see if I can get you some?"

"Oh, please," cried both girls.

"If you can do so, Mr. Stirling, we should like to see the interesting part," said Miss De Voe.

"I'll try."

"Send word back by Oliver." The carriage had drawn up at the cottage, and farewells were made.

As soon as Peter reached the hotel, he went to the New York City delegation room, and saw Costell. He easily secured admissions, and pencilling on a card, "At headquarters they tell me that the nominations will begin at the afternoon session, about two o'clock," he sent them back by the carriage. Then bearding the terrors of the colored "monarch of all he surveys," who guards the dining-room of every well-ordered Saratoga hotel, he satisfied as large an appetite as he remembered in a long time.

The morning proceedings in the convention were purely formal. The election of the chairman, the roll-call, the naming of the committees, and other routine matter was gotten through with, but the real interest centred in the undertone of political talk going on with little regard to the business in hand. After the committees were named, an unknown man came up to Peter, and introduced himself by a name which Peter at once recognized as that of one of the committee on the platform.

"Mr. Costell thinks you might like to see this, and can perhaps suggest a change," explained Mr. Talcott, laying several sheets of manuscript on Peter's desk and indicating with his finger a certain paragraph.

Peter read it twice before saying anything. "I think I can better it," he said. "If you can give me time. I'm very slow about such things."

"All right. Get it in shape as quickly as possible, and send it to the committee-room."

Left alone Peter looked round for a blank wall. Failing in his search, he put his head into his hands, and tried to shut out the seething, excited mass of men about him. After a time he took a sheet of paper and wrote a paragraph for the platform. It pledged the party to investigate the food and tenement questions, and to pass such remedial legislation as should seem best. It pledged the party to do this, with as little disturbance and interference with present conditions as possible, "but fully recognizing the danger of State interference, we place human life above money profits, and human health above annual incomes, and shall use the law to its utmost to protect both." When it appeared in the platform, there was an addition that charged the failure to obtain legislation "which should have rendered impossible the recent terrible lesson in New York City" to "the obstruction in the last legislature in the interest of the moneyed classes and landlords, by the Republican party." That had not been in Peter's draft and he was sorry to see it. Still, the paragraph had a real ring of honesty and feeling in it. That was what others thought too. "Gad, that Stirling, knows how to sling English," said one of the committee, when the paragraph was read aloud. "He makes it take right hold." Many an orator in that fall's campaign read the nineteenth section of the Democratic platform aloud, feeling that it was ammunition of the right kind. It is in all the New York papers of September 24th, of that year.

Immediately after the morning adjournment, Green came up to Peter.

"We've had a count, and can't carry Catlin. So we shan't even put him up. What do you think of Milton?"

"I don't know him personally, but he has a very good record, I believe."

"He isn't what we want, but that's not the question. We must take what we can get."

"I suppose you think Porter has a chance."

"Not if we take Milton."

"Between the two I have no choice."

An hour later, the convention was called to order by the chairman. A few moments sufficed to complete the unfinished business, and then the chairman's gavel fell, and every one knew without his announcement that the crucial moment had been reached.

Much to Peter's surprise, Kennedy was one of the members who was instantly on his feet, and was the one selected for recognition by the chairman. He was still more surprised when Kennedy launched at once into a glowing eulogium of Porter. Peter was sitting next Kennedy, and though he sat quietly, a sad look came into the face usually so expressionless. He felt wronged. He felt that he had been an instrument in the deceiving of others. Most of all he grieved to think that a delegate of his ward, largely through his own interference, was acting discreditably. Peter wanted others to do right, and he felt that that was not what Kennedy was doing.

The moment Kennedy finished, Peter rose, as did

Maguire. The convention was cheering for Porter, and it took some time to quiet it to a condition when it was worth while recognizing any one. During this time the chairman leaned forward and talked with Green, who sat right below him, for a moment. Green in turn spoke to Costell, and a little slip of paper was presently handed up to the chairman, who from that moment became absolutely oblivious of the fact that Maguire was on his feet. When silence finally came, in spite of Maguire's, "Mr. Chairman," that individual said, "Mr. Stirling."

Peter began in a low voice, "In rising, Mr. Chairman, to second the nomination of Mr. Porter, I feel that it would be idle in me to praise one so well known to all of us, even if he had not just been the subject of so appreciative a speech from my colleague——"

Here cries of "louder" interrupted Peter, during which interruption Green said to Costell, "We've been tricked."

"I'm not so sure," replied Costell, "Maguire's on his feet yet, and doesn't look happy. Something's happening which has not been slated."

When Peter resumed, there were no more cries of "louder." His introduction had been a matter of trouble and doubt to him, for he liked Porter, and feared he might not show it. But now he merely had something to tell his audience, and that was easy work. So, his voice ringing very clear and distinct, he told them of the original election of the delegates; of the feeling of his ward; of the attempts to obtain a city nomination of Porter; of Maguire's promise. "Gad, he hits from the shoulder," said Green. As soon as the trend of his remarks was realized, Porter's supporters began to hiss and hoot. Peter at once stopped, but the moment silence came he began again, and after a repetition of this a few times, they saw they could neither embarrass nor anger him, so they let him have his say. He brought his speech to an end by saying:

"I have already expressed my admiration of Mr. Porter, and as soon as I had made up my mind to vote for him I made no secret of that intention. But he should not have been nominated by a city delegate, for he is not the choice of New York City, and any attempt to show that he is, or that he has any true backing there, is only an attempt to deceive. In seconding his nomination therefore, I wish it to be distinctly understood that both his nomination and seconding are personal acts, and in no sense the act of the delegates of the city of New York."

There was a mingling of hoots and cheers as Peter sat down, though neither was very strong. In truth, the larger part of the delegates were very much in the dark as to the tendency of Peter's speech. "Was it friendly or unfriendly to Porter?" they wondered.

"Mr. Maguire," said the chairman.

"Mr. Chairman, the gentleman who has just sat down is to be complimented on his speech. In my whole life I have never heard so deceptive and blinding a narration. We know of Brutus stabbing his friends. But what shall we say of a pretended Brutus who caresses while he stabs?"

Here the Porter adherents became absolutely sure of the character of Peter's speech, and hissed.

"Nor is it Imperial Cæsar alone," continued Maguire, "against whom he turns his poniard. Not content with one foul murder, he turns against Cæsar's friends. By devilish innuendo, he charges the honorable Mr. Kennedy and myself with bargaining to deceive the American people. I call on him for proof or retraction."

The convention laughed. Peter rose and said: "Mr. Chairman, I gave a truthful account of what actually took place last evening in the United States Hotel. I made no charges."

"But you left the impression that Mr. Kennedy and I had made a deal," shrieked Maguire.

"If the gentleman draws that conclusion from what passed, it is not my fault."

The convention laughed. "Do you mean to charge such a bargain?" angrily shouted Maguire.

"Will you deny it?" asked Peter calmly.

"Then you do charge it?"

Here the convention laughed for the third time. Green shouted "deny it," and the cry was taken up by many of the delegates.

"Yes," screamed Maguire. "I do deny it."

Peter turned to Kennedy. "Do you too, deny it?"

"Yes," shouted Kennedy, loudly.

Again the convention laughed.

"Then," said Peter, "if I had charged you with a bargain, I should now find it necessary to apologize."

The convention roared. Maguire screamed something, but it could not be heard. The tenor of his remarks was indicated by his red face and clinched fist.

Costell smiled his deep smile. "I'm very glad," he said to the man next him, "that we didn't pick Stirling up."

Then Milton was nominated and seconded, as were also Catlin, and four minor stars. That done, a ballot was taken and the vote stood:

Porter	206
Milton	197
Catlin	52
Scattering	29

A second ballot showed:

Porter	206
Milton	202
Catlin	54
Scattering	22

A third ballot gave:

Porter	206
Milton	210
Catlin	52
Scattering	16

"Porter's done for on the next," was whispered round the hall, though where it started, no one knew. Evidently his adherents thought so, for one made a motion to adjourn. It was voted down, and once more the roll call started.

"I shall vote for Milton," Peter told Schlurger, and the changes in the delegations as the call proceeded, proved that many changes were being made the same way. Yet the fourth ballot showed:

Porter	125
Milton	128
Catlin	208
Scattering	14

The wildest excitement broke out in the Porter delegates. "They've beaten us," screamed Kennedy, as much to himself as to those about. "They've used Milton to break our ranks, meaning Catlin all the time." So in truth, it was. Milton had been put up to draw off Porter's delegates, but the moment they had begun to turn to Milton, enough New York City delegates had been transferred to Catlin to prevent Milton being chosen. Amid protests and angry words on all sides another ballot was taken:

Catlin	256
Porter	118
Milton	110

Before the result was announced, Green was at Peter's elbow.

"Will you move to make it unanimous?" he asked.

"Yes." And Peter made the formal motion, which was carried by acclamation. Half an hour served to choose the Lieutenant-Governor and the rest of the ticket, for the bulk of it had already been slated. The platform was adopted, and the convention dissolved.

"Well," said Kennedy angrily to Peter, "I guess you've messed it this time. A man can't please both sides, but he needn't get cussed by both."

Peter went out and walked to his hotel. "I'm afraid I did mess it," he thought, "yet I don't see what else I could have done."

CHAPTER XXIV

MISUNDERSTANDINGS AND UNDERSTANDINGS

"Did you understand what it all meant, Cousin Anneke?" asked Dorothy, as they were coming downstairs.

"No. The man who got so angry seemed to think Mr. Stirling had——"

She stopped short. A group of men on the sidewalk were talking, and she paused to hear one say:

"To see that young chap Stirling handling Maguire was an eye-opener."

Another man laughed, rather a deep, quiet laugh. "Maguire understands everything but honesty," he said. "You can always beat him with that."

Miss De Voe would have liked to stay and listen, but there were too many men. So the ladies entered the carriage.

"At least we know that he said he was trying to tell the truth," she went on, "and you just heard what that man said. I don't know why they all laughed."

"He didn't seem to mind a bit."

"No. Hasn't he a funny half-embarrassed, half-cool manner?"

"He wasn't embarrassed after he was fairly speaking. You know he was really fine-looking, when he spoke."

"Yes," said Dorothy. "You said he had a dull, heavy face."

"That was the first time I saw him, Dorothy. It's a face which varies very much. Oliver, drive to the United States. We will take him home to dinner."

"Oh, good," cried the youngest. "Then he will tell us why they laughed."

As they drove up to the hotel, Peter had just reached the steps. He turned to the carriage, the moment he saw that they wanted him.

"We wish to carry you off to a simple country dinner," Miss De Voe told him.

"I am going to take the special to New York, and that leaves in half an hour."

"Take a later train."

"My ticket wouldn't be good on it."

Most men Miss De Voe would have snubbed on the spot, but to Peter she said: "Then get another ticket."

"I don't care to do that," said Peter.

"Oh, please, Mr. Stirling," said Minna. "I want to ask you a lot of questions about the convention."

"Hush, Minna," said Miss De Voe. She was nettled that Peter should refuse, and that her niece could stoop to beg of "a criminal lawyer and ward politician," as she put it mentally. But she was determined not to show it. "We are sorry. Good-evening. Home, Oliver."

So they did not learn from Peter why the convention

laughed. The subject was brought up at dinner, and Dorothy asked the opinion of the voters of the family.

"Probably he had made a fluke of some kind," one said.

"More probably he had out-sharped the other side," suggested a second.

"It will be in the papers to-morrow," said the first suggestor.

The three women looked in the next day's papers, but the reporters were as much at sea in regard to the Stirling-sixth-ward incident, as had been the rank-and-file in the convention. Three took their views from Maguire, and called it "shameful treason," and the like. Two called it "unprincipled and contradictory conduct." One alone said that "Mr. Stirling seemed to be acting conscientiously, if erratically." Just what effect it had had on the candidates none of the papers agreed in. One said it had killed Porter. Another, that "it was a purely personal matter without influence on the main question." The other papers shaded between these, though two called it "a laughable incident." The opposition press naturally saw in it an entire discrediting of both factions of the Democratic party, and absolute proof that the nominee finally selected was unfit for office.

Unable to sift out the truth, the ladies again appealed to the voters of the family.

"Oh," said one, "Stirling did something tricky and was caught in it."

"I don't believe that," said Miss De Voe.

"Nor I," said Dorothy.

"Well, if you want to make your political heeler an angel, I have no objection," laughed the enfranchised being.

"I don't think a man who made that speech about the children can be a scoundrel," said Dorothy.

"I don't either," said Minna.

"That's the way you women reason," responded he of the masculine intellect. "Because a man looks out for some sick kittens, ergo, he is a political saint. If you must take up with politicians, do take Republicans, for then, at least, you have a small percentage of chance in your favor that they are gentlemen."

"Don't be a Pharisee, Lispenard," said Miss De Voe, utilizing Peter's rebuke.

"Then don't trouble me with political questions. Politics are so vulgar in this country that no gentleman keeps up with them."

Miss De Voe and the two girls dropped the "vulgar" subject, but Miss De Voe said later:

"I should like to know what they laughed at?"

"Do ask him—if he comes to call on you, this winter, Cousin Anneke."

"No. I asked him once and he did not come." Miss De Voe paused a moment. "I shall not ask him again," she added.

"I don't think he intends to be rude," said Dorothy.

"No," responded Miss De Voe. "I don't think he knows what he is doing. He is absolutely without our standards, and it is just as well for both that he shouldn't call." Woman-like, Miss De Voe forgot that she had said Peter was a gentleman.

If Peter had found himself a marked man in the trip up, he was doubly so on the return train. He sat most of the time by himself, pondering on what had happened, but he could not be unconscious of the number of people to whom he was pointed out. He was conscious too, that his course had not been understood, and that many of those who looked at him with interest, did so without approbation. He was not buoyed up either, by a sense that he had succeeded in doing the best. He had certainly hurt Porter, and had made enemies of Maguire and Kennedy. Except for the fact that he had tried to do right, he could see no compensating balance.

Naturally the newspapers the next morning did not cheer him, though perhaps he cared less for what they said than he ought. He sent them, good, bad, and indifferent, to his mother, writing her at the same time a long letter, telling her how and why he had taken this course. He wrote also a long letter to Porter, explaining his conduct. Porter had already been told that Peter was largely responsible for his defeat, but after reading Peter's letter, he wrote him a very kind reply, thanking him for his support and for his letter. "It is not always easy to do what one wants in politics," he wrote, "but if one tries with high motives, for high things, even defeat loses its bitterness. I shall not be able to help you, in your wished-for reforms as greatly as I hoped, but I am not quite a nonentity in politics even now, and if at any time you think my aid worth the asking, do not hesitate to call on me for it. I shall always be glad to see you at my house for a meal or a night, whether you come on political matters or merely for a chat."

Peter found his constituents torn with dissensions over his and Kennedy's course in the convention. He did not answer in kind the blame and criticism industriously sowed by Kennedy; but he dropped into a half-a-dozen saloons in the next few days, and told "the b'ys" a pretty full history of the "behind-the-scenes" part.

"I'm afraid I made mistakes," he frankly acknowledged, "yet even now I don't see how I could have done differently. I certainly thought I was doing right."

"An' so yez were," shouted Dennis. "An' if that dirty beast Kennedy shows his dirty face inside these doors, it's a washin' it will git wid the drainin' av the beer-glasses. We wants none av his dirty bargains here."

"I don't know that he had made any bargain," said Peter.

"But we do," shouted one of the men. "It's a bargain he's always makin'."

"Yes," said Dennis. "It's Kennedy looks out for himself, an' we'll let him do it next time all by himself." It could not be traced to its origin, but in less than a week the consensus of opinion in the ward was that: "Kennedy voted for himself, but Stirling for us."

The ward, too, was rather proud of the celebrity it had achieved. The papers had not merely paragraphed Peter, and the peculiar position of the "district" in the convention, but they had begun now asking questions as to how the ward would behave. "Would it support Catlin?" "Was it true that the ward machine had split, and intended to nominate rival tickets?" "Had one faction made a deal with the Republicans?"

"Begobs," said Dennis, "it's the leaders an' the papers are just afther discoverin' there is a sixth ward, an' it's Misther Stirling's made them do it."

The chief party leaders had stayed over at Saratoga, but Peter had a call from Costell before the week was out.

"The papers gave it to you rather rough," Costell said kindly, "but they didn't understand it. We thought you behaved very square."

"They tell me I did Porter harm."

"No. It was Maguire did the harm. You simply told about it. Of course you get the blame."

"My constituents stand by me."

"How do they like Catlin?"

"I think they are entirely satisfied. I'm afraid they never cared much who got it."

"I'm told Kennedy is growling, and running amuck?"

"He's down on Catlin and me."

"Well, if you think best, we'll placate him? But Gallagher seemed to think he couldn't do much?"

"I don't think he has much of a following. Even Moriarty, who was his strong card, has gone back on him."

"Will you make a couple of speeches for us in this ward?"

"If you'll let me say what I want?"

"You can support us?"

"Yes."

"Then we'll leave it to you. Only beware of making too many statements. You'll get dates and places from the committee as soon as they are settled. We pay twenty-five dollars a night. If you hit the right key, we may want you in some of the other wards, too."

"I shall be glad to talk. It's what I've been doing to small crowds in the saloons."

"So I'm told. You'll never get a better place. Men listen there, as they never will at a mass-meeting." Costell rose. "If you are free next Sunday, come up into Westchester and take a two o'clock dinner with me. We won't talk politics, but you shall see a nice little woman, who's good enough to make my life happier, and after we've looked over my stables, I'll bring you back to the city behind a gray mare that will pass about anything there is on the road."

So Peter had a half day in the country and enjoyed it very much. He looked over Mrs. Costell's flower-garden, in which she spent almost her whole time, and chatted with her about it. He saw the beautiful stables, and their still more beautiful occupants. He liked the couple very much. Both were simple and silent people, of little culture, but it seemed to Peter that the atmosphere had a gentle, homely tone that was very pleasing. As he got into the light buggy, he said to Mrs. Costell:

"I'll get the seed of that mottled gillyflower from my mother as soon as possible. Perhaps you'll let me bring it up myself?"

"Do," she said. "Come again, whether you get the seed or not."

After they had started, Mr. Costell said: "I'm glad you asked that. Mrs. Costell doesn't take kindly to many of the men who are in politics with me, but she liked you, I could see."

Peter spoke twice in the next week in small halls in his ward. He had good audiences, and he spoke well, if simply.

"There ain't no fireworks in his stuff," said the ward satirist. "He don't unfurl the American flag, nor talk about liberty and the constitution. He don't even speak of us as noble freemen. He talks just as if he thought we was in a saloon. A feller that made that speech about the babies ought to treat us to something moving."

That was what many of the ward thought. Still they went because they wanted to see if he wouldn't burst out suddenly. They felt that Peter had unlimited potentialities in the way of eloquence (for eloquence to them meant the ability to move the emotions) and merely saved his powers. Without quite knowing it they found what he had to say interesting. He brought the questions at issue straight back to elementary forms. He showed just how each paragraph in the platform would directly affect, not the state, but the "district."

"He's thoroughly good," the party leaders were told.

"If he would abuse the other side a little more, and stick in a little tinsel and calcium light he would be great."

So he was called upon to speak elsewhere in the city. He worked at one of the polls on election day, and was pleased to find that he was able to prevent a little of the "trading" for which Kennedy had arranged. His ward went Democratic, as was a foregone conclusion, but by an unusually large majority, and Peter found that he and Dennis were given the credit for it, both in the ward, and at headquarters. Catlin was elected, and the Assembly had been won. So Peter felt that his three months' work had not been an entire failure. The proceeds of his speeches had added also two hundred and fifty dollars to his savings bank account, and one hundred more to the account of "Peter Stirling, Trustee."

CHAPTER XXV

VARIOUS KINDS OF SOCIETY

PETER spent Christmas with his mother, and found her very much worried over his "salooning."

"It's first steps, Peter, that do the mischief," she told him.

"But, mother, I only go to talk with the men. Not to drink."

"You'll come to that later. The devil's paths always start straight, my boy, but they end in wickedness. Promise me you won't go any more."

"I can't do that, mother. I am trying to help the men, and you ought not to ask me to stop doing what may aid others."

"Oh, my boy, my boy!" sobbed the mother.

"If you could only understand it, mother, as I have come to, you wouldn't mind. Here, the saloon is chiefly a loafing place for the lazy and shiftless, but in New York, it's very different. It's the poor man's club. If you could see the dark, cold, foul-aired tenements where they live, and then the bright, warm, cheerful saloons, that are open to all, you would see that it isn't the drink that draws the men. I even wish the women could come. The bulk of the men are temperate, and only take a glass or two of beer or whisky, to pay for their welcome. They really go for the social part, and sit and talk, or read the papers. Of course a man gets drunk, sometimes, but usually it is not a regular customer, and even such cases would be fewer, if we didn't tax whisky so outrageously that the dishonest barkeepers are tempted to doctor their whisky with drugs which drive men frantic if they drink. But most of the men are too sensible, and too poor, to drink so as really to harm themselves."

"Peter, Peter! To think that three years in New York should bring you to talk so! I knew New York was a sink-hole of iniquity, but I thought you were too good a boy to be misled."

"Mother, New York has less evil in it than most places. Here, after the mills shut down, there's no recreation for the men, and so they amuse themselves with viciousness. But in a great place like New York, there are a thousand amusements specially planned for the evening hours. Exhibitions, theatres, concerts, libraries, lectures —everything to tempt one away from wrong-doing to fine things. And there wickedness is kept out of sight as it never is here. In New York you must go to it, but in these small places it hunts one out and tempts one."

"Oh, Peter! Here, where there's room in church of a Sabbath for all the folks, while they say that in New York there isn't enough seats in churches for mor'n a quarter of the people. A missionary was saying only last week that we ought to help raise money to build churches in New York. Just think of there being mor'n ten saloons for every church! And that my son should speak for them and spend nights in them!"

"I'm sorry it troubles you so. If I felt I had any right to stop, I'd do it."

"You haven't drunk in them yet, Peter?"

"No."

"And you'll promise to write me if you do."

"I'll promise you I won't drink in them, mother."

"Thank you, Peter." Still his mother was terrified at

the mere thought, and at her request, her clergyman spoke also to Peter. He was easier to deal with, and after a chat with Peter, he told Mrs. Stirling:

"I think he is doing no harm, and may do much good. Let him do what he thinks best."

"It's dreadful though, to have your son's first refusal be about going to saloons," sighed the mother.

"From the way he spoke I think his refusal was as hard to him as to you. He's a good boy, and you had better let him judge of what's right."

On Peter's return to the city, he found an invitation from Mrs. Bohlmann to come to a holiday festivity of which the Germans are so fond. He was too late to go, but he called promptly, to explain why he had not responded. He was very much surprised, on getting out his dress-suit, now donned for the first time in three years, to find how badly it fitted him.

"Mother is right," he had to acknowledge. "I have grown much thinner."

However, the ill-fit did not spoil his evening. He was taken into the family room, and passed a very pleasant hour with the jolly brewer, his friendly wife, and the two "nice girls." They were all delighted with Catlin's election, and Peter had to tell them about his part in it. They did not let him go when he rose, but took him into the dining-room, where a supper was served at ten. In leaving, a box of candy, saved for him from the Christmas tree, was given him.

"You will come again, Mr. Stirling?" asked Mrs. Bohlmann, warmly.

"Thank you," said Peter. "I shall be very glad to."

"Yah," said Mr. Bohlmann. "You coom choost as ofden as you blease."

Peter took his dress-suit to a tailor the next day, and ordered it to be taken in. That individual protested loudly on the ground that the coat was so old-fashioned that it would be better to make a new suit. Peter told him that he wore evening dress too rarely to make a new suit worth the having, and the tailor yielded rather than lose the job. Scarcely had it been put in order, when Peter was asked to dine at his clergyman's and the next day came another

invitation, to dine with Justice Gallagher. Peter began to
wonder if he had decided wisely in vamping the old suit.

He had one of the pleasantest evenings of his life at Dr.
Purple's. It was a dinner of ten, and Peter was conscious
that a real compliment had been paid him in being included, for the rest of the men were not merely older than
himself, but they were the "strong" men of the church.
Two were trustees. All were prominent in the business
world. And it pleased Peter to find that he was not treated
as the youngster of the party, but had his opinions asked.
At one point of the meal the talk drifted to a Bethel church
then under consideration, and this in turn brought up the
tenement-house question. Peter had been studying this,
both practically and in books, for the last three months.
Before long, the whole table was listening to what he
had to say. When the ladies had withdrawn, there was
political talk, in which Peter was much more a listener,
but it was from preference rather than ignorance. One
of the men, a wholesale dealer in provisions, spoke of the
new governor's recommendation for food legislation.

"The leaders tell me that the legislature will do something about it," Peter said.

"They'll probably make it worse," said Mr. Avery.

"Don't you think it can be bettered?" asked Peter.

"Not by politicians."

"I'm studying the subject," Peter said. "Will you let
me come down some day, and talk with you about it?"

"Yes, by all means. You'd better call about lunch hour,
when I'm free, and we can talk without interruption."

Peter would much have preferred to go on discussing
with the men, when they all joined the ladies, but Mrs.
Purple took him off, and placed him between two women.
They wanted to hear about "the case" so Peter patiently
went over that well-worn subject. Perhaps he had his
pay by being asked to call upon both. More probably
the requests were due to what Mrs. Purple had said of him
during the smoking time:

"He seems such a nice, solid, sensible fellow. I wish
some of you would ask him to call on you. He has no
friends, apparently."

The dinner at Justice Gallagher's was a horse of a very

different color. The men did not impress him very highly, and the women not at all. There was more to eat and drink, and the talk was fast and lively. Peter was very silent. So quiet, that Mrs. Gallagher told her "take in" that she "guessed that young Stirling wasn't used to real fashionable dinners," and Peter's partner quite disregarded him for the rattling, breezy talker on her other side. After the dinner Peter had a pleasant chat with the Justice's seventeen-year-old daughter, who was just from a Catholic convent, and the two tried to talk in French. It is wonderful what rubbish is tolerable if only talked in a foreign tongue.

"I don't see what you wanted to have that Stirling for?" said Honorable Mrs. Justice Gallagher, to him who conferred that proud title upon her, after the guests had departed.

"You are clever, aren't you?" said Gallagher, bitingly.

"That's living with you," retorted the H. M. J., who was not easily put down.

"Then you see that you treat Stirling as if he was somebody. He's getting to be a power in the ward, and if you want to remain Mrs. Justice Gallagher and spend eight thousand—and pickings—a year, you see that you keep him friendly."

"Oh, I'll be friendly, but he's awful dull."

"Oh, no, mamma," said Monica. "He really isn't. He's read a great many more French books than I have."

Peter lunched with the wholesale provision-dealer as planned. The lunch hour proving insufficient for the discussion, a family dinner, a few days later, served to continue it. The dealer's family were not very enthusiastic about Peter.

"He knows nothing but grub talk," grumbled the heir apparent, who from the proud altitude of a broker's office, had come to scorn the family trade.

"He doesn't know any fashionable people," said one of the girls, who having unfulfilled ambitions concerning that class, was doubly interested and influenced by its standards and idols.

"He certainly is not brilliant," remarked the mother.

"Humph," growled the pater-familias, "that's the way

all you women go on. Brilliant! Fashionable! I don't
wonder marriage is a failure when I see what you like
in men. That Stirling is worth all your dancing men, but
just because he holds his tongue when he hasn't a sensible
thing to say, you think he's no good."

"Still he is 'a nobody.'"

"He's the fellow who made that big speech in the
stump-tail milk case."

"Not that man?"

"Exactly. But of course he isn't 'brilliant.'"

"I never should have dreamed it."

"Still," said the heir, "he keeps his eloquence for cows,
and not for dinners."

"He talked very well at Dr. Purple's," said the mamma,
whose opinion of Peter had undergone a change.

"And he was invited to call by Mrs. Dupont and Mrs.
Sizer, which is more than you've ever been," said Avery
senior to Avery junior.

"That's because of the prog," growled the son, seeing
his opportunity to square accounts quickly.

Coming out of church the next Sunday, Peter was laid
hold of by the Bohlmanns and carried off to a mid-day
dinner, at which were a lot of pleasant Germans, who
made it very jolly with their kindly humor. He did not
contribute much to the laughter, but every one seemed to
think him an addition to the big table.

Thus it came to pass that late in January Peter dedi-
cated a week of evenings to "Society," and nightly donning his dress suit, called dutifully on Mrs. Dupont, Mrs.
Sizer, Mrs. Purple, Mrs. Avery, Mrs. Costell, Mrs. Gallagher and Mrs. Bohlmann. Peter was becoming very
frivolous.

CHAPTER XXVI

AN EVENING CALL

BUT Peter's social gadding did not end with these bread-
and-butter calls. One afternoon in March, he went into
the shop of a famous picture-dealer, to look over an exhi-

bition then advertised, and had nearly finished his patient examination of each picture, which always involved quite as much mental gymnastics as æsthetic pleasure to Peter, when he heard a pleasant:

"How do you do, Mr. Stirling?"

Turning, he found Miss De Voe and a well-dressed man at his elbow. Peter's face lighted up in a way which made the lady say to herself: "I wonder why he wouldn't buy another ticket?" Aloud she said, "I want you to know another of my cousins. Mr. Ogden, Mr. Stirling."

"Charmed," said Mr. Ogden genially. Any expression which Peter had thought of using seemed so absolutely tame, beside this passive particle, that he merely bowed.

"I did not know you cared for pictures," said Miss De Voe.

"I see most of the public exhibitions," Peter told her. "I try to like them."

Miss De Voe looked puzzled.

"Don't," said Mr. Ogden. "I tried once, when I first began. But it's much easier to notice what women say and answer 'yes' and 'no' at the right points."

Peter looked puzzled.

"Nonsense, Lispenard," said Miss De Voe. "He's really one of the best connoisseurs I know, Mr. Stirling."

"There," said Lispenard. "You see. Only agree with people, and they think you know everything."

"I suppose you have seen the pictures, and so won't care to go round with us?" inquired Miss De Voe.

"I've looked at them, but I should like to go over again with you," said Peter. Then he added, "if I shan't be in the way."

"Not a bit," said Lispenard heartily. "My cousin always wants a listener. It will be a charity to her tongue and my ears." Miss De Voe merely gave him a very pleasant smile. "I wonder why he wouldn't buy a ticket?" she thought.

Peter was rather astonished at the way they looked at the pictures. They would pass by a dozen without giving them a second glance, and then stop at one, and chat about it for ten minutes. He found that Miss De Voe had not exaggerated her cousin's art knowledge. He talked familiarly and brilliantly, though making constant fun of his own opinions, and often jeering at the faults of the picture. Miss De Voe also talked well, so Peter really did supply the ears for the party. He was very much pleased when they both praised a certain picture.

"I liked that," he told them, making the first remark (not a question) which he had yet made. "It seemed to me the best here."

"Unquestionably," said Lispenard. "There is poetry and feeling in it."

Miss De Voe said: "That is not the one I should have thought of your liking."

"That's womanly," said Lispenard, "they are always deciding what a man should like."

"No," denied Miss De Voe. "But I should think with your liking for children, that you would have preferred that piece of Brown's, rather than this sad, desolate sand-dune."

"I cannot say why I like it, except that I feel as if it had something to do with my own mood at times."

"Are you very lonely?" asked Miss De Voe, in a voice too low for Lispenard to hear.

"Sometimes," said Peter, simply.

"I wish," said Miss De Voe, still speaking low, "that the next time you feel so you would come and see me."

"I will," said Peter.

When they parted at the door, Peter thanked Lispenard: "I have really learned a good deal, thanks to Miss De Voe and you. I've seen the pictures with eyes that know much more about them than mine do."

"Well, we'll have to have another turn some day. We're always in search of listeners."

"If you come and see me, Mr. Stirling," said Miss De Voe, "you shall see my pictures. Good-bye."

"So that is your Democratic heeler?" said Lispenard, eyeing Peter's retreating figure through the carriage window.

"Don't call him that, Lispenard," said Miss De Voe, wincing.

Lispenard laughed, and leaned back into a comfortable

attitude. "Then that's your protector of sick kittens?"

Miss De Voe made no reply. She was thinking of that dreary wintry stretch of sand and dune.

Thus it came to pass that a week later, when a north-easter had met a south-wester overhead and both in combination had turned New York streets into a series of funnels, in and through which wind, sleet and snow fought for possession, to the almost absolute dispossession of humanity and horses, that Peter ended a long stare at his blank wall by putting on his dress-suit, and plunging into the streets. He had, very foolishly, decided to omit dinner, a couple of hours before, rather than face the storm, and a north-east wind and an empty stomach are enough to set any man staring at nothing, if that dangerous inclination is at all habitual. Peter realized this, for the opium eater is always keenly alive to the dangers of the drug. Usually he fought the tendency bravely, but this night he felt too tired to fight himself, and preferred to battle with a little thing like a New York storm. So he struggled through the deserted streets until he had reached his objective point in the broad Second Avenue house. Miss De Voe was at home, but was "still at dinner."

Peter vacillated, wondering what the correct thing was under the circumstances. The footman, remembering him of old, and servants in those simple days being still open to impressions, suggested that he wait. Peter gladly accepted the idea. But he did not wait, for hardly had the footman left him than that functionary returned, to tell Peter that Miss De Voe would see him in the dining-room.

"I asked you to come in here, because I'm sure, after venturing out such a night, you would like an extra cup of coffee," Miss De Voe explained. "You need not sit at the table. Morden, put a chair by the fire."

So Peter found himself sitting in front of a big wood-fire, drinking a cup of coffee decidedly better in quality than his home-brew. Blank walls ceased to have any particular value for the time.

In a moment Miss De Voe joined him at the fire. A small table was moved up, and a plate of fruit, and a cup of coffee placed upon it.

"That is all, Morden," she said. "It is so nice of you

to have come this evening. I was promising myself a very solitary time, and was dawdling over my dinner to kill some of it. Isn't it a dreadful night?"

"It's blowing hard. Two or three times I thought I should have to give it up."

"You didn't walk?"

"Yes. I could have taken a solitary car that passed, but the horses were so done up that I thought I was better able to walk."

Miss De Voe touched the bell. "Another cup of coffee, Morden, and bring the cognac," she said. "I am not going to let you please your mother to-night," she told Peter. "I am going to make you do what I wish." So she poured a liberal portion of the eau-de-vie into Peter's second cup, and he most dutifully drank it. "How funny that he should be so obstinate sometimes, and so obedient at others," thought Miss De Voe. "I don't generally let men smoke, but I'm going to make an exception to-night in your case," she continued.

It was a sore temptation to Peter, but he answered quickly, "Thank you for the thought, but I won't this evening."

"You have smoked after dinner already?"

"No. I tried to keep my pipe lighted in the street, but it blew and sleeted too hard."

"Then you had better."

"Thank you, no."

Miss De Voe thought her former thought again. "Where do you generally dine?" she asked.

"I have no regular place. Just where I happen to be."

"And to-night?"

Peter was not good at dodging. He was silent for a moment. Then he said, "I saw rather a curious thing, as I was walking up. Would you like to hear about it?"

Miss De Voe looked at him curiously, but she did not seem particularly interested in what Peter had to tell her, in response to her "yes." It concerned an arrest on the streets for drunkenness.

"I didn't think the fellow was half as drunk as frozen," Peter concluded, "and I told the policeman it was a case for an ambulance rather than a station-house. He didn't agree, so I had to go with them both to the precinct and speak to the superintendent."

"That was before your dinner?" asked Miss De Voe, calmly.

It was a very easily answered question, apparently, but Peter was silent again.

"It was coming up here," he said finally.

"What is he trying to keep back?" asked Miss De Voe mentally. "I suppose some of the down-town places are not quite—but he wouldn't—" then she said out loud: "I wonder if you men do as women do, when they dine alone? Just live on slops. Now, what did you order to-night? Were you an ascetic or a sybarite?"

"Usually," said Peter, "I eat a very simple dinner."

"And to-night?"

"Why do you want to know about to-day?"

"Because I wish to learn where you dined, and thought I could form some conclusion from your menu." Miss De Voe laughed, so as to make it appear a joke, but she knew very well that she was misbehaving.

"I didn't reply to your question," said Peter, "because I would have preferred not. But if you really wish to know, I'll answer it."

"Yes. I should like to know." Miss De Voe still smiled.

"I haven't dined."

"Mr. Stirling! You are joking?" Miss De Voe's smile had ended, and she was sitting up very straight in her chair. Women will do without eating for an indefinite period, and think nothing of it, but the thought of a hungry man fills them with horror—unless they have the wherewithal to mitigate the consequent appetite. Hunger with woman, as regards herself, is "a theory." As regards a man it is "a condition."

"No," said Peter.

Miss De Voe touched the bell again, but quickly as Morden answered it, Peter was already speaking.

"You are not to trouble yourself on my account, Miss De Voe. I wish for nothing."

"You must have——"

Peter was rude enough to interrupt with the word "Nothing."

"But I shall not have a moment's pleasure in your call if I think of you as——"

Peter interrupted again. "If that is so," he said, rising, "I had better go."

"No," cried Miss De Voe. "Oh, won't you please? It's no trouble. I'll not order much."

"Nothing, thank you," said Peter.

"Just a chop or——"

Peter held out his hand.

"No, no. Sit down. Of course you are to do as you please. But I should be so happy if——?" and Miss De Voe looked at Peter appealingly.

"No. Thank you."

"Nothing, Morden." They sat down again. "Why, didn't you dine?" asked Miss De Voe.

"I didn't care to face the storm."

"Yet you came out?"

"Yes. I got blue, and thought it foolish to stay in-doors by myself."

"I'm very glad you came here. It's a great compliment to find an evening with me put above dinner. You know I had the feeling that you didn't like me."

"I'm sorry for that. It's not so."

"If not, why did you insist on my twice asking you to call on me?"

"I did not want to call on you without being sure that you really wished to have me."

"Then why wouldn't you stay and dine at Saratoga?"

"Because my ticket wouldn't have been good."

"But a new ticket would only cost seven dollars."

"In my neighborhood, we don't say 'only seven dollars.'"

"But you don't need to think of seven dollars."

"I do. I never have spent seven dollars on a dinner in my life."

"But you should have, this time, after making seven hundred and fifty dollars in one month. I know men who would give that amount to dine with me." It was a foolish brag, but Miss De Voe felt that her usual means of inspiring respect were not working,—not even realized.

"Very likely. But I can't afford such luxuries. I had spent more than usual and had to be careful."

"Then it was economy?"

"Yes."

"I had no idea my dinner invitations would ever be held in so little respect that a man would decline one to save seven dollars." Miss De Voe was hurt. "I had given him five hundred dollars," she told herself, "and he ought to have been willing to spend such a small amount of it to please me." Then she said: "A great many people economize in foolish ways."

"I suppose so," said Peter. "I'm sorry if I disappointed you. I really didn't think I ought to spend the money."

"Never mind," said Miss De Voe. "Were you pleased with the nomination and election of Catlin?"

"I was pleased at the election, but I should have preferred Porter."

"I thought you tried to prevent Porter's nomination?"

"That's what the papers said, but they didn't understand."

"I wasn't thinking of the papers. You know I heard your speech in the convention."

"A great many people seem to have misunderstood me. I tried to make it clear."

"Did you intend that the convention should laugh?"

"No. That surprised and grieved me very much!"

Miss De Voe gathered from this and from what the papers had said that it must be a mortifying subject to Peter, and knew that she ought to discontinue it. But she could not help saying, "Why?"

"It's difficult to explain, I'm afraid. I had a feeling that a man was trying to do wrong, but I hoped that I was mistaken. It seemed to me that circumstances compelled me to tell the convention all about it, but I was very careful not to hint at my suspicion. Yet the moment I told them they laughed."

"Why?"

"Because they felt sure that the man had done wrong."

"Oh!" It was a small exclamation, but the expression

Miss De Voe put into it gave it a big meaning. "Then they were laughing at Maguire?"

"At the time they were. Really, though, they were laughing at human weakness. Most people seem to find that amusing."

"And that is why you were grieved?"

"Yes."

"But why did the papers treat you so badly?"

"Mr. Costell tells me that I told too much truth for people to understand. I ought to have said nothing, or charged a bargain right out, for then they would have understood. A friend of—a fellow I used to know, said I was the best chap for bungling he ever knew, and I'm afraid it's true."

"Do you know Costell? I thought he was such a dishonest politician?"

"I know Mr. Costell. I haven't met the dishonest politician yet."

"You mean?"

"He hasn't shown me the side the papers talk about."

"And when he does?"

"I shall be very sorry, for I like him, and I like his wife." Then Peter told about the little woman who hated politics and loved flowers, and about the cool, able manager of men, who could not restrain himself from putting his arms about the necks of his favorite horses, and who had told about the death of one of his mares with tears in his eyes. "He had his cheek cut open by a kick from one of his horses once, and he speaks of it just as we would speak of some unintentional fault of a child."

"Has he a great scar on his cheek?"

"Yes. Have you seen him?"

"Once. Just as we were coming out of the convention. He said something about you to a group of men which called my attention to him." Miss De Voe thought Peter would ask her what it was. "Would you like to know what he said?" she asked, when Peter failed to do so.

"I think he would have said it to me, if he wished me to hear it."

Miss De Voe's mind reverted to her criticism of Peter. "He is so absolutely without our standards." Her chair suddenly ceased to be comfortable. She rose, saying, "Let us go to the library. I shall not show you my pictures now. The gallery is too big to be pleasant such a night. You must come again for that. Won't you tell be about some of the other men you are meeting in politics?" she asked when they had sat down before another open fire. "It seems as if all the people I know are just alike—I suppose it's because we are all so conventional—and I am very much interested in hearing about other kinds."

So Peter told about Dennis and Blunkers, and the "b'ys" in the saloons; about Green and his fellow delegates; about the Honorable Mr., Mrs., and Miss Gallagher, and their dinner companions. He did not satirize in the least. He merely told various incidents and conversations, in a sober, serious way; but Miss De Voe was quietly amused by much of the narrative and said to herself, "I think he has humor, but is too serious-minded to yield to it." She must have enjoyed his talk for she would not let Peter go early, and he was still too ignorant of social usages to know how to get away, whether a woman wished or no. Finally he insisted that he must leave when the clock pointed dangerously near eleven.

"Mr. Stirling," said Miss De Voe, in a doubtful, "won't-you-please" voice, such as few men had ever heard from her, "I want you to let me send you home? It will only take a moment to have the carriage here."

"I wouldn't take a horse out in such weather," said Peter, in a very settling kind of voice.

"He's obstinate," thought Miss De Voe. "And he makes his obstinacy so dreadfully—dreadfully pronounced!" Aloud she said: "You will come again?"

"If you will let me."

"Do. I am very much alone too, as perhaps you know?" Miss De Voe did not choose to say that her rooms could be filled nightly and that everywhere she was welcome.

"No. I really know nothing about you, except what you have told me, and what I have seen."

Miss De Voe laughed merrily at Peter's frankness. "I feel as if I knew all about you," she said.

"But you have asked questions," replied Peter.

Miss De Voe caught her breath again. Try as she would, she could not get accustomed to Peter. All her social experience failed to bridge the chasm opened by his speech. "What did he mean by that plain statement, spoken in such a matter-of-fact voice?" she asked herself. Of course the pause could not continue indefinitely, and she finally said: "I have lived alone ever since my father's death. I have relatives, but prefer to stay here. I am so much more independent. I suppose I shall have to move some day. This part of the city is beginning to change so." Miss De Voe was merely talking against time, and was not sorry when Peter shook hands, and left her alone.

"He's very different from most men," she said to the blazing logs. "He is so uncomplimentary and out-spoken! How can he succeed in politics? Still, after the conventional society men he is—he is—very refreshing. I think I must help him a little socially."

CHAPTER XXVII

A DINNER

THE last remark made by Miss De Voe to her fire resulted, after a few days, in Peter's receiving a formal dinner invitation, which he accepted with a promptness not to be surpassed by the best-bred diner-out. He regretted now his vamping of the old suit. Peter understood that he was in for quite another affair than the Avery, the Gallagher, or even the Purple dinner. He did not worry, however, and if in the dressing-room he looked furtively at the coats of the other men, he entirely forgot the subject the moment he started downstairs, and thought no further of it till he came to take off the suit in his own room.

When Peter entered the drawing-room, he found it well filled with young people, and for a moment a little of the bewildered feeling of four years before came over him. But he found himself chatting with Miss De Voe, and the feeling left him as quickly as it had come. In a moment he was introduced to a "Miss Lenox," who began talking in an easy way which gave Peter just as much or as little to say as he chose. Peter wondered if many girls were as easy to talk to as—as—Miss Lenox.

He took Miss De Voe in, and found Dorothy Ogden sitting on his other side. He had barely exchanged greetings with her, when he heard his name spoken from across the table, and looking up, he found Miss Leroy sitting opposite.

"I hope you haven't entirely forgotten me," that girl said, the moment his attention was caught.

"Not at all," said Peter.

"Nor my dress," laughed Miss Leroy.

"I remember the style, material, and train."

"Especially the train I am sure."

"Do explain these mysterious remarks," said Dorothy.

"Mr. Stirling and I officiated at a wedding, and I was in such mortal terror lest some usher should step on my gown, that it became a joke."

"Whose wedding was that?" asked Miss De Voe.

"Miss Pierce's and Watts D'Alloi's," said the bridesmaid.

"Do you know Watts D'Alloi?" exclaimed Miss De Voe to Peter.

"Yes."

"Indeed! When?"

"At college."

"Are you a Harvard man?"

"Yes."

"You were Mr. D'Alloi's chum, weren't you?" said Miss Leroy.

"Yes."

"Watts D'Alloi?" again exclaimed Miss De Voe.

"Yes."

"But he's a mere boy."

"He's two years my senior."

"You don't mean it?"

"Yes."

"I thought you were over thirty."

"Most people do."

Miss De Voe said to herself, "I don't know as much about him as I thought I did. He may be very frank, but he doesn't tell all he thinks. Now I know where he gets his nice manner. I ought to have recognized the Harvard finish."

"When did you last hear from the D'Allois?" asked Miss Leroy.

"Not since they sailed," said Peter, wincing internally.

"Not really?" said the bridesmaid. "Surely you've heard of the baby?"

"No." Lines were coming into Peter's face which Miss De Voe had never before seen.

"How strange. The letters must have gone astray. But you have written him?"

"I did not know his address."

"Then you really haven't heard of the little baby—why, it was born two—no, three years ago—and of Helen's long ill-health, and of their taking a villa on the Riviera, and of how they hope to come home this spring?"

"No."

"Yes. They will sail in June if Helen is well enough. I'm to be god-mother."

"If you were Mr. D'Alloi's chum, you must have known Ray Rivington," said Dorothy.

"Yes. But I've not seen him since we graduated. He went out West."

"He has just returned. Ranching is not to his taste."

"Will you, if you see him, say that I'm in New York and should like to run across him?"

"I will. He and Laurence—my second brother—are old cronies, and he often drops in on us. I want you to know my brothers. They are both here this evening."

"I have met the elder one, I suppose."

"No. That was a cousin, Lispenard Ogden. He spoke of meeting you. You would be amused to hear his comment about you."

"Mr. Stirling doesn't like to have speeches repeated to him, Dorothy," said Miss De Voe.

"What do you mean?" asked Dorothy, looking from one to the other.

"He snubbed me the other evening when I tried to

tell him what we heard, coming out of the convention last autumn," explained Miss De Voe, smiling slightly at the thought of treating Peter with a dose of his own medicine.

Peter looked at Miss De Voe. "I hope you don't mean that?"

"How else could I take it?"

"You asked me if I wished something, and I merely declined, I think."

"Oh, no. You reproved me."

"I'm very sorry if I did. I'm always blundering."

"Tell us what Lispenard said, Dorothy. I'm curious myself."

"May I, Mr. Stirling?"

"I would rather not," said Peter.

And Dorothy did not tell him, but in the drawing-room she told Miss De Voe:

"He said that except his professor of archæology at Heidelberg, Mr. Stirling was the nicest old dullard he'd ever met, and that he must be a very good chap to smoke with."

"He said that, Dorothy?" exclaimed Miss De Voe, contemptuously.

"Yes."

"How ridiculous," said Miss De Voe. "Lispenard's always trying to hit things off in epigrams, and sometimes he's very foolish." Then she turned to Miss Leroy. "It was very nice, your knowing Mr. Stirling."

"I only met him that once. But he's the kind of man somehow that you remember. It's curious I've never heard of him since then."

"You know he's the man who made that splendid speech when the poor children were poisoned summer before last."

"I can't believe it!"

"It's so. That is the way I came to know him."

Miss Leroy laughed. "And Helen said he was a man who needed help in talking!"

"Was Mrs. D'Alloi a great friend of his?"

"No. She told me that Watts had brought him to see them only once. I don't think Mr. Pierce liked him."

"He evidently was very much hurt at Watts's not writing him."

"Yes. I was really sorry I spoke, when I saw how he took it."

"Watts is a nice boy, but he always was thoughtless."

In passing out of the dining-room, Dorothy had spoken to a man for a moment, and he at once joined Peter.

"You know my sister, Miss Ogden, who's the best representative of us," he said. "Now I'll show you the worst. I don't know whether she exploited her brother Ogden to you?"

"Yes. She talked about you and your brother this evening."

"Trust her to stand by her family. There's more loyalty in her than there was in the army of the Potomac. My cousin Lispenard says it's wrecking his nervous system to live up to the reputation she makes for him."

"I never had a sister, but it must be rather a good thing to live up to."

"Yes. And to live with. Especially other fellows' sisters."

"Are you ready to part with yours for that purpose?"

"No. That's asking too much. By the way, I think we are in the same work. I'm in the office of Jarvis, Redburn and Saltus."

"I'm trying it by myself."

"You've been very lucky."

"Yes. I've succeeded much better than I hoped for. But I've had very few clients."

"Fortunately it doesn't take many. Two or three rich steady clients will keep a fellow running. I know a man who's only got one, but he runs him for all he's worth, and gets a pretty good living out of him."

"My clients haven't been of that sort." Peter smiled a little at the thought of making a steady living out of the Blacketts, Dooleys or Milligans.

"It's all a matter of friends."

Peter had a different theory, but he did not say so. Just at that point they were joined by Laurence Ogden, who was duly introduced, and in a moment the conversation at their end of the table became general.   Peter listened, enjoying his Havana.

When they joined the ladies, they found Lispenard Ogden there, and he intercepted Peter.

"Look here," he said.   "A friend of mine has just come back from Europe, with a lot of prints.   He's a fellow who thinks he has discrimination, and he wants me to come up and look them over to-morrow evening. He hopes to have his own taste approved and flattered. I'm not a bit good at that, with men.   Won't you go with me, and help me lie?"

"Of course I should like to."

"All right.   Dine with me at six at the Union Club."

"I'm not going to let you talk to each other," said Miss De Voe.   "Lispenard, go and talk with Miss McDougal."

"See how quickly lying brings its own punishment," laughed Lispenard, walking away.

"What does he mean?" asked Miss De Voe.

"The opposite of what he says, I think," said Peter.

"That is a very good description of Lispenard.   Almost good enough to have been said by himself.   If you don't mind, I'll tell him."

"No."

"Do tell me, Mr. Stirling, how you and Watts D'Alloi came to room together?"

"He asked me."

"Yes.   But what ever made him do that?"

"I've often wondered myself."

"I can easily understand his asking you, but what first threw you together?"

"A college scrape."

"Were you in a college scrape?"

"Yes.   I was up before the faculty twice."

"Do tell me what you had done?"

"I was charged with stealing the chapel Bible, and with painting a front door of one of the professors."

"And had you done these things?"

"No."

The guests began to say good-night, so the dialogue was interrupted.   When it came Peter's turn to go, Miss De Voe said:

"I hope you will not again refuse my dinner invitations."

"I have had a very pleasant evening," said Peter. "But I had a pleasanter one, the other night."

"Good-evening," said Miss De Voe mechanically. She was really thinking "What a very nice speech. He couldn't have meant anything by his remark about the questions."

Peter dined the next evening with Lispenard, who in the course of the meal turned the conversation to Miss De Voe. Lispenard was curious to learn just what Peter knew of her.

"She's a great swell, of course," he said incidentally.

"I suppose so. I really know nothing about her, but the moment I saw her I felt that she was different from any other woman I had ever met."

"But you've found out about her since?"

"No. I was tempted to question Dr. Purple, but I didn't like to ask about a friend."

Lispenard laughed. "You've got a pretty bad case of conscience, I'm afraid. It's a poor thing to have in New York, too. Well, my cousin is one of the richest, best born women in this country, though I say it. You can't do better than cultivate her."

"Is that what you do?"

"No. You have me there. She doesn't approve of me at all. You see, women in this country expect a man to be serious and work. I can't do either. I suppose it's my foreign education. She likes my company, and finds my escortage very convenient. But while she thinks I'm a pretty good companion, she is sure I'm a poor sort of a man. If she takes a shine to you, make the most of it. She can give you anything she pleases socially."

"I suppose you have anything you please socially?"

"Pretty much."

"And would you advise me to spend time to get it?"

"Um. I wouldn't give the toss of a copper for it—but I can have it. It's not being able to have it that's the bad thing."

"So I have found," said Peter gravely.

Lispenard laughed heartily, as he sipped his "Court France." "I wish," he said, "that a lot of people, whose lives are given to nothing else, could have heard you say that, in that tone of voice. You don't spell Society with a capital, do you?"

"Possibly," said Peter, "if I had more capital, I should use some on society."

"Good," said Lispenard. "Heavens," he said to himself, "he's made a joke! Cousin Anneke will never believe it."

He told her the next day, and his statement proved correct.

"I know you made the joke," she said. "He didn't."

"And why shouldn't he joke as well as I?"

"It doesn't suit him."

"Why not?"

"Parlor tricks are all right in a lap-dog, but they only belittle a mastiff."

Lispenard laughed good-naturedly. He was used to his cousin's hits at his do-nothingness, and rather enjoyed them. "He is a big beast, isn't he? But he's a nice fellow. We had such a good time over Le Grand's etchings last night. Didn't get away till after one. It's really a pleasure to find a man who can smoke and keep quiet, and yet enjoy things strongly. Le Grand was taken with him too. We just fitted each other."

"I'm glad you took him. I'm going to give him some society."

"Did you ever hear the story of Dr. Brown?"

"No. What is it?"

"A certain widow announced to her son that she was to marry Dr. Brown. 'Bully for you, Ma,' said the son, 'Does Dr. Brown know it?'"

"What do you mean?"

Lispenard laughed. "Does Stirling know it? Because I advise you to tell him before you decide to do anything with him. He's not easy to drive."

"Of course he'll be glad to meet nice people."

"Try him."

"What do you mean?"

"I mean that Peter Stirling won't give a raparee for all the society you can give him."

"You don't know what you are talking about."

But Lispenard was right. Peter had enjoyed the dinner at Miss De Voe's and the evening at Mr. Le Grand's. Yet each night on reaching his rooms, he had sat long hours in his straight office chair, in the dark. He was thinking of what Miss Leroy had told him of—of—— He was not thinking of "Society."

CHAPTER XXVIII

COMMISSIONS

PETER made his dinner call at Miss De Voe's, but did not find her at home. He received a very pleasant letter expressing her regret at missing him, and a request to lunch with her two days later, and to go with some friends to an afternoon piano recital, "if you care for music. If not, merely lunch with us." Peter replied that he was very sorry, but business called him to Albany on that day.

"I really regret it," said Miss De Voe to Dorothy. "It is getting so late in the season, that unless he makes his call quickly, I shall hardly be able to give him more than one other chance."

Peter's business in Albany had been sprung on him suddenly. It was neither more nor less than a request sent verbally through Costell from Governor Catlin, to come up and see him.

"It's about the Food and Tenement Commission bills," Costell told him. "They'll be passed by the Senate to-day or to-morrow, and be in Catlin's hands."

"I hope he'll make good appointments," said Peter, anxiously.

"I think he will," said Costell, smiling quietly. "But I don't believe they will be able to do much. Commissions are commonly a way of staving off legislation."

Peter went up to Albany and saw Catlin. Much to his surprise he found the Governor asking his advice about the bills and the personnel of the Commissions. But after a few minutes he found that this seeking for aid and support in all matters was chronic, and meant nothing special in his own case.

"Mr. Schlurger tells me, though he introduced the bills, that you drafted both. Do you think I had better sign them?"

"Yes."

"Mr. Costell told me to take your advice. You really think I had better?"

"Yes."

The Governor evidently found something solacing in the firm voice in which Peter spoke his "yes." He drew two papers towards him.

"You really think I had better?"

"Yes."

The Governor dipped his pen in the ink, but hesitated. "The amendments haven't hurt them?" he queried.

"Not much."

"But they have been hurt?"

"They have been made better in some ways."

"Really?"

"Yes.

Still the Governor hesitated, but finally began a big G. Having committed himself, he wrote the rest rapidly. He paused for a moment over the second bill, and fingered it nervously. Then he signed it quickly. "That's done." He shoved them both away much as if they were dangerous.

"I wonder," thought Peter, "if he enjoys politics?"

"There's been a great deal of trouble about the Commissioners," said the Governor.

"I suppose so," said Peter.

"Even now, I can't decide. The leaders all want different men."

"The decision rests with you."

"That's the trouble," sighed the Governor. "If only they'd agree."

"You should make your own choice. You will be held responsible if the appointments are bad.'

"I know I shall. Just look over those lists, and see if you think they'll do.'

Peter took the slips of paper and read them.

"I needn't say I'm pleased to see my name," he said. "I had no idea you would think of me."

"That was done by Costell," said the Governor, hastening to shift the responsibility.

"I really don't know any of the rest well enough to express an opinion. Personally, I should like to see some scientific men on each Commission."

"Scientific! But we have none in politics."

"No? But this isn't politics."

"I hoped you'd think these lists right."

"I think they are good. And the bills give us the power to take evidence; perhaps we can get the scientific part that way."

Peter did his best to brace Catlin up; and his talk or other pressure seemed to have partially galvanized the backbone of that limp individual, for a week later the papers announced the naming of the two Commissions. The lists had been changed, however. That on food consisted of Green, a wholesale grocer, and a member of the Health Board. Peter's name had been dropped. That on tenements, of five members, was made up of Peter; a very large property-owner in New York, who was a member as well of the Assembly; a professional labor agitator; a well-known politician of the better type, and a public contractor. Peter, who had been studying some reports of a British Royal Commission on the same subject, looked grave, thinking that what the trained men in England had failed in doing, he could hardly hope to accomplish with such ill-assorted instruments. The papers were rather down on the lists. "The appointments have destroyed any chance of possible benefit," was their general conclusion, and Peter feared they were right.

Costell laughed when Peter spoke of the Commissions. "If you want Catlin to do anything well, you've got to stand over him till it's done. I wanted you on both commissions, so that you could see how useless they all are, and not blame us politicians for failing in our duty. Green promises to get you appointed Secretary of the Food Commission, which is the next best thing, and will give you a good salary for a time."

The Tenement Commission met with little delay, and

Peter had a chance to examine its motley members. The big landlord was a great swell, who had political ambitions, but was too exclusive, and too much of a dilettante to be a real force. Peter took a prejudice against him before meeting him, for he knew just how his election to the Assembly had been obtained—even the size of the check—and Peter thought buying an election was not a very creditable business. He did not like what he knew of the labor agitator, for such of the latter's utterances and opinions as he had read seemed to be the cheapest kind of demagogism. The politician he had met and liked. Of the contractor he knew nothing.

The Commission organized by electing the politician as chairman. Then the naming of a secretary was discussed, each member but Peter having a candidate. Much to Peter's surprise, the landlord, Mr. Pell, named Ray Rivington.

"I thought he was studying law?" Peter said.

"He is," said Pell. "But he can easily arrange to get off for the few hours we shall meet a week, and the five dollars a day will be a very nice addition to his income. Do you know him?"

"We were in college together. I thought he was rich."

"No. He's of good family, but the Rivingtons are growing poorer every year. They try to live on their traditions, and traditions don't pay grocers. I hope you'll help him. He's a very decent fellow."

"I shall vote for him," replied Peter, marvelling that he should be able to give a lift to the man who, in the Harvard days, had seemed so thoroughly the mate of Watts and the other rich fellows of the "gang." Rivington being the only candidate who had two votes, he was promptly selected.

Thirty arduous minutes were spent in waiting for the arrival of the fifth member of the Commission, and in the election of chairman and secretary. A motion was then made to adjourn, on the ground that the Commission could not proceed without the secretary.

Peter promptly objected. He had been named secretary for this particular meeting, and offered to act until

Rivington could be notified. "I think," he said, "that we ought to lay out our programme."

The labor agitator agreed with him, and rising, delivered an extempore speech, declaring that "we must not delay. The leeches (here he looked at Mr. Pell) are sucking the life-blood of the people," etc.

The chairman started to call him to order, but Peter put his hand on the chairman's arm. "If you stop him," he said in a low voice, "he'll think we are against him, and he'll say so outside."

"But it's such foolishness."

"And so harmless! While he's talking, look over this." Peter produce an outline of action which he had drawn up, and having written it in duplicate, he passed one draft over to Mr. Pell.

They all let the speech go on, Peter, Mr. Pell and the chairman chatting over the plan, while the contractor went to sleep. The agitator tried to continue, but as the inattention became more and more evident, his speech became tamer and tamer. Finally he said, "That is my opinion," and sat down.

The cessation of the oration waked up the contractor, and Peter's outline was read aloud.

"I don't move its adoption," said Peter. "I merely submit it as a basis."

Not one of the members had come prepared with knowledge of how to go to work, except the chairman, who had served on other commissions. He said:

"I think Mr. Stirling's scheme shows very careful thought, and is admirable. We cannot do better than adopt it."

"It is chiefly copied from the German committee of three years ago," Peter told them. "But I have tried to modify it to suit the different conditions."

Mr. Pell objected to the proposed frequent sittings. Thereupon the agitator praised that feature. The hour of meeting caused discussion. But finally the scheme was adopted, and the date of the first session fixed.

Peter went downstairs with Mr. Pell, and the latter offered to drop him at his office. So they drove off together, and talked about the Commission.

"That Kurfeldt is going to be a nuisance," said Pell.

"I can't say yet. He evidently has no idea of what our aim is. Perhaps, though, when we really get to work, he'll prove useful."

Peter had a call the next day from Rivington. It was made up of thanks, of college chat, and of inquiry as to duties. Peter outlined the preliminary work, drafted the "Inquiries" and other printed papers necessary to be sent out before the first meeting, and told him about the procedure at the meetings.

"I know I shall get into all kinds of pickles," said Ray. "I write such a bad hand that often I can't read it myself. How the deuce am I to take down evidence?"

"I shall make notes for my own use, and you will be welcome to them, if they will help you."

"Thanks, Peter. That's like you."

The Commission began its inquiry, on the date fixed, and met three times a week from that time on. Peter did not try to push himself forward, but he was by far the best prepared on the subject, and was able to suggest the best sources of information. He asked good questions, too, of the various witnesses summoned. Finally he was the one regular attendant, and therefore was the one appealed to for information elicited at previous meetings. He found the politician his best helper. Pell was useful when he attended, which was not very often, and even this intermittent attendance ceased in June. "I'm going to Newport," he explained, and did not appear again till late in the fall. The contractor really took no part in the proceedings beyond a fairly frequent attendance, and an occasional fit of attention whenever the inquiry related to building. The labor-agitator proved quite a good man. He had, it is true, no memory, and caused them to waste much time in reading over the minutes of previous meetings. But he was in earnest, and proved to be perfectly reasonable as soon as he found that the Commissioners' duties were to inquire and not to make speeches. Peter walked home with him several times, and they spent evenings together in Peter's rooms, talking over the evidence, and the possibilities.

Peter met a great many different men in the course of the inquiry; landlords, real-estate agents, architects, engineers, builders, plumbers, health officials, doctors and tenants. In many cases he went to see these persons after they had been before the Commission, and talked with them, finding that they were quite willing to give facts in private which they did not care to have put on record.

He had been appointed the Secretary of the Food Commission, and spent much time on that work. He was glad to find that he had considerable influence, and that Green not merely acted on his suggestions, but encouraged him to make them. The two inquiries were so germane that they helped him reciprocally. No reports were needed till the next meeting of the Legislature, in the following January, and so the two commissions took enough evidence to swamp them. Poor Ray was reduced almost to despair over the mass of "rubbish" as he called it, which he would subsequently have to put in order.

Between the two tasks, Peter's time was well-nigh used up. It was especially drawn upon when the taking of evidence ceased and the drafting of the reports began. Ray's notes proved hopeless, so Peter copied out his neatly, and let Ray have them, rather glad that irrelevant and useless evidence was thus omitted. It was left to Peter to draw the report, and when his draft was submitted, it was accompanied by a proposed General Tenement-house Bill. Both report and bill were slightly amended, but not in a way that Peter minded.

Peter drew the Food Commission report as well, although it went before the Commission as Green's. To this, too, a proposed bill was attached, which had undergone the scrutiny of the Health Board, and had been conformed to their suggestions.

In November Peter carried both reports to Albany, and had a long talk with Catlin over them. That official would have preferred no reports, but since they were made, there was nothing to do but to submit them to the Legislature. Peter did not get much encouragement from him about the chances for the bills. But Costell told him that they could be "whipped through. The only danger is of their being amended so as to spoil them."

"Well," said Peter, "I hope they will be passed. I've done my best, whatever happens."

A very satisfactory thing to be able to say of yourself, if you believe in your own truthfulness.

CHAPTER XXIX

IN THE MEANTIME

In spite of nine months' hard work on the two Commissions, it is not to be supposed that Peter's time was thus entirely monopolized. If one spends but seven hours of the twenty-four in sleep, and but two more on meals, there is considerable remaining time, and even so slow a worker as Peter found spare hours not merely for society and saloons, but for what else he chose to undertake.

Socially he had an evening with Miss De Voe, just before she left the city for the summer; a dinner with Mr. Pell, who seemed to have taken a liking to Peter; a call on Lispenard; another on Le Grand; and a family meal at the Rivingtons, where he was made much of in return for his aid to Ray.

In the saloons he worked hard over the coming primary, and spent evenings as well on doorsteps in the district, talking over objects and candidates. In the same cause, he saw much of Costell, Green, Gallagher, Schlurger and many other party men of greater or less note in the city's politics. He had become a recognized quantity in the control of the district, and the various ward factions tried hard to gain his support. When the primary met, the proceedings, if exciting, were never for a moment doubtful, for Gallagher, Peter, Moriarty and Blunkers had been able to agree on both programme and candidates. An attempt had been made to "turn down" Schlurger, but Peter had opposed it, and had carried his point, to the great gratitude of the silent, honest German. What was more important to him, this had all been done without exciting hard feelings.

"Stirling's a reasonable fellow," Gallagher told Costell,

not knowing how much Peter was seeing of the big leader, "and he isn't dead set on carrying his own schemes. We've never had so little talk of mutiny and sulking as we have had this spring. Moriarty and Blunkers swear by him. It's queer. They've always been on opposite sides till now."

When the weather became pleasant, Peter took up his "angle" visitings again, though not with quite the former regularity. Yet he rarely let a week pass without having spent a couple of evenings there. The spontaneous welcome accorded him was payment enough for the time, let alone the pleasure and enjoyment he derived from the imps. There was little that could raise Peter in their estimation, but they understood very well that he had become a man of vast importance, as it seemed to them. They had sharp little minds and ears, and had caught what the "district" said and thought of Peter.

"Cheese it, the cop, Tim," cried an urchin one evening to another, who was about to "play ball."

"Cheese it yerself. He won't dare tech me," shouted Tim, "so long as Mister Peter's here."

That speech alone showed the magnitude of his position in their eyes. He was now not merely, "friends wid de perlice;" he was held in fear by that awesome body!

"If I was as big as him," said one, "I'd fire all the peelers."

"Wouldn't that be dandy!" cried another.

He won their hearts still further by something he did in midsummer. Blunkers had asked him to attend what brilliant posters throughout that part of the city announced as:

HO FOR THE SEA-SHORE!

SIXTH ANNUAL

CLAM BAKE

OF THE

PATRICK N. BLUNKERS'S ASSOCIATION

When Peter asked, he found that it was to consist of a barge party (tickets fifty cents) to a bit of sand not far away from the city, with music, clams, bathing and danc-

ing included in the price of the ticket, and unlimited beer
for those who could afford that beverage.

"The beer just pays for it," Blunkers explained. "I
don't give um whisky cause some —— cusses don't drink
like as dey orter." Then catching a look in Peter's face,
he laughed rather shamefacedly. "I forgits," he explained. "Yer see I'm so da——" he checked himself—
"I swears widout knowin' it."

"I shall be very glad to go," said Peter.

"Dat's bully," said Blunkers. Then he added anxiously:
"Dere's somethin' else, too, since yer goin'. Ginerally
some feller makes a speech. Yer wouldn't want to do it
dis time, would yer?"

"What do they talk about?"

"Just what dey——" Blunkers swallowed a word, nearly
choking in so doing, and ended "please."

"Yes. I shall be glad to talk, if you don't mind my
taking a dull subject?"

"Yer just talk what yer want. We'll listen."

After Peter had thought it over for a day, he went to
Blunkers's gin palace.

"Look here," he said. "Would it be possible to hire
one more barge, and take the children free? I'll pay for
the boat, and for the extra food, if they won't be in the
way."

"I'm damned if yer do," shouted Blunkers. "Yer don't
pay for nothinks, but der childers shall go, or my name
ain't Blunkers."

And go they did, Blunkers making no secret of the fact
that it was Peter's idea. So every child who went, nearly
wild with delight, felt that the sail, the sand, the sea, and
the big feed, was all owed to Peter.

It was rather an amusing experience to Peter. He
found many of his party friends in the district, not ex-
cluding such men as Gallagher, Kennedy and others of the
more prominent rank. He made himself very pleasant to
those whom he knew, chatting with them on the trip down.
He went into the water with the men and boys, and
though there were many good swimmers, Peter's country
and river training made it possible for him to give even
the "wharf rats," a point or two in the way of water

feats. Then came the regulation clam-bake, after which Peter talked about the Tenement-house question for twenty minutes. The speech was very different from what they expected, and rather disappointed them all. However, he won back their good opinions in closing, for he ended with a very pleasant "thank you," to Blunkers, so neatly worded, and containing such a thoroughly apt local joke, that it put all in a good humor, and gave them something to tell their neighbors, on their return home. The advantage of seldom joking is that people remember the joke, and it gets repeated. Peter almost got the reputation of a wit on that one joke, merely because it came after a serious harangue, and happened to be quotable. Blunkers was so pleased with the end of the speech that he got Peter to write it out, and to this day the "thank you" part of the address, in Peter's neat handwriting, handsomely framed, is to be seen in Blunkers's saloon.

Peter also did a little writing this summer. He had gone to see three or four of the reporters, whom he had met in "the case," to get them to write up the Food and Tenement subjects, wishing thereby to stir up public feeling. He was successful to a certain degree, and they not merely wrote articles themselves, but printed three or four which Peter wrote. In two cases, he was introduced to "staff" writers, and even wrote an editorial, for which he was paid fifteen dollars. This money was all he received for the time spent, but he was not working for shekels. All the men told him to let them know when he had more "stories" for them, and promised him assistance when the reports should go in to the Legislature.

Peter visited his mother as usual during August. Before going, he called on Dr. Plumb, and after an evening with him, went to two tenements in the district. As the result of these calls, he carried three children with him when he went home. Rather pale, thin little waifs. It is a serious matter to charge any one with so grave a crime as changeling, but Peter laid himself open to it, for when he came back, after two weeks, he returned very different children to the parents. The fact that they did not prosecute for the substitution only proves how little the really poor care for their offspring.

But this was not his only summering. He spent four days with the Costells, as well as two afternoons later, thoroughly enjoying, not merely the long, silent drives over the country behind the fast horses, but the pottering round the flower-garden with Mrs. Costell. He had been reading up a little on flowers and gardening, and he was glad to swap his theoretical for her practical knowledge. Candor compels the statement that he enjoyed the long hours stretched on the turf, or sitting idly on the veranda, puffing Mr. Costell's good Havanas.

Twice Mr. Bohlmann stopped at Peter's office of a Saturday and took him out to stay over Sunday at his villa in one of the Oranges. The family all liked Peter and did not hesitate to show it. Mr. Bohlmann told him:

"I sbend about dree dousand a year on law und law-babers. Misder Dummer id does for me, but ven he does nod any longer it do, I gifts id you."

On the second visit Mrs. Bohlmann said:

"I tell my good man that with all the law-business he has, he must get a lawyer for a son-in-law."

Peter had not heard Mrs. Bohlmann say to her husband the evening before, as they were prinking for dinner:

"Have you told Mr. Stirling about your law business?"

Nor Mr. Bohlmann's prompt:

"Yah. I dells him der last dime."

Yet Peter wondered if there were any connection between the two statements. He liked the two girls. They were nice-looking, sweet, sincere women. He knew that Mr. Bohlmann was ranked as a millionaire already, and was growing richer fast. Yet—Peter needed no blank walls.

During this summer, Peter had a little more law practice. A small grocer in one of the tenements came to him about a row with his landlord. Peter heard him through, and then said: "I don't see that you have any case; but if you will leave it to me to do as I think best, I'll try if I can do something," and the man agreeing, Peter went to see the landlord, a retail tobacconist up-town. "I don't think my client has any legal grounds," he told the landlord, "but he thinks that he has, and the case does seem a little hard. Such material repairs could not have been foreseen when the lease was made."

The tobacconist was rather obstinate at first. Finally he said, "I'll tell you what I'll do. I'll contribute one hundred dollars towards the repairs, if you'll make a tenant named Podds in the same building pay his rent; or dispossess him if he doesn't, so that it shan't cost me anything."

Peter agreed, and went to see the tenant in arrears. He found that the man had a bad rheumatism and consequently was unable to work. The wife was doing what she could, and even the children had been sent on the streets to sell papers, or by other means, to earn what they could. They also owed a doctor and the above-mentioned grocer. Peter went back to the landlord and told him the story.

"Yes," he said, "it's a hard case, I know, but, Mr. Stirling, I owe a mortgage on the place, and the interest falls due in September. I'm out four months' rent, and really can't afford any more." So Peter took thirty-two dollars from his "Trustee" fund, and sent it to the tobacconist. "I have deducted eight dollars for collection," he wrote. Then he saw his first client, and told him of his landlord's concession.

"How much do I owe you?" inquired the grocer.

"The Podds tell me they owe you sixteen dollars."

"Yes. I shan't get it."

"My fee is twenty-five. Mark off their bill and give me the balance."

The grocer smiled cheerfully. He had charged the Podds roundly for their credit, taking his chance of pay, and now got it paid in an equivalent of cash. He gave the nine dollars with alacrity.

Peter took it upstairs and gave it to Mrs. Podds. "If things look up with you later," he said, "you can pay it back. If not, don't trouble about it. I'll look in in a couple of weeks to see how things are going."

When this somewhat complicated matter was ended, he wrote about it to his mother:

"Many such cases would bankrupt me. As it is, my fund is dwindling faster than I like to see, though every lessening of it means a lessening of real trouble to some one. I should like to tell Miss De Voe what good her money has done already, but fear she would not understand what I told her. It has enabled me to do so much that otherwise I could not have afforded. There is only one hundred and seventy-six dollars left. Most of it though, is merely loaned and perhaps will be repaid. Anyway, I shall have nearly six hundred dollars for my work as secretary of the Food Commission, and I shall give half of it to this fund."

CHAPTER XXX

A "COMEDY"

WHEN the season began again, Miss De Voe seriously undertook her self-imposed work of introducing Peter. He was twice invited to dinner and was twice taken with opera parties to sit in her box, besides receiving a number of less important attentions. Peter accepted dutifully all that she offered him. Even ordered a new dress-suit of a tailor recommended by Lispenard. He was asked by some of the people he met to call, probably on Miss De Voe's suggestion, and he dutifully called. Yet at the end of three months Miss De Voe shook her head.

"He is absolutely a gentleman, and people seem to like him. Yet somehow—I don't understand it."

"Exactly," laughed Lispenard. "You can't make a silk purse out of a sow's ear."

"Lispenard," angrily said Miss De Voe, "Mr. Stirling is as much better than——"

"That's it," said Lispenard. "Don't think I'm depreciating Peter. The trouble is that he is much too good a chap to make into a society or a lady's man."

"I believe you are right. I don't think he cares for it at all."

"No," said Lispenard. " 'Barkis is not willin'.' I think he likes you, and simply goes to please you."

"Do you really think that's it?"

Lispenard laughed at the earnestness with which the question was asked. "No," he replied. "I was joking. Peter cultivates you, because he wants to know your swell friends."

Either this conversation or Miss De Voe's own thoughts, led to a change in her course. Invitations to formal dinners and to the opera suddenly ceased, and instead, little family dinners, afternoons in galleries, and evenings at concerts took their place. Sometimes Lispenard went with them, sometimes one of the Ogden girls, sometimes they went alone. It was an unusual week when Peter's mail did not now bring at least one little note giving him a chance to see Miss De Voe if he chose.

In February came a request for him to call. "I want to talk with you about something," it said. That same evening he was shown into her drawing-rooms. She thanked him with warmth for coming so quickly, and Peter saw that only the other visitors prevented her from showing some strong feeling. He had stumbled in on her evening—for at that time people still had evenings—but knowing her wishes, he stayed till they were left alone together.

"Come into the library," she said. As they passed across the hall she told Morden, "I shall not receive any more to-night."

The moment they were in the smaller and cosier room, without waiting to sit even, she began: "Mr. Stirling, I dined at the Manfreys yesterday." She spoke in a voice evidently endeavoring not to break. Peter looked puzzled.

"Mr. Lapham, the bank president, was there."

Peter still looked puzzled.

"And he told the table about a young lawyer who had very little money, yet who put five hundred dollars—his first fee—into his bank, and had used it to help——" Miss De Voe broke down, and leaning against the mantel, buried her face in her handkerchief.

"It's curious you should have heard of it," said Peter.

"He—he didn't mention names, b-bu-but I knew, of course."

"I didn't like to speak of it because—well—I've wanted to tell you the good it's done. Suppose you sit down." Peter brought a chair, and Miss De Voe took it.

"You must think I'm very foolish," she said, wiping her eyes.

"It's nothing to cry about." And Peter began telling

her of some of the things which he had been able to do:
—of the surgical brace it had bought; of the lessons in
wood-engraving it had given; of the sewing-machine it
had helped to pay for; of the arrears in rent it had settled.
"You see," he explained, "these people are too self-re-
specting to go to the big charities, or to rich people. But
their troubles are talked over in the saloons and on the
door-steps, so I hear of them, and can learn whether
they really deserve help. They'll take it from me, because they feel that I'm one of them."

Miss De Voe was too much shaken by her tears to talk
that evening. Miss De Voe's life and surroundings were
not exactly weepy ones, and when tears came they meant
much. She said little, till Peter rose to go, and then only:
"I shall want to talk with you, to see what I can do
to help you in your work. Please come again soon. I
ought not to have brought you here this evening, only
to see me cry like a baby. But—I had done you such
injustice in my mind about that seven dollars, and then
to find that—Oh!" Miss De Voe showed signs of a recur-
ring break-down, but mastered herself. "Good-evening."

Peter gone, Miss De Voe had another "good" cry—
which is a feminine phrase, quite incomprehensible to
men—and, going to her room, bathed her eyes. Then she
sat before her boudoir fire, thinking. Finally she rose.
In leaving the fire, she remarked aloud to it:

"Yes. He shall have Dorothy, if I can do it."

So Dorothy became a pretty regular addition to the in-
formal meals, exhibitions and concerts. Peter was once
more taken to the opera, but Dorothy and Miss De Voe
formed with him the party in the box on such nights.
Miss De Voe took him to call on Mrs. Ogden, and sang
his praises to both parents. She even went so far as to
say frankly to them what was in her mind.

Mr. Ogden said, "Those who know him speak very
well of him. I heard 'Van' Pell praise him highly at Newport last summer. Said all the politicians thought of him
as a rising man."

"He seems a nice steady fellow," said the mamma. "I
don't suppose he has much practice?"

"Oh, don't think of the money," said Miss De Voe.

"What is that compared to getting a really fine man whom one can truly love?"

"Still, money is an essential," said the papa.

"Yes. But you both know what I intend to do for Dorothy and Minna. They need not think of money. If he and Dorothy only will care for each other!"

Peter and Dorothy did like each other. Dorothy was very pretty, and had all the qualities which make a girl a strong magnet to men. Peter could not help liking her. As for Dorothy, she was like other women. She enjoyed the talking, joking, "good-time" men in society, and chatted and danced with them with relish. But like other women, when she thought of marriage, she did not find these gingerbread ornamentations so attractive. The average woman loves a man, aside from his love for her, for his physical strength, and his stiff truth-telling. The first is attractive to her because she has it not. Far be it from man to say why the second attracts. So Dorothy liked Peter. She admired many qualities in him which she would not have tolerated in other men. It is true that she laughed at him, too, for many things, but it was the laughter of that peculiar nature which implies admiration and approval, rather than the lower feelings. When the spring separation came, Miss De Voe was really quite hopeful.

"I think things have gone very well. Now, Mr. Stirling has promised to spend a week with me at Newport. I shall have Dorothy there at the same time," she told Mrs. Ogden.

Lispenard, who was present, laughed as usual. "So you are tired of your new plaything already?"

"What do you mean?"

"Aren't you marrying him so as to get rid of his calls, and his escortage?"

"Of course not. We shall go on just the same."

"Bully for you, Ma. Does Dr. Brown know it?"

Miss De Voe flushed angrily, and put an end to her call. "What a foolish fellow Lispenard is!" she remarked unconsciously to Wellington at the carriage door.

"Beg pardon, mum?" said Wellington, blank wonderment filling his face.

"Home, Wellington," said Miss De Voe crossly.

Peter took his week at Newport on his way back from his regular August visit to his mother. Miss De Voe had told him casually that Dorothy would be there, and Dorothy was there. Yet he saw wonderfully little of her. It is true that he could have seen more if he had tried, but Peter was not used to practicing finesse to win minutes and hours with a girl, and did not feel called upon, bluntly, to take such opportunities. His stay was not so pleasant as he had expected. He had thought a week in the same house with Miss De Voe, Dorothy and Lispenard, without much regard to other possible guests, could not but be a continual pleasure. But he was conscious that something was amiss with his three friends. Nor was Peter the only one who felt it. Dorothy said to her family when she went home:

"I can't imagine what is the matter with Cousin Anneke. All last spring she was nicer to me than she has ever been before, but from the moment I arrived at Newport, and before I could possibly have said or done anything to offend her, she treated me in the snippiest way. After two days I asked her what the matter was, but she insisted there was nothing, and really lost her temper at my suggesting the idea. There was something, I know, for when I said I was coming home sooner than I had at first intended, she didn't try to make me stay."

"Perhaps," said Mrs. Ogden, "she was disappointed in something, and so vented her feeling on you."

"But she wasn't cross—except when I asked her what the matter was. She was just—just snippy."

"Was Mr. Stirling there?"

"Yes. And a lot of other people. I don't think anybody had a good time, unless it was Cousin Lispenard. And he wasn't a bit nice. He had some joke to himself, and kept making remarks that nobody could understand, and chuckling over them. I told him once that he was rude, but he said that 'when people went to a play they should laugh at the right points.' That's the nice thing about Mr. Stirling. You know that what he says is the real truth."

"Lispenard's always trying to be clever."

"Yes. What do you suppose he said to me as I came away!"

"What?"

"He shook my hand, laughing, and said, 'Exit villain. It is to be a comedy, not a tragedy.' What could he mean?"

Lispenard stayed on to see the "comedy," and seemed to enjoy it, if the amused expression on his face when he occasionally gave himself up to meditation was any criterion. Peter had been pressed to stay beyond the original week, and had so far yielded as to add three days to his visit. These last three days were much pleasanter than those which had gone before, although Dorothy had departed and Peter liked Dorothy. But he saw much more of Miss De Voe, and Miss De Voe was in a much pleasanter mood. They took long drives and walks together, and had long hours of talk in and about the pleasant house and grounds. Miss De Voe had cut down her social duties for the ten days Peter was there, giving far more time for them to kill than usually fell to Newporters even in those comparatively simple days.

In one of these talks, Miss De Voe spoke of Dorothy.

"She is a such a nice, sweet girl," she said. "We all hope she'll marry Lispenard."

"Do you think cousins ought to marry?"

Miss De·Voe had looked at Peter when she made her remark. Peter had replied quietly, but his question, as Miss De Voe understood it, was purely scientific, not personal. Miss De Voe replied:

"I suppose it is not right, but it is so much better than what may happen, that it really seems best. It is so hard for a girl in Dorothy's position to marry as we should altogether wish."

"Why?" asked Peter, who did not see that a girl with prospective wealth, fine social position, and personal charm, was not necessarily well situated to get the right kind of a husband.

"It is hard to make it clear—but—I'll tell you my own story, so that you can understand. Since you don't ask questions, I will take the initiative. That is, unless your

not asking them means you are not interested?" Miss De
Voe laughed in the last part of this speech.

"I should like to hear it."

People, no matter what Peter stated, never said
"Really?" "You are in earnest?" or "You really mean
it?" So Miss De Voe took him at his word.

"Both my father and mother were rich before they
married, and the rise in New York real estate made them
in time, much richer. They both belonged to old families.
I was the only child—Lispenard says old families are so
proud of themselves that they don't dare to have large
families for fear of making the name common. Of course
they lavished all their thought, devotion and anxiety on
me. I was not spoiled; but I was watched and tended
as if I were the most precious thing the world contained.
When I grew up, and went into society, I question if I
ever was a half-hour out of the sight of one or the other
of my parents. I had plenty of society, of course, but
it was restricted entirely to our set. None other was
good enough for me! My father never had any business,
so brought no new element into our household. It was
old families, year in and year out! From the moment
I entered society I was sought for. I had many suitors.
I had been brought up to fear fortune-hunting, and suspected the motives of many men. Others did not seem
my equals—for I had been taught pride in my birth.
Those who were fit as regarded family were, many of
them, unfit in brains or morals—qualities not conspic-
uous in old families. Perhaps I might have found one to
love—if it had not been for the others. I was surrounded
wherever I went and if by chance I found a pleasant man
to talk to, *téte-à-téte,* we were interrupted by other men
coming up. Only a few even of the men whom I met
could gain an *entrée* to our house.—They weren't thought
good enough. If a working, serious man had ever been
able to see enough of me to love me, he probably would
have had very little opportunity to press his suit. But
the few men I might have cared for were frightened off
by my money, or discouraged by my popularity and ex-
clusiveness. They did not even try. Of course I did not
understand it then. I gloried in my success and did not

see the wrong it was doing me. I was absolutely happy at home, and really had not the slightest inducement to marry—especially among the men I saw the most. I led this life for six years. Then my mother's death put me in mourning. When I went back into society, an almost entirely new set of men had appeared. Those whom I had known were many of them married—others were gone. Society had lost its first charm to me. So my father and I travelled three years. We had barely returned when he died. I did not take up my social duties again till I was thirty-two. Then it was as the spinster aunt, as you have known me. Now do you understand how hard it is for such a girl as Dorothy to marry rightly?"

"Yes. Unless the man is in love. Let a man care enough for a woman, and money or position will not frighten him off."

"Such men are rare. Or perhaps it is because I did not attract them. I did not understand men as well then as I do now. Of some whom I thought unlovable or dull at that time, I have learned to think better. A woman does not marry to be entertained—or should not."

"I think," said Peter, "that one marries for love and sympathy."

"Yes. And if they are given, it does not matter about the rest. Even now, thirty-seven though I am, if I could find a true man who could love me as I wish to be loved, I could love him with my whole heart. It would be my happiness not merely to give him social position and wealth, but to make his every hope and wish mine also."

All this had been said in the same natural manner in which they both usually spoke. Miss De Voe had talked without apparent emotion. But when she began the last remark, she had stopped looking at Peter, and had gazed off through the window at the green lawn, merely showing him her profile. As a consequence she did not see how pale he suddenly became, nor the look of great suffering that came into his face. She did not see this look pass and his face, and especially his mouth, settle into a rigid determination, even while the eyes remained sad.

Miss De Voe ended the pause by beginning, "Don't you"—but Peter interrupted her there, by saying:

"It is a very sad story to me—because I—I once craved love and sympathy."

Miss De Voe turned and looked at him quickly. She saw the look of suffering on his face, but read it amiss. "You mean?" she questioned.

"There was a girl I loved," said Peter softly, "who did not love me."

"And you love her still?"

"I have no right to."

"She is married?"

"Yes."

"Will you tell me about it?"

"I—I would rather not."

Miss De Voe sat quietly for a moment, and then rose. "Dear friend," she said, laying her hand on Peter's shoulder, "we have both missed the great prize in life. Your lot is harder than the one I have told you about. It is very,"—Miss De Voe paused a moment,—"it is very sad to love—without being loved."

And so ended Lispenard's comedy.

CHAPTER XXXI

CONFLICTS

LISPENARD went back with Peter to the city. He gave his reason on the train:

"You see I go back to the city occasionally in the summer, so as to make the country bearable, and then I go back to the country, so as to make the city endurable. I shall be in Newport again in a week. When will you come back?"

"My summering's over."

"Indeed. I thought my cousin would want you again!"

"She did not say so."

"The deuce she didn't. It must be the only thing she didn't say, then, in your long confabs?"

Peter made no reply, though Lispenard looked as well as asked a question.

"Perhaps," continued Lispenard, "she talked too much, and so did not remember to ask you?"

Still Peter said nothing.

"Are you sure she didn't give you a chance to have more of her society?" Lispenard was smiling.

"Ogden," said Peter gently, "you are behaving contemptibly and you know it."

The color blazed up into Lispenard's face and he rose, saying:

"Did I understand you aright?" The manner and attitude were both threatening though repressed.

"If you tell me that I misunderstood you, I will apologize. If you think the statement insulting, I will withdraw it. I did not speak to insult you; but because I wished you to know how your questions impressed me."

"When a man tells another he is contemptible, he cannot expect to escape results. This is no place to have a scene. You may send me your apology when we reach New York——"

Peter interrupted. "I shall, if you will tell me I wronged you in supposing your questions to be malicious."

Lispenard paid no attention to the interjection. "Otherwise," he finished, "we will consider our relations ended." He walked away.

Peter wrote Lispenard that evening a long letter. He did not apologize in it, but it ended:

"There should be no quarrel between us, for we ought to be friends. If alienation has come, it is due to what has occurred to-day, and that shall not cause unkind feelings, if I can help it. An apology is due somewhere. You either asked questions you had no right to ask, or else I misjudged you. I have written you my point of view. You have your own. I leave the matter to your fairness. Think it over, and if you still find me in the wrong, and will tell me so, I will apologize."

He did not receive a reply. Meeting Ogden Ogden a few days later, he was told that Lispenard had gone west for a hunting trip, quite unexpectedly. "He said not to expect him back till he came. He seemed out of sorts at something." In September Peter had a letter from Miss De Voe. Merely a few lines saying that she had decided to spend the winter abroad, and was on the point of sailing. "I am too hurried to see my friends, but did not like to go without some good-byes, so I write them." On the whole, as in the case of most comedies, there was little amusement for the actual performers. A great essayist has defined laughter as a "feeling of superiority in the laughter over the object laughed at." If this is correct, it makes all humor despicable. Certainly much coarseness, meanness and cruelty are every day tolerated, because of the comic covering with which it is draped.

It is not to be supposed that this comedy nor its winter prologue had diverted Peter from other things. In spite of Miss De Voe's demands on his time he had enough left to spend many days in Albany when the legislature took up the reports of the Commissions. He found strong lobbies against both bills, and had a long struggle with them. He had the help of the newspapers, and he had the help of Costell, yet even with this powerful backing, the bills were first badly mangled, and finally were sidetracked. In the actual fight, Pell helped him most, and Peter began to think that a man might buy an election and yet not be entirely bad. Second only to Pell, was his whilom enemy, the former District Attorney, now a state senator, who battled himself into Peter's reluctant admiration and friendship by his devotion and loyalty to the bills. Peter concluded that he had not entirely done the man justice in the past. Curiously enough, his chief antagonist was Maguire.

Peter did not give up the fight with this defeat. His work for the bills had revealed to him the real undercurrents in the legislative body, and when it adjourned, making further work in Albany only a waste of time, he availed himself of the secret knowledge that had come to him, to single out the real forces which stood behind and paid the lobby, and to interview them. He saw the actual principals in the opposition, and spoke with utmost frankness. He told them that the fight would be renewed, on his part, at every session of the legislature till the bills were passed; that he was willing to consider pro-

posed amendments, and would accept any that were
honest. He made the fact very clear to them that they
would have to pay yearly to keep the bills off the statute
book. Some laughed at him, others quarrelled. But a
few, after listening to him, stated their true objections to
the bills, and Peter tried to meet them.

When the fall elections came, Peter endeavored to further his cause in another way. Three of the city's
assemblymen and one of her senators had voted against
the bills. Peter now invaded their districts, and talked
against them in saloons and elsewhere. It very quickly
stirred up hard feeling, which resulted in attempts to down
him. But Peter's blood warmed up as the fight thick-
ened, and hisses, eggs, or actual attempts to injure him
physically did not deter him. The big leaders were appealed to to call him off, but Costell declined to interfere.

"He wouldn't stop anyway," he told Green, "so we
should do no good. Let them fight it out by themselves."
Both of which sentences showed that Mr. Costell understood his business.

Peter had challenged his opponents to a joint debate,
and when that was declined by them, he hired halls for
evenings and spoke on the subject. He argued well,
with much more feeling than he had shown since his
speech in "the case." After the first attempt of this kind
he had no difficulty in filling his halls. The rumor came
back to his own district that he was "talkin' foin," and
many of his friends there turned out to hear him. The
same news went through other wards of the city and
drew men from them. People were actually excluded,
for want of room, and therefore every one became anxious
to hear his speeches. Finally, by subscription of a number of people who had become interested, headed by Mr.
Pell, the Cooper Union was hired, and Peter made a really
great speech to nearly three thousand people.

The papers came to his help too, and stood by him
manfully. By their aid, it was made very clear that this
was a fight against a selfish body. By their aid, it became one of the real questions of the local campaign, and
was carried beyond the borders of the city, so as to play
a part in the county elections. Peter met many of the

editors, and between his expert knowledge, acquired on the Commissions, and his practical knowledge, learned at Albany, proved a valuable man to them. They repaid his help by kind words, and praise in their columns, and brought him forward as the chief man in the movement. Mrs. Stirling concluded that the conspiracy to keep Peter in the background had been abandoned.

"Those New York papers couldn't help my Peter's getting on," was the way she put it.

The results of this fight were even better than he had hoped. One Assemblyman gave in and agreed no longer to oppose the bills. Another was defeated. The Senator had his majority so cut down that he retired from the opposition. The questions too had become so much more discussed and watched, and the blame so fastened upon the lobby that many members from the country no longer dared to oppose legislation on the subject. Hence it was that the bills, newly drawn by Peter, to reduce opposition as far as possible, when introduced by Schlurger soon after the opening of the legislature, went through with a rush, not even ayes and nays being taken. Aided by Mr. Costell, Peter secured their prompt signing by Catlin; his long fight had ended in victory.

The "sixt" was wild with joy over the triumph. Whether it was because it was a tenement ward, or because Peter had talked there so much about it, or because his success was felt to redound to their credit, the voters got up a display of fireworks on the night when the news of the signing of the bills reached New York. When Peter returned to the city, he was called down to a hall one evening, to witness a torchlight procession and receive resolutions "engrossed and framed" from his admiring friends. Blunkers was chairman and made a plain speech which set the boys cheering by its combination of strong feeling and lack of grammar. Then Justice Gallagher made a fine-sounding, big-worded presentation. In the enthusiasm of the moment, Dennis broke the programme by rising and giving vent to a wild burst of feeling, telling his audience all that they owed to Peter, and though they knew already what he told them, they cheered and cheered the strong, natural eloquence.

"Yer was out a order," said Blunkers, at the end of the speech.

"Yez loi!" said Dennis, jumping on his feet again. "It's never out av order to praise Misther Stirling."

The crowd applauded his sentiment.

CHAPTER XXXII

THE END OF THE CONFLICT

PETER had had some rough experiences two or three times in his fall campaign, and Dennis, who had insisted on escorting him, took him to task about his "physical culture."

"It's thirty pounds yez are too heavy, sir," he told Peter. "An' it's too little intirely yez afther knowin' av hittin'."

Peter asked his advice, bought Indian clubs, dumb-bells, and boxing-gloves, and under Dennis's tutelage began to learn the art of self-defence. He was rather surprised, at the end of two months, to find how much flesh he had taken off, how much more easily he moved, how much more he was eating, and how much more he was able to do, both mentally and physically.

"It seems as if somebody had oiled my body and brain," he told Dennis.

Dennis let him into another thing, by persuading him to join the militia regiment most patronized by the "sixth," and in which Dennis was already a sergeant. Peter received a warm welcome from the regiment, for Dennis, who was extremely popular, had heralded his fame, and Peter's physical strength and friendly way did the rest. Ogden Ogden laughed at him for joining a "Mick" regiment, and wanted to put Peter into the Seventh. Peter only said that he thought his place was where he was.

Society did not see much of Peter this winter. He called on his friends dutifully, but his long visits to Albany, his evenings with Dennis, and his drill nights, interfered badly with his acceptance of the invitations sent him. He had, too, made many friends in his commission work and politics, so that he had relatively less time to give to his older ones. The absence of Miss De Voe and Lispenard somewhat reduced his social obligations it is true, but the demands on his time were multiplying fast.

One of these demands was actual law work. The first real case to come to him was from the contractor who had served on the tenement-commission. He was also employed by the Health Board as special counsel in a number of prosecutions, to enforce clauses of his Food Bill. The papers said it was because of his familiarity with the subject, but Peter knew it was the influence of Green, who had become a member of that Board. Then he began to get cases from the "district," and though there was not much money in each case, before long the number of them made a very respectable total.

The growth of his practice was well proven by a suggestion from Dummer that they should join forces. "Mr. Bohlmann wants to give you some of his work, and it's easier to go into partnership than to divide his practice."

Peter knew that Dummer had a very lucrative business of a certain kind, but he declined the offer.

"I have decided never to take a case which has not right on its side."

"A lawyer is just as much bound to try a case as a physician is bound to take a patient."

"That is what lawyers say outside, but they know better."

"Well, have your scruples. We'll make the firm cases only such as you choose. I'll manage the others."

"I should like to," said Peter. "I'm very grateful for the offer—but we could hardly do that successfully. If the firm was good for anything, we should be known as belonging to it, and the public could not well discriminate."

So that chance of success was passed. But every now and then Bohlmann sent him something to do, and Dummer helped him to a joint case occasionally.

So, though friends grew steadily in numbers, society

saw less and less of Peter. Those who cared to study his tastes came to recognize that to force formal entertaining on him was no kindness, and left it to Peter to drop in when he chose, making him welcome when he came.

He was pleased to get a letter from Lispenard during the winter, from Japan. It was long, but only the first paragraph need be quoted, for the rest related merely to his travels:

"The breezes of the Pacific have blown away all my bad temper," he wrote, "and I want to say that I was wrong, and regret my original fault, as well as what it later led me into. You are quite right. We must continue friends."

Peter wrote a reply, which led to a regular correspondence. He sent Miss De Voe, also, a line of Christmas greetings, and received a long letter from her at Nice, which told him something of Watts and Helen:

"She is now well again, but having been six years in Europe, she and her husband have become wedded to the life. I question if they ever return. I spoke of you, and they both inquired with great warmth about you."

Peter replied, sending his "remembrance to Mr. and Mrs. D'Alloi in case you again meet them." From that time on Miss De Voe and he corresponded, she telling him of her Italian, Greek and Egyptian wanderings, and he writing of his doings, especially in regard to a certain savings bank fund standing in the name of "Peter Stirling, trustee" to which Miss De Voe had, the winter before, arranged to contribute a thousand dollars yearly.

As his practice increased he began to indulge himself a little. Through the instrumentality of Mr. Pell, he was put first into one and later into a second of the New York clubs, and his dinners became far less simple in consequence. He used these comforters of men, indeed, almost wholly for dining, and, though by no means a club-man in other senses, it was still a tendency to the luxurious. To counteract this danger he asked Mr. Costell to pick him up a saddle-horse, whereupon that friend promptly presented him with one. He went regularly now to a good tailor, which conduct ought to have ruined him with the "b'ys," but it didn't. He still smoked a pipe occasionally in the saloons or on the doorsteps of the district, yet candor compels us to add that he now had in his room a box of cigars labelled "Habana." These were creature pleasures, however, which he only allowed himself on rare occasions. And most of these luxuries did not appear till his practice had broadened beyond the point already noted.

Broaden it did. In time many city cases were thrown in his way. As he became more and more a factor in politics, the judges began to send him very profitable referee cases. Presently a great local corporation, with many damage suits, asked him to accept its work on a yearly salary.

"Of course we shall want you to look out for us at Albany," it was added.

"I'll do what I can to prevent unfair legislation. That must be all, though. As for the practice, you must let me settle every case where I think the right is with the plaintiff." This caused demur at first, but eventually he was employed, and it was found that money was saved in the long run, for Peter was very successful in getting people to settle out of court.

Then the savings bank, for which Peter had done his best (not merely as recorded, but at other times), turned over its law business to him, giving him many real estate transactions to look into, besides papers to draw. "He brings us a good many depositors," Mr. Lapham told his trustees, "and is getting to be a large depositor himself."

Peter began to find help necessary, and took a partner. He did this at the suggestion of Ogden Ogden who had concluded his clerkship, and who said to Peter:

"I have a lot of friends who promise me their work. I don't know how much it will be, but I should like to try it with you. Of course, yours is the bigger practice, but we can arrange that."

So after considerable discussion, the sign on Peter's door became "Stirling and Ogden," and the firm blossomed out with an office boy—one of Peter's original "angle" friends, now six years older than when Peter and he had first met.

Ogden's friends did materialize, and brought good paying cases. As the city, referee, corporation and bank work increased, their joint practice needed more help, and Ray Rivington was, on Ogden's request, taken in.

"He doesn't get on with his law studies, though he pretends to work over them hard. In fact he'll never be a good lawyer. He hasn't a legal mind. But he'll bring cases, for he's very popular in society, and he'll do all the palavering and running round very well. He's just the fellow to please people." This was what Ogden urged, adding, "I might as well tell you that I'm interested for another reason, too. He and Dorothy will marry, if he can ever get to the marrying point. This, of course, is to be between us."

"I'll be very glad to have him, both for his own sake, and for what you've just told me," said Peter.

Thus it was that the firm again changed its name, becoming "Stirling, Ogden and Rivington," and actually spread into two other rooms, Peter's original little "ten by twelve" being left to the possession of the office boy. That functionary gazed long hours at the map of Italy on the blank wall, but it did not trouble him. He only whistled and sang street songs at it. As for Peter, he was too busy to need blank walls. He had fought two great opponents. The world and himself. He had conquered them both.

CHAPTER XXXIII

A RENEWAL

IF the American people had anglicized themselves as thoroughly into liking three-volume stories, as they have in other things, it would be a pleasure to trace the next ten years of Peter's life; for his growing reputation makes this period a far easier matter to chronicle than the more obscure beginnings already recorded. If his own life did not supply enough material we could multiply our characters, as did Dickens, or journey sideways, into little essays, as did Thackeray. His life and his biographer's pen might fail to give interest to such devices, but the plea is now for "realism," which most writers take to mean microscopical examination of minutia. If the physical and psychical emotions of a heroine as she drinks a glass of water can properly be elaborated so as to fill two printed pages, Peter's life could be extended endlessly. There were big cases, political fights, globe trottings, and new friends, all of which have unlimited potentialities for numerous chapters. But Americans are peculiar people, and do not buy a pound of sugar any the quicker because its bulk has been raised by a skilful admixture of moisture and sand. So it seems best partly to take the advice of the Bellman, in the "Hunting of the Snark," to skip sundry years. In resuming, it is to find Peter at his desk, reading a letter. He has a very curious look on his face, due to the letter, the contents of which are as follows:

March 22.

DEAR OLD CHUM—

Here is the wretched old sixpence, just as bad as ever—if not worse—come back after all these years.

And as of yore, the sixpence is in a dreadful pickle, and appeals to the old chum, who always used to pull him out of his scrapes, to do it once more. Please come and see me as quickly as possible, for every moment is important. You see I feel sure that I do not appeal in vain. "Changeless as the pyramids" ought to be your motto.

Helen and our dear little girl will be delighted to see you, as will

Yours affectionately,

WATTS.

Peter opened a drawer and put the letter into it. Then he examined his diary calendar. After this he went to a door, and, opening it, said:

"I am going uptown for the afternoon. If Mr. Murtha comes, Mr. Ogden will see him."

Peter went down and took a cab, giving the driver a number in Gramercy Park.

The footman hesitated on Peter's inquiry. "Mr. D'Alloi is in, sir, but is having his afternoon nap, and we have orders he's not to be disturbed."

"Take him my card. He will see me."

The footman showed Peter into the drawing-room, and disappeared. Peter heard low voices for a moment, then the curtains of the back room were quickly parted, and, with hands extended to meet him, Helen appeared.

"This is nice of you—and so unexpected!"

Peter took the hand, but said nothing. They sat down and Mrs. D'Alloi continued:

"Watts is asleep, and I have given word that he is not to be disturbed. I want to see you for a moment myself. You have plenty of time?"

"Yes."

"That's very nice. I don't want you to be formal with us. Do say that you can stay to dinner?"

"I would, if I were not already engaged."

"Then we'll merely postpone it. It's very good of you to come to see us. I've tried to get Watts to look you up, but he is so lazy! It's just as well since you've found us out. Only you should have asked for both of us."

"I came on business," said Peter.

Mrs. D'Alloi laughed. "Watts is the poorest man in the world for that, but he'll do anything he can to help you, I know. He has the warmest feeling for you."

Peter gathered from this that Mrs. D'Alloi did not know of the "scrape," whatever it was, and with a lawyer's caution, he did not attempt to disabuse her of the impression that he had called about his own affairs.

"How you have changed!" Mrs. D'Alloi continued. "If I had not known who it was from the card, I am not sure that I should have recognized you."

It was just what Peter had been saying to himself of Mrs. D'Alloi. Was it her long ill-health, or was it the mere lapse of years, which had wrought such changes in her? Except for the eyes, everything had altered. The cheeks had lost their roundness and color; the hair had thinned noticeably; lines of years and pain had taken away the sweet expression that formerly had counted for so much; the pretty roundness of the figure was gone, and what charm it now had was due to the modiste's skill. Peter felt puzzled. Was this the woman for whom he had so suffered? Was it this memory that had kept him, at thirty-eight, still a bachelor? Like many another man, he found that he had been loving an ideal—a creation of his own mind. He had, on a boyish fancy, built a dream of a woman with every beauty and attraction, and had been loving it for many years, to the exclusion of all other womankind. Now he saw the original of his dream, with the freshness and glamour gone, not merely from the dream, but from his own eyes. Peter had met many pretty girls, and many sweet ones since that week at the Pierces. He had gained a very different point of view of women from that callow time.

Peter was not blunderer enough to tell Mrs. D'Alloi that he too, saw a change. His years had brought tact, if they had not made him less straightforward. So he merely said, "You think so?"

"Ever so much. You've really grown slender, in spite of your broad shoulders—and your face is so—so different."

There was no doubt about it. For his height and breadth of shoulder, Peter was now by no means heavy. His face, too, had undergone a great change. As the roundness had left it, the eyes and the forehead had both become more prominent features, and both were good. The square, firm jaw still remained, but the heaviness of the cheek and nose had melted into lines which gave only strength and character, and destroyed the dulness which people used to comment upon. The face would never be called handsome, in the sense that regular features are supposed to give beauty, but it was strong and speaking, with lines of thought and feeling.

"You know," laughed Mrs. D'Alloi, "you have actually become good-looking, and I never dreamed that was possible!"

"How long have you been here?"

"A month. We are staying with papa, till the house in Fifty-seventh Street can be put in order. It has been closed since Mrs. D'Alloi's death. But don't let's talk houses. Tell me about yourself."

"There is little to tell. I have worked at my profession, with success."

"But I see your name in politics. And I've met many

people in Europe who have said you were getting very famous."

"I spend a good deal of time in politics. I cannot say whether I have made myself famous, or infamous. It seems to depend on which paper I read."

"Yes, I saw a paper on the steamer, that——" Mrs. D'Alloi hesitated, remembering that it had charged Peter with about every known sin of which man is capable. Then she continued, "But I knew it was wrong." Yet there was quite as much of question as of assertion in her remark. In truth, Mrs. D'Alloi was by no means sure that Peter was all that was desirable, for any charge made against a politician in this country has a peculiar vitality and persistence. She had been told that Peter was an open supporter of saloons, and that New York politics battened on all forms of vice. So a favorite son could hardly have retained the purity that women take as a standard of measurement. "Don't you find ward politics very hard?" she asked, dropping an experimental plummet, to see what depths of iniquity there might be.

"I haven't yet."

"But that kind of politics must be very disagreeable to gentlemen. The men must have such dirty hands!"

"It's not the dirty hands which make American politics disagreeable. It's the dirty consciences."

"Are—are politics so corrupt and immoral?"

"Politics are what the people make them."

"Really?"

"I suppose your life has not been of a kind to make you very familiar with it all. Tell me what these long years have brought you?"

"Perfect happiness! Oh, Mr. Stirling—may I call you Peter?—thank you. Peter, I have the finest, noblest husband that ever lived! He is everything that is good and kind!" Mrs. D'Alloi's face lighted up with happiness and tenderness.

"And your children?"

"We have only one. The sweetest, loveliest child you can imagine."

"Fie, fie, Rosebud," cried a voice from the doorway. "You shouldn't speak of yourself so, even if it is the truth. Leave that to me. How are you, Peter, old fellow? I'd apologize for keeping you waiting, but if you've had Helen, there's no occasion. Isn't it Boileau who said that: 'The best thing about many a man is his wife'?"

Mrs. D'Alloi beamed, but said, "It isn't so, Peter. He's much better than I."

Watts laughed. "You'll have to excuse this, old man. Will happen sometimes, even in the properest of families, if one marries an angel."

"There, you see," said Mrs. D'Alloi. "He just spoils me, Peter."

"And she thrives on it, doesn't she, Peter?" said Watts. "Isn't she prettier even than she was in the old days?"

Mrs. D'Alloi colored with pleasure, even while saying: "Now, Watts dear, I won't swallow such palpable flattery. There's one kiss for it—Peter won't mind—and now I know you two want to talk old times, so I'll leave you together. Good-bye, Peter—or rather *au revoir*—for you must be a regular visitor now. Watts, arrange with Peter to dine with us some day this week."

Mrs. D'Alloi disappeared through the doorway. Peter's pulse did not change a beat.

CHAPTER XXXIV

HELP

THE moment she was gone, Watts held out his hand, saying: "Here, old man, let us shake hands again. It's almost like going back to college days to see my old chum. Come to the snuggery, where we shan't be interrupted." They went through two rooms, to one fitted up as a smoking-room and office. "It's papa-in-law's work-shop. He can't drop his work at the bank, so he brings it home and goes on here. Sit down. Here, take a cigar. Now, are you comfortable?"

"Yes."

"*Maintenant,* I suppose you want to know why I wrote you to come so quickly?"

"Yes."

"Well, the truth of it is, I'm in an awful mess. Yesterday I was so desperate I thought I should blow my brains out. I went round to the club to see if I couldn't forget or drown my trouble, just as sick as a man could be. Fellows talking. First thing I heard was your name. 'Just won a great case.' 'One of the best lawyers in New York.' Thinks I to myself, 'That's a special providence.' Peter always was the fellow to pull me through my college scrapes. I'll write him.' Did it, and played billiards for the rest of the evening, secure in the belief that you would come to my help, just as you used to."

"Tell me what it is?"

"Even that isn't easy, chum. It's a devilish hard thing to tell even to you."

"Is it money trou——?"

"No, no!" Watts interrupted. "It isn't that. The truth is I've a great deal more money than is good for me, and apparently always shall have. I wish it were only that!"

"How can I help you?" began Peter.

"I knew you would," cried Watts, joyfully. "Just the same old reliable you always were. Here. Draw up nearer. That's it. Now then, here goes. I shan't mind if you are shocked at first. Be as hard on me as you like."

"Well?"

"Well, to make a long story short, I'm entangled with a woman, and there's the devil to pay. Now you'll pull me through, old man, won't you?"

"No."

"Don't say that, Peter! You must help me. You're my only hope."

"I do not care to mix myself in such a business," said Peter, very quietly. "I would rather know nothing about it." Peter rose.

"Don't desert me," cried Watts, springing to his feet, and putting his hand on Peter's shoulder, so as to prevent his progress to the door. "Don't. She's going to expose me. Think of the disgrace! My God, Peter, think——"

"Take your hand off my shoulder."

"But, Peter, think——"

"The time to think was before—not now, Watts. I will not concern myself in this."

"But, old man. I can't face it. It will kill Helen!"

Peter had already thrown aside the arm, and had taken a step towards the doorway. He stopped and turned. "She does not know?"

"Not a suspicion. And nothing but absolute proof will make her believe it. She worships me. Oh, Peter, save her! Save Leonore—if you won't save me!"

"Can they be saved?"

"That's what I want to know. Here—sit down, please! I'll tell you all about it."

Peter hesitated a moment, and then sat down.

"It began in Paris twelve years ago. Such affairs have a way of beginning in Paris, old man. It's in the atmosphere. She——"

"Stop. I will ask questions. There's no good going over the whole story." Peter tried to speak calmly, and to keep his voice and face from showing what he felt. He paused a moment, and then said: "She threatens to expose you. Why?"

"Well, after three years I tired of it, and tried to end it. Then she used it to blackmail me for ten years, till, in desperation, I came to America, to see if I couldn't escape her."

"And she followed you?"

"Yes. She was always tracking me in Europe, and making my life a hell on earth, and now she's followed me here."

"If it's merely a question of money, I don't see what you want of me."

"She says she doesn't want money now—but revenge. She's perfectly furious over my coming off without telling her—always had an awful temper—and—well, you know an infuriated woman is capable of anything. The Spaniard was right who said it was easier to take care of a peck of fleas than one woman, eh, chum?"

"So she threatens to tell your wife?"

"No. She says she's going to summon me into court."

"On what grounds?"

"That's the worst part of it. You see, chum, there's a child, and she says she's going to apply for a proper support for it. Proper support! Heavens! The money I've paid her would support ten children. It's only temper."

Peter said, "Watts, Watts," in a sad voice.

"Pretty bad, isn't it? If it wasn't for the child I could——"

Peter interrupted. "Has she any proofs of paternity besides——?"

Watts interrupted in turn. "Yes. Confound it! I was fool enough to write letters during my infatuation. Talleyrand was right when he said only fools and women wrote letters."

"How could you?"

"That's what I've asked myself a hundred times. Oh, I'm sorry enough. I've sworn never to put pen to paper again. *Jamais!*"

"I did not mean the letters. But your vow."

"My vow?"

"Your marriage vow."

"Oh, yes. I know. But you know, chum, before you promise to love one woman for all time you should have seen them all."

"And that display ten minutes ago was all mockery?"

"No, no! Really, Peter, I'm awfully fond of the little woman. Really I am. And you know Daudet says a man can love two women at the same time."

"And if so, how about his honor?" Peter was trying to repress his emotion, but it would jerk out questions.

"Yes, I know. I've said that to myself over and over again. Why, look here." Watts pulled a small revolver from his hip pocket. "This will show you how close to the desperation point I have come. I've carried that for two days, so that if worse comes to worst—well. Phut! —*Voila tout.*"

Peter rose, speaking in a voice ringing with scorn. "You would escape your sin, to leave it with added disgrace for your wife and daughter to bear! Put up your pistol, Watts D'Alloi. If I am to help you, I want to help a man—not a skulker. What do you want me to do?"

"That's what I wish to know. What can I do?"

"You have offered her money?"

"Yes. I told her that——"

"Never mind details," interrupted Peter. "Was it enough to put further offers out of the question?"

"Yes. She won't hear of money. She wants revenge."

"Give me her name and address."

"Celestine——" The rest was interrupted by a knock at the door. "Well?" said Watts.

The door was opened, and a footman entered. "If you please, Mr. D'Alloi, there's a Frenchwoman at the door who wants to see you. She won't give me her name, but says you'll know who it is."

"Say I won't see her. That I'm busy."

"She told me to say that if you were engaged, she'd see Mrs. D'Alloi."

"My God!" said Watts, under his breath.

"Ask the woman to come in here," said Peter, quietly, but in a way which made the man leave the room without waiting to see if Watts demurred.

A complete silence followed. Then came the rustle of skirts, and a woman entered the room. Peter, who stood aside, motioned to the footman to go, and closed the door himself, turning the key.

The woman came to the middle of the room. "So, Monsieur D'Alloi," she said in French, speaking very low and distinctly, "you thought it best not to order your groom to turn me out, as you did that last day in Paris, when you supposed your flight to America left you free to do as you pleased? But you did not escape me. Here I am."

Watts sat down in an easy-chair, and striking a match, lighted a cigarette. "That, Celestine," he said in French, "is what in English we call a self-evident proposition."

Celestine's foot began to tap the floor. "You needn't pretend you expected I would follow you. You thought you could drop me, like an old slipper."

Watts blew a whiff of tobacco from his mouth. "It

was a remark of Ricard's, I believe, 'that in woman, one
should always expect the unexpected.'"

"Mon Dieu!" shrieked Celestine. "If I—if I could kill
you—you——"

She was interrupted by Peter's bringing a chair to her
and saying in French, "Will you not sit down, please?"

She turned in surprise, for she had been too wrought up
to notice that Peter was in the room. She stared at him
and then sat down.

"That's right," said Watts. "Take it easy. No occasion to get excited."

"Ah!" screamed Celestine, springing to her feet, "your
name shall be in all the papers. You shall——"

Peter again interrupted. "Madame, will you allow me
to say something?" He spoke gently and deferentially.

Celestine looked at him again, saying rapidly: "Why
should I listen to you? What are you to me? I don't
even know you. My mind's made up. I tell you——"
The woman was lashing herself into a fury, and Peter
interrupted her again:

"Pardon me. We are strangers. If I ask anything of
you for myself, I should expect a refusal. But I ask it
for humanity, to which we all owe help. Only hear what
I have to say. I do not claim it as a right, but as a
favor."

Celestine sat down. "I listen," she said. She turned
her chair from Watts and faced Peter, as he stood at the
study table.

Peter paused a moment, and then said: "After what I
have seen, I feel sure you wish only to revenge yourself
on Mr. D'Alloi?"

"Yes."

"Now let me show you what you will do. For the
last two days Mr. D'Alloi has carried a pistol in his pocket,
and if you disgrace him he will probably shoot himself."

"Bon!"

"But where is your revenge? He will be beyond your
reach, and you will only have a human life upon your
conscience ever after."

"I shall not grieve!"

"Nor is that all. In revenging yourself on him, you

do one of the cruelest acts possible. A wife, who trusts and believes in him, will have her faith and love shattered. His daughter—a young girl, with all her life before her—must ever after despise her father and blush at her name. Do not punish the weak and innocent for the sin of the guilty!" Peter spoke with an earnestness almost terrible. Tears came into his eyes as he made his appeal, and his two auditors both rose to their feet, under the impulse of his voice even more than of his words. So earnest was he, and so spell-bound were the others, that they failed to hear the door from the dining-room move, or notice the entrance of Mrs. D'Alloi, as Peter ended his plea.

A moment's silence followed Peter's outburst of feeling. Then the Frenchwoman cried:

"Truly, truly. But what will you do for me and my child? Haven't we been ill-treated? Don't you owe us help, too? Justice! Don't we deserve tenderness and protection?"

"Yes," said Peter. "But you wish revenge. Ask for justice, ask for help, and I will do what is within my power to aid you."

"Watts," cried Mrs. D'Alloi, coming forward, "of what child are you talking? Whose child? Who is this woman?"

Watts jumped as if he had been shot. Celestine even retreated before the terrible voice and face with which Mrs. D'Alloi asked her questions. A sad, weary look came into Peter's eyes. No one answered Mrs. D'Alloi.

"Answer me," she cried.

"My dear little woman. Don't get excited. It's all right." Watts managed to say this much. But he did not look his last remark.

"Answer me, I say. Who is this woman? Speak!"

"It's all right, really, it's all right. Here. Peter will tell you it's all right."

"Peter," cried Mrs. D'Alloi. "Of whose child were you speaking?"

Peter was still standing by the desk. He looked sad and broken, as he said:

"This is the mother, Mrs. D'Alloi."

"Yes? Yes?"

Peter raised his eyes to Helen's, and looked at her. Then he said quietly:

"And Watts—will tell you that—I am its father."

CHAPTER XXXV

RUNNING AWAY

THE dramatic pause which followed Peter's statement was first broken by Mrs. D'Alloi, who threw her arms about Watts's neck, and cried: "Oh! my husband. Forgive me, forgive me for the suspicion!"

Peter turned to Celestine. "Madame," he said, "we are not wanted here." He unlocked the door into the hall, and stood aside while she passed out, which she did quietly. Another moment found the two on the sidewalk. "I will walk with you to your hotel, if you will permit me?" Peter said to her.

"Certainly," Celestine replied. Nothing more was said in the walk of ten blocks. When they reached the hotel entrance, Peter asked: "Can you see me for a few moments?"

"Yes. Come to my private parlor." They took the elevator, and were but a moment in reaching that apartment.

Peter spoke the moment the door was closed. "Madame," he said, "you saw that scene. Spare his wife and child? He is not worth your anger."

"Ah, Ciel!" cried Celestine, emotionally. "Do you think so lowly of me, that you can imagine I would destroy your sacrifice? Your romantic, your dramatic, *mon Dieu!* your noble sacrifice? Non, non. Celestine Lacour could never do so. She will suffer cruelty, penury, insults, before she behaves so shamefully, so perfidiously."

Peter did not entirely sympathize with the Frenchwoman's admiration for the dramatic element, but he was too good a lawyer not to accept an admission, no matter upon what grounds. He held out his hand promptly.

"Madame," he said, "accept my thanks and admiration for your generous conduct."

Celestine took it and shook it warmly.

"Of course," said Peter. "Mr. D'Alloi owes you an ample income."

"Ah!" cried Celestine, shrugging her shoulders. "Do not talk of him—I leave it to you to make him do what is right."

"And you will return to France?"

"Yes, yes. If you say so?" Celestine looked at Peter in a manner known only to the Latin races. Just then a side door was thrown open, and a boy of about twelve years of age dashed into the room, followed by a French poodle.

"Little villain!" cried Celestine. "How dare you approach without knocking? Go. Go. Quickly."

"Pardon, Madame," said the child. "I thought you still absent."

"Is that the child?" asked Peter.

"Yes," said Celestine.

"Does he know?"

"Nothing. I do not tell him even that I am his mother."

"Then you are not prepared to give him a mother's care and tenderness?"

"Never. I love him not. He is too like his father. And I cannot have it known that I am the mother of a child of twelve. It would not be believed, even." Celestine took a look at herself in the tall mirror.

"Then I suppose you would like some arrangement about him?"

"Yes."

Peter stayed for nearly an hour with the woman. He stayed so long, that for one of the few times in his life he was late at a dinner engagement. But when he had left Celestine, every detail had been settled. Peter did not have an expression of pleasure on his face as he rode down-town, nor was he very good company at the dinner which he attended that evening.

The next day did not find him in any better mood. He

went down-town, and called on an insurance company and talked for a while with the president. Then he called at a steamship office. After that he spent twenty minutes with the head of one of the large schools for boys in the city. Then he returned to his office.

"A Mr. D'Alloi is waiting for you in your private office, sir," he was told. "He said that he was an old friend and insisted on going in there."

Peter passed into his office.

Watts cried: "My dear boy, how can I ever——"

He was holding out his hand, but Peter failed to take it, and interrupted him.

"I have arranged it all with Madame Lacour," Peter said coldly. "She sails on La Bretagne on Thursday. You are to buy an annuity for three thousand dollars a year. In addition, you are to buy an annuity for the boy till he is twenty-five, of one thousand dollars a year, payable to me as his guardian. This will cost you between forty and fifty thousand dollars. I will notify you of the amount when the insurance company sends it to me. In return for your check, I shall send you the letters and other things you sent Madame Lacour, or burn them, as you direct. Except for this, the affair is ended. I need not detain you further."

"Oh, I say, chum. Don't take it this way," cried Watts. "Do you think——?"

"I end it as suits me," said Peter. "Good-day."

"But, at least you must let me pay you a fee for your work?"

Peter turned on Watts quickly, but checked the movement and the words on his tongue. He only reiterated, "Good-day."

"Well, if you will have it so," Watts went to the door, but hesitated. "Just as you please. If, later, you change your mind, send me word. I shan't cherish any feeling for this. I want to be friends."

"Good-day," said Peter. Watts passed out, closing the door.

Peter sat down at his desk, doing nothing, for nearly an hour. How long he would have sat will never be known,

if his brown study had not been ended by Rivington's
entrance. "The Appeals have just handed down their
decision in the Henley case. We win."

"I thought we should," said Peter mechanically.

"Why, Peter! What's the matter with you? You look
as seedy as——"

"As I feel," said Peter. "I'm going to stop work and
take a ride, to see if I can't knock some of my dulness
out of me." Within an hour he was at the Riding Club.

"Hello," said the stable man. "Twice in one day?
You're not often here at this hour, sir. Which horse will
you have?"

"Give me whichever has the most life in him."

"It's Mutineer has the devil in him always, sir. Though
it's not yourself need fear any horse. Only look out for
the ice."

Peter rode into the Park in ten minutes. He met Lispenard at the first turn.

"Hello! It's not often you are here at this hour."
Lispenard reined his horse up alongside.

"No," said Peter. "I've been through a very revolt—
a very disagreeable experience, and I've come up here to
get some fresh air. I don't want to be sociable."

"That's right. Truthful as ever. But one word before
we separate. Keppel has just received two proofs of
Haden's last job. He asks awful prices for them, but
you ought to see them."

"Thanks." And the two friends separated as only true
friends can separate.

Peter rode on, buried in his own thoughts. The park
was rather empty, for dark comes on early in March, and
dusk was already in the air. He shook himself presently,
and set Mutineer at a sharp canter round the larger circle
of the bridle path. But before they had half swung the
circle, he was deep in thought again, and Mutineer was
taking his own pace. Peter deserved to get a stumble and
a broken neck or leg, but he didn't. He was saved from
it by an incident which never won any credit for its good
results to Peter, however much credit it gained him.

Peter was so deeply engrossed in his own thoughts that
he did not hear the clatter of a horse's feet behind him,

just as he struck the long stretch of the comparatively straight path along the Reservoir. But Mutineer did, and pricked up his ears. Mutineer could not talk articulately, but all true lovers of horses understand their language. Mutineer's cogitations, transmitted into human speech, were something to this effect:

"Hello. What's that horse trying to do? He can't for a moment expect to pass me!"

But the next moment a roan mare actually did pass him, going at a swift gallop.

Mutineer laid his ears back. "The impudence!" he said. "Does that little whiffet of a roan mare think she's going to show me her heels? I'll teach her!" It is a curious fact that both the men and horses who are most seldom passed by their kind, object to it most when it happens.

Peter suddenly came back to affairs earthly to find Mutineer just settling into a gait not permitted by Park regulations. He drew rein, and Mutineer, knowing that the fun was up, danced round the path in his bad temper.

"Really," he said to himself, "if I wasn't so fond of you, I'd give you and that mare an awful lesson. Hello! not another? This is too much!"

The last remarks had relation to more clattering of hoofs. In a moment a groom was in view, going also at a gallop.

"Hout of the way," cried the groom, to Peter, for Mutineer was waltzing round the path in a way that suggested "no thoroughfare." "Hi'm after that runaway."

Peter looked after the first horse, already a hundred feet away. He said nothing to groom nor horse, but Mutineer understood the sudden change in the reins, even before he felt that maddening prick of the spurs. There was a moment's wild grinding of horse's feet on the slippery road and then Mutineer had settled to his long, tremendous stride.

"Now, I'll show you," he remarked, "but if only he wouldn't hold me so damned tight." We must forgive Mutineer for swearing. He lived so much with the stablemen, that, gentleman though he was, evil communications could not be entirely resisted.

Peter was riding "cool." He knew he could run the mare down, but he noticed that the woman, who formed the mount, was sitting straight, and he could tell from the position of her elbows that she was still pulling on her reins, if ineffectually. He thought it best therefore to let the mare wind herself before he forced himself up, lest he should only make the runaway horse the wilder. So after a hundred yards' run, he drew Mutineer down to the mare's pace, about thirty feet behind her.

They ran thus for another hundred yards. Then suddenly Peter saw the woman drop her reins, and catch at the saddle. His quick eye told him in a moment what had happened. The saddle-girth had broken, or the saddle was turning. He dug his spurs into Mutineer, so that the horse, who had never had such treatment, thought that he had been touched by two branding irons. He gave a furious shake of his ears, and really showed the blood of his racing Kentucky forebears. In fifteen seconds the horse was running even with the mare.

Peter had intended merely to catch the reins of the runaway, trusting to his strength to do what a woman's could not. But when he came up alongside, he saw that the saddle had turned so far that the rider could not keep her seat ten seconds longer. So he dropped his reins, bent over, and putting his arms about the woman lifted her off the precarious seat, and put her in front of him. He held her there with one arm, and reached for his reins. But Mutineer had tossed them over his head.

"Mutineer!" said Peter, with an inflection of voice decidedly commanding.

"I covered a hundred yards to your seventy," Mutineer told the roan mare. "On a mile track I could go round you twice, without getting out of breath. I could beat you now, even with double mount easily. But my Peter has dropped the reins and that puts me on my honor. Good-bye." Mutineer checked his great racing stride, broke to a canter; dropped to a trot; altered that to a walk, and stopped.

Peter had been rather astonished at the weight he had lifted. Peter had never lifted a woman before. His chief experience in the weight of human-kind had been in

wrestling matches at the armory, and only the largest and
most muscular men in the regiment cared to try a bout
with him. Of course Peter knew as a fact that women
were lighter than men, but after bracing himself, much as
he would have done to try the cross-buttock with two
hundred pounds of bone and brawn, he marvelled much
at the ease with which he transferred the rider. "She
can't weigh over eighty pounds," he thought. Which
was foolish, for the woman actually weighed one hundred
and eighteen, as Peter afterwards learned.

The woman also surprised Peter in another way.
Scarcely had she been placed in front of him, than she
put her arms about his neck and buried her face in his
shoulder. She was not crying, but she was drawing her
breath in great gasps in a manner which scared Peter
terribly. Peter had never had a woman cling to him in
that way, and frightened as he was, he made three very
interesting discoveries:

1. That a man's shoulder seems planned by nature as
a resting place for a woman's head.

2. That a man's arm about a woman's waist is a very
pleasant position for the arm.

3. That a pair of woman's arms round a man's neck,
with the clasped hands, even if gloved, just resting on the
back of his neck, is very satisfying.

Peter could not see much of the woman. His arm told
him that she was decidedly slender, and he could just
catch sight of a small ear and a cheek, whose roundness
proved the youth of the person. Otherwise he could only
see a head of very pretty brown hair, the smooth dressing
of which could not entirely conceal its longing to curl.

When Mutineer stopped, Peter did not quite know what
to do. Of course it was his duty to hold the woman till
she recovered herself. That was a plain duty—and pleasant. Peter said to himself that he really was sorry for
her, and thought his sensations were merely the satisfaction of a father in aiding his daughter. We must forgive his foolishness, for Peter had never been a father,
and so did not know the parental feeling.

It had taken Mutineer twenty seconds to come to a
stand, and for ten seconds after, no change in the con-

dition occurred. Then suddenly the woman stopped her gasps. Peter, who was looking down at her, saw the pale cheeks redden. The next moment, the arms were taken from his neck and the woman was sitting up straight in front of him. He got a downward look at the face, and he thought it was the most charming he had ever seen.

The girl kept her eyes lowered, while she said firmly, though with traces of breathlessness and tremolo in her voice, "Please help me down."

Peter was out of his saddle in a moment, and lifted the girl down. She staggered slightly on reaching the ground, so that Peter said: "You had better lean on me."

"No," said the girl, still looking down, "I will lean against the horse." She rested against Mutineer, who looked around to see who was taking this insulting liberty with a Kentucky gentleman. Having looked at her he said: "You're quite welcome, you pretty dear!" Peter thought he would like to be a horse, but then it occurred to him that equines could not have had what he had just had, so he became reconciled to his lot.

The girl went on flushing, even after she was safely leaning against Mutineer. There was another ten seconds' pause, and then she said, still with downcast eyes, "I was so frightened, that I did not know what I was doing."

"You behaved very well," said Peter, in the most comforting voice he could command. "You held your horse splendidly."

"I wasn't a bit frightened, till the saddle began to turn." The girl still kept her eyes on the ground, and still blushed. She was undergoing almost the keenest mortification possible for a woman. She had for a moment been horrified by the thought that she had behaved in this way to a groom. But a stranger—a gentleman—was worse! She had not looked at Peter's face, but his irreproachable riding-rig had been noticed. "If it had only been a policeman," she thought. "What can I say to him?"

Peter saw the mortification without quite understanding it. He knew, however, it was his duty to ease it, and took the best way by giving her something else to think about.

"As soon as you feel able to walk, you had better take my arm. We can get a cab at the 72d Street entrance, probably. If you don't feel able to walk, sit down on that stone, and I'll bring a cab. It oughtn't to take me ten minutes."

"You are very good," said the girl, raising her eyes, and taking a look at Peter's face for the first time.

A thrill went through Peter.

The girl had slate-colored eyes!!

CHAPTER XXXVI

A DREAM

SOMETHING in Peter's face seemed to reassure the girl, for though she looked down after the glance, she ceased leaning against the horse, and said, "I behaved very foolishly, of course. Now I will do whatever you think best."

Before Peter had recovered enough from his thrill to put what he thought into speech, a policeman came riding towards them, leading the roan mare. "Any harm done?" he called.

"None, fortunately. Where can we get a cab? Or can you bring one here?"

"I'm afraid there'll be none nearer than Fifty-ninth Street. They leave the other entrances before it's as dark as this."

"Never mind the cab," said the girl. "If you'll help me to mount, I'll ride home."

"That's the pluck!" said the policeman.

"Do you think you had better?" asked Peter.

"Yes. I'm not a bit afraid. If you'll just tighten the girth."

It seemed to Peter he had never encountered such a marvellously fascinating combination as was indicated by the clinging position of a minute ago and the erect one of the present moment. He tightened the girth with a pull

that made the roan mare wonder if a steam-winch had
hold of the end, and then had the pleasure of the little
foot being placed in his hand for a moment, as he lifted
the girl into the saddle.

"I shall ride with you," he said, mounting instantly.

"Beg pardon," said the policeman. "I must take your
names. We are required to report all such things to headquarters."

"Why, Williams, don't you know me?" asked Peter.

Williams looked at Peter, now for the first time on a
level with him. "I beg your pardon, Mr. Stirling. It
was so dark, and you are so seldom here afternoons that
I didn't know you."

"Tell the chief that this needn't go on record, nor be
given to the reporters."

"Very well, Mr. Stirling."

"I beg your pardon," said the girl in a frank yet shy
way, "but will you tell me your first name?"

Peter was rather astonished, but he said "Peter."

"Oh!" cried the girl, looking Peter in the face. "I
understand it now. I didn't think I could behave so to a
stranger! I must have felt it was you." She was smiling
joyfully, and she did not drop her eyes from his. On the
contrary she held out her hand to him.

Of course Peter took it. He did not stop to ask if it
was right or wrong to hold a young girl's hand. If it was
wrong, it was certainly a very small one, judging from
the size of the hand.

"I was so mortified! But if it's you it's all right."

Peter thought this mood of the girl was both delightful
and complimentary, but he failed to understand anything
of it, except its general friendliness. His manner may
have suggested this, for suddenly the girl said:

"But of course, you do not know who I am? How
foolish of me! I am Leonore D'Alloi."

It was Peter's turn to gasp. "Not——?" he began
and then stopped.

"Yes," said the girl joyfully, as if Peter's "not" had
had something delightful in it.

"But—she's a child."

"I'll be eighteen next week," said Leonore, with all

the readiness of that number of years to proclaim its age.

Peter concluded that he must accept the fact. Watts could have a child that old. Having reached this conclusion, he said, "I ought to have known you by your likeness to your mother." Which was an unintentional lie. Her mother's eyes she had, as well as the long lashes; and she had her mother's pretty figure, though she was taller. But otherwise she was far more like Watts. Her curly hair, her curvy mouth, the dimple, and the contour of the face were his. Leonore D'Alloi was a far greater beauty than her mother had ever been. But to Peter, it was merely a renewal of his dream.

Just at this point the groom rode up. "Beg pardon, Miss D'Alloi," he said, touching his cap. "My 'orse went down on a bit of hice."

"You are not hurt, Belden?" said Miss D'Alloi.

Peter thought the anxious tone heavenly. He rather wished he had broken something himself.

"No. Nor the 'orse."

"Then it's all right. Mr. Stirling, we need not interrupt your ride. Belden will see me home."

Belden see her home! Peter would see him do it! That was what Peter thought. He said, "I shall ride with you, of course." So they started their horses, the groom dropping behind.

"Do you want to try it again?" asked Mutineer of the roan.

"No," said the mare. "You are too big and strong."

Leonore was just saying: "I could hear the pound of a horse's feet behind me, but I thought it was the groom, and knew he could never overtake Fly-away. So when I felt the saddle begin to slip, I thought I was—was going to be dragged—as I once saw a woman in England—Oh!—and then suddenly I saw a horse's head, and then I felt some one take hold of me so firmly that I didn't have to hold myself at all, and I knew I was safe. Oh, how nice it is to be big and strong!"

Peter thought so too.

So it is the world over. Peter and Mutineer felt happy and proud in their strength, and Leonore and Fly-away glorified them for it. Yet in spite of this, as Peter looked down at the curly head, from his own and Mutineer's altitude, he felt no superiority, and knew that the slightest wish expressed by that small mouth, would be as strong with him as if a European army obeyed its commands.

"What a tremendous horse you have!" said Leonore.

"Isn't he," assented Peter. "He's got a bad temper, I'm sorry to say, but I'm very fond of him. He was given me by my regiment, and was the choice of a very dear friend now dead."

"Who was that?"

"No one you know. A Mr. Costell."

"Oh, yes I do. I've heard all about him."

"What do you know of Mr. Costell?"

"What Miss De Voe told me."

"Miss De Voe?"

"Yes. We saw her both times in Europe. Once at Nice, and once in—in 1882—at Maggiore. The first time, I was only six, but she used to tell me stories about you and the little children in the angle. The last time she told me all she could remember about you. We used to drift about the lake moonlight nights, and talk about you."

"What made that worth doing to you?"

"Oh, from the very beginning, that I can remember, papa was always talking about 'dear old Peter' "—the talker said the last three words in such a tone, and shot such a look up at Peter, half laughing and half timid, that in combination they nearly made Peter reel in his saddle—"and you seemed almost the only one of his friends he did speak of, so I became very curious about you as a little girl, and then Miss De Voe made me more interested, so that I began questioning Americans, because I was really anxious to learn things concerning you. Nearly every one did know something, so I found out a great deal about you."

Peter was realizing for the first time in his life, how champagne made one feel.

"Tell me whom you found who knew anything about me?"

"Oh, nearly everybody knew something. That is,

every one we've met in the last five years. Before that, there was Miss De Voe, and grandpapa, of course, when he came over in 1879——"

"But," interrupted Peter, "I don't think I had met him once before that time, except at the Shrubberies."

"No, he hadn't seen you. But he knew a lot about you, from Mr. Lapham and Mr. Avery, and some other men who had met you."

"Who else?"

"Miss Leroy, mamma's bridesmaid, who spent two weeks at our villa near Florence, and Dr. Purple, your clergyman, who was in the same house with us at Oberammergau, and—and—oh the best were Mr. and Mrs. Rivington. They were in Jersey, having their honeymoon. They told me more than all the rest put together."

"I feel quite safe in their hands. Dorothy and I formed a mutual admiration society a good many years ago."

"She and Mr. Rivington couldn't say enough good of you."

"You must make allowance for the fact that they were on their wedding journey, and probably saw everything rose-colored."

"That was it. Dorothy told me about your giving Mr. Rivington a full partnership, in order that Mr. Ogden should give his consent."

Peter laughed.

"Ray swore that he wouldn't tell. And Dorothy has always appeared ignorant. And yet she knew it on her wedding trip."

"She couldn't help it. She said she must tell some one, she was so happy. So she told mamma and me. She showed us your photograph. Papa and mamma said it was like you, but I don't think it is."

Again Leonore looked up at him. Leonore, when she glanced at a man, had the same frank, fearless gaze that her mother had of yore. But she did not look as often nor as long, and did not seem so wrapped up in the man's remarks when she looked. We are afraid even at seventeen that Leonore had discovered that she had very fetching eyes, and did not intend to cheapen them, by showing them too much. During the whole of this dialogue, Peter

had had only "come-and-go" glimpses of those eyes. He
wanted to see more of them. He longed to lean over and
turn the face up and really look down into them. Still,
he could see the curly hair, and the little ear, and the
round of the cheek, and the long lashes. For the moment
Peter did not agree with Mr. Weller that "life isn't all
beer and skittles."

"I've been so anxious to meet you. I've begged papa
ever since we landed to take me to see you. And he's
promised me, over and over again, to do it, but something
always interfered. You see, I felt very strange and—and
queer, not knowing people of my own country, and I felt
that I really knew you, and wouldn't have to begin new
as I do with other people. I do so dread next winter
when I'm to go into society. I don't know what I shall
do. I'll not know any one."

"You'll know me."

"But you don't go into society."

"Oh, yes, I do. Sometimes, that is. I shall probably
go more next winter. I've shut myself up too much."
This was a discovery of Peter's made in the last ten
seconds.

"How nice that will be! And will you promise to
give me a great deal of attention?"

"You'll probably want very little. I don't dance."
Peter suddenly became conscious that Mr. Weller was
right.

"But you can learn. Please. I do so love valsing."

Peter almost reeled again at the thought of waltzing
with Leonore. Was it possible life had such richness in
it? Then he said with a bitter note in his voice very unusual to him:

"I'm afraid I'm too old to learn."

"Not a bit," said Leonore. "You don't look any
older than lots of men I've seen valsing. Young men I
mean. And I've seen men seventy years old dancing in
Europe."

Whether Peter could have kept his seat much longer is
to be questioned. But fortunately for him, the horses
here came to a stop in front of a stable.

"Why," said Leonore, "here we are already! What a short ride it has been."

Peter thought so too, and groaned over the end of it. But then he suddenly remembered that Leonore was to be lifted from her horse. He became cold with the thought that she might jump before he could get to her, and he was off his horse, and by her side with the quickness of a military training. He put his hands up, and for a moment had—well, Peter could usually express himself but he could not put that moment into words. And it was not merely that Leonore had been in his arms for a moment, but that he had got a good look up into her eyes.

"I wish you would take my horse round to the Riding Club," he told the groom. "I wish to see Miss D'Alloi home."

"Thank you very much, but my maid is here in the brougham, so I need not trouble you. Good-bye, and thank you. Oh, thank you so much!" She stood very close to Peter, and looked up into his eyes with her own. "There's no one I would rather have had save me."

She stepped into the brougham, and Peter closed the door. He mounted his horse again, and straightening himself up, rode away.

"Hi thought," remarked the groom to the stableman, "that 'e didn't know 'ow to sit 'is 'orse, but 'e's all right, arter all. 'E rides like ha 'orse guards capting, w'en 'e don't 'ave a girl to bother 'im."

Would that girl bother him?

CHAPTER XXXVII

"FRIENDS"

At first blush, judging from Peter's behavior, the girl was not going to bother him. Peter left his horse at the stable, and taking a hansom, went to his club. There he spent a calm half hour over the evening papers. His dinner was eaten with equal coolness. Not till he had reached his study did he vary his ordinary daily routine. Then, instead of working or reading, he rolled a comfortable chair up to the fire, put on a fresh log or two, opened a new box of Bock's, and lighting one, settled back in the chair. How many hours he sat and how many cigars he smoked are not recorded, lest the statement should make people skeptical of the narrative.

Of course Peter knew that life had not lost its troubles. He was not fooling himself as to what lay before him. He was not callous to the sufferings already endured. But he put them, past, and to come, from him for one evening, and sat smoking lazily with a dreamy look on his face. He had lately been studying the subject of Asiatic cholera, but he did not seem to be thinking of that. He had just been through what he called a "revolting experience," but it is doubtful if he was thinking of that. Whatever his thoughts were, they put a very different look on his face than that which it used to wear while he studied blank walls.

When Peter sat down, rather later than usual at his office desk the next morning, he took a sheet of paper, and wrote, "Dear sir," upon it. Then he tore it up. He took another and wrote, "My dear Mr. D'Alloi." He tore that up. Another he began, "Dear Watts." A moment later it was in the paper basket. "My dear friend," served to bring a similar fate to the fourth. Then Peter rose and strolled about his office aimlessly. Finally he went out into a gallery running along the various rooms, and, opening a door, put his head in.

"You hypocritical scoundrel," he said. "You swore to me that you would never tell a living soul."

"Well?" came a very guilty voice back.

"And Dorothy's known all this time."

Dead silence.

"And you've both been as innocent as—as you were guilty."

"Look here, Peter, I can't make you understand, because you've—you've never been on a honeymoon. Really, old fellow, I was so happy over your generosity in giving me a full share, when I didn't bring a tenth of the business, and so happy over Dorothy, that if I hadn't told her, I should have simply—bust. She swore she'd never tell. And now she's told you!"

"No, but she told some one else."

"Never!"

"Yes."

"Then she's broken her word. She——"

"The Pot called the Kettle black."

"But to tell one's own wife is different. I thought she could keep a secret."

"How can you expect a person to keep a secret when you can't keep it yourself?" Peter and Ray were both laughing.

Ray said to himself, "Peter has some awfully knotty point on hand, and is resting the brain tissue for a moment." Ray had noticed, when Peter interrupted him during office hours, on matters not relating to business, that he had a big or complex question in hand.

Peter closed the door and went back to his room. Then he took a fifth sheet of paper, and wrote:

WATTS: A day's thought has brought a change of feeling on my part. Neither can be the better for alienation or unkind thoughts. I regret already my attitude of yesterday. Let us cancel all that has happened since our college days, and put it aside as if it had never occurred.

PETER.

Just as he had finished this, his door opened softly. Peter did not hear it, but took the letter up and read it slowly.

"Boo!"

Peter did not jump at the Boo. He looked up very calmly, but the moment he looked up, jump he did. He jumped so that he was shaking hands before the impetus was lost.

"This is the nicest kind of a surprise," he said.

"Bother you, you phlegmatic old cow," cried a merry voice. "Here we have spent ten minutes palavering your boy, in order to make him let us surprise you, and then when we spring it on you, you don't budge. Wasn't it shabby treatment, Dot?"

"You've disappointed us awfully, Mr. Stirling."

Peter was shaking hands more deliberately with Leonore than he had with Watts. He had been rather clever in shaking hands with him first, so that he need not hurry himself over the second. So he had a very nice moment —all too short—while Leonore's hand lay in his. He said, in order to prolong the moment, without making it too marked, "It will take something more frightful than you, Miss D'Alloi, to make me jump." Then Peter was sorry he had said it, for Leonore dropped her eyes.

"Now, old man, give an account of yourself." Watts was speaking jauntily, but not quite as easily as he usually did. "Here Leonore and I waited all last evening, and you never came. So she insisted that we come this morning."

"I don't understand?" Peter was looking at Leonore as if she had made the remark. Leonore was calmly examining Peter's room.

"Why, even a stranger would have called last night to inquire about Dot's health, after such an accident. But for you not to do it, was criminal. If you have aught to say why sentence should not now be passed on you, speak now or forever—no—that's the wedding ceremony, isn't it? Not criminal sentence—though, on second thought, there's not much difference."

"Did you expect me, Miss D'Alloi?"

Miss D'Alloi was looking at a shelf of law books with her back to Peter, and was pretending great interest in them. She did not turn, but said "Yes."

"I wish I had known that," said Peter, with the sincerest regret in his voice.

Miss D'Alloi's interest in legal literature suddenly ceased. She turned and Peter had a momentary glimpse of those wonderful eyes. Either his words or tone had evidently pleased Miss D'Alloi. The corners of her mouth were curving upwards. She made a deep courtesy to him and said: "You will be glad to know, Mr. Stirling, that Miss D'Alloi has suffered no serious shock from her runaway, and passed a good night. It seemed to Miss D'Alloi that the least return she could make for Mr. Stirling's kindness, was to save him the trouble of coming to inquire about Miss D'Alloi's health, and so leave Mr. Stirling more time to his grimy old law books."

"There, sir, I hope you are properly crushed for your wrong-doing," cried Watts.

"I'm not going to apologize for not coming," said Peter, "for that is my loss; but I can say that I'm sorry."

"That's quite enough," said Leonore. "I thought perhaps you didn't want to be friends. And as I like to have such things right out, I made papa bring me down this morning so that I could see for myself." She spoke with a frankness that seemed to Peter heavenly, even while he grew cold at the thought that she should for a moment question his desire to be friends.

"Of course you and Peter will be friends," said Watts.

"But mamma told me last night—after we went upstairs, that she was sure Mr. Stirling would never call."

"Never, Dot?" cried Watts.

"Yes. And when I asked her why, she wouldn't tell me at first, but at last she said it was because he was so unsociable. I shan't be friends with any one who won't come to see me." Leonore was apparently looking at the floor, but from under her lashes she was looking at something else.

Whatever Peter may have felt, he looked perfectly cool. Too cool, Leonore thought. "I'm not going to make any vows or protestations of friendship," he said. "I won't even pledge myself to come and see you, Miss D'Alloi. Remember, friendship comes from the word free. If we are to be friends, we must each leave the other to act freely."

"Well," said Leonore, "that is, I suppose, a polite way of saying that you don't intend to come. Now I want to know why you won't?"

"The reasons will take too long to explain to you now, so I'll defer the telling till the first time I call on you." Peter was smiling down at her.

Miss D'Alloi looked up at Peter, to see what meaning his face gave his last remark. Then she held out her two hands. "Of course we are to be the best of friends," she said. Peter got a really good look down into those eyes as they shook hands.

The moment this matter had been settled, Leonore's manner changed. "So this is the office of the great Peter Stirling?" she said, with the nicest tone of interest in her voice, as it seemed to Peter.

"It doesn't look it," said Watts. "By George, with the business people say your firm does, you ought to do better than this. It's worse even than our old Harvard quarters, and those were puritanical enough."

"There is a method in its plainness. If you want style, go into Ogden's and Rivington's rooms."

"Why do you have the plain office, Mr. Stirling?"

"I have a lot of plain people to deal with, and so I try to keep my room simple, to put them at their ease. I've never heard of my losing a client yet because my room is as it is, while I should have frightened away some if I had gone in for the same magnificence as my partners."

"But I say, chum, I should think that is the sort you would want to frighten away. There can't be any money in their business?"

"We weren't talking of money. We were talking of people. I am very glad to say, that with my success, there has been no change in my relations with my ward. They all come to me here, and feel perfectly at home, whether they come as clients, as co-workers, or merely as friends."

"Ho, ho," laughed Watts. "You wily old fox! See the four bare walls. The one shelf of law books. The one cheap cabinet of drawers. The four simple chairs, and the plain desk. Behold the great politician! The man of the people."

Peter made no reply. But Leonore said to him, "I'm glad you help the poor people still, Mr. Stirling," and gave Peter another glimpse of those eyes. Peter didn't mind after that.

"Look here, Dot," said Watts. "You mustn't call chum Mr. Stirling. That won't do. Call him—um—call him Uncle Peter."

"I won't," said Leonore, delighting Peter thereby. "Let me see. What shall I call you?" she asked of Peter.

"Honey," laughed Watts.

"What shall I call you?" Miss D'Alloi put her head on

one side, and looked at Peter out of the corners of her eyes.

"You must decide that, Miss D'Alloi."

"I suppose I must. I—think—I—shall—call—you—Peter." She spoke hesitatingly till she said his name, but that went very smoothly. Peter on the spot fell in love with the five letters as she pronounced them.

"Plain Peter?" inquired Watts.

"Now what will you call me?"

"Miss D'Alloi," said Peter.

"No. You—are—to—call—me—call—me——"

"Miss D'Alloi," re-affirmed Peter.

"Then I will call you Mr. Stirling, Peter."

"No, you won't."

"Why?"

"Because you said you'd call me Peter."

"But not if you won't——"

"You made no condition at the time of promise. Shall I show you the law?"

"No. And I shall not call you Peter, any more, Peter."

"Then I shall prosecute you."

"But I should win the case, for I should hire a friend of mine to defend me. A man named Peter." Leonore sat down in Peter's chair. "I'm going to write him at once about it." She took one of his printed letter sheets and his pen, and, putting the tip of the holder to her lips (Peter has that pen still), thought for a moment. Then she wrote:

DEAR PETER:
I am threatened with a prosecution. Will you defend me? Address your reply to "Dear Leonore."

LEONORE D'ALLOI.

"Now," she said to Peter, "you must write me a letter in reply. Then you can have this note." Leonore rose with the missive in her hand.

"I never answer letters till I've received them." Peter took hold of the slender wrist, and possessed himself of the paper. Then he sat down at his desk and wrote on another sheet:

Dear Miss D'Alloi:
I will defend you faithfully and always.

PETER STIRLING.

"That isn't what I said," remarked Miss D'Alloi. "But I suppose it will have to do."

"You forgot one important thing."

"What is that?"

"My retaining fee."

"Oh, dear," sighed Leonore. "My allowance is nearly gone. Don't you ever do work for very, very poor people, for nothing?"

"Not if their poverty is pretence."

"Oh, but mine isn't. Really. See. Here is my purse. Look for yourself. That's all I shall have till the first of the month."

She gave Peter her purse. He was still sitting at his desk, and he very deliberately proceeded to empty the contents out on his blotter. He handled each article. There was a crisp ten-dollar bill, evidently the last of those given by the bank at the beginning of the month. There were two one-dollar bills. There was a fifty-cent piece, two quarters and a dime. A gold German twenty-mark piece, about eight inches of narrow crimson ribbon, and a glove button, completed the contents. Peter returned the American money and the glove button to the purse and handed it back to Miss D'Alloi.

"You've forgotten the ribbon and the gold piece," said Leonore.

"You were never more mistaken in your life," replied Peter, with anything but legal guardedness concerning unprovable statements. He folded up the ribbon neatly and put it, with the coin, in his waistcoat pocket.

"Oh," said Leonore, "I can't let you have that. That's my luck-piece."

"Is it?" Peter expressed much surprise blended with satisfaction in his tone.

"Yes. You don't want to take my good luck."

"I will think it over, and write you a legal opinion later."

"Please!" Miss D'Alloi pleaded.

"That is just what I have succeeded in doing—for myself."

"But I want my luck-piece. I found it in a crack of the rocks crossing the Ghemi. And I must have the ribbon. I need it to match for a gown it goes with." Miss D'Alloi put true anxiety into her voice, whatever she really felt.

"I shall be glad to help you match it," said Peter, "and any time you send me word, I will go shopping with you. As for your luck, I shall keep that for the present."

"Now I know," said Leonore crossly, "why lawyers have such a bad reputation. They are perfect thieves!" She looked at Peter with the corners of her mouth drawn down. He gazed at her with a very grave look on his face. They eyed each other steadily for a moment, and then the corners of Leonore's mouth suddenly curled upwards. She tried hard for a moment to keep serious. Then she gave up and laughed. Then they both laughed.

Many people will only see an amusing side to the dialogue here so carefully recorded. If so, look back to the time when everything that he or she said was worth listening to. Or if there has never been a he or a she, imitate Peter, and wait. It is worth waiting for.

CHAPTER XXXVIII

THE HERMITAGE

IT is not to be supposed from this last reflection of ours, that Leonore was not heart-whole. Leonore had merely had a few true friends, owing to her roving life, and at seventeen a girl craves friends. When, therefore, the return to America was determined upon, she had at once decided that Peter and she would be the closest of friends. That she would tell him all her confidences, and take all her troubles to him. Miss De Voe and Dorothy had told her about Peter, and from their descriptions, as well as from her father's reminiscences, Leonore had concluded that Peter was just the friend she had wanted for so long. That Leonore held her eyes down, and tried to

charm yet tantalize her intended friend, was because
Leonore could not help it, being only seventeen and a
girl. If Leonore had felt anything but a friendly interest
and liking, blended with much curiosity, in Peter, she
never would have gone to see him in his office, and would
never have talked and laughed so frankly with him.

As for Peter, he did not put his feelings into good
docketed shape. He did not attempt to label them at all.
He had had a delicious half-hour yesterday. He had
decided, the evening before, that he must see those slate-
colored eyes again, if he had to go round the world in
pursuit of them. How he should do it, he had not even
thought out, till the next morning. He had understood
very clearly that the owner of those slate-colored eyes
was really an unknown quantity to him. He had understood, too, that the chances were very much against his
caring to pursue those eyes after he knew them better.
But he was adamant that he must see those eyes again,
and prove for himself whether they were but an *ignis
fatuus,* or the radiant stars that Providence had cast for
the horoscope of Peter Stirling. He was studying those
eyes, with their concomitants, at the present time. He
was studying them very coolly, to judge from his appearance and conduct. Yet he was enjoying the study in a
way that he had never enjoyed the study of somebody
"On Torts." Somebody "On Torts," never looked like
that. Somebody "On Torts," never had luck-pieces, and
silk ribbons. Somebody "On Torts," never wrote letters
and touched the end of pens to its lips. Somebody "On
Torts," never courtesied, nor looked out from under its
eyelashes, nor called him Peter.

While this investigation had been progressing, Watts
had looked at the shelf of law books, had looked out of
the window, had whistled, and had yawned. Finally, in
sheer *ennui* he had thrown open a door, and looked to
see what lay behind.

"Ha, ha!" he cried. "All is discovered. See! Here
sits Peter Stirling, the ward politician, enthroned in Jef-
fersonian simplicity. But here, behind the arras, sits
Peter Stirling, the counsellor of banks and railroads, in

the midst of all the gorgeousness of the golden East."
Watts passed into the room beyond.

"What does he mean, Peter?"

"He has gone into my study. Would you like——"
He was interrupted by Watts calling, "Come in here,
Dot, and see how the unsociable old hermit bestows him-
self."

So Leonore and Peter followed Watts's lead. The room
into which they went was rather a curious one. It was at
least twenty-five feet square, having four windows, two
looking out on Broadway, and two on the side street. It
had one other door besides that by which they had entered. Here the ordinary quality ended. Except for the
six openings already noted and a large fireplace, the
walls were shelved from floor to ceiling (which was not
a low one), with dusky oak shelving. The ceiling was
panelled in dark oak, and the floor was covered with a
smooth surface of the same wood. Yet though the
shelves were filled with books, few could be seen, for on
every upright of the shelving, were several frames of oak,
hinged as one sees them in public galleries occasionally,
and these frames contained etchings, engravings, and
paintings. Some were folded back against the shelves.
Others stood out at right angles to them, and showed that
the frames were double ones, both sides containing something. Four easy-chairs, three less easy chairs, and a
large table desk, likewise of dusky oak, were the sole other
fittings of the room, if we except two large polar bear
skins.

"Oh," cried Leonore, looking about, "I'm so glad to
see this. People have told me so much about your rooms.
And no two of them ever agreed."

"No," said Peter. "It seems a continual bone of
contention with my friends. They scold me because I
shelved it to the ceiling, because I put it in one-colored
wood, because I framed my pictures and engravings this
way, and because I haven't gone in for rugs, and bric-à-
brac, and the usual furnishings. At times I have really
wondered, from their determination to change things,
whether it was for them to live in, or for my use?"

"It is unusual," said Leonore, reluctantly, and evidently selecting a word that should not offend Peter.

"You ought to be hung for treating fine pictures so," said Watts.

"I had to give them those broad flat mats, because the books gave no background."

"It's—it's—" Leonore hesitated. "It's not so startling, after a moment."

"You see they had to hang this way, or go unhung. I hadn't wall space for both pictures and books. And by giving a few frames a turn, occasionally, I can always have fresh pictures to look at."

"Look here, Dot, here's a genuine Rembrandt's 'Three Crosses,'" called Watts. "I didn't know, old man, that you were such a connoisseur."

"I'm not," said Peter. "I'm fond of such things, but I never should have had taste or time to gather these."

"Then how did you get them?"

"A friend of mine—a man of exquisite taste—gathered them. He lost his money, and I bought them of him."

"That was Mr. Le Grand?" asked Leonore, ceasing her study of the "Three Crosses."

"Yes."

"Mrs. Rivington told me about it."

"It must have been devilish hard for him to part with such a collection," said Watts.

"He hasn't really parted with them. He comes down here constantly, and has a good time over them. It was partly his scheme to arrange them this way."

"And are the paintings his, too, Peter?"

Peter could have hugged her for the way she said Peter. "No," he managed to remark. "I bought some of them, and Miss De Voe and Lispenard Ogden the others. People tell me I spoil them by the flat framing, and the plain, broad gold mats. But it doesn't spoil them to me. I think the mixture of gold mats and white mats breaks the monotony. And the variation just neutralizes the monotone which the rest of the room has. But of course that is my personal equation."

"Then this room is the real taste of the 'plain man,' eh?" inquired Watts.

"Really, papa, it is plain. Just as simple as can be."

"Simple! Yes, sweet simplicity! Three-thousand-dollar-etching simplicity! Millet simplicity! Oh, yes, Peter's a simple old dog."

"No, but the woodwork and the furniture. Isn't this an enticing chair? I must try it." And Leonore almost dissolved from view in its depths. Peter has that chair still. He would probably knock the man down who offered to buy it.

It occurred to Peter that since Leonore was so extremely near the ground, and was leaning back so far, that she could hardly help but be looking up. So he went and stood in front of the fireplace, and looked down at her. He pretended that his hands were cold. Watts perhaps was right. Peter was not as simple as people thought.

It seemed to Peter that he had never had so much to see, all at once, in his life. There were the occasional glimpses of the eyes (for Leonore, in spite of her position, did manage to cover the larger part of them) not one of which must be missed. Then there was her mouth. That would have been very restful to the eye; if it hadn't been for the distracting chin below it. Then there were the little feet, just sticking out from underneath the tailor-made gown, making Peter think of Herrick's famous lines. Finally there were those two hands! Leonore was very deliberately taking off her gloves. Peter had not seen those hands ungloved yet, and waited almost breathlessly for the unveiling. He decided that he must watch and shake hands at parting before Leonore put those gloves on again.

"I say," said Watts, "how did you ever manage to get such a place here?"

"I was a tenant for a good many years of the insurance company that owns the building, and when it came to rebuild, it had the architect fit this floor for me just as I wished it. So I put our law-offices in front and arranged my other rooms along the side street. Would you like to see them?" Peter asked this last question very obviously of Leonore.

"Very much."

So they passed through the other door, to a little square

hall, lighted by a skylight, with a stairway going up to the roof.

"I took the upper floor, so as to get good air and the view of the city and the bay, which is very fine," Peter said. "And I have a staircase to the roof, so that in good weather I can go up there."

"I wondered what the great firm was doing up ten stories," said Watts.

"Ogden and Rivington have been very good in yielding to my idiosyncrasies. This is my mealing closet."

It was a room nine feet square, panelled, ceiled and floored in mahogany, and the table and six chairs were made of the same material.

"So this is what the papers call the 'Stirling political incubator?' It doesn't look like a place for hatching dark plots," said Watts.

"Sometimes I have a little dinner here. Never more than six, however, for it's too small."

"I say, Dot, doesn't this have a jolly cosy feeling? Couldn't one sit here blowy nights, with the candles lit, eating nuts and telling stories? It makes me think of the expression, 'snug as a bug.'"

"Miss Leroy told me, Peter, what a reputation your dinners had, and how every one was anxious to be invited just once," said Leonore.

"But not a second time, old man. You caught Dot's inference, I hope? Once is quite enough."

"Peter, will you invite me some day?"

Would he! Peter longed to tell her that the place and everything it contained, including its owner— Then Peter said to himself, "You really don't know anything about her. Stop your foolishness." Still Peter knew that —that foolishness was nice. He said, "People only care for my dinners because they are few and far between, and their being way down here in the city, after business hours, makes them something to talk about. Society wants badly something to talk about most of the time. Of course, my friends are invited." Peter looked down at Leonore, and she understood, without his saying so, that she was to be a future guest.

"How do you manage about the prog, chum?"

"Mr. Le Grand had a man—a Maryland darky—whom
he turned over to me. He looks after me generally, but
his true forte is cooking. For oysters and fish and game
I can't find his equal. And, as I never attempt very elaborate dinners, he cooks and serves for a party of six in
very good shape. We are not much in haste down here
after six, because it's so still and quiet. The hurry's gone
up-town to the social slaves. Suppose you stay and try
his skill at lunch to-day? My partners generally are with
me, and Jenifer always has something good for them."

"By all means," said Watts.

But Leonore said: "No. We mustn't make a nuisance
of ourselves the first time we come." Peter and Watts
tried to persuade her, but she was not persuadable. Leonore had no intention, no matter how good a time it
meant, of lunching solo with four men.

"I think we must be going," she said.

"You mustn't go without seeing the rest of my quarters," said Peter, hoping to prolong the visit.

Leonore was complaisant to that extent. So they went
into the pantry, and Leonore proceeded, apparently, to
show her absolute ignorance of food matters under the
pretext that she was displaying great housekeeping knowledge. She told Peter that he ought to keep his champagne on ice. "That champagne will spoil if it isn't
kept on ice." She complained because some bottles of
Burgundy had dust on them. "That's not merely untidy," she said, "but it's bad for the wine. It ought to
be stood on end, so that the sediment can settle." She
criticised the fact that a brace of canvasbacks were on
ice. "All your game should be hung," she said. She
put her finger or her eyes into every drawer and cup-
board, and found nothing to praise. She was absolutely
grave over it, but before long Peter saw the joke and entered into it. It was wonderful how good some of the
things that she touched tasted later.

Then they went into Peter's sleeping-room. Leonore
said it was very ordinary, but promptly found two things
to interest her.

"Do you take care of your window flowers?"

"No. Mrs. Costell comes down to lunch with me once

a week, and potters with them. She keeps all the windows full of flowers—perhaps you have noticed them in the other rooms, as well?"

"Yes. I liked them, but I didn't think they could be yours. They grow too well for a man."

"It seems as if Mrs. Costell had only to look at a plant, and it breaks out blossoming," Peter replied.

"What a nice speech," said Leonore.

"It's on a nice subject," Peter told her. "When you have that, it's very easy to make a nice speech."

"I want to meet Mrs. Costell. I've heard all about her."

The second point of interest concerned the contents of what had evidently been planned as an umbrella-stand.

"Why do you have three swords?" she asked, taking the handsomest from its resting place.

"So that I can kill more people."

"Why, Dot, you ought to know that an officer wants a service sword and a dress-sword."

"But these are all dress-swords. I'm afraid you are very proud of your majorship."

Peter only smiled a reply down at her.

"Yes," said Leonore, "I have found out your weakness at last. You like gold lace and fixings."

Still Peter only smiled.

"This sword is presented to Captain Peter Stirling in recognition of his gallant conduct at Hornellsville, July 25, 1877," Leonore read on the scabbard. "What did you do at Hornellsville?"

"Various things."

"But what did you do to get the sword?"

"My duty!"

"Tell me?"

"I thought you knew all about me."

"I don't know this."

Peter only smiled at her.

"Tell me. If you don't, somebody else will. Please."

"Why, Dot, these are all presentation swords."

"Yes," said Peter; "and so gorgeous that I don't dare use them. I keep the swords I wear at the armory."

"Are you going to tell me what you did to get them?"

"That one was given me by my company when I was

made captain. That was subscribed for by some friends. The one you have was given me by a railroad."

"For what?"

"For doing my duty."

"Come, papa. We'll go home."

Peter surrendered. "There were some substitutes for strikers in freight cars that were fitted up with bunks. The strikers fastened the doors on them, and pushed them into a car-shed."

"And what did you do?"

"We rolled the cars back."

"I don't think that was much. Nothing to give a sword for. Now, have you anything more to show us?"

"No. I have a spare room, and Jenifer has a kitchen and sleeping place beyond, but they are not worth showing."

They went out into the little square hall, and so into the study. Leonore began unfolding her gloves.

"I've had a very nice time," she said. "I think I shall come again very often. I like down-town New York." Leonore was making her first trip to it, so that she spoke from vast knowledge.

"I can't tell you how pleasant it has been to me. It isn't often that such sunshine gets in here," said Peter.

"Then you do prefer sunshine to grimy old law books?" inquired Leonore, smiling demurely.

"Some sunshine," said Peter, meaningly.

"Wherever there has been sunshine there ought to be lots of flowers. I have a good mind—yes, I will—leave you these violets." Leonore took a little bunch that she had worn near her throat and put them and her hand in Peter's. And she hadn't put her glove on yet! Then she put her gloves on, and Peter shook hands. Then he remembered that he ought to see them to the elevator, so he took them out—and shook hands again. After that he concluded it was his duty to see them to the carriage— and he shook hands again.

Peter was not an experienced hand, but he was doing very well.

CHAPTER XXXIX

THE DUDE

JUST as Peter came back to his office, his lunch was announced.

"What makes you look so happy?" asked Ray.

"Being so," said Peter, calmly.

"What a funny old chap he is," Ray remarked to Ogden, as they went back to work. "He brought me his opinion, just after lunch, in the Hall-Seelye case. I suppose he had been grubbing all the morning over those awful figures, and a tougher or dryer job, you couldn't make. Yet he came in to lunch looking as if he was walking on air."

When Peter returned to his office, he would have preferred to stop work and think for a bit. He wanted to hold those violets, and smell them now and then. He wished to read that letter over again. He longed to have a look at that bit of ribbon and gold. But he resisted temptation. He said: "Peter Stirling, go to work." So all the treasures were put in a drawer of his study table, and Peter sat down at his office desk. First, after tearing up his note to Watts, he wrote another, as follows:

WATTS:
   You can understand why I did not call last night, or bind myself as to the future. I shall hope to receive an invitation to call from Mrs. D'Alloi. How, I must leave to you; but you owe me this much, and it is the only payment I ask of you. Otherwise let us bury all that has occurred since our college days, forever.
                                                PETER.

Then he ground at the law till six, when he swung his clubs and dumb-bells for ten minutes; took a shower; dressed himself, and dined. Then he went into his study, and opened a drawer. Did he find therein a box of cigars, or a bunch of violets, gold-piece, ribbon and sheet of paper? One thing is certain. Peter passed another evening without reading or working. And two such idle evenings could not be shown in another week of his life for the last twenty years.

The next day Peter was considerably nearer earth. Not that he didn't think those eyes just as lovely, and had he been thrown within their radius, he would probably have been as strongly influenced as ever. But he was not thrown within their influence, and so his strong nature and common sense reasserted themselves. He took his coffee, his early morning ride, and then his work, in their due order. After dinner, that evening, he only smoked one cigar. When he had done that, he remarked to himself—apropos of the cigars, presumably—"Peter, keep to your work. Don't burn yourself again." Then his face grew very firm, and he read a frivolous book entitled: "Neun atiologische und prophylactische Satze . . . uber die Choleræpidemien in Ostindien," till nearly one o'clock.

The following day was Sunday. Peter went to church, and in the afternoon rode out to Westchester to pass the evening there with Mrs. Costell. Peter thought his balance was quite recovered. Other men have said the same thing. The fact that they said so, proved that they were by no means sure of themselves.

This was shown very markedly on Monday in Peter's case, for after lunch he did not work as steadily as he had done in the morning hours. He was restless. Twice he pressed his lips, and started into work very, very hard —and did it for a time. Then the restlessness would come on again. Presently he took to looking at his watch. Then he would snap it to, and go to work again, with a great determination in his face, only to look at the watch again before long. Finally he touched his bell.

"Jenifer," he said, "I wish you would rub off my spurs, and clean up my riding trousers."

"For lohd, sar, I done dat dis day yesserday."

"Never mind, then," said Peter. "Tell Curzon to ring me up a hansom."

When Peter rode into the park he did not vacillate. He put his horse at a sharp canter, and started round the path. But he had not ridden far when he suddenly checked his horse, and reined him up with a couple of riders. "I've been looking for you," he said frankly. Peter had not ceased to be straightforward.

"Hello! This is nice," said Watts

"Don't you think it's about time?" said Leonore. Leonore had her own opinion of what friendship consisted. She was not angry with Peter—not at all. But she did not look at him.

Peter had drawn his horse up to the side on which Leonore was riding. "That is just what I thought," he said deliberately, "and that's why I'm here now."

"How long ago did that occur to you, please?" said Leonore, with dignity.

"About the time it occurred to me that you might ride here regularly afternoons."

"Don't you?" Leonore was mollifying.

"No. I like the early morning, when there are fewer people."

"You unsociable old hermit," exclaimed Watts.

"But now?" asked Leonore.

When Leonore said those two words Peter had not yet had a sight of those eyes. And he was getting desperately anxious to see them. So he replied: "Now I shall ride in the afternoons."

He was rewarded by a look. The sweetest kind of a look. "Now, that is very nice, Peter," said Leonore. "If we see each other every day in the Park, we can tell each other everything that we are doing or thinking about. So we will be very good friends for sure." Leonore spoke and looked as if this was the pleasantest of possibilities, and Peter was certain it was.

"I say, Peter," said Watts. "What a tremendous dude we have come out. I wanted to joke you on it the first time I saw you, but this afternoon it's positively appalling. I would have taken my Bible oath that it was the last thing old Peter would become. Just look at him, Dot. Doesn't he fill you with 'wonder, awe and praise?'"

Leonore looked at Peter a little shyly, but she said frankly:

"I've wondered about that, Peter. People told me you were a man absolutely without style."

Peter smiled. "Do you remember what Friar Bacon's brass head said?"

"Time is: Time was: Time will never be again?" asked Leonore.

"That fits my lack of style, I think."

"Pell and Ogden, and the rest of them, have made you what I never could, dig at you as I would. So you've yielded to the demands of your toney friends?"

"Of course I tried to dress correctly for my up-town friends, when I was with them. But it was not they who made me careful, though they helped me to find a good tailor, when I decided that I must dress better."

"Then it was the big law practice, eh? Must keep up appearances?"

"I fancy my dressing would no more affect my practice, than does the furnishing of my office."

"Then who is she? Out with it, you sly dog."

"Of course I shan't tell you that."

"Peter, will you tell me?" asked Leonore.

Peter smiled into the frank eyes. "Who she is?"

"No. Why you dress so nicely. Please?"

"You'll laugh when I tell you it is my ward."

"Oh, nonsense," laughed Watts. "That's too thin. Come off that roof. Unless you're guardian of some bewitching girl?"

"Your ward, Peter?"

"Yes. I don't know whether I can make you understand it. I didn't at first. You see I became associated with the ward, in people's minds, after I had been in politics for a few years. So I was sometimes put in positions to a certain extent representative of it. I never thought much how I dressed, and it seems that sometimes at public meetings, and parades, and that sort of thing, I wasn't dressed quite as well as the other men. So when the people of my ward, who were present, were asked to point me out to strangers, they were mortified about the way I looked. It seemed to reflect on the ward. The first inkling I had of it was after one of these parades, in which, without thinking, I had worn a soft hat. I was the only man who did not wear a silk one, and my ward felt very badly about it. So they made up a purse, and came to me to ask me to buy a new suit and silk hat and gloves. Of course that set me asking questions, and though they didn't want to hurt my feelings, I wormed enough out of them to learn how they felt.

Since then I've spent a good deal of money on tailors, and dress very carefully."

"Good for 'de sixt'! Hurrah for the unwashed democracy, where one man's as good as another! So a 'Mick' ward wants its great man to put on all the frills? I tell you, chum, we may talk about equality, but the lower classes can't but admire and worship the tinsel and flummery of aristocracy."

"You are mistaken. They may like to see brilliant sights: Soldiers, ball-rooms or the like, and who does not? Beauty is æsthetic, not aristocratic. But they judge people less by their dress or money than is usually supposed. Far less than the people up-town do. They wanted me to dress better, because it was appropriate. But let a man in the ward try to dress beyond his station, and he'd be jeered out of it, or the ward, if nothing worse happened."

"Oh, of course they'd hoot at their own kind," said Watts. "The hardest thing to forgive in this world is your equal's success. But they wouldn't say anything to one of us."

"If you, or Pell, or Ogden should go into Blunkers's place in my ward, this evening, dressed as you are, or better, you probably would be told to get out. I don't believe you could get a drink. And you would stand a chance of pretty rough usage. Last week I went right from a dinner to Blunkers's to say a word to him. I was in evening dress, Newcastle, and crush hat—even a bunch of lilies of the valley—yet every man there was willing to shake hands and have me sit down and stay. Blunkers couldn't have been dressed so, because it didn't belong to him. For the same reason, you would have no business in Blunkers's place, because you don't belong there. But the men know I dressed for a reason, and came to the saloon for a reason. I wasn't putting on airs. I wasn't intruding my wealth on them."

"Look here, chum, will you take me into Blunkers's place some night, and let me hear you powwow the 'b'ys?' I should like to see how you do it."

"Yes," Peter said deliberately, "if some night you'll let me bring Blunkers up to watch one of your formal dinners. He would enjoy the sight, I'm sure."

Leonore cocked her little nose up in the air, and laughed merrily.

"Oh, but that's very different," said Watts.

"It's just as different as the two men with the tooth-ache," said Peter. "They both met at the dentist's, who it seems had only time to pull one tooth. The question arose as to which it should be. 'I'm so brave,' said one, 'that I can wait till to-morrow.' 'I'm such a coward,' said the other, 'that I don't dare have it done to-day.' "

"Haven't you ever taken people to those places, Peter?" asked Leonore.

"No. I've always refused. It's a society fad now to have what are called 'slumming parties,' and of course I've been asked to help. It makes my blood tingle when I hear them talk over the 'fun' as they call it. They get detectives to protect them, and then go through the tene-ments—the homes of the poor—and pry into their privacy and poverty, just out of curiosity. Then they go home and over a chafing dish of lobster or terrapin, and champagne, they laugh at the funny things they saw. If the poor could get detectives, and look in on the luxury and comfort of the rich they wouldn't see much fun in it, and there's less fun in a down-town tenement than there is in a Fifth Avenue palace. I heard a girl tell the other night about breaking in on a wake by chance. 'Weren't we lucky?' she said. 'It was so funny to see the poor people weeping and drinking whisky at the same time. Isn't it heartless?' Yet the dead—perhaps the bread-win-ner of the family, fallen in the struggle—perhaps the last little comer, not strong enough to fight this earth's battle —must have lain there in plain view of that girl. Who was the most heartless? The family and friends who had gathered over that body, according to their customs, or the party who looked in on them and laughed?" Peter had forgotten where he was, or to whom he was talking.

Leonore had listened breathlessly. But the moment he ceased speaking, she bowed her head and began to sob. Peter came down from his indignant tirade like a flash. "Miss D'Alloi," he cried, "forgive me. I forgot. Don't cry so." Peter was pleading in an anxious voice. He felt as if he had committed murder.

"There, there, Dot. Don't cry. It's nothing to cry about."

Miss D'Alloi was crying and endeavoring at the same time to solve the most intricate puzzle ever yet propounded by man or woman—that is, to find a woman's pocket. She complicated things even more by trying to talk. "I —I—know I'm ver-ver-very foooooooolish," she managed to get out, however much she failed in a similar result with her pocket-handkerchief.

"Since I caused the tears, you must let me stop them," said Peter. He had produced his own handkerchief, and was made happy by seeing Leonore bury her face in it, and re-appear not quite so woe-begone.

"I—only—didn't—know—you—could—talk—like—like that," explained Leonore.

"Let this be a lesson for you," said Watts. "Don't come any more of your jury-pathos on my little girl."

"Papa! You—I—Peter, I'm so glad you told me—I'll never go to one."

Watts laughed. "Now I know why you charm all the women whom I hear talking about you. I tell you, when you rear your head up like that, and your eyes blaze so, and you put that husk in your voice, I don't wonder you fetch them. By George, you were really splendid to look at."

That was the reason why Leonore had not cried till Peter had finished his speech. We don't charge women with crying whenever they wish, but we are sure that they never cry when they have anything better to do.

CHAPTER XL

OPINIONS

WHEN the ride was ended, Leonore was sent home in the carriage, Watts saying he would go with Peter to his club. As soon as they were in the cab, he said:

"I wanted to see you about your letter."

"Well?"

"Everything's going as well as can be expected. Of course the little woman's scandalized over your supposed iniquity, but I'm working the heavy sentimental 'saved-our-little-girl's-life' business for all it's worth. I had her crying last night on my shoulder over it, and no woman can do that and be obstinate long. She'll come round before a great while."

Peter winced. He almost felt like calling Watts off from the endeavor. But he thought of Leonore. He must see her—just to prove to himself that she was not for him, be it understood—and how could he see enough of her to do that—for Peter recognized that it would take a good deal of that charming face and figure and manner to pall on him—if he was excluded from her home? So he justified the continuance of the attempt by saying to himself: "She only excludes me because of something of which I am guiltless, and I've saved her from far greater suffering than my presence can ever give her. I have earned the privilege if ever man earned it." Most people can prove to themselves what they wish to prove. The successful orator is always the man who imposes his frame of mind on his audience. We call it "saying what the people want said." But many of the greatest speakers first suggest an idea to their listeners, and when they say it in plain English, a moment later, the audience say, mentally, "That's just what we thought a moment ago," and are convinced that the speaker is right.

Peter remained silent, and Watts continued: "We get into our own house to-morrow, and give Leonore a birthday dinner Tuesday week as a combined house-warming and celebration. Save that day, for I'm determined you shall be asked. Only the invitation may come a little late. You won't mind that?"

"No. But don't send me too many of these formal things. I keep out of them as much as I can. I'm not a society man and probably won't fit in with your friends."

"I should know you were not *de societé* by that single speech. If there's one thing easy to talk to, or fit in with, it's a society man or woman. It's their business to be chatty and pleasant, and they would be polite and en-

tertaining to a kangaroo, if they found one next them at
dinner. That's what society is for. We are the yolk of
the egg, which holds and blends all the discordant, untrained elements: the oil, vinegar, salt, and mustard. We
don't add much flavor to life, but people wouldn't mix
without us."

"I know," said Peter, "if you want to talk petty personalities and trivialities, that it's easy enough to get
through endless hours of time. But I have other things
to do."

"Exactly. But we have a purpose, too. You mustn't
think society is all frivolity. It's one of the hardest working professions."

"And the most brainless."

"No. Don't you see, that society is like any other kind
of work, and that the people who will centre their whole
life on it must be the leaders of it? To you, the spending
hours over a new *entrée,* or over a cotillion figure, seems
rubbish, but it's the exact equivalent of your spending
hours over who shall be nominated for a certain office.
Because you are willing to do that, you are one of the
"big four." Because we are willing to do our task, we
differentiate into the "four hundred." You mustn't think
society doesn't grind up brain-tissue. But we use so
much in running it, that we don't have enough for other
subjects, and so you think we are stupid. I remember a
woman once saying she didn't like conversazioni, 'because
they are really brain-parties, and there is never enough
to go round, and give a second help.' Anyway, how can
you expect society to talk anything but society, when men
like yourself stay away from it."

"I don't ask you to talk anything else. But let me
keep out of it."

" 'He's not the man for Galway'," hummed Watts.
"He prefers talking to 'heelers,' and 'b'ys,' and 'toughs,'
and other clever, intellectual men."

"I like to talk to any one who is working with a purpose in life."

"I say, Peter, what do those fellows really say of us?"

"I can best describe it by something Miss De Voe once
said. We were at a dinner together, where there was a

Chicago man who became irritated at one or two bits of ignorance displayed by some of the other guests over the size and prominence of his abiding place. Finally he said: 'Why, look here, you people are so ignorant of my city, that you don't even know how to pronounce its name.' He turned to Miss De Voe and said, 'We say Chicawgo. Now, how do you pronounce it in New York?' Miss De Voe put on that quiet, crushing manner she has when a man displeases her, and said, 'We never pronounce it in New York.'"

"Good for our Dutch-Huguenot stock! I tell you, Peter, blood does tell."

"It wasn't a speech I should care to make, because it did no good, and could only mortify. But it does describe the position of the lower wards of New York towards society. I've been working in them for nearly sixteen years, and I've never even heard the subject mentioned."

"But I thought the anarchists and socialists were always taking a whack at us?"

"They cry out against over-rich men—not against society. Don't confuse the constituents with the compound. Citric acid is a deadly poison, but weakened down with water and sugar, it is only lemonade. They growl at the poison, not at the water and sugar. Before there can be hate, there must be strength."

The next day Peter turned up in the park about four, and had a ride—with Watts. The day after that, he was there a little earlier, and had a ride—with the groom. The day following he had another ride—with the groom. Peter thought they were very wonderful rides. Some one told him a great many interesting things. About some one's European life, some one's thoughts, some one's hopes, and some one's feelings. Some one really wanted a friend to pour it all out to, and Peter listened well, and encouraged well.

"He doesn't laugh at me, as papa does," some one told herself, "and so it's much easier to tell him. And he shows that he really is interested. Oh, I always said he and I should be good friends, and we are going to be."

This put some one in a very nice frame of mind, and

Peter thought he had never met such a wonderful combination of frankness, of confidence, and yet of a certain girlish shyness and timidity. Some one would tell him something, and then appeal to him, if he didn't think that was so? Peter generally thought it was. Some one did not drop her little touch of coquetry, for that was ingrain, as it is in most pretty girls. But it was the most harmless kind of coquetry imaginable. Some one was not thinking at all of winning men's hearts. That might come later. At present, all she wanted was that they should think her pretty, and delightful, so that—that they should want to be friends.

When Peter joined Watts and Leonore, however, on the fourth day, there was a noticeable change in Leonore's manner to him. He did not get any welcome except a formal "Good-afternoon," and for ten minutes Watts and he had to sustain the conversation by firing remarks at each other past a very silent intermediary. Peter had no idea what was wrong, but when he found that she did not mollify at the end of that time, he said to her:

"What is the matter?"

"Matter with what?" asked Leonore, calmly.

"With you."

"Nothing."

"I shan't take that for an answer. Remember, we have sworn to be friends."

"Friends come to see each other."

Peter felt relieved, and smiled. "They do," he said, "when they can."

"No, they don't, sometimes," said Leonore severely. Then she unbent a little. "Why haven't you been to see us? You've had a full week."

"Yes," said Peter, "I have had a very full week."

"Are you going to call on us, Mr. Stirling?"

"To whom are you talking?"

"To you."

"My name's Peter."

"That depends. Are you going to call on us?"

"That is my hope and wish."

Leonore unbent a little more. "If you are," she said, "I wish you would do it soon, because mamma said to-day she thought of asking you to my birthday dinner next Tuesday, but I said you oughtn't to be asked till you had called."

"Did you know that bribery is unlawful?"

"Are you going to call?"

"Of course I am."

"That's better. When?"

"What evening are you to be at home?"

"To-morrow," said Leonore, beginning to curl up the corners of her mouth.

"Well," said Peter, "I wish you had said this evening, because that's nearer, but to-morrow isn't so far away."

"That's right. Now we'll be friends again."

"I hope so."

"Are you willing to be good friends—not make believe, or half friends, but—real friends?"

"Absolutely."

"Don't you think friends should tell each other everything?"

"Yes." Peter was quite willing, even anxious, that Leonore should tell him everything.

"You are quite sure?"

"Yes."

"Then," said Leonore, "tell me about the way you got that sword."

Watts laughed. "She's been asking every one she's met about that. Do tell her, just for my sake."

"I've told you already."

"Not the way I want it. I know you didn't try to make it interesting. Some of the people remembered there was something very fine, but I haven't found anybody yet who could really tell it to me. Please tell about it nicely, Peter." Leonore was looking at Peter with the most pleading of looks.

"It was during the great railroad strike. The Erie had brought some men up from New York to fill the strikers' places. The new hands were lodged in freight cars, when off work, for it wasn't safe for them to pass outside the guard lines of soldiers. Some of the strikers applied for work, and were re-instated. They only did it to get inside our lines. At night, when the substitutes in the cars were fast asleep, tired out with the double work they had done, the strikers locked the car-doors. They pulled the two cars into a shed full of freight, broke open a petroleum tank, and with it wet the cars and some others loaded with jute. They set fire to the cars and barricaded the shed doors. Of course we didn't know till the flames burst through the roof of the shed, when by the light, one of the superintendents found the bunk cars gone. The fire-department was useless, for the strikers two days before, had cut all the hose. So we were ordered up to get the cars out. Some strikers had concealed themselves in buildings where they could overlook the shed, and while we were working at the door, they kept firing on us. We were in the light of the blazing shed, and they were in the dark, which gave them a big advantage over us, and we couldn't spare the time to attend to them. We tore up some rails and with them smashed in the door. The men in the cars were screaming, so we knew which to take, and fortunately they were the nearest to the door. We took our muskets—for the frames of the cars were blazing, and the metal part too hot to touch —and fixing bayonets, drove them into the woodwork and so pushed the cars out. When we were outside, we used the rails again, to smash an opening in the ends of the cars which were burning the least. We got the men out unharmed, but pretty badly frightened."

"And were you not hurt?"

"We had eight wounded and a good many badly burned."

"And you?"

"I had my share of the burns."

"I wish you would tell me what you did—not what the others did."

Peter would have told her anything while she looked like that at him.

"I was in command at that point. I merely directed things, except taking up the rails. I happened to know how to get a rail up quickly, without waiting to unscrew the bolts. I had read it, years before, in a book on railroad construction. I didn't think that paragraph would ever help me to save forty lives—for five minutes' delay would have been fatal. The inside of the shed was one sheet of flame. After we broke the door down, I only stood and superintended the moving of the cars. The men did the real work."

"But you said the inside of the shed was a sheet of flame."

"Yes. The railroad had to give us all fresh uniforms. So we made new toggery out of that night's work. I've heard people say militia are no good. If they could have stood by me that night, and seen my company working over those blazing cars, in that mass of burning freight, with the roof liable to fall any minute, and the strikers firing every time a man showed himself, I think they would have altered their opinion."

"Oh," said Leonore, her eyes flashing with enthusiasm. "How splendid it is to be a man, and be able to do real things! I wish I had known about it in Europe."

"Why?"

"Because the officers were always laughing about our army. I used to get perfectly wild at them, but I couldn't say anything in reply. If I could only have told them about that."

"Hear the little Frenchwoman talk," said Watts.

"I'm not French."

"Yes, you are, Dot."

"I'm all American. I haven't a feeling that isn't all American. Doesn't that make me an American, Peter, no matter where I was born?"

"I think you are an American under the law."

"Am I really?" said Leonore, incredulously.

"Yes. You were born of American parents, and you will be living in this country when you become of age. That constitutes nationality."

"Oh, how lovely! I knew I was an American, really, but papa was always teasing me and saying I was a foreigner. I hate foreigners."

"Confound you, chum, you've spoiled one of my best jokes! It's been such fun to see Dot bristle when I teased her. She's the hottest little patriot that ever lived."

"I think Miss D'Alloi's nationality is akin to that of a case of which I once heard," said Peter, smiling. "A man was bragging about the number of famous men who were born in his native town. He mentioned a well-known personage, among others, and one of his auditors said: 'I didn't know he was born there.' 'Oh, yes, he was,' replied the man. 'He was born there, but during the temporary absence of his parents!'"

"Peter, how much does a written opinion cost?" asked Leonore, eagerly.

"It has a range about equal to the woman's statement that a certain object was as long as a piece of string."

"But your opinions?"

"I have given an opinion for nothing. The other day I gave one to a syndicate, and charged eight thousand dollars."

"Oh, dear!" said Leonore. "I wonder if I can afford to get your opinion on my being an American? I should like to frame it and hang it in my room. Would it be expensive?"

"It is usual with lawyers," said Peter gravely, "to find out how much a client has, and then make the bill for a little less. How much do you have?"

"I really haven't any now. I shall have two hundred dollars on the first. But then I owe some bills."

"You forget your grandmamma's money, Dot."

"Oh! Of course. I shall be rich, Peter. I come into the income of my property on Tuesday. I forget how much it is, but I'm sure I can afford to have an opinion."

"Why, Dot, we must get those papers out, and you must find some one to put the trust in legal shape, and take care of it for you," said Watts.

"I suppose," said Leonore to Peter, "if you have one lawyer to do all your work, that he does each thing cheaper, doesn't he?"

"Yes. Because he divides what his client has, on several jobs, instead of on one," Peter told her.

"Then I think I'll have you do it all. We'll come down and see you about it. But write out that opinion at once, so that I can prove that I'm an American."

"Very well. But there's a safer way, even, of making sure that you're an American."

"What is that?" said Leonore, eagerly.

"Marry one," said Peter.

"Oh, yes," said Leonore. "I've always intended to do that, but not for a great many years."

CHAPTER XLI

CALLS

PETER dressed himself the next evening with particular care, even for him. As Peter dressed, he was rather down on life. He had been kept from his ride that afternoon by taking evidence in a referee case. "I really needed the exercise badly," he said. He had tried to work his dissatisfaction off on his clubs and dumb-bells, but whatever they had done for his blood and tissue, they had not eased his frame of mind. Dinner made him a little pleasanter, for few men can remain cross over a proper meal. Still, he did not look happy, when, on rising from his coffee, he glanced at his watch and found that it was but ten minutes past eight.

He vacillated for a moment, and then getting into his outside trappings, he went out and turned eastward, down the first side street. He walked four blocks, and then threw open the swing door of a brilliantly lighted place, stepping at once into a blaze of light and warmth which was most attractive after the keen March wind blowing outside.

He nodded to the three barkeepers. "Is Dennis inside?" he asked.

"Yes, Misther Stirling. The regulars are all there."

Peter passed through the room, and went into another without knocking. In it were some twenty men, sitting for the most part in attitudes denoting ease. Two, at a small table in the corner, were playing dominoes. Three others, in another corner, were amusing themselves with "High, Low, Jack." Two were reading papers. The rest were collected round the centre table, most of them smoking. Some beer mugs and tumblers were standing about, but not more than a third of the twenty were drinking anything. The moment Peter entered, one of the men jumped to his feet.

"B'ys," he cried, "here's Misther Stirling. Begobs, sir, it's fine to see yez. It's very scarce yez been lately." He had shaken hands, and then put a chair in place for Peter.

The cards, papers, and dominoes had been abandoned the moment Dennis announced Peter's advent, and when Peter had finished shaking the hands held out to him, and had seated himself, the men were all gathered round the big table.

Peter laid his hat on the table, threw back his New-castle and lit a cigar. "I've been very short of time, Dennis. But I had my choice this evening before going up-town, of smoking a cigar in my own quarters, or here. So I came over to talk with you all about Denton."

"An' what's he been doin'?" inquired Dennis.

"I saw him to-day about the Hummel franchise that comes up in the Board next Tuesday. He won't vote for it, he says. I told him I thought it was in the interest of the city to multiply means of transit, and asked him why he refused. He replied that he thought the Hummel gang had been offering money, and that he would vote against bribers."

"He didn't have the face to say that?" shouted one of the listeners.

"Yes."

"Oi never!" said Dennis. "An' he workin' night an' day to get the Board to vote the rival road."

"I don't think there's much doubt that money is being spent by both sides," said Peter. "I fear no bill could ever pass without it. But the Hummel crowd are really responsible people, who offer the city a good percentage. The other men are merely trying to get the franchise, to sell it out at a profit to Hummel. I don't like the methods of either, but there's a road needed, and there'll be a road voted, so it's simply a choice between the two. I shouldn't mind if Denton voted against both schemes, but to say he'll vote against Hummel for that reason, and yet vote for the other franchise shows that he's not square. I didn't say so to him, because I wanted to talk it over with the ward a little first to see if they stood with me."

"That we do, sir," said Dennis, with a sureness which was cool, if nothing more. Fortunately for the boldness of the speaker, no one dissented, and two or three couples nodded heads or pipes at each other.

Peter looked at his watch. "Then I can put the screws on him safely, you think?"

"Yes," cried several.

Peter rose. "Dennis, will you see Blunkers and Driscoll this evening, or some time to-morrow, and ask if they think so too? And if they don't tell them to drop in on me, when they have leisure."

"Begobs, sir, Oi'll see them inside av ten minutes. An' if they don't agree wid us, sure, Oi'll make them."

"Thank you. Good-night."

"Good-night, Mr. Stirling," came a chorus, and Peter passed into the street by the much maligned side-door.

Dennis turned to the group with his face shining with enthusiasm. "Did yez see him, b'ys? There was style for yez. Isn't he somethin' for the ward to be proud av?"

Peter turned to Broadway, and fell into a long rapid stride. In spite of the cold he threw open his coat, and carried his outer covering on his arm. Peter had no intention of going into an up-town drawing-room with any suggestion of "sixt" ward tobacco. So he walked till he reached Madison Square, when, after a glance at his watch, he jumped into a cab.

It was a quarter-past nine when the footman opened the door of the Fifty-seventh Street house, in reply to Peter's ring. Yet he was told that, "The ladies are still at dinner."

Peter turned and went down the stoop. He walked to the Avenue, and stopped at a house not far off.

"Is Mrs. Pell at home?" he asked, and procured entrance for both his pasteboard and himself.

"Welcome, little stranger," was his greeting. "And it is so nice that you came this evening. Here is Van, on from Washington for two days."

"I was going to look you up, and see what 'we, the people' were talking about, so that I could enlighten our legislators when I go back," said a man of forty.

"I wrote Pope a long letter to-day, which I asked him to show you," said Peter. "Things are in a bad shape, and getting worse."

"But, Peter," queried the woman, "if you are the leader, why do you let them get so?"

"So as to remain the leader," said Peter, smiling quietly.

"Now that's what comes of ward politics," cried Mrs. Pell. "You are beginning to make Irish bulls."

"No," replied Peter, "I am serious, and because people don't understand what I mean, they don't understand American politics."

"But you say in effect that the way you retain your leadership, is by not leading. That's absurd!"

"No. Contradiction though it may seem the way to lose authority, is to exercise it too much. Christ enunciated the great truth of democratic government, when he said, 'He that would be the greatest among you, shall be the servant of all.'"

"I hope you won't carry your theory so far as to let them nominate Maguire?" said Mr. Pell, anxiously.

"Now, please don't begin on politics," said the woman. "Here is Van, whom I haven't seen for nine weeks, and here is Peter, whom I haven't seen for time out of mind, and just as I think I have a red-letter evening before me, you begin your everlasting politics."

"I merely stopped in to shake hands," said Peter. "I have a call to make elsewhere, and can stay but twenty minutes. For that time we choose you speaker, and you can make us do as it pleases you."

Twenty minutes later Peter passed into the D'Alloi drawing-room. He shook Mrs. D'Alloi's hand steadily, which was more than she did with his. Then he was made happy for a moment, with that of Leonore. Then he was introduced to a Madame Mellerie, whom he placed at once as the half-governess, half-companion, who had charge of Leonore's education; a Mr. Maxwell, and a Marquis de somebody. They were both good-looking young fellows; and greeted Peter in a friendly way. But Peter did not like them.

He liked them less when Mrs. D'Alloi told him to sit in a given place, and then put Madame Mellerie down by him. Peter had not called to see Madame Mellerie. But he made a virtue of necessity, and he was too instinctively courteous not to treat the Frenchwoman with the same touch of deference his manner towards women always had. After they had been chatting for a little on French literature, it occurred to Peter that her opinion of him might have some influence with Leonore, so he decided that he would try and please her. But this thought turned his mind to Leonore, and speaking of her to her governess, he at once became so interested in the facts she began to pour out to him, that he forgot entirely about his diplomatic scheme.

This arrangement continued half an hour, when a dislocation of the *status quo* was made by the departure of Mr. Maxwell. When the exit was completed, Mrs. D'Alloi turned to place her puppets properly again. But she found a decided bar to her intentions. Peter had formed his own conclusions as to why he had been set to entertain Madame Mellerie, not merely from the fact itself, but from the manner in which it had been done, and most of all, from the way Mrs. D'Alloi had managed to stand between Leonore and himself, as if protecting the former, till she had been able to force her arrangements. So with the first stir Peter had risen, and when the little bustle had ceased he was already standing by Leonore, talking to her. Mrs. D'Alloi did not look happy, but for the moment she was helpless.

Peter had had to skirt the group to get to Leonore, and so had stood behind her during the farewells. She apparently had not noticed his advent, but the moment she had done the daughter-of-the-house duty, she turned to him, and said: "I wondered if you would go away without seeing me. I was so afraid you were one of the men who just say, 'How d'ye do' and 'Good-bye,' and think they've paid a call."

"I called to see you to-night, and I should not have gone till I had seen you. I'm rather a persistent man in some things."

"Yes," said Leonore, bobbing her head in a very knowing manner, "Miss De Voe told me."

"Mr. Stirling," said Mrs. D'Alloi, "can't you tell us the

meaning of the Latin motto on this seal?" Mrs. D'Alloi held a letter towards him, but did not stir from her position across the room.

Peter understood the device. He was to be drawn off, and made to sit by Mrs. D'Alloi, not because she wanted to see him, but because she did not want him to talk to Leonore. Peter had no intention of being dragooned. So he said: "Madame Mellerie has been telling me what a good Latin scholar Miss D'Alloi is. I certainly shan't display my ignorance, till she has looked at it." Then he carried the envelope over to Leonore, and in handing it to her, moved a chair for her, not neglecting one for himself. Mrs. D'Alloi looked discouraged, the more when Peter and Leonore put their heads close together to examine the envelope.

"*'In bonam partem,'*" read Leonore. "That's easy, mamma. It's—why, she isn't listening!"

"You can tell her later. I have something to talk to you about."

"What is that?"

"Your dinner in my quarters. Whom would you like to have there?"

"Will you really give me a dinner?"

"Yes."

"And let me have just whom I want?"

"Oh, lovely! Let me see. Mamma and papa, of course."

"That's four. Now you can have two more."

"Peter. Would you mind—I mean—" Leonore hesitated a moment and then said in an apologetic tone— "Would you like to invite madame? I've been telling her about your rooms—and you—and I think it would please her so."

"That makes five," said Peter.

"Oh, goody!" said Leonore, "I mean," she said, correcting herself, "that that is very kind of you."

"And now the sixth?"

"That must be a man of course," said Leonore, wrinkling up her forehead in the intensity of puzzlement. "And I know so few men." She looked out into space, and Peter had a moment's fear lest she should see the marquis and name him. "There's one friend of yours I'm very anxious to meet. I wonder if you would be willing to ask him?"

"Who is that?"

"Mr. Moriarty."

"No, I can't ask him. I don't want to cheapen him by making a show of him."

"Oh! I haven't that feeling about him. I——"

"I think you would understand him and see the fine qualities. But do you think others would?" Peter mentioned no names, but Leonore understood.

"No," she said. "You are quite right."

"You shall meet him some day," said Peter, "if you wish, but when we can have only people who won't embarrass or laugh at him."

"Really, I don't know whom to select."

"Perhaps you would like to meet Le Grand?"

"Very much. He is just the man."

"Then we'll consider that settled. Are you free for the ninth?"

"Yes. I'm not going out this spring, and mamma and papa haven't really begun yet, and it's so late in the season that I'm sure we are free."

"Then I will ice the canvas-backs and champagne and dust off the Burgundy for that day, if your mamma accedes."

"Peter, I wanted to ask you the other day about that. I thought you didn't drink wine."

"I don't. But I give my friends a glass, when they are good enough to come to me. I live my own life, to please myself, but for that very reason, I want others to live their lives to please themselves. Trying to live other people's lives for them, is a pretty dog-in-the-manger business."

Just then Mrs. D'Alloi joined them. "Were you able to translate it?" she asked, sitting down by them.

"Yes, indeed," said Leonore. "It means 'Towards the right side,' or as a motto it might be translated, 'For the right side.'"

Mrs. D'Alloi had clearly, to use a western expression, come determined to "settle down and grow up with the country." So Peter broached the subject of the dinner, and when she hesitated, Leonore called Watts into the group. He threw the casting ballot in favor of the dinner, and so it was agreed upon. Peter was asked to come to Leonore's birthday festival, "If you don't mind such short notice," and he didn't mind, apparently. Then the conversation wandered at will till Peter rose. In doing so, he turned to Leonore, and said:

"I looked the question of nationality up to-day, and found I was right. I've written out a legal opinion in my best hand, and will deliver it to you, on receiving my fee."

"How much is that?" said Leonore, eagerly.

"That you come and get it."

CHAPTER XLII

DOWN-TOWN NEW YORK

PETER had not been working long the next morning when he was told that "The Honorable Terence Denton wishes to see you." "Very well," he said, and that worthy was ushered in.

"Good-morning, Denton. I'm glad to see you. I was going down to the Hall to-day to say something, but you've saved me the trouble."

"I know you was. So I thought I'd get ahead of you," said Denton, with a surly tone and manner.

"Sit down," said Peter. Peter had learned that, with a certain class of individuals, a distance and a seat have a very dampening effect on anger. It is curious, man's instinctive desire to stand up to and be near the object for which anger is felt.

"You've been talking against me in the ward, and makin' them down on me."

"No, I didn't talk against you. I've spoken with some of the people about the way you think of voting on the franchises."

"Yes. I wasn't round, but a friend heard Dennis and Blunkers a-going over it last night. And it's you did it."

"Yes. But you know me well enough to be sure, after my talk with you yesterday, that I wouldn't stop there."

"So you try to set the pack on me."

"No. I try to see how the ward wants its alderman to vote on the franchises."

"Look a-here. What are you so set on the Hummel crowd for?"

"I'm not."

"Is it because Hummel's a big contractor and gives you lots of law business?"

"No," said Peter, smiling. "And you don't think it is, either."

"Has they offered you some stock cheap?"

"Come, come, Denton. You know the *tu quoque* won't do here."

Denton shifted in his seat uneasily, not knowing what reply to make. Those two little Latin words had such unlimited powers of concealment in them. He did not know whether *tu quoque* meant something about votes, an insulting charge, or merely a reply, and feared to make himself ridiculous by his response to them. He was not the first man who has been hampered and floored by his own ignorance. He concluded he must make an entire change of subject to be safe. So he said, "I ain't goin' to be no boss's puppy dog."

"No," said Peter, finding it difficult not to smile, "you are not that kind of a man."

"I takes my orders from no one."

"Denton, no one wants you to vote by order. We elected you alderman to do what was best for the ward and city, as it seems to you. You are responsible for your votes to us, and no other man can be. I don't care who orders you or advises you; in the end, you must vote yourself, and you yourself will be held to account by us."

"Yes. But if I don't vote as you wants, you'll sour the boys on me."

"I shall tell them what I think. You can do the same. It's a fair game between us."

"No, it ain't. You're rich and you can talk more."

"You know my money has nothing to do with it. You know I don't try to deceive the men in talking to them.

If they trust what I tell them, it's because it's reasonable, and because I haven't tricked them before."

"Well, are you goin' to drive me out?"

"I hope not. I think you've made a good alderman, Denton, and you'll find I've said so."

"But now?"

"If you vote for that franchise, I shall certainly tell the ward that I think you've done wrong. Then the ward will do as they please."

"As you please, you mean."

"No. You've been long enough in politics to know that unless I can make the ward think as I do, I couldn't do anything. What would you care for my opinion, if you didn't know that the votes are back of it?"

Just then the door swung open, and Dennis came in. "Tim said yez was alone wid Denton, sir, so Oi came right in. It's a good-mornin', sir. How are yez, Terence?"

"You are just the man I want, Dennis. Tell Denton how the ward feels about the franchises."

"Shure. It's one man they is. An' if Denton will step down to my place this night, he'll find out how they think."

"They never would have felt so, if Mister Stirling hadn't talked to them. Not one in twenty knew the question was up."

"That's because they are most of them too hard working to keep track of all the things. Come, Denton; I don't attempt to say how you shall vote. I only tell you how it seems to me. Go round the ward, and talk with others. Then you can tell whether I can give you trouble in the future or not. I don't want to fight you. We've been good friends in the past, and we can do more by pulling in double harness than by kicking. I don't know a man I would rather see at the Hall." Peter held out his hand, and Denton took it.

"All right, Mister Stirling. I'll do my best to stay friends," he said, and went out.

Peter turned and smiled at Dennis. "They can't find out that it's not I, but the ward. So every time there's trouble they lay it against me, and it's hard to keep them friendly. And I hate quarrels and surliness."

"It's yezself can do it, though. Shure, Denton was in a great state av mind this mornin', they was tellin' me, but he's all right now, an' will vote right, or my name isn't Dennis Moriarty."

"Yes. He doesn't know it yet, but he'll vote square on Tuesday."

Just then Tim brought in the cards of Watts and Leonore, and strangely enough, Peter said they were to be shown in at once. In they came, and after the greetings, Peter said:

"Miss D'Alloi, this is my dear friend, Dennis Moriarty. Dennis, Miss D'Alloi has wanted to know you because she's heard of your being such a friend to me."

"Shure," said Dennis, taking the little hand so eagerly offered him, "Oi'm thinkin' we're both lucky to be in the thoughts at all, at all, av such a sweet young lady."

"Oh, Mr. Moriarty, you've kissed the blarney stone."

"Begobs," responded Dennis, "it needs no blarney stone to say that. It's afther sayin' itself."

"Peter, have you that opinion?"

"Yes." Peter handed her out a beautifully written sheet of script, all in due form, and given an appearance of vast learning, by red ink marginal references to such solid works as "Wheaton," "Story," and "Cranch's" and "Wallace's" reports. Peter had taken it practically from a "Digest," but many apparently learned opinions come from the same source. And the whole was given value by the last two lines, which read, "Respectfully submitted, Peter Stirling." Peter's name had value at the bottom of a legal opinion, or a check, if nowhere else.

"Look, Mr. Moriarty," cried Leonore, too full of happiness over this decision of her nationality not to wish for some one with whom to share it, "I've always thought I was French—though I didn't feel so a bit—and now Mr. Stirling has made me an American, and I'm so happy. I hate foreigners."

Watts laughed. "Why, Dot. You mustn't say that to Mr. Moriarty. He's a foreigner himself."

"Oh, I forgot. I didn't think that——" Poor Leonore stopped there, horrified at what she had said.

"No," said Peter, "Dennis is not a foreigner. He's

one of the most ardent Americans I know. As far as my experience goes, to make one of Dennis's bulls, the hottest American we have to-day is the Irish-American."

"Oh, come," said Watts. "You know every Irishman pins his loyalty to the 'owld counthry.'"

"Shure," said Dennis, "an' if they do, what then? Sometimes a man finds a full-grown woman, fine, an' sweet, an' strong, an' helpful to him, an' he comes to love her big like. But does that make him forget his old weak mother, who's had a hard life av it, yet has done her best by him? Begobs! If he forgot her, he wouldn't be the man to make a good husband. Oi don't say Oi'm a good American, for it's small Oi feel besides Misther Stirling. But Oi love her, an' if she ever wants the arm, or the blood, or the life, av Dennis Moriarty, she's only got to say so."

"Well," said Watts, "this is very interesting, both as a point of view and as oratory; but it isn't business. Peter, we came down this morning to take whatever legal steps are necessary to put Dot in possession of her grandmother's money, of which I have been trustee. Here is a lot of papers about it. I suppose everything is there relating to it."

"Papa seemed to think it would be very wise to ask you to take care of it, and pay me the income. I can't have the principal till I'm twenty-five."

"You must tie it up some way, Peter, or Dot will make ducks and drakes of it. She has about as much idea of the value of money as she has of the value of foreigners. When we had our villa at Florence, she supported the entire pauper population of the city."

Peter had declined heretofore the care of trust funds. But it struck him that this was really a chance—from a business standpoint entirely! It is true, the amount was only ninety-two thousand, and, as a trust company would handle that sum of money for four hundred and odd dollars, he was bound to do the same; and this would certainly not pay him for his time. "Sometimes, however," said Peter to himself, "these trusteeships have very handsome pickings, aside from the half per cent." Peter did not say that the "pickings," as they framed themselves in his mind, were sundry calls on him at his office, and a justifiable reason at all times for calling on Leonore; to say nothing of letters and other unearned increment. So Peter was not obstinate this time. "It's such a simple matter that I can have the papers drawn while you wait, if you've half an hour to spare." Peter did this, thinking it would keep them longer, but later it occurred to him it would have been better to find some other reason, and leave the papers, because then Leonore would have had to come again soon. Peter was not quite as cool and far-seeing as he was normally.

He regretted his error the more when they all took his suggestion that they go into his study. Peter rang for his head clerk, and explained what was needed with great rapidity, and then left the latter and went into the study.

"I wonder what he's in such a hurry for?" said the clerk, retiring with the papers.

When Peter entered the library he found Leonore and Watts reposing in chairs, and Dennis standing in front of them, speaking. This was what Dennis was saying:

"'Schatter, boys, an' find me a sledge.' Shure, we thought it was demented he was, but he was the only cool man, an' orders were orders. Dooley, he found one, an' then the captain went to the rails an' gave it a swing, an' struck the bolts crosswise like, so that the heads flew off, like they was shootin' stars. Then he struck the rails sideways, so as to loosen them from the ties. Then says he: 'Half a dozen av yez take off yez belts an' strap these rails together!' Even then we didn't understand, but we did it. All this time the dirty spal—Oi ask yez pardon, miss—all this time the strikers were pluggin' at us, an' bullets flyin' like fun. 'Drop your muskets,' says the captain, when we had done; 'fall in along those rails. Pick them up, and double-quick for the shed door,' says he, just as if he was on parade. Then we saw what he was afther, and double-quick we went. Begobs, that door went down as if it was paper. He was the first in. 'Stand back,' says he, 'till Oi see what's needed.' Yez should have seen him walk into that sheet av flame, an' stand theer, quiet-like, thinkin', an' it so hot that we at the door were coverin' our faces to save them from scorchin'. Then he says: 'Get your muskets!' We went, an' Moike says to me: 'It's no good. No man can touch them cars. He's goin' to attind to the strikers.' But not he. He came out, an' he says: 'B'ys, it's hot in there, but, if you don't mind a bit av a burn, we can get the poor fellows out. Will yez try?' 'Yes!' we shouted. So he explained how we could push cars widout touchin' them. 'Fall in,' says he. 'Fix bayonets. First file to the right av the cars, second rank to the left. Forward march!' An' we went into that hell, an' rolled them cars out just as if we was marchin' down Broadway, wid flags, an' music, an' women clappin' hands.''

"But weren't you dreadfully burnt?"

"Oh, miss, yez should have seen us! We was blacker thin the divil himsilf. Hardly one av us but didn't have the hair burnt off the part his cap didn't cover; an', as for eyelashes, an' mustaches, an' blisters, no one thought av them the next day. Shure, the whole company was in bed, except them as couldn't lie easy."

"And Mr. Stirling?"

"Shure, don't yez know about him?"

"No."

"Why, he was dreadful burnt, an' the doctors thought it would be blind he'd be; but he went to Paris, an' they did somethin' to him there that saved him. Oh, miss, the boys were nearly crazy wid fear av losin' him. They'd rather be afther losin' the regimental cat.''

Peter had been tempted to interrupt two or three times, but it was so absorbing to watch Leonore's face, and its changing expression, as, unconscious of his presence, she listened to Dennis, that Peter had not the heart to do it. But now Watts spoke up.

"Do you hear that, Peter? There's value for you! You're better than the cat."

So the scenes were shifted, and they all sat and chatted till Dennis left. Then the necessary papers were brought in and looked over at Peter's study-table, and Miss D'Alloi took another of his pens. Peter hoped she'd stop and think a little, again, but she didn't. Just as she had begun an L she hesitated, however.

"Why," she said, "this paper calls me 'Leonore D'Alloi, spinster!' I'm not going to sign that."

"That is merely the legal term," Peter explained. Leonore pouted for some time over it, but finally signed. "I shan't be a spinster, anyway, even if the paper does say so," she said.

Peter agreed with her.

"See what a great blot I've made on your clean blotter," said Leonore, who had rested the pen-point there. "I'm very sorry." Then she wrote on the blotter, "Leonore D'Alloi. Her very untidy mark." "That was what Madame Mellerie always made me write on my exercises."

Then they said "Good-bye." "I like down-town New York better and better," said Leonore.

So did Peter.

CHAPTER XLIII

A BIRTHDAY EVENING

PETER went into Ray's office on Monday. "I want your advice," he said. "I'm going to a birthday dinner to-morrow. A girl for whom I'm trustee. Now, how handsome a present may I send her?"

"H'm. How well do you know her?"

"We are good friends."

"Just about what you please, I should say, if you know her well, and make money out of her?"

"That is, jewelry?"

"Ye-es."

"Thanks." Peter turned.

"Who is she, Peter? I thought you never did anything so small as that. Nothing, or four figures, has always seemed your rule?"

"This had extenuating circumstances," smiled Peter.

So when Peter shook hands, the next evening, with the very swagger young lady who stood beside her mother, receiving, he was told:

"It's perfectly lovely! Look." And the little wrist was held up to him. "And so were the flowers. I couldn't carry a tenth of them, so I decided to only take papa's. But I put yours up in my room, and shall keep them there." Then Peter had to give place to another, just as he had decided that he would have one of the flowers from the bunch she was carrying, or—he left the awful consequences of failure blank.

Peter stood for a moment unconscious of the other people, looking at the pretty rounded figure in the dainty evening dress of French open-work embroidery. "I didn't think she could be lovelier than she was in her street and riding dresses but she is made for evening dress," was his thought. He knew this observation wasn't right, however, so he glanced round the room, and then walked up to a couple.

"There, I told Mr. Beekman that I was trying to magnetize you, and though your back was turned, you came to me at once."

"Er—really, quite wonderful, you know," said Mr. Beekman. "I positively sharn't dare to be left alone with you, Miss De Voe."

"You needn't fear me. I shall never try to magnetize you, Mr. Beekman," said Miss De Voe. "I was so pleased," she continued, turning to Peter, "to see you take that deliberate survey of the room, and then come over here."

Peter smiled. "I go out so little now, that I have turned selfish. I don't go to entertain people. I go to be entertained. Tell me what you have been doing?"

But as Peter spoke, there was a little stir, and Peter had to say "excuse me." He crossed the room, and said, "I am to have the pleasure, Mrs. Grinnell," and a moment later the two were walking towards the dining-room. Miss De Voe gave her arm to Beekman calmly, but her eyes followed Peter. They both could have made a better arrangement. Most dinner guests can.

It was a large dinner, and so was served in the ballroom. The sixty people gathered were divided into little groups, and seated at small tables holding six or eight. Peter knew all but one at his table, to the extent of having had previous meetings. They were all fashionables, and the talk took the usual literary-artistic-musical turn

customary with that set. "Men, not principles" is the
way society words the old cry, or perhaps "personalities,
not generalities" is a better form. So Peter ate his
dinner quietly, the conversation being general enough not
to force him to do more than respond, when appealed
to. He was, it is true, appealed to frequently. Peter had
the reputation, as many quiet men have, of being brainy.
Furthermore he knew the right kind of people, was known
to enjoy a large income, was an eligible bachelor, and
was "interesting and unusual." So society no longer
rolled its Juggernaut over him regardlessly, as of yore.
A man who was close friends with half a dozen exclusives of the exclusives, was a man not to be disregarded,
simply because he didn't talk. Society people applied much
the same test as did the little angle children, only in place
of "He's friends wid der perlice," they substituted "He's
very intimate with Miss De Voe, and the Ogdens and the
Pells."

Peter had dimly hoped that he would find himself seated
at Leonore's table—he had too much self-depreciation
to think for a moment that he would take her in—but
hers was a young table, he saw, and he would not have
minded so much if it hadn't been for that Marquis. Peter
began to have a very low opinion of foreigners. Then
he remembered that Leonore had the same prejudice, so
he became more reconciled to the fact that the Marquis
was sitting next her. And when Leonore sent him a look
and a smile, and held up the wrist, so as to show the pearl
bracelet, Peter suddenly thought what a delicious *rissole*
he was eating.

As the dinner waned, one of the footmen brought him a
card, on which Watts had written: "They want me to say
a few words of welcome and of Dot. Will you respond?"
Peter read the note and then wrote below it: "Dear Miss
D'Alloi: You see the above. May I pay you a compliment? Only one? Or will it embarrass you?" When
the card came back a new line said: "Dear Peter: I am
not afraid of your compliment, and am very curious to
hear it." Peter said, "Tell Mr. D'Alloi that I will with
pleasure." Then he tucked the card in his pocket. That
card was not going to be wasted.

So presently the glasses were filled up, even Peter saying, "You may give me a glass," and Watts was on his feet. He gave "our friends" a pleasant welcome, and after apologizing for their absence, said that at least, "like the little wife in the children's play, 'We too have not been idle,' for we bring you a new friend and introduce her to you to-night."

Then Peter rose, and told the host: "Your friends have been grieved at your long withdrawal from them, as the happy faces and welcome we tender you this evening, show. We feared that the fascination of European art, with its beauty and ease and finish, had come to overweigh the love of American nature, despite its life and strength and freshness; that we had lost you for all time. But to-night we can hardly regret even this long interlude, if to that circumstance we owe the happiest and most charming combination of American nature and European art—Miss D'Alloi."

Then there was applause, and a drinking of Miss D'Alloi's health, and the ladies passed out of the room—to enjoy themselves, be it understood, leaving the men in the gloomy, quarrelsome frame of mind it always does.

Peter apparently became much abstracted over his cigar, but the abstraction was not perhaps very deep, for he was on his feet the moment Watts rose, and was the first to cross the hall into the drawing-room. He took a quick glance round the room, and then crossed to a sofa. Dorothy and—and some one else were sitting on it.

"Speaking of angels," said Dorothy.

"I wasn't speaking of you," said Peter. "Only thinking."

"There," said Leonore. "Now if Mrs. Grinnell had only heard that."

Peter looked a question, so Leonore continued:

"We were talking about you. I don't understand you. You are so different from what I had been told to think you. Every one said you were very silent and very uncomplimentary, and never joked, but you are not a bit as they said, and I thought you had probably changed, just as you had about the clothes. But Mrs. Grinnell says she never heard you make a joke or a compliment in her life, and that at the Knickerbocker they call you 'Peter, the silent.' You are a great puzzle."

Dorothy laughed. "Here we four women—Mrs. Grinnell, and Mrs. Winthrop and Leonore and myself—have been quarrelling over you, and each insisting you are something different. I believe you are not a bit firm and stable, as people say you are, but a perfect chameleon, changing your tint according to the color of the tree you are on. Leonore was the worst, though! She says that you talk and joke a great deal. We could have stood anything but that!"

"I am sorry my conversation and humor are held in such low estimation."

"There," said Leonore. "See. Didn't I tell you he joked? And, Peter, do you dislike women?"

"Unquestionably," said Peter.

"Please tell me. I told them of your speech about the sunshine, and Mrs. Winthrop says that she knows you didn't mean it. That you are a woman-hater and despise all women, and like to get off by yourself."

"That's the reason I joined you and Dorothy," said Peter.

"Do you hate women?" persisted Leonore.

"A man is not bound to incriminate himself," replied Peter, smiling.

"Then that's the reason why you don't like society, and why you are so untalkative to women. I don't like men who think badly of women. Now, I want to know why you don't like them?"

"Supposing," said Peter, "you were asked to sit down to a game of whist, without knowing anything of the game. Do you think you could like it?"

"No. Of course not!"

"Well, that is my situation toward women. They have never liked me, nor treated me as they do other men. And so, when I am put with a small-talk woman, I feel all at sea, and, try as I may, I can't please her. They are never friendly with me as they are with other men."

"Rubbish!" said Dorothy. "It's what you do, not what she does, that makes the trouble. You look at a woman with those grave eyes and that stern jaw of yours, and we all feel that we are fools on the spot, and really become so. I never stopped being afraid of you till I found out that in reality you were afraid of me. You know you are. You are afraid of all women."

"He isn't a bit afraid of women," affirmed Leonore.

Just then Mr. Beekman came up. "Er—Mrs. Rivington. You know this is—er—a sort of house-warming, and they tell me we are to go over the house, don't you know, if we wish. May I harve the pleasure?"

Dorothy conferred the boon. Peter looked down at Leonore with a laugh in his eyes. "Er—Miss D'Alloi," he said, with the broadest of accents, "you know this,—er—is a sort of house-warming and——" He only imitated so far and then they both laughed.

Leonore rose. "With pleasure, I only wish Mrs. Grinnell had heard you. I didn't know you could mimic?"

"I oughtn't. It's a small business. But I am so happy that I couldn't resist the temptation."

Leonore asked, "What makes you so happy?"

"My new friend," said Peter.

Leonore went on up the stairs without saying anything. At the top, however, she said, enthusiastically: "You do say the nicest things! What room would you like to see first?"

"Yours," said Peter.

So they went into the little bedroom, and boudoir, and looked over them. Of course Peter found a tremendous number of things of interest. There were her pictures, most of them her own purchases in Europe; and her books and what she thought of them; and her thousand little knick-knacks of one kind and another. Peter wasn't at all in a hurry to see the rest of the house.

"These are the photographs of my real friends," said Leonore, "except yours. I want you to give me one to complete my rack."

"I haven't had a photograph taken in eight years, and am afraid I have none left."

"Then you must sit."

"Very well. But it must be an exchange." Peter almost trembled at his boldness, and at the thought of a possible granting.

"Do you want mine?"

"Very much."

"I have dozens," said Leonore, going over to her desk, and pulling open a drawer. "I'm very fond of being taken. You may have your choice."

"That's very difficult," said Peter, looking at the different varieties. "Each has something the rest haven't. You don't want to be generous, and let me have these four?"

"Oh, you greedy!" said Leonore, laughing. "Yes, if you'll do something I'm going to ask you."

Peter pocketed the four. "That is a bargain," he said, with a brashness simply disgraceful in a good business man. "Now, what is it?"

"Miss De Voe told me long ago about your savings-bank fund for helping the poor people. Now that I have come into my money, I want to do what she does. Give a thousand dollars a year to it—and then you are to tell me just what you do with it."

"Of course I'm bound to take it, if you insist. But it won't do any good. Even Miss De Voe has stopped giving now, and I haven't added anything to it for over five years."

"Why is that?"

"You see, I began by loaning the fund to people who were in trouble, or who could be boosted a little by help, and for three or four years, I found the money went pretty fast. By that time people began to pay it back, with interest often, and there has hardly been a case when it hasn't been repaid. So what with Miss De Voe's contributions, and the return of the money, I really have more than I can properly use already. There's only about eight thousand loaned at present, and nearly five thousand in bank."

"I'm so sorry!" said Leonore. "But couldn't you give some of the money, so that it wouldn't come back?"

"That does more harm than good. It's like giving opium to kill temporary pain. It stops the pain for the moment, but only to weaken the system so as to make the person less able to bear pain in the future. That's the trouble with most of our charity. It weakens quite as much as it helps."

"I have thought about this for five years as something I should do. I'm so grieved." And Leonore looked her words.

Peter could not stand that look. "I've been thinking of sending a thousand dollars of the fund, that I didn't think there was much chance of using, to a Fresh Air fund and the Day Nursery. If you wish I'll send two thousand instead and then take your thousand? Then I can use that for whatever I have a chance."

"That will do nicely. But I thought you didn't think regular charities did much good?"

"Some don't. But it's different with children. They don't feel the stigma and are not humiliated or made indolent by help. We can't do too much to help them. The future of this country depends on its poor children. If they are to do right, they must be saved from ill-health, and ignorance, and vice; and the first step is to give them good food and air, so that they shall have strong little bodies. A sound man, physically, may not be a strong man in other ways, but he stands a much better chance."

"Oh, it's very interesting," said Leonore. "Tell me some more about the poor people."

"What shall I tell you?" said Peter.

"How to help them."

"I'll speak about something I have had in mind for a long time, trying to find some way to do it. I think the finest opportunity for benevolence, not already attempted, would be a company to lend money to the poor, just as I have attempted, on a small scale, in my ward. You see there are thousands of perfectly honest people who are living on day wages, and many of them can lay up little or no money. Then comes sickness, or loss of employment, or a fire which burns up all their furniture and clothes, or some other mischance, and they can turn only to pawnbrokers and usurers, with their fearful charges; or charity, with its shame. Then there are hundreds of people whom a loan of a little money would help wonderfully. This boy can get a place if he had a respectable suit of clothes. Another can obtain work by learning a trade, but can't live while he learns it. A woman can support herself if she can buy a sewing-machine, but hasn't the money to buy it. Another can get a job at something, but is required to make a deposit to the value of the goods intrusted to her. Now, if all these people could go to some company, and tell their story, and get their notes discounted, according to their reputation, just as the merchant does at his bank, don't you see what a help it would be?"

"How much would it take, Peter?"

"One cannot say, because, till it is tested, there would be no way of knowing how much would be asked for. But a hundred thousand dollars would do to start with."

"Why, that's only a hundred people giving a thousand each," cried Leonore eagerly. "Peter, I'll give a thousand, and I'll make mamma and papa give a thousand, and I'll speak to my friends and——"

"Money isn't the difficult part," said Peter, longing to a fearful degree to take Leonore in his arms. "If it were only money, I could do it myself—or if I did not choose to do it alone, Miss De Voe and Pell would help me."

"What is it, then?"

"It's finding the right man to run such a company. I can't give the time, for I can do more good in other directions. It needs a good business man, yet one who must have many other qualities which rarely go with a business training. He must understand the poor, because he must look into every case, to see if it is a safe risk—or rather if the past life of the applicant indicates that he is entitled to help. Now if your grandfather, who is such an able banker, were to go into my ward, and ask about the standing of a man in it, he wouldn't get any real information. But if I ask, every one will tell me what he thinks. The man in control of such a bank must be able to draw out the truth. Unless the management was just what it ought to be, it would be bankrupt in a few months, or else would not lend to one quarter of the people who deserve help. Yet from my own experience, I know, that money can be loaned to these people, so that the legal interest more than pays for the occasional loss, and that most of these losses are due to inability, more than to dishonesty."

"I wish we could go on talking," sighed Leonore. "But the people are beginning to go downstairs. I suppose I must go, so as to say good-bye. I only wish I could help you in charity."

"You have given *me* a great charity this evening," said Peter.

"You mean the photographs," smiled Leonore.

"No."

"What else?"

"You have shown me the warmest and most loving of hearts," said Peter, "and that is the best charity in the world."

On the way down they met Lispenard coming up. "I've just said good-night to your mother. I would have spoken to you while we were in your room, but you were so engrossed that Miss Winthrop and I thought we had better not interrupt."

"I didn't see you," said Leonore.

"Indeed!" said Lispenard, with immense wonderment. "I can believe that. You know you were cutting us." Then he turned to Peter. "You old scamp, you," he whispered, "you are worse than the Standard Oil."

"I sent for you some time ago, Leonore," said her mother, disapprovingly. "The guests have been going and you were not here."

"I'm sorry, mamma. I was showing Peter the house."

"Good-night," said that individual. "I dread formal dinners usually, but this one has been the pleasantest of my life."

"That's very nice. And thank you, Peter, for the bracelet, and the flowers, and the compliment. They were all lovely. Would you like a rose?"

Would he? He said nothing, but he looked enough to get it.

"Can't we put you down?" said a man at the door. "It's not so far from Washington Square to your place, that your company won't repay us."

"Thank you," said Peter, "but I have a hansom here."

Yet Peter did not ride. He dismissed the cabby, and

walked down the Avenue. Peter was not going to com-
press his happiness inside a carriage that evening. He
needed the whole atmosphere to contain it.

As he strode along he said:

"It isn't her beauty and grace alone"—(It never is with
a man, oh, no!)—"but her truth and frankness and friendliness. And then she doesn't care for money, and she
isn't eaten up with ambition. She is absolutely untouched
by the world yet. Then she is natural, yet reserved, with
other men. She's not husband-hunting, like so many of
them. And she's loving, not merely of those about her,
but of everything."

Musicians will take a simple theme and on it build unlimited variations. This was what Peter proceeded to
do. From Fifty-seventh Street to Peter's rooms was a
matter of four miles. Peter had not half finished his the-
matic treatment of Leonore when he reached his quarters.
He sat down before his fire, however, and went on, not
with hope of exhausting all possible variations, but merely
for his own pleasure.

Finally, however, he rose and put photographs, rose,
and card away.

"I've not allowed myself to yield to it," he said (which
was a whopper) "till I was sure she was what I could
always love. Now I shall do my best to make her love
me."

CHAPTER XLIV

A GOOD DAY

THE next day it was raining torrents, but despite this,
and to the utter neglect of his law business, Peter drove
up-town immediately after lunch, to the house in Fifty-
seventh Street. He asked for Watts, but while he was
waiting for the return of the servant, he heard a light foot-
step, and turning, he found Leonore fussing over some
flowers. At the same moment she became conscious of
his presence.

"Good-day," said Peter.

"It isn't a good day at all," said Leonore, in a disconsolate voice, holding out her hand nevertheless.

"Why not?"

"It's a horrid day, and I'm in disgrace."

"For what?"

"For misbehaving last night. Both mamma and madame say I did very wrong. I never thought I couldn't be real friends with you." The little lips were trembling slightly.

Peter felt a great temptation to say something strong. "Why can't the women let such an innocent child alone?" he thought to himself. Aloud he said, "If any wrong was done, which I don't think, it was my fault. Can I do anything?"

"I don't believe so," said Leonore, with a slight unsteadiness in her voice. "They say that men will always monopolize a girl if she will allow it, and that a really well-mannered one won't permit it for a moment."

Peter longed to take her in his arms and lay the little downcast head against his shoulder, but he had to be content with saying: "I am so sorry they blame you. If I could only save you from it." He evidently said it in a comforting voice, for the head was raised a trifle.

"You see," said Leonore, "I've always been very particular with men, but with you it seemed different. Yet they both say I stayed too long upstairs, and were dreadfully shocked about the photographs. They said I ought to treat you like other men. Don't you think you are different?"

Yes. Peter thought he was very different.

"Mr. D'Alloi will see you in the library," announced the footman at this point.

Peter turned to go, but in leaving he said: "Is there any pleasure or service I can do, to make up for the trouble I've caused you?"

Leonore put her head on one side, and looked a little less grief-stricken. "May I save that up?" she asked.

"Yes."

A moment later Peter was shaking hands with Watts.

"This is nice of you. Quite like old times. Will you smoke?"

"No. But please yourself. I've something to talk about."

"Fire away."

"Watts, I want to try and win the love of your little girl."

"Dear old man," cried Watts, "there isn't any one in God's earth whom I would rather see her choose, or to whom I would sooner trust her."

"Thank you, Watts," said Peter, gratefully. "Watts is weak, but he is a good fellow," was his mental remark. Peter entirely forgot his opinion of two weeks ago. It is marvellous what a change a different point of view makes in most people.

"But if I give you my little Dot, you must promise me one thing."

"What is that?"

"That you will never tell her? Ah! Peter, if you knew how I love the little woman, and how she loves me. From no other man can she learn what will alter that love. Don't make my consent bring us both suffering?"

"Watts, I give my word she shall never know the truth from me."

"God bless you, Peter. True as ever. Then that is settled. You shall have a clear field and every chance."

"I fear not. There's something more. Mrs. D'Alloi won't pardon that incident—nor do I blame her. I can't force my presence here if she does not give her consent. It would be too cruel, even if I could hope to succeed in spite of her. I want to see her this morning. You can tell better than I whether you had best speak to her first, or whether I shall tell her."

"H'm. That is a corker, isn't it? Don't you think you had better let things drift?"

"No. I'm not going to try and win a girl's love behind the mother's back. Remember, Watts, the mother is the only one to whom a girl can go at such a time. We mustn't try to take advantage of either."

"Well, I'll speak to her, and do my best. Then I'll send her to you. Help yourself to the tobacco if you get tired of waiting *tout seul.*"

Watts went upstairs and knocked at a door. "Yes,"

said a voice. Watts put his head in. "Is my Rosebud so busy that she can't spare her lover a few moments?"

"Watts, you know I live for you."

Watts dropped down on the lounge. "Come here, then, like a loving little wife, and let me say my little say."

No woman nearing forty can resist a little tenderness in her husband, and Mrs. D'Alloi snuggled up to Watts in the pleasantest frame of mind. Watts leaned over and kissed her cheek. Then Mrs. D'Alloi snuggled some more.

"Now, I want to talk with you seriously, dear," he said. "Who do you think is downstairs?"

"Who?"

"Dear old Peter. And what do you think he's come for!"

"What?"

"Dot."

"For what?"

"He wants our consent, dear, to pay his addresses to Leonore."

"Oh, Watts!" Mrs. D'Alloi ceased to snuggle, and turned a horrified face to her husband.

"I've thought she attracted him, but he's such an impassive, cool old chap, that I wasn't sure."

"That's what I've been so afraid of. I've worried so over it."

"You dear, foolish little woman. What was there to worry over?"

"Watts! You won't give your consent?"

"Of course we will. Why, what more do you want? Money, reputation, brains, health." (That was the order in which Peter's advantages ranged themselves in Watts's mind.) "I don't see what more you can ask, short of a title, and titles not only never have all those qualities combined, but they are really getting decidedly *nouveau richey* and not respectable enough for a Huguenot family, who've lived two hundred and fifty years in New York. What a greedy mamma she is for her little girl."

"Oh, Watts! But think!"

"It's hard work, dear, with your eyes to look at. But I will, if you'll tell me what to think about."

"My husband! You cannot have forgotten? Oh, no! It is too horrible for you to have forgotten that day."

"You heavenly little Puritan! So you are going to refuse Peter as a son-in-law, because he—ah—he's not a Catholic monk. Why, Rosebud, if you are going to apply that rule to all Dot's lovers, you had better post a sign: 'Wanted, a husband. P. S. No man need apply.'"

"Watts! Don't talk so."

"Dear little woman. I'm only trying to show you that we can't do better than trust our little girl to Peter."

"With that stain! Oh, Watts, give him our pure, innocent, spotless child!"

"Oh, well. If you want a spotless wedding, let her marry the Church. She'll never find one elsewhere, my darling."

"Watts! How can you talk so? And with yourself as an example. Oh, husband! I want our child—our only child—to marry a man as noble and true as her father. Surely there must be others like you?"

"Yes. I think there are a great many men as good as I, Rosebud. But I'm no better than I should be, and it's nothing but your love that makes you think I am."

"I won't hear you say such things of yourself. You know you are the best and purest man that ever lived. You know you are."

"If there's any good in me, it's because I married you."

"Watts, you couldn't be bad if you tried." And Mrs. D'Alloi put her arms round Watts's neck and kissed him.

Watts fondled her for a moment in true lover's fashion. Then he said, "Dear little wife, a pure woman can never quite know what this world is. I love Dot next to you, and would not give her to a man whom I believe would not be true to her, or make her happy. I know every circumstance of Peter's connection with that woman, and he is as blameless as man ever was. Such as it was, it was ended years ago, and can never give him more trouble. He is a strong man, and will be true to Dot. She might get a man who would make her life one long torture. She may be won by a man who only cares for her money, and will not even give her the husks of love. But Peter loves her, and has outgrown his mistakes. And don't forget that but for him we might now have nothing but some horribly mangled remains to remember of our little darling. Dear, I love Dot twenty times more than I love Peter. For her sake, and yours, I am trying to do my best for her."

So presently Mrs. D'Alloi came into the library, where Peter sat. She held out her hand to him, but Peter said:

"Let me say something first. Mrs. D'Alloi, I would not have had that occurrence happen in your home or presence if I had been able to prevent it. It grieves me more than I can tell you. I am not a roué. In spite of appearances I have lived a clean life. I shall never live any other in the future. I—I love Leonore. Love her very dearly. And if you will give her to me, should I win her, I pledge you my word that I will give her the love, and tenderness, and truth which she deserves. Now, will you give me your hand?"

"He is speaking the truth," thought Mrs. D'Alloi, as Peter spoke. She held out her hand. "I will trust her to you if she chooses you."

Half an hour later, Peter went back to the drawing-room, to find Leonore reposing in an exceedingly undignified position before the fire on a big tiger-skin, and stroking a Persian cat, who, in delight at this enviable treatment, purred and dug its claws into the rug. Peter stood for a time watching the pretty tableau, wishing he was a cat.

"Yes. Tawny-eye," said Leonore, in heartrending tones, "it isn't a good day at all."

"I'm going to quarrel with you on that," said Peter. "It's a glorious day."

Leonore rose from the skin. "Tawny-eye and I don't think so."

"But you will. In the first place I've explained about the monopoly and the photographs to your mamma, and she says she did not understand it, and that no one is to blame. Secondly, she says I'm to stay to dinner and am to monopolize you till then. Thirdly, she says we may be just as good friends as we please. Fourthly, she has asked me to come and stay for a week at Grey-Court this summer. Now, what kind of a day is it?"

"Simply glorious! Isn't it, Tawny-eye?" And the young lady again forgot her "papas, proprieties, potatoes, prunes and prisms," and dropping down on the rug, buried her face in the cat's long silky hair. Then she reappeared long enough to say:

"You are such a comforting person! I'm so glad you were born."

CHAPTER XLV

THE BOSS

AFTER this statement, so satisfying to both, Leonore recovered her dignity enough to rise, and say, "Now, I want to pay you for your niceness. What do you wish to do?"

"Suppose we do what pleases you."

"No. I want to please you."

"That *is* the way to please me," said Peter emphatically. Just then a clock struck four. "I know," said Leonore. "Come to the tea-table, and we'll have afternoon tea together. It's the day of all others for afternoon tea."

"I just said it was a glorious day."

"Oh, yes. It's a nice day. But it's dark and cold and rainy all the same."

"But that makes it all the better. We shan't be interrupted."

"Do you know," said Leonore, "that Miss De Voe told me once that you were a man who found good in everything, and I see what she meant."

"I can't hold a candle to Dennis. He says it's 'a foine day' so that you feel that it really is. I never saw him in my life, when it wasn't 'a foine day.' I tell him he carries his sunshine round in his heart."

"You are so different," said Leonore, "from what every one said. I never knew a man pay such nice compliments. That's the seventh I've heard you make."

"You know I'm a politician, and want to become popular."

"Oh, Peter! Will you let me ask you something?"

"Anything," said Peter, rashly, though speaking the absolute truth. Peter just then was willing to promise anything. Perhaps it was the warm cup of tea; perhaps it was the blazing logs; perhaps it was the shade of the lamp, which cast such a pleasant rosy tint over everything; perhaps it was the comfortable chair; perhaps it was that charming face; perhaps it was what Mr. Mantalini called the "demd total."

"You see," said Leonore, shaking her head in a puzzled way, "I've begun to read the papers—the political part, I mean—and there are so many things I don't understand which I want to ask you to explain."

"That is very nice," said Peter, "because there are a great many things of which I want to tell you."

"Goody!" said Leonore, forgetting again she was now bound to conduct herself as befit a society girl. "And you'll not laugh at me if I ask foolish questions?"

"No."

"Then what do the papers mean by calling you a boss?"

"That I am supposed to have sufficient political power to dictate to a certain extent."

"But don't they speak of a boss as something not nice?" asked Leonore, a little timidly, as if afraid of hurting Peter's feelings.

"Usually it is used as a stigma," said Peter, smiling. "At least by the kind of papers you probably read."

"But you are not a bad boss, are you?" said Leonore, very earnestly.

"Some of the papers say so."

"That's what surprised me. Of course I knew they were wrong, but are bosses bad, and are you a boss?"

"You are asking me one of the biggest questions in American politics. I probably can't answer it, but I'll try to show you why I can't. Are there not friends whose advice or wish would influence you?"

"Yes. Like you," said Leonore, giving Peter a glimpse of her eyes.

"Really," thought Peter, "if she does that often, I can't talk abstract politics." Then he rallied and said: "Well, that is the condition of men as well, and it is that condition, which creates the so-called boss. In every community there are men who influence more or less the rest. It may be that one can only influence half a dozen other intimates. Another may exert power over fifty. A third may sway a thousand. One may do it by mere physical superiority. Another by a friendly manner. A third by being better informed. A fourth by a deception or bribery. A fifth by honesty. Each has something that dominates the weaker men about him. Take my ward. Burton is a prize-fighter, and physically a splendid man. So he has his little court. Driscoll is a humorist, and can talk, and he has his admirers. Sloftky is popular with the Jews, because he is of their race. Burrows is a policeman, who is liked by the whole ward, because of his kindness and good-nature. So I could go on telling you of men who are a little more marked than the rest, who have power to influence the opinions of men about them, and therefore have power to influence votes. That is the first step in the ladder."

"But isn't Mr. Moriarty one?"

"He comes in the next grade. Each of the men I have mentioned can usually affect an average of twenty-five votes. But now we get to another rung of the ladder. Here we have Dennis, and such men as Blunkers, Denton, Kennedy, Schlurger and others. They not merely have their own set of followers, but they have more or less power to dominate the little bosses of whom I have already spoken. Take Dennis for instance. He has fifty adherents who stick to him absolutely, two hundred and fifty who listen to him with interest, and a dozen of the smaller bosses, who pass his opinions to their followers. So he can thus have some effect on about five hundred votes. Of course it takes more force and popularity to do this and in this way we have a better grade of men."

"Yes. I like Mr. Moriarty, and can understand why others do. He is so ugly, and so honest, and so jolly. He's lovely."

"Then we get another grade. Usually men of a good

deal of brain force, though not of necessity well educated. They influence all below them by being better informed, and by being more far-seeing. Such men as Gallagher and Dummer. They, too, are usually in politics for a living, and so can take the trouble to work for ends for which the men with other work have no time. They don't need the great personal popularity of those I have just mentioned, but they need far more skill and brain. Now you can see, that these last, in order to carry out their intentions, must meet and try to arrange to pull together, for otherwise they can do nothing. Naturally, in a dozen or twenty men, there will be grades, and very often a single man will be able to dominate them all, just as the smaller bosses dominate the smaller men. And this man the papers call a boss of a ward. Then when these various ward bosses endeavor to unite for general purposes, the strongest man will sway them, and he is boss of the city."

"And that is what you are?"

"Yes. By that I mean that nothing is attempted in the ward or city without consultation with me. But of course I am more dependent on the voters than they are on me, for if they choose to do differently from what I advise, they have the power, while I am helpless."

"You mean the smaller bosses?"

"Not so much them as the actual voters. A few times I have shot right over the heads of the bosses and appealed directly to the voters."

"Then you can make them do what you want?"

"Within limits, yes. As I told you, I am absolutely dependent on the voters. If they should defeat what I want three times running, every one would laugh at me, and my power would be gone. So you see that a boss is only a boss so long as he can influence votes."

"But they haven't defeated you?"

"No, not yet."

"But if the voters took their opinions from the other bosses how did you do anything?"

"There comes in the problem of practical politics. The question of who can affect the voters most. Take my own ward. Suppose that I want something done so much that I insist. And suppose that some of the other leaders

are equally determined that it shan't be done. The ward
splits on the question and each faction tries to gain control in the primary. When I have had to interfere, I go
right down among the voters and tell them why and what
I want to do. Then the men I have had to antagonize
do the same, and the voters decide between us. It then
is a question as to which side can win the majority of
the voters. Because I have been very successful in this,
I am the so-called boss. That is, I can make the voters
feel that I am right."

"How?"

"For many reasons. First, I have always tried to tell
the voters the truth, and never have been afraid to acknowledge I was wrong, when I found I had made a mistake, so people trust what I say. Then, unlike most of the
leaders in politics, I am not trying to get myself office
or profit, and so the men feel that I am disinterested.
Then I try to be friendly with the whole ward, so that if
I have to do what they don't like, their personal feeling
for me will do what my arguments never could. With
these simple, strong-feeling, and unreasoning folk, one
can get ten times the influence by a warm hand-shake
and word that one can by a logical argument. We are so
used to believing what we read, if it seems reasonable,
that it is hard for us to understand that men who spell
out editorials with difficulty, and who have not been
trained to reason from facts, are not swayed by what to
us seems an obvious argument. But, on the contrary, if
a man they trust, puts it in plain language to them, they
see it at once. I might write a careful editorial, and ask
my ward to read it, and unless they knew I wrote it, they
probably wouldn't be convinced in the least. But let me
go into the saloons, and tell the men just the same thing,
and there isn't a man who wouldn't be influenced by it."

"You are so popular in the ward?" asked Leonore.

"I think so. I find kind words and welcome everywhere. But then I have tried very hard to be popular.
I have endeavored to make a friend of every man in it
with whom one could be friendly, because I wished to be
as powerful as possible, so that the men would side with

me whenever I put my foot down on something wrong."

"Do you ever tell the ward how they are to vote?"

"I tell them my views. But never how to vote. Once I came very near it, though."

"How was that?"

"I was laid up for eight months by my eyes, part of the time in Paris. The primary in the meantime had put up a pretty poor man for an office. A fellow who had been sentenced for murder, but had been pardoned by political influence. When I was able to take a hand, I felt that I could do better by interfering, so I came out for the Republican candidate, who was a really fine fellow. I tried to see and talk to every man in the ward, and on election day I asked a good many men, as a personal favor, to vote for the Republican, and my friends asked others. Even Dennis Moriarty worked and voted for what he calls a 'dirty Republican,' though he said 'he never thought he'd soil his hands wid one av their ballots.' That is the nearest I ever came to telling them how to vote."

"And did they do as you asked?"

"The only Republican the ward has chosen since 1862 was elected in that year. It was a great surprise to every one—even to myself—for the ward is Democratic by about four thousand majority. But I couldn't do that sort of thing often, for the men wouldn't stand it. In other words, I can only do what I want myself, by doing enough else that the men wish. That is, the more I can do to please the men, the more they yield their opinions to mine."

"Then the bosses really can't do what they want?"

"No. Or at least not for long. That is a newspaper fallacy. A relic of the old idea that great things are done by one-man power. If you will go over the men who are said to control—the bosses, as they are called—in this city, you will find that they all have worked their way into influence slowly, and have been many years kept in power, though they could be turned out in a single fight. Yet this power is obtained only by the wish of a majority, for the day they lose the consent of a majority of the voters that day their power ends. We are really more dependent than the representatives, for they are elected for a certain time, while our tenure can be ended at any moment. Why am I a power in my ward? Because I am supposed to represent a given number of votes, which are influenced by my opinions. It would be perfectly immaterial to my importance how I influenced those votes, so long as I could control them. But because I can influence them, the other leaders don't dare to antagonize me, and so I can have my way up to a certain point. And because I can control the ward I have made it a great power in city politics."

"How did you do that?"

"By keeping down the factional feeling. You see there are always more men struggling for power or office, than can have it, and so there cannot but be bad blood between the contestants. For instance, when I first became interested in politics, Moriarty and Blunkers were quite as anxious to down each other as to down the Republicans. Now they are sworn friends, made so in this case, by mere personal liking for me. Some have been quieted in this way. Others by being held in check. Still others by different means. Each man has to be studied and understood, and the particular course taken which seems best in his particular case. But I succeeded even with some who were pretty bitter antagonists at first, and from being one of the most uncertain wards in the city, the sixth has been known at headquarters for the last five years as 'old reliability' from the big majority it always polls. So at headquarters I am looked up to and consulted. Now do you understand why and what a boss is?"

"Yes, Peter. Except why bosses are bad."

"Don't you see that it depends on what kind of men they are, and what kind of voters are back of them? A good man, with honest votes back of him, is a good boss, and *vice versa.*"

"Then I know you are a good boss. It's a great pity that all the bosses can't be good?"

"I have not found them so bad. They are quite as honest, unselfish, and reasonable as the average of mankind. Now and then there is a bad man, as there is likely to be anywhere. But in my whole political career, I have never known a man who could control a thousand votes for five years, who was not a better man, all in all, than the voters whom he influenced. More one cannot expect. The people are not quick, but they find out a knave or a demagogue if you give them time."

"It's the old saying: 'You can fool all of the people, some of the time, and some of the people all of the time, but you can't fool all of the people all of the time,'" laughed a voice.

Peter took his eyes off Leonore's face, where they had been resting restfully, and glanced up. Watts had entered the room.

"Go on," said Watts. "Don't let me interrupt your political disquisitions; I have only come in for a cup of tea."

"Miss D'Alloi and I were merely discussing bosses," said Peter. "Miss D'Alloi, when women get the ballot, as I hope they will, I trust you will be a good boss, for I am sure you will influence a great many votes."

"Oh!" said Leonore, laughing, "I shan't be a boss at all. You'll be my boss, I think, and I'll always vote for you."

Peter thought the day even more glorious than he had before.

CHAPTER XLVI

THE BETTER ELEMENT

THE evening after this glorious day, Peter came in from his ride, but instead of going at once to his room, he passed down a little passage, and stood in a doorway.

"Is everything going right, Jenifer?" he queried.

"Yissah!"

"The flowers came from Thorley's?"

"Yissah!"

"And the candies and ices from Maillard?"

"Yissah!"

"And you've *frappéd* the champagne?"

"Yissah!"

"Jenifer, don't put quite so much onion juice as usual in the Queen Isabella dressing. Ladies don't like it as much as men."

"Yissah!"

"And you stood the Burgundy in the sun?"

"Yissah! Wha' foh yo' think I doan do as I ginl'y do?"

Jenifer was combining into a stuffing bread crumbs, chopped broiled oysters, onions, and many other mysterious ingredients, and was becoming irritated at such evident doubt of his abilities.

Peter ought to have been satisfied, but he only looked worried. He glanced round the little closet that served as a kitchen, in search of possible sources for slips, but did not see them. All he was able to say was, "That broth smells very nice, Jenifer."

"Yissah. Dar ain't nuffin in dat sup buh a quart a thick cream, and de squeezin's of a hunerd clams, sah. Dat sup will make de angels sorry dey died. Dey'll just tink you'se dreful unkine not to offer dem a secon' help. Buh doan yo' do it, sah, foh when dey gits to dem prayhens, dey'll be pow'ful glad yo' didn't." To himself, Jenifer remarked: "Who he gwine hab dis day? He neber so anxious befoh, not even when de Presidint and Guv'nor Pohter dey dun dine hyah."

Peter went to his room and, after a due course of clubbing and tubbing, dressed himself with the utmost care. Truth compels the confession that he looked in his glass for some minutes. Not, however, apparently with much pleasure, for an anxious look came into his face, and he remarked aloud, as he turned away, "I don't look so old, but I once heard Watts say that I should never take a prize for my looks, and he was right. I wonder if she cares for handsome men?"

Peter forgot his worry in the opening of a box in the dining-room and the taking out of the flowers. He placed the bunches at the different places, raising one of the bouquets of violets to his lips, before he laid it down. Then he took the cut flowers, and smilax, and spread them loosely in the centre of the little table, which otherwise had nothing on it, except the furnishings placed at each seat.   After that he again kissed a bunch of violets. History doesn't state whether it was the same bunch. Peter must have been very fond of flowers!

"Peter," called a voice.

"Is that you, Le Grand? Go right into my room."

"I've done that already.   You see I feel at home.   How are you?" he continued, as Peter joined him in the study.

"As always."

"I thought I would run in early, so as to have a bit of you before the rest.   Peter, here's a letter from Muller. He's got that 'Descent' in its first state, in the most brilliant condition.   You had better get it, and trash your present impression.   It has always looked cheap beside the rest."

"Very well.   Will you attend to it?"

Just then came the sound of voices and the rustle of draperies in the little hall.

"Hello!   Ladies?" said Le Grand.   "This is to be one of what Lispenard calls your 'often, frequently, only once' affairs, is it?"

"I'm afraid we are early," said Mrs. D'Alloi.   "We did not know how much time to allow."

"No.   Such old friends cannot come too soon."

"And as it is, I'm really starved," said another personage, shaking hands with Peter as if she had not seen him for a twelve-month instead of parting with him but two hours before.   "What an appetite riding in the Park does give one!   Especially when afterwards you drive, and drive, and drive, over New York stones."

"Ah," cried Madame.   *"C'est très bien!"*

"Isn't it jolly?" responded Leonore.

"But it is not American.   It is Parisian."

"Oh, no, it isn't!   It's all American.   Isn't it, Peter?"

But Peter was telling Jenifer to hasten the serving of dinner.   So Leonore had to fight her country's battles by herself.

"What's all this to-day's papers are saying, Peter?" asked Watts, as soon as they were seated.

"That's rather a large subject even for a slow dinner."

"I mean about the row in the Democratic organization over the nomination for governor?"

"The papers seem to know more about it than I do," said Peter calmly.

Le Grand laughed. "Miss De Voe, Ogden, Rivington —all of us, have tried to get Peter, first and last, to talk politics, but not a fact do we get. They say it's his ability to hold his tongue which made Costell trust him and push him, and that that was the reason he was chosen to fill Costell's place."

"I don't fill his place," said Peter. "No one can do that. I merely succeeded him. And Miss D'Alloi will tell you that the papers calling me 'Taciturnity Junior' is a libel. Am I not a talker, Miss D'Alloi?"

"I really can't find out," responded Leonore, with a puzzled look. "People say you are not."

"I didn't think you would fail me after the other night."

"Ah," said madame. "The quiet men are the great men. Look at the French."

"Oh, madame!" exclaimed Leonore.

"You are joking," cried Mrs. D'Alloi.

"That's delicious," laughed Watts.

"Whew," said Le Grand, under his breath.

"Ah! Why do you cry out? Mr. Stirling, am I not right?" Madame appealed to the one face on which no amusement or skepticism was shown.

"I think it is rather dangerous to ascribe any particular trait to any nationality. It is usually misleading. But most men who think much, talk little, and the French have many thinkers."

"I always liked Von Moltke, just for it being said of him that he could be silent in seven languages," said Le Grand.

"Yes," said Leonore. "It's so restful. We crossed on the steamer with a French Marquis who can speak six languages, and can't say one thing worth listening to in any."

Peter thought the soup all Jenifer had cracked it up to be.

"Peter," said Leonore, turning to him, "Mr. Le Grand said that you never will talk politics with anybody. That doesn't include me, of course?"

"No," said Peter promptly.

"I thought it didn't," said Leonore, her eyes dancing with pleasure, however, at the reply. "We had Mr. Pell to lunch to-day and I spoke to him as to what you said about the bosses, and he told me that bosses could never be really good, unless the better element were allowed to vote, and not the saloon-keepers and roughs. I could see he was right, at once."

"From his point of view. Or rather the view of his class."

"Don't you think so?"

"No."

"Why not?"

"Broadly speaking, all persons of sound mind are entitled to vote on the men and the laws which are to govern them. Aside from this, every ounce of brain or experience you can add to the ballot, makes it more certain. Suppose you say that half the people are too ignorant to vote sensibly. Don't you see that there is an even chance, at least, that they'll vote rightly, and if the wrong half carries the election, it is because more intelligent people have voted wrongly, have not voted, or have not taken the trouble to try and show the people the right way, but have left them to the mercies of the demagogue. If we grant that every man who takes care of himself has some brain, and some experience, his vote is of some value, even if not a high one. Suppose we have an eagle, and a thousand pennies. Are we any better off by tossing away the coppers, because each is worth so little? That is why I have always advocated giving the franchise to women. If we can add ten million voters to an election, we have added just so much knowledge to it, and made it just so much the harder to mislead or buy enough votes to change results."

"You evidently believe," said Watts, "in the saying, 'Everybody knows more than anybody?'"

Peter had forgotten all about his company in his interest over—over the franchise. So he started slightly at this question, and looked up from—from his subject.

"Yes," said Le Grand. "We've been listening and longing to ask questions. When we see such a fit of loquacity, we want to seize the opportunity."

"No," said Leonore, "I haven't finished. Tell me. Can't you make the men do what you want, so as to have them choose only the best men?"

"If I had the actual power I would not," said Peter.

"Why?"

"Because I would not dare to become responsible for so much, and because a government of the 'best' men is not an American government."

"Why not?"

"That is the aristocratic idea. That the better element, so called, shall compel the masses to be good, whether they wish it or no. Just as one makes a child behave without regard to its own desires. With grown men, such a system only results in widening the distance between the classes and masses, making the latter more dependent and unthinking. Whereas, if we make every man vote he must think a little for himself, because different people advise him contrarily, and thus we bring him nearer to the more educated. He even educates himself by his own mistakes; for every bad man elected, and every bad law passed, make him suffer the results, and he can only blame himself. Of course we don't get as good a government or laws, but then we have other off-setting advantages."

"What are those?"

"We get men and laws which are the wish of the majority. Such are almost self-supporting and self-administering. It is not a mere combination of words, printing ink, and white paper which makes a law. It is the popular sentiment back of it which enforces it, and unless a law is the wish of a majority of the people who are to be governed by it, it is either a dead letter, or must be enforced by elaborate police systems, supported oftentimes with great armies. Even then it does not succeed, if the people choose to resist. Look at the attempt to govern Ireland by force, in the face of popular sentiment. Then, too, we get a stability almost unknown in governments which do not conform to the people. This country has altered its system of government less than any other great country in the last hundred years. And there is less socialistic legislation and propaganda here than any-where else. That is, less discontent."

"But, Peter, if the American people are as sensible as you think, how do you account for the kind of men who exercise control?" said Le Grand.

"By better men not trying."

"But we have reform movements all the time, led by good men. Why aren't these men elected?"

"Who are as absolutely inexperienced and blind as to the way to influence votes, as well can be. Look at it, as a contest, without regard to the merit of the cause. On one side we have bosses, who know and understand the men in their wards, have usually made themselves popular, are in politics for a living, have made it a life-study, and by dear experience have learned that they must sur-render their own opinions in order to produce harmony and a solid vote. The reformer, on the contrary, is usually a man who has other occupations, and, if I may say so, has usually met with only partial success in them. By that I mean that the really successful merchant, or banker, or professional man cannot take time to work in politics, and so only the less successful try. Each re-former, too, is sure that he himself is right, and as his bread and butter is not in the issue, he quarrels to his heart's content with his associates, so that they rarely can unite all their force. Most of the reform movements in this city have been attempted in a way that is simply laughable. What should we say if a hundred busy men were to get together to-morrow, and decide that they would open a great bank, to fight the clearing-house banks of New York? Yet this, in effect, is what the reformers have done over and over again in politics. They say to the men who have been kept in power for years by the people, 'You are scoundrels. The people who elected you are ignorant. We know how to do it better. Now we'll turn you out.' In short, they tell the majority they are fools, but ask their votes. The average reformer endorses thoroughly the theory, 'that every man is as good as another, and a little better.' And he himself always is the better man. The people won't stand that. The 'holier than thou' will defeat a man quicker in this country than will any rascality he may have done."

"But don't you think the reformer is right in principle?"

"In nine cases out of ten. But politics does not consist in being right. It's in making other people think you are. Men don't like to be told that they are ignorant and wrong, and this assumption is the basis of most of the so-called educational campaigns. To give impetus to a new movement takes immense experience, shrewdness, tact, and many other qualities. The people are obstructive—that is conservative—in most things, and need plenty of time."

"Unless *you* tell them what they are to do," laughed Watts. "Then they know quick enough."

"Well, that has taken them fifteen years to learn. Don't you see how absurd it is to suppose that the people are going to take the opinions of the better element offhand? At the end of a three months' campaign? Men have come into my ward and spoken to empty halls; they've flooded it with campaign literature, which has served to light fires; their papers have argued, and nobody read them. But the ward knows me. There's hardly a voter who doesn't. They've tested me. Most of them like me. I've lived among them for years. I've gone on their summer excursions. I've talked with them all over the district. I have helped them in their troubles. I have said a kind word over their dead. I'm godfather to many. With others I've stood shoulder to shoulder when the bullets were flying. Why, the voters who were children when I first came here, with whom I used to sit in the angle, are almost numerous enough now to carry an election as I advise. Do you suppose, because speakers, unknown to them, say I'm wrong, and because the three-cent papers, which they never see, abuse me, that they are going to turn from me unless I make them? That is the true secret of the failure of reformers. A logical argument is all right in a court of appeals, but when it comes to swaying five thousand votes, give me five thousand loving hearts rather than five thousand logical reasons."

"Yet you have carried reforms."

"I have tried, but always in a practical way. That is, by not antagonizing the popular men in politics, but by becoming one of them and making them help me. I have gained political power by recognizing that I could

only have my own way by making it suit the voters.
You see there are a great many methods of doing about
the same thing. And the boss who does the most things
that the people want, can do the most things that the
people don't want. Every time I have surrendered my
own wishes, and done about what the people desire, I
have added to my power, and so have been able to do
something that the people or politicians do not care about
or did not like."

"And as a result you are called all sorts of names."

"Yes. The papers call me a boss. If the voters didn't
agree with me, they would call me a reformer."

"But, Peter," said Le Grand, "would you not like to
see such a type of man as George William Curtis in
office?"

"Mr. Curtis probably stood for the noblest political
ideas this country has ever produced. But he held a
beacon only to a small class. A man who writes from
an easy-chair, will only sway easy-chair people. And
easy-chair people never carried an election in this country,
and never will. This country cannot have a government
of the best. It will always be a government of the average. Mr. Curtis was only a leader to his own grade, just
as Tim Sullivan is the leader of his. Mr. Curtis, in his
editorials, spoke the feelings of one element in America.
Sullivan, in Germania Hall, voices another. Each is representative, the one of five per cent. of New York; the
other of ninety-five per cent. If the American people
have decided one thing, it is that they will not be taken
care of, nor coercively ruled, by their better element, or
minorities."

"Yet you will acknowledge that Curtis ought to rule,
rather than Sullivan?"

"Not if our government is to be representative. I
need not say that I wish such a type as Mr. Curtis was
representative."

"I suppose if he had tried to be a boss he would have
failed?"

"I think so. For it requires as unusual a combination
of qualities to be a successful boss, as to be a successful
merchant or banker. Yet one cannot tell. I myself have

never been able to say what elements make a boss, except that he must be in sympathy with the men whom he tries to guide, and that he must be meeting them. Mr. Curtis had a broad, loving nature and sympathies, and if the people had discovered them, they would have liked him. But the reserve which comes with culture makes one largely conceal one's true feelings. Super-refinements puts a man out of sympathy with much that is basic in humanity, and it needs a great love, or a great sacrifice of feeling, to condone it. It is hard work for what Watts calls a touch, and such a man, to understand and admire one another."

"But don't you think," said Mrs. D'Alloi, "that the people of our class are better and finer?"

"The expression 'noblesse oblige' shows that," said madame.

"My experience has led me to think otherwise," said Peter. "Of course there is a difference of standards, of ideals, and of education, in people, and therefore there are differences in conduct. But for their knowledge of what is right and wrong, I do not think the so-called better classes, which should, in truth, be called the prosperous classes, live up to their own standards of right any more than do the poor."

"Oh, I say, draw it mild. At least exclude the criminal classes," cried Watts. "They know better."

"We all know better. But we don't live up to our knowledge. I crossed on one of the big Atlantic liners lately, with five hundred other saloon passengers. They were naturally people of intelligence, and presumably of easy circumstances. Yet at least half of those people were plotting to rob our government of money by contriving plans to avoid paying duties truly owed. To do this all of them had to break our laws, and in most cases had, in addition, to lie deliberately. Many of them were planning to accomplish this theft by the bribery of the custom-house inspectors, thus not merely making thieves of themselves, but bribing other men to do wrong. In this city I can show you blocks so densely inhabited that they are election districts in themselves. Blocks in which twenty people live and sleep in a single room, year after year; where the birth of a little life into the world means that all must eat less and be less warm; where man and woman, old and young, must shiver in winter, and stifle in summer; where there is not room to bury the people who live in the block within the ground on which they dwell. But I cannot find you, in the poorest and vilest parts of this city, any block where the percentage of liars and thieves and bribe-givers is as large as was that among the first-class passengers of that floating palace. Each condition of society has its own misdoings, and I believe varies little in the percentage of wrong-doers to the whole."

"To hear Peter talk you would think the whole of us ought to be sentenced to life terms," laughed Watts. "I believe it's only an attempt on his part to increase the practice of lawyers."

"Do you really think people are so bad, Peter?" asked Leonore, sadly.

"No. I have not, ten times in my life, met a man whom I should now call bad. I have met men whom I thought so, but when I knew them better I found the good in them more than balancing the evil. Our mistake is in supposing that some men are 'good' and others 'bad,' and that a sharp line can be drawn between them. The truth is, that every man has both qualities in him and in very few does the evil overbalance the good. I marvel at the goodness I find in humanity, when I see the temptation and opportunity there is to do wrong."

"Some men are really depraved, though," said Mrs. D'Alloi.

"Yes," said madame. "Think of those strikers!"

Peter felt a thrill of pleasure pass through him, but he did not show it. "Let me tell you something in connection with that. A high light in place of a dark shadow. There was an attempt to convict some of the strikers, but it failed, for want of positive evidence. The moral proof, however, against a fellow named Connelly was so strong that there could be no doubt that he was guilty. Two years later that man started out in charge of a long express, up a seven-mile grade, where one of our railroads crosses the Alleghanies. By the lay of the land every inch of that seven miles of track can be seen throughout its entire length, and when he had pulled half way up, he saw a section of a freight train coming down the grade at a tremendous speed. A coupling had broken, and this part of the train was without a man to put on the brakes. To go on was death. To stand still was the same. No speed which he could give his train by backing would enable it to escape those uncontrolled cars. He sent his fireman back to the first car, with orders to uncouple the engine. He whistled 'on brakes' to his train, so that it should be held on the grade safely. And he, and the engine alone, went on up that grade, and met that flying mass of freight. He saved two hundred people's lives. Yet that man, two years before, had tried to burn alive forty of his fellow-men. Was that man good or bad?"

"Really, chum, if you ask it as a conundrum, I give it up. But there are thoroughly and wholly good things in this world, and one of them is this stuffing. Would it be possible for a fellow to have a second help?"

Peter smiled. "Jenifer always makes the portions according to what is to follow, and I don't believe he'll think you had better. Jenifer, can Mr. D'Alloi have some more stuffing?"

"Yissah," said Jenifer, grinning the true darkey grin, "if de gentmun want t' sell his ap'tite foh a mess ob potash."

"Never mind," said Watts. "I'm not a dyspeptic, and so don't need potash. But you might wrap the rest up in a piece of newspaper, and I'll take it home."

"Peter, you must have met a great many men in politics whom you knew to be dishonest?" said Mrs. D'Alloi.

"No. I have known few men whom I could call dishonest. But then I make a great distinction between the doer of a dishonest act and a dishonest man."

"That is what the English call 'a fine-spun' distinction, I think," said madame.

"I hope not. A dishonest man I hold to be one who works steadily and persistently with bad means and motives. But there are many men whose lives tell far more for good than for evil in the whole, yet who are not above doing wrong at moments or under certain circumstances.

This man will lie under given conditions or temptations. Another will bribe, if the inducement is strong enough. A third will merely trick. Almost every man has a weak spot somewhere. Yet why let this one weakness—a partial moral obliquity or imperfection—make us cast him aside as useless and evil. As soon say that man physically is spoiled, because he is near-sighted, lame or stupid. If we had our choice between a new, bright, keen tool, or a worn, dull one, of poor material, we should not hesitate which to use. But if we only have the latter, how foolish to refuse to employ it as we may, because we know there are in the world a few better ones."

"Is not condoning a man's sins, by failing to blame him, direct encouragement to them?" said Mrs. D'Alloi.

"One need not condone the sin. My rule has been, in politics, or elsewhere, to fight dishonesty wherever I found it. But I try to fight the act, not the man. And if I find the evil done beyond hope of correction, I do not antagonize the doer of it. More can be done by amity and forbearance than by embittering and alienating. Man is not bettered by being told that he is bad. I had an alderman in here three or four days ago who was up to mischief. I could have called him a scoundrel, without telling him untruth. But I didn't. I told him what I thought was right, in a friendly way, and succeeded in straightening him out, so that he dropped his intention, yet went away my friend. If I had quarrelled with him, we should have parted company, he would have done the wrong, I should have fought him when election time came—and defeated him. But he, and probably fifty of his adherents in the ward would have become my bitter enemies, and opposed everything I tried in the future. If I quarrelled with enough such men, I should in time entirely lose my influence in the ward, or have it generally lessened. But by dealing as a friend with him, I actually prevented his doing what he intended, and we shall continue to work together. Of course a man can be so bad that this course is impossible, but they are as few in politics as they are elsewhere."

"Taciturnity Stirling in his great circus feat of riding a whole ward at once," said Watts.

"I don't claim that I'm right," said Peter. "I once thought very differently. I started out very hotly as a reformer when I began life. But I have learned that humanity is not reformed with a club, and that if most people gave the energy they spend in reforming the world, or their friends, to reforming themselves, there would be no need of reformers."

"The old English saying that 'people who can't mind their own business invariably mind some one's else,' seems applicable," said Watts.

"But is it not very humiliating to you to have to be friends with such men?" said Mrs. D'Alloi.

"You know Mr. Drewitt?" asked Peter.

"Yes," said all but madame.

"Do you take pleasure in knowing him?"

"Of course," said Watts. "He's very amusing and a regular parlor pet."

"That is the reason I took him. For ten years that man was notoriously one of the worst influences in New York State politics. At Albany, in the interest of a great corporation, he was responsible for every job and bit of lobbying done in its behalf. I don't mean to say that he really bribed men himself, for he had lieutenants for the actual dirty work, but every dollar spent passed through his hands, and he knew for what purpose it was used. At the end of that time, so well had he done his work, that he was made president of the corporation. Because of that position, and because he is clever, New York society swallowed him and has ever since delighted to fête him. I find it no harder to shake hands and associate with the men he bribed, than you do to shake hands and associate with the man who gave the bribe."

"Even supposing the great breweries, and railroads, and other interests to be chiefly responsible for bribery, that makes it all the more necessary to elect men above the possibility of being bribed," said Le Grand. "Why not do as they do in Parliament? Elect only men of such high character and wealth, that money has no temptation for them."

"The rich man is no better than the poor man, except that in place of being bribed by other men's money, he allows his own money to bribe him. Look at the course of the House of Lords on the corn-laws. The slave-holders' course on secession. The millionaire silver senators' course on silver. The one was willing to make every poor man in England pay a half more for his bread than need be, in order that land might rent for higher prices. The slave-owner was willing to destroy his own country, rather than see justice done. The last are willing to force a great commercial panic, ruining hundreds and throwing thousands out of employment, if they can only get a few cents more per ounce for their silver. Were they voting honestly in the interest of their fellow-men? Or were their votes bribed?"

Mrs. D'Alloi rose, saying, "Peter, we came early and we must go early. I'm afraid we've disgraced ourselves both ways."

Peter went down with them to their carriage. He said to Leonore in the descent, "I'm afraid the politics were rather dull to you. I lectured because I wanted to make some things clear to you."

"Why?" questioned Leonore.

"Because, in the next few months you'll see a great deal about bosses in the papers, and I don't want you to think so badly of us as many do."

"I shan't think badly of you, Peter," said Leonore, in the nicest tone.

"Thank you," said Peter. "And if you see things said of me that trouble you, will you ask me about them?"

"Yes. But I thought you wouldn't talk politics?"

"I will talk with you, because, you know, friends must tell each other everything."

When Leonore had settled back in the carriage for the long drive, she cogitated: "Mr. Le Grand said that he and Miss De Voe, and Mr. Ogden had all tried to get Peter to talk about politics, but that he never would. Yet, he's known them for years, and is great friends with them. It's very puzzling!"

Probably Leonore was thinking of American politics.

CHAPTER XLVII

THE BLUE-PETER

LEONORE'S puzzle went on increasing in complexity, but there is a limit to all intricacy, and after a time Leonore began to get an inkling of the secret. She first noticed that Peter seemed to spend an undue amount of time with her. He not merely turned up in the Park daily, but they were constantly meeting elsewhere. Leonore went to a gallery. There was Peter! She went to a concert. Ditto, Peter! She visited the flower-show. So did Peter! She came out of church. Behold Peter! In each case with nothing better to do than to see her home. At first Leonore merely thought these meetings were coincidences, but their frequency soon ended this theory, and then Leonore noticed that Peter had a habit of questioning her about her plans beforehand, and of evidently shaping his accordingly.

Nor was this all. Peter seemed to be constantly trying to get her to spend time with him. Though the real summer was fast coming, he had another dinner. He had a box at the theatre. He borrowed a drag from Mr. Pell, and took them all up for a lunch at Mrs. Costell's in Westchester. Then nothing would do but to have another drive, ending in a dinner at the Country Club.

Flowers, too, seemed as frequent as their meetings. Peter had always smiled inwardly at bribing a girl's love with flowers and bon-bons, but he had now discovered that flowers are just the thing to send a girl, if you love her, and that there is no bribing about it. So none could be too beautiful and costly for his purse. Then Leonore wanted a dog—a mastiff. The legal practice of the great firm and the politics of the city nearly stopped till the finest of its kind had been obtained for her.

Another incriminating fact came to her through Dorothy.

"I had a great surprise to-day," she told Leonore. "One that fills me with delight, and that will please you."

"What is that?"

"Peter asked me at dinner, if we weren't to have An-nekes' house at Newport for the summer, and when I said 'yes,' he told me that if I would save a room for him, he would come down Friday nights and stay over Sunday, right through the summer. He has been a simply impossible man hitherto to entice into a visit. Ray and I felt like giving three cheers."

"He seemed glad enough to be invited to visit Grey-Court," thought Leonore.

But even without all this, Peter carried the answer to the puzzle about with him in his own person. Leonore could not but feel the difference in the way he treated, and talked, and looked at her, as compared to all about her. It is true he was no more demonstrative, than with others; his face held its quiet, passive look, and he spoke in much the usual, quiet, even tone of voice. Yet Leonore was at first dimly conscious, and later certain, that there was a shade of eagerness in his manner, a ten-derness in his voice, and a look in his eye, when he was with her, that was there in the presence of no one else.

So Leonore ceased to puzzle over the problem at a given point, having found the answer. But the solving did not bring her much apparent pleasure.

"Oh, dear!" she remarked to herself. "I thought we were going to be such good friends! That we could tell each other everything. And now he's gone and spoiled it. Probably, too, he'll be bothering me later, and then he'll be disappointed, and cross, and we shan't be good friends any more. Oh, dear! Why do men have to be-have so? Why can't they just be friends?"

It is a question which many women have asked. The query indicates a degree of modesty which should make the average masculine blush at his own self-love. The best answer to the problem we can recommend to the average women is a careful and long study of a mirror.

As a result of this cogitation Leonore decided that she would nip Peter's troublesomeness in the bud, that she would put up a sign, "Trespassing forbidden;" by which he might take warning. Many women have done the same thing to would-be lovers, and have saved the lovers much trouble and needless expense. But Leonore, after planning out a dialogue in her room, rather messed it when she came to put it into actual public performance. Few girls of eighteen are cool over a love-affair. And so it occurred thusly:

Leonore said to Peter one day, when he had dropped in for a cup of afternoon tea after his ride with her:

"If I ask you a question, I wonder if you will tell me what you think, without misunderstanding why I tell you something?"

"I will try."

"Well," said Leonore, "there is a very nice Englishman whom I knew in London, who has followed me over here, and is troubling me. He's dreadfully poor, and papa says he thinks he is after my money. Do you think that can be so?"

So far the public performance could not have gone better if it had been rehearsed. But at this point, the whole programme went to pieces. Peter's cup of tea fell to the floor with a crash, and he was leaning back in his chair, with a look of suffering on his face.

"Peter," cried Leonore, "what is it?"

"Excuse me," said Peter, rallying a little. "Ever since an operation on my eyes they sometimes misbehave themselves. It's neuralgia of the optic nerve. Sometimes it pains me badly. Don't mind me. It will be all right in a minute if I'm quiet."

"Can't I do anything?"

"No. I have an eye-wash which I used to carry with me, but it is so long since I have had a return of my trouble that I have stopped carrying it."

"What causes it?"

"Usually a shock. It's purely nervous."

"But there was no shock now, was there?" said Leonore, feeling so guilty that she felt it necessary to pretend innocence.

Peter pulled himself together instantly and, leaning over, began deliberately to gather up the fragments of the cup. Then he laid the pieces on the tea-table and said: "I was dreadfully frightened when I felt the cup slipping. It was very stupid in me. Will you try to forgive me for breaking one of your pretty set?"

"That's nothing," said Leonore. To herself that young lady remarked, "Oh, dear! It's much worse than I thought. I shan't dare say it to him, after all."

But she did, for Peter helped her, by going back to her original question, saying bravely: "I don't know enough about Mr. Max—— the Englishman, to speak of him, but I think I would not suspect men of that, even if they are poor."

"Why not?"

"Because it would be much easier, to most men, to love you than to love your money."

"You think so?"

"Yes."

"I'm so glad. I felt so worried over it. Not about this case, for I don't care for him, a bit. But I wondered if I had to suspect every man who came near me."

Peter's eyes ceased to burn, and his second cup of tea, which a moment before was well-nigh choking him, suddenly became nectar for the gods.

Then at last Leonore made the remark towards which she had been working. At twenty-five Leonore would have been able to say it without so dangerous a preamble.

"I don't want to be bothered by men, and wish they would let me alone," she said. "I haven't the slightest intention of marrying for at least five years, and shall say no to whomever asks me before then."

Five years! Peter sipped his tea quietly, but with a hopeless feeling. He would like to claim that bit of womanhood as his own that moment, and she could talk of five years! It was the clearest possible indication to Peter that Leonore was heart-whole. "No one, who is in love," he thought, "could possibly talk of five years, or five months even." When Peter got back to his chambers that afternoon, he was as near being despairing as he had been since—since—a long time ago. Even the obvious fact, that, if Leonore was not in love with him, she was also not in love with any one else, did not cheer him. There is a flag in the navy known as the Blue-Peter. That evening, Peter could have supplied our whole marine, with considerable bunting to spare.

But even worse was in store for him on the morrow.

When he joined Leonore in the Park that day, she proved to him that woman has as much absolute brutality as the lowest of prize-fighters. Women get the reputation of being less brutal, because of their dread of blood-letting. Yet when it comes to torturing the opposite sex in its feelings, they are brutes compared with their sufferers.

"Do you know," said Leonore, "that this is almost our last ride together?"

"Don't jerk the reins needlessly, Peter," said Mutineer, crossly.

"I hope not," said Peter.

"We have changed our plans. Instead of going to Newport next week, I have at last persuaded papa to travel a little, so that I can see something of my own country, and not be so shamefully ignorant. We are going to Washington on Saturday, and from there to California, and then through the Yellowstone, and back by Niagara. We shan't be in Newport till the middle of August."

Peter did not die at once. He caught at a life-preserver of a most delightful description. "That will be a very enjoyable trip," he said. "I should like to go myself."

"There is no one I would rather have than you," said Leonore, laying her little hand softly on the wound she had herself just made, in a way which women have. Then she stabbed again. "But we think it pleasanter to have it just a party of four."

"How long shall you be in Washington?" asked Peter, catching wildly at a straw this time.

"For a week. Why?"

"The President has been wanting to see me, and I thought I might run down next week."

"Dear me," thought Leonore. "How very persistent he is!"

"Where will you put up?" said Peter.

"We haven't decided. Where shall you stay?" she had the brutality to ask.

"The President wants me with him, but I may go to a hotel. It leaves one so much freer." Peter was a lawyer, and saw no need of committing himself. "If I am there when you are, I can perhaps help you enjoy yourself. I

think I can get you a lunch at the White House, and, as I
know most of the officials, I have an 'open sesame' to some
other nice things." Poor Peter! He was trying to tempt
Leonore to tolerate his company by offering attractions in
connection therewith. A chromo with the pound of tea.
And this from the man who had thought flowers and bon-
bons bribery!

"Why does the President want to see you?"

"To talk politics."

"About the governorship?"

"Yes. Though we don't say so."

"Is it true, Peter, that you can decide who it is to be,
as the papers say?"

"No. I would give twenty-five thousand dollars to-
day if I could name the Democratic nominee."

"Why?"

"Would you mind my not telling you?"

"Yes. I want to know. And you are to tell me," said
her majesty, calmly.

"I will tell you, though it is a secret, if you will tell
me a secret of yours which I want to know."

"No," said Leonore. "I don't think that's necessary.
You are to tell me without making me promise anything."
Leonore might deprecate a man's falling in love with her,
but she had no objection to the power and perquisites it
involved.

"Then I shan't tell you," said Peter, making a tremendous rally.

Leonore looked out from under her lashes to see just
how much of Peter's sudden firmness was real and how
much pretence. Then she became unconscious of his
presence.

Peter said something.

Silence.

Peter said something else.

Silence.

"Are you really so anxious to know?" he asked, sur-
rendering without terms.

He had a glorious look at those glorious eyes. "Yes,"
said the dearest of all mouths.

"The great panic," said Peter, "has led to the forma-

tion of a so-called Labor party, and, from present indica-
tions, they are going to nominate a bad man. Now,
there is a great attempt on foot to get the Democratic
convention to endorse whomever the Labor party nominates."

"Who will that be?"

"A Stephen Maguire."

"And you don't want him?"

"No. I have never crossed his path without finding
him engaged in something discreditable. But he's truckled
himself into a kind of popularity and power, and, having
always been 'a Democrat,' he hopes to get the party to
endorse him."

"Can't you order the convention not to do it?"

Peter smiled down into the eyes. "We don't order
men in this country with any success."

"But can't you prevent them?"

"I hope so. But it looks now as if I should have to do
it in a way very disagreeable to myself."

"How?"

"This is a great secret, you understand?"

"Yes," said Leonore, all interest and eagerness. "I can
keep a secret splendidly."

"You are sure?" asked Peter.

"Sure."

"So can I," said Peter.

Leonore perfectly bristled with indignation. "I won't
be treated so," she said. "Are you going to tell me?"
She put on her severest manner.

"No," said Peter.

"He is obstinate," thought Leonore to herself. Then
aloud she said: "Then I shan't be friends any more."

"That is very nice," said Peter, soberly.

"What?" said Leonore, looking at him in surprise.

"I have come to the conclusion," said Peter, "that there
is no use in our trying to be friends. So we had better
give up at once. Don't you think so?"

"What a pretty horse Miss Winthrop has?" said Leonore. And she never obtained an answer to her question,
nor answered Peter's.

CHAPTER XLVIII

A MUTINEER

AFTER Peter's return from Washington, there was a settled gloom about him positively appalling. He could not be wooed, on any plea, by his closest friends, to journey up-town into the social world. He failed entirely to avail himself of the room in the Rivington's Newport villa, though Dorothy wrote appealingly, and cited his own words to him. Even to his partners he became almost silent, except on law matters. Jenifer found that no delicacy, however rare or however well cooked and served, seemed to be noticed any more than if it was mess-pork. The only moments that this atmosphere seemed to yield at all was when Peter took a very miscellaneous collection of rubbish out of a little sachet, meant for handkerchiefs, which he now carried in his breast-pocket, and touched the various articles to his lips. Then for a time he would look a little less suicidal.

But it was astonishing the amount of work he did, the amount of reading he got through, the amount of politics he bossed, and the cigars he smoked, between the first of June, and the middle of August. The party-leaders had come to the conclusion that Peter did not intend to take a hand in this campaign, but, after his return from Washington, they decided otherwise. "The President must have asked him to interfere," was their whispered conclusion, "but it's too late late now. It's all cut and dried."

Peter found, as this remark suggested, that his two months' devotion to the dearest of eyes and sweetest of lips, had had serious results. As with Mutineer once, he had dropped his bridle, but there was no use in uttering, as he had then, the trisyllable which had reduced the horse to order. He had a very different kind of creature with which to deal, than a Kentucky gentleman of lengthy lineage. A creature called sometimes a "tiger." Yet curiously enough, the same firm voice, and the same firm manner, and a "mutineer," though this time a man instead of a horse, was effective here. All New York knew

that something had been done, and wanted to know what.
There was not a newspaper in the city that would have
refused to give five thousand dollars for an authentic
stenographic report of what actually was said in a space
of time not longer than three hours in all. Indeed, so
intensely were people interested, that several papers felt
called upon to fabricate and print most absurd versions
of what did occur, all the accounts reaching conclusions
as absolutely different as the press portraits of celebrities.
From three of them it is a temptation to quote the display
headlines or "scare-heads," which ushered these reports
to the world. The first read:

"THE BOSSES AT WAR"[2]

"HOT WORDS AND LOOKS"

"BUT THEY'LL CRAWL LATER"

"There's beauty in the bellow of the blast,
  There's grandeur in the growling of the gale;
But there's eloquence-appalling, when Stirling is aroaring,
  And the Tiger's getting modest with his tail."

That was a Republican account. The second was:

"MAGUIRE ON TOP!"

**"The Old Man is Friendly. A Peace-making
Dinner at the Manhattan Club. Friends in
Council. Labor and Democracy Shoulder
to Shoulder. A United Front to the Enemy."**

The third, printed in an insignificant little penny paper
never read and almost unknown by reading people, yet
which had more city advertising than all the other papers
put together, and a circulation to match the largest, announced:

"TACITURNITY JUNIOR'S"

"ONCE MORE AT THE BAT!"

"NO MORE NONSENSE"

"HE PUTS MAGUIRE OUT ON THIRD BASE"

"NOW PLAY BALL!"

And unintelligible as this latter sounds, it was near enough the truth to suggest inspiration. But there is no need to reprint the article that followed, for now it is possible, for the first time, to tell what actually occurred; and this contribution should alone permit this work to rank, as no doubt it is otherwise fully qualified to, in the dullest class of all books, that of the historical novel.

The facts are, that Peter alighted from a hansom one evening, in the middle of July, and went into the Manhattan Club. He exchanged greetings with a number of men in the halls, and with more who came in while he was reading the evening papers. A man came up to him while he still read, and said:

"Well, Stirling. Reading about your own iniquity?"

"No," said Peter, rising and shaking hands. "I gave up reading about that ten years ago. Life is too short."

"Pelton and Webber were checking their respectability in the coat-room, as I came up. I suppose they are in the café."

Peter said nothing, but turned, and the two entered that room. Peter shook hands with three men who were there, and they all drew up round one of the little tables. A good many men who saw that group, nudged each other, and whispered remarks:

"A reporter from the *Sun* is in the strangers' room, Mr. Stirling, and asks to see you," said a servant.

"I cannot see him," said Peter, quietly. "But say to him that I may possibly have something to tell him, about eleven o'clock."

The four men at the table exchanged glances.

"I can't imagine a newspaper getting an interview out of you, Stirling," laughed one of them, a little nervously.

Peter smiled. "Very few of us are absolutely consistent. I can't imagine any of you, for instance, making a political mistake, but perhaps you may some day."

A pause of a curious kind came after this, which was only interrupted by the arrival of three more men. They all shook hands, and Peter rang a bell.

"What shall it be?" he asked.

There was a moment's hesitation, and then one said, "Order for us. You're host. Just what you like."

Peter smiled. "Thomas," he said, "bring us eight Apollinaris cocktails."

The men all laughed, and Thomas said, "Beg pardon, Mr. Stirling?" in a bewildered way. Thomas had served the club many years, but he had never heard of that cocktail.

"Well, Thomas," said Peter, "if you don't have that in stock, make it seven Blackthorns."

Then presently eight men packed themselves into the elevator, and a moment later were sitting in one of the private dining-rooms. For an hour and a half they chatted over the meal, very much as if it were nothing more than a social dinner. But the moment the servant had passed the cigars and light, and had withdrawn, the chat suddenly ceased, and a silence came for a moment. Then a man said:

"It's a pity it can't please all, but the majority's got to rule."

"Yes," promptly said another, "this is really a Maguire ratification meeting."

"There's nothing else to do," affirmed a third.

But a fourth said: "Then what are we here for?"

No one seemed to find an answer. After a moment's silence, the original speaker said:

"It's the only way we can be sure of winning."

"He gives us every pledge," echoed the second.

"And we've agreed, anyways, so we are bound," continued the first speaker.

Peter took his cigar out of his mouth. "Who are bound?" he asked, quietly.

"Why, the organization is—the party," said Number Two, with a "deny-it-if-you-dare" in his voice.

"I don't see how we can back out now, Stirling," said Number One.

"Who wants to?" said another. "The Labor party promises to support us on our local nominations, and Maguire is not merely a Democrat, but he gives us every pledge."

"There's no good of talking of anything else anyhow," said Number One, "for there will be a clean majority for Maguire in the convention."

"And no other candidate can poll fifty votes on the first ballot," said Number Two.

Then they all looked at Peter, and became silent. Peter puffed his cigar thoughtfully.

"What do you say?" said Number One.

Peter merely shook his head.

"But I tell you it's done," cried one of the men, a little excitedly. "It's too late to backslide! We want to please you, Stirling, but we can't this time. We must do what's right for the party."

"I'm not letting my own feeling decide it," said Peter. "I'm thinking of the party. For every vote the Labor people give Maguire, the support of that party will lose us a Democratic vote."

"But we can't win with a triangular fight. The Republicans will simply walk over the course."

If Peter had been a hot-headed reformer, he would have said: "Better that than that such a scoundrel shall win." But Peter was a politician, and so saw no need of saying the unpleasantest thing that occurred to him, even if he felt it. Instead, he said: "The Labor party will get as many votes from the Republicans as from us, and, for every vote the Labor party takes from us, we shall get a Republican vote, if we put up the right kind of a man."

"Nonsense," cried Number One.

"How do you figure that?" asked another.

"In these panic times, the nomination of such a man as Maguire, with his truckling to the lowest passions and his socialistic speeches, will frighten conservative men enough to make them break party lines, and unite on the most certain candidate. That will be ours."

"But why risk it, when, with Maguire, it's certain?"

Peter wanted to say: "Maguire shall not be endorsed, and that ends it." Instead, he said: "We can win with our own man, and don't need to trade with or endorse the Labor party. We can elect Maguire by the aid of the worst votes in this city, or we can elect our own man by the aid of the best. The one weakens our party in the future; the other strengthens it."

"You think that possible?" asked the man who had sought information as to what they "were here for."

"Yes. The Labor party makes a stir, but it wouldn't give us the oyster and be content with the shells if it really felt strong. See what it offers us. All the local and State ticket except six assemblymen, two senators, and a governor, tied hand and foot to us, whose proudest claim for years has been that he's a Democrat."

"But all this leaves out of sight the fact that the thing's done," said Number One.

Peter puffed his cigar.

"Yes. It's too late. The polls are closed," said another.

Peter stopped puffing. "The convention hasn't met," he remarked, quietly.

That remark, however, seemed to have a sting in it, for Number Two cried:

"Come. We've decided. Now, put up or shut up. No more beating about the bush."

Peter puffed his cigar.

"Tell us what you intend, Stirling," said Number One. "We are committed beyond retreat. Come in with us, or stay outside the breastworks."

"Perhaps," said Peter, "since you've taken your own position, without consulting me, you will allow me the same privilege."

"Go to—where you please," said Number Six, crossly.

Peter puffed his cigar.

"Well, what do you intend to do?" asked Number One.

Peter knocked the ash off his cigar. "You consider yourselves pledged to support Maguire?"

"Yes. We are pledged," said four voices in unison.

"So am I," said Peter.

"How?"

"To oppose him," said Peter.

"But I tell you the majority of the convention is for him," said Number One. "Don't you believe me?"

"Yes."

"Then what good will your opposition do?"

"It will defeat Maguire."

"No power on earth can do that."

Peter puffed his cigar.

"You can't beat him in the convention, Stirling. The delegates pledged to him, and those we can give him elect him on the first ballot."

"How about November fourth?" asked Peter.

Number One sprang to his feet. "You don't mean?" he cried.

"Never!" said Number Three.

Peter puffed his cigar.

"Come, Stirling, say what you intend!"

"I intend," said Peter, "if the Democratic convention endorses Stephen Maguire, to speak against him in every ward of this city, and ask every man in it, whom I can influence, to vote for the Republican candidate."

Dead silence reigned.

Peter puffed his cigar.

"You'll go back on the party?" finally said one, in awe-struck tones.

"You'll be a traitor?" cried another.

"I'd have believed anything but that you would be a dashed Mugwump!" groaned the third.

Peter puffed his cigar.

"Say you are fooling?" begged Number Seven.

"No," said Peter. "Nor am I more a traitor to my party than you. You insist on supporting the Labor candidate and I shall support the Republican candidate. We are both breaking our party."

"We'll win," said Number One.

Peter puffed his cigar.

"I'm not so sure," said the gentleman of the previous questions. "How many votes can you hurt us, Stirling?"

"I don't know." Peter looked very contented.

"You can't expect to beat us single?"

Peter smiled quietly. "I haven't had time to see many men. But—I'm not single. Bohlmann says the brewers will back me, Hummel says he'll be guided by me, and the President won't interfere."

"You might as well give up," continued the previous questioner. "The Sixth is a sure thirty-five hundred to the bad, and between Stirling's friends, and the Hummel crowd, and Bohlmann's people, you'll lose twenty-five thousand in the rest of the city, besides the Democrats you'll frighten off by the Labor party. You can't put it less than thirty-five thousand, to say nothing of the hole in the campaign fund."

The beauty about a practical politician is that votes count for more than his own wishes. Number One said:

"Well, that's ended. You've smashed our slate. What have you got in its place?"

"Porter?" suggested Peter.

"No," said three voices.

"We can't stand any more of him," said Number One.

"He's an honest, square man," said Peter.

"Can't help that. One dose of a man who's got as little gumption as he, is all we can stand. He may have education, but I'll be hanged if he has intellect. Why don't you ask us to choose a college professor, and have done with it."

"Come, Stirling," said the previous questioner, "the thing's been messed so that we've got to go into convention with just the right man to rally the delegates. There's only one man we can do it with, and you know it."

Peter rose, and dropped his cigar-stump into the ash-receiver. "I don't see anything else," he said, gloomily. "Do any of you?"

A moment's silence, and then Number One said: "No."

"Well," said Peter, "I'll take the nomination if necessary, but keep it back for a time, till we see if something better can't be hit upon."

"No danger," said Number One, holding out his hand, gleefully.

"There's more ways of killing a pig than choking it with butter," said Number Three, laughing and doing the same.

"It's a pity Costell isn't here," added the previous questioner. "After your not yielding to him, he'd never believe we had forced you to take it."

And that was what actually took place at that very-much-talked-about dinner.

Peter went downstairs with a very serious look on his face. At the door, the keeper of it said: "There are six reporters in the strangers' room, Mr. Stirling, who wish to see you."

A man who had just come in said: "I'm sorry for you, Peter."

Peter smiled quietly. "Tell them our wishes are not mutual." Then he turned to the newcomer. "It's all right," he said, "so far as the party is concerned, Hummel. But I'm to foot the bill to do it."

"The devil! You don't mean——?"

Peter nodded his head.

"I'll give twenty-five thousand to the fund," said Hummel, gleefully. "See if I don't."

"Excuse me, Mr. Stirling," said a man who had just come in.

"Certainly," said Peter promptly. "But I must ask the same favor of you, as I am going down-town at once." Peter had the brutality to pass out of the front door instantly, leaving the reporter with a disappointed look on his face.

"If he only would have said something?" groaned the reporter to himself. "Anything that could be spun into a column. He needn't have told me what he didn't care to tell, yet he could have helped me to pay my month's rent as easily as could be."

As for Peter, he fell into a long stride, and his face nearly equalled his stride in length. After he reached his quarters he sat and smoked, with the same serious look.

He did not look cross. He did not have the gloom in his face which had been so fixed an expression for the last month. But he looked as a man might look who knew he had but a few hours to live, yet to whom death had no terror.

"I am giving up," Peter thought, "everything that has been my true life till now. My profession, my friends, my chance to help others, my books, and my quiet. I shall be misunderstood, reviled and hated. Everything I do will be distorted for partisan purposes. Friends will misjudge. Enemies will become the more bitter. I give up fifty thousand dollars a year in order to become a slave, with toadies, trappers, lobbyists and favor-seekers as my daily quota of humanity. I even sacrifice the larger part of my power."

So ran Peter's thoughts, and they were the thoughts of a man who had not worked seventeen years in politics for nothing. He saw alienation of friends, income, peace, and independence, and the only return a mere title, which to him meant a loss, rather than a gain of power. Yet this was one of the dozen prizes thought the best worth striving for in our politics. Is it a wonder that our government and office-holding is left to the foreign element? That the native American should prefer any otner work, rather than run the gauntlet of public opinion and press, with loss of income and peace, that he may hold some difficult office for a brief term?

But finally Peter rose. "Perhaps she'll like it," he said aloud, and presumably, since no woman is allowed a voice in American politics, he was thinking of Miss Columbia. Then he looked at some photographs, a scrap of ribbon, a gold coin (Peter clearly was becoming a money worshipper), three letters, a card, a small piece of blotting-paper, a handkerchief (which Leonore and Peter had spent nearly ten minutes in trying to find one day), a glove, and some dried rose-leaves and violets. Yet this was the man who had grappled an angry tiger but two hours before and had brought it to lick his hand.

He went to bed very happy.

CHAPTER XLIX

CLOUDS

BUT a month later he was far happier, for one morning towards the end of August, his mail brought him a letter from Watts, announcing that they had been four days installed in their Newport home, and that Peter would now be welcome any time. "I have purposely not filled Grey-Court this summer, so that you should have every chance. Between you and me and the post, I think there have been moments when mademoiselle missed 'her friend' far more than she confessed."

"Dat's stronory," thought Jenifer. "He dun eat mo' dis yar hot mo'nin' dan he dun in two mumfs."

Then Jenifer was sent out with a telegram, which merely said: "May I come to-day by Shore line limited? P. S."

"When you get back, Jenifer," said Peter, "you may pack my trunk and your own. We may start for New-port at two." Evidently Peter did not intend to run any risks of missing the train, in case the answer should be favorable.

Peter passed into his office, and set to work to put the loose ends in such shape that nothing should go wrong during his absence. He had not worked long, when one of the boys told him that:

"Mr. Cassius Curlew wants to see you, Mr. Stirling."

Peter stopped his writing, looking up quickly: "Did he say on what business?"

"No."

"Ask him, please." And Peter went on writing till the boy returned.

"He says it's about the convention."

"Tell him he must be more specific."

The boy returned in a moment with a folded scrap of paper.

"He said that would tell you, Mr. Stirling."

Peter unfolded the scrap, and read upon it: "A message from Maguire."

"Show him in." Peter touched a little knob on his desk on which was stamped "Chief Clerk." A moment later a man opened a door. "Samuels," said Peter, "I wish you would stay here for a moment. I want you to listen to what's said."

The next moment a man crossed the threshold of another door. "Good-morning, Mr. Stirling," he said.

"Mr. Curlew," said Peter, without rising and with a cold inclination of his head.

"I have a message for you, Mr. Stirling," said the man, pulling a chair into a position that suited him, and sitting, "but it's private."

Peter said nothing, but began to write.

"Do you understand? I want a word with you private," said the man after a pause.

"Mr. Samuels is my confidential clerk. You can speak with perfect freedom before him." Peter spoke without raising his eyes from his writing.

"But I don't want any one round. It's just between you and me."

"When I got your message," said Peter, still writing, "I sent for Mr. Samuels. If you have anything to say, say it now. Otherwise leave it unsaid."

"Well, then," said the man, "your party's been tricking us, and we won't stand it."

Peter wrote diligently.

"And we know who's back of it. It was all pie down to that dinner of yours."

"Is that Maguire's message?" asked Peter, though with no cessation of his labors.

"Nop," said the man. "That's the introduction. Now, we know what it means. You needn't deny it. You're squinting at the governorship yourself. And you've made the rest go back on Maguire, and work for you on the quiet. Oh, we know what's going on."

"Tell me when you begin on the message," said Peter, still writing.

"Maguire's sent me to you, to tell you to back water. To stop bucking."

"Tell Mr. Maguire I have received his message."

"Oh, that isn't all, and don't you forget it! Maguire's

in this for fur and feathers, and if you go before the convention as a candidate, we'll fill the air with them."

"Is that part of the message?" asked Peter.

"By that we mean that half an hour after you accept
the nomination, we'll have a force of detectives at work
on your past life, and we'll hunt down and expose every
discreditable thing you've ever done."

Peter rose, and the man did the same instantly, putting
one of his hands on his hip-pocket. But even before he
did it, Peter had begun speaking, in a quiet, self-contained
voice: "That sounds so like Mr. Maguire, that I think
we have the message at last. Go to him, and say that I
have received his message. That I know him, and I
know his methods. That I understand his hopes of
driving me, as he has some, from his path, by threats of
private scandal. That, judging others by himself, he
believes no man's life can bear probing. Tell him that
he has misjudged for once. Tell him that he has himself
decided me in my determination to accept the nomination.
That rather than see him the nominee of the Democratic
party, I will take it myself. Tell him to set on his blood-
hounds. They are welcome to all they can unearth in my
life."

Peter turned towards his door, intending to leave the
room, for he was not quite sure that he could sustain this
attitude, if he saw more of the man. But as his hand was
on the knob, Curlew spoke again.

"One moment," he called. "We've got something more
to say to you. We have proof already."

Peter turned, with an amused look on his face. "I
was wondering," he said, "if Maguire really expected to
drive me with such vague threats."

"No siree," said Curlew with a self-assured manner, but
at the same time putting Peter's desk between the clerk
and himself, so that his flank could not be turned. "We've
got some evidence that won't be sweet reading for you,
and we're going to print it, if you take the nomination."

"Tell Mr. Maguire he had better put his evidence in
print at once. That I shall take the nomination."

"And disgrace one of your best friends?" asked Curlew.

Peter started slightly, and looked sharply at the man.

"Ho, ho," said Curlew. "That bites, eh? Well, it will bite worse before it's through with."

Peter stood silent for a moment, but his hands trembled slightly, and any one who understood anatomy could have recognized that every muscle in his body was at full tension. But all he said was: "Well?"

"It's about that trip of yours on the 'Majestic.'"

Peter looked bewildered.

"We've got sworn affidavits of two stewards," Curlew continued, "about yours and some one else's goings on. I guess Mr. and Mrs. Rivington won't thank you for having them printed."

Instantly came a cry of fright, and the crack of a revolver, which brought Peter's partners and the clerks crowding into the room. It was to find Curlew lying back on the desk, held there by Peter with one hand, while his other, clasping the heavy glass inkstand, was swung aloft. There was a look on Peter's face that did not become it. An insurance company would not have considered Curlew's life at that moment a fair risk.

But when Peter's arm descended it did so gently, put the inkstand back on the desk, and taking a pocket-handkerchief wiped a splash of ink from the hand that had a moment before been throttling Curlew. That worthy struggled up from his back-breaking attitude and the few parts of his face not drenched with ink, were very white, while his hands trembled more than had Peter's a moment before.

"Peter!" cried Ogden. "What is it?"

"I lost my temper for a moment," said Peter.

"But who fired that shot?"

Peter turned to the clerks. "Leave the room," he said, "all of you. And keep this to yourselves. I don't think the other floors could have heard anything through the fire-proof brick, but if any one comes, refer them to me." As the office cleared, Peter turned to his partners and said: "Mr. Curlew came here with a message which he thought needed the protection of a revolver. He judged rightly, it seems."

"Are you hit?"

"I felt something strike." Peter put his hand to his

side. He unbuttoned his coat and felt again. Then he pulled out a little sachet from his breast-pocket, and as he did so, a flattened bullet dropped to the floor. Peter looked into the sachet anxiously. The bullet had only gone through the lower corner of the four photographs and the glove! Peter laughed happily. "I had a gold coin in my pocket, and the bullet struck that. Who says that a luck-piece is nothing but a superstition?"

"But, Peter, shan't we call the police?" demanded Ogden, still looking stunned.

Curlew moved towards the door.

"One moment," said Peter, and Curlew stopped.

"Ray," Peter continued, "I am faced with a terrible question. I want your advice?"

"What, Peter?"

"A man is trying to force me to stand aside and permit a political wrong. To do this, he threatens to publish lying affidavits of worthless scoundrels, to prove a shameful intimacy between a married woman and me."

"Bosh," laughed Ray. "He can publish a thousand and no one would believe them of you."

"He knows that. But he knows, too, that no matter how untrue, it would connect her name with a subject shameful to the purest woman that ever lived. He knows that the scavengers of gossip will repeat it, and gloat over it. That the filthy society papers will harp on it for years. That in the heat of a political contest, the partisans will be only too glad to believe it and repeat it. That no criminal prosecution, no court vindication, will ever quite kill the story as regards her. And so he hopes that, rather than entail this on a woman whom I love, and on her husband and family, I will refuse a nomination. I know of such a case in Massachusetts, where, rather than expose a woman to such a danger, the man withdrew. What should I do?"

"Do? Fight him. Tell him to do his worst."

Peter put his hand on Ray's shoulder.

"Even if—if—it is one dear to us both?"

"Peter!"

"Yes. Do you remember your being called home in our Spanish trip, unexpectedly? You left me to bring

Miss De Voe, and— Well. They've bribed, or forged affidavits of two of the stewards of the 'Majestic.' "

Ray tried to spring forward towards Curlew. But Peter's hand still rested on his shoulder, and held him back. "I started to kill him," Peter said quietly, "but I remembered he was nothing but the miserable go-between."

"My God, Peter! What can I say?"

"Ray. The stepping aside is nothing to me. It was an office which I was ready to take, but only as a sacrifice and a duty. It is to prevent wrong that I interfered. So do not think it means a loss to me to retire."

"Peter, do what you intended to do. We must not compromise with wrong even for her sake."

The two shook hands. "I do not think they will ever use it, Ray," said Peter. "But I may be mistaken, and cannot involve you in the possibility, without your consent."

"Of course they'll use it," cried Ogden. "Scoundrels who could think of such a thing, will use it without hesitation."

"No," said Peter. "A man who uses a coward's weapons, is a coward at heart. We can prevent it, I think." Then he turned to Curlew. "Tell Mr. Maguire about this interview. Tell him that I spared you, because you are not the principal. But tell him from me, that if a word is breathed against Mrs. Rivington, I swear that I'll search for him till I find him, and when I find him I'll kill him with as little compunction as I would a rattlesnake." Peter turned and going to his dressing-room, washed away the ink from his hands.

Curlew shuffled out of the room, and, black as he was, went straight to the Labor headquarters and told his story.

"And he'll do it too, Mr. Maguire," he said. "You should have seen his look as he said it, and as he stood over me. I feel it yet."

"Do you think he means it?" said Ray to Ogden, when they were back in Ray's room.

"I wouldn't think so if I hadn't seen his face as he stood over that skunk. But if ever a man looked murder he did at that moment. And quiet old Peter of all men!"

"We must talk to him. Do tell him that——"

"Do you dare do it?"

"But you——?"

"I don't. Unless he speaks I shall——"

"Ray and Ogden," said a quiet voice, "I wish you would write out what you have just seen and heard. It may be needed in the future."

"Peter, let me speak," cried Ray. "You mustn't do what you said. Think of such an end to your life. No matter what that scoundrel does don't end your life on a gallows. It——"

Peter held up his hand. "You don't know the American people, Ray. If Maguire uses that lying story, I can kill him, and there isn't a jury in the country which, when the truth was told, wouldn't acquit me. Maguire knows it, too. We have heard the last of that threat, I'm sure."

Peter went back to his office. "I don't wonder," he thought, as he stood looking at the ink-stains on his desk and floor, "that people think politics nothing but trickery and scoundrelism. Yet such vile weapons and slanders would not be used if there were not people vile and mean enough at heart to let such things influence them. The fault is not in politics. It is in humanity."

CHAPTER L

SUNSHINE

But just as Peter was about to continue this rather unsatisfactory train of thought, his eye caught sight of a flattened bullet lying on the floor. He picked it up, with a smile. "I knew she was my good luck," he said. Then he took out the sachet again, and kissed the dented and bent coin. Then he examined the photographs. "Not even the dress is cut through," he said gleefully, looking at the full length. "It couldn't have hit in a better place." When he came to the glove, however, he grieved a little over it. Even this ceased to trouble him the next moment, for a telegram was laid on his desk. It merely said, "Come by all means. W. C. D'A." Yet that was enough to make Peter drop thoughts, work, and everything for a time. He sat at his desk, gazing at a blank wall, and thinking of a pair of slate-colored eyes. But his expression bore no resemblance to the one formerly assumed when that particular practice had been habitual.

Nor was this expression the only difference in this day, to mark the change from Peter past to Peter present. For instead of manœuvring to make Watts sit on the back seat, when he was met by the trap late that afternoon, at Newport, he took possession of that seat in the coolest possible manner, leaving the one by the driver to Watts. Nor did Peter look away from the girl on that back seat. Quite the contrary. It did not seem to him that a thousand eyes would have been any too much. Peter's three months of gloom vanished, and became merely a contrast to heighten his present joy. A sort of "shadow-box."

He had had the nicest kind of welcome from his "friend." If the manner had not been quite so absolutely frank as of yore, yet there was no doubt as to her pleasure in seeing Peter. "It's very nice to see you again," she had said while shaking hands. "I hoped you would come quickly." Peter was too happy to say anything in reply. He merely took possession of that vacant seat, and rested his eyes in silence till Watts, after climbing into place, asked him how the journey to Newport had been.

"Lovelier than ever," said Peter, abstractedly. "I didn't think it was possible."

"Eh?" said Watts, turning with surprise on his face.

But Leonore did not look surprised. She only looked the other way, and the corners of her mouth were curving upwards.

"The journey?" queried Watts.

"You mean Newport, don't you?" said Leonore helpfully, when Peter said nothing. Leonore was looking out from under her lashes—at things in general, of course.

Peter said nothing. Peter was not going to lie about what he had meant, and Leonore liked him all the better for not using the deceiving loophole she had opened.

Watts said, "Oh, of course. It improves every year. But wasn't the journey hot, old man?"

"I didn't notice," said Peter.

"Didn't notice! And this one of the hottest days of the year."

"I had something else to think about," explained Peter.

"Politics?" asked Watts.

"Oh, Peter," said Leonore, "we've been so interested in all the talk. It was just as maddening as could be, how hard it was to get New York papers way out west. I'm awfully in the dark about some things. I've asked a lot of people here about it, but nobody seems to know anything. Or if they do, they laugh at me. I met Congressman Pell yesterday at the Tennis Tournament, and thought he would tell me all about it. But he was horrid! His whole manner said: 'I can't waste real talk on a girl.' I told him I was a great friend of yours, and that you would tell me when you came, but he only laughed and said, he had no doubt you would, for you were famous for your indiscretion. I hate men who laugh at women the moment they try to talk as men do."

"I think," said Peter, "we'll have to turn Pell down. A Congressman who laughs at one of my friends won't do."

"I really wish you would. That would teach him," said Leonore, vindictively. "A man who laughs at women can't be a good Congressman."

"I tell you what we'll do," said Peter. "I don't want to retire him, because—because I like his mother. But I will tell you something for you to tell him, that will astonish him very much, and make him want to know who told you, and so you can tease him endlessly."

"Oh, Peter!" said Leonore. "You are the nicest man."

"What's that?" asked Watts.

"It's a great secret," said Peter. "I shall only tell it to Miss D'Alloi, so that if it leaks beyond Pell, I shall know whom to blame for it."

"Goody!" cried Leonore, giving a little bounce for joy.

"Is it about that famous dinner?" inquired Watts.

"No."

"Peter, I'm so curious about that. Will you tell me what you did?"

"I ate a dinner," said Peter smiling.

"Now don't be like Mr. Pell," said Leonore, reprovingly, "or I'll take back what I just said."

"Did you roar, and did the tiger put its tail between its legs?" asked Watts.

"That is the last thing our friends, the enemies, have found," said Peter.

"You will tell me about it, won't you, Peter?" said Leonore, ingratiatingly.

"Have you a mount for me, Watts, for to-morrow? Mutineer comes by boat to-night, but won't be here till noon."

"Yes. I've one chap up to your weight, I think."

"I don't like dodgers," said Leonore, the corners of her mouth drawn down.

"I was not dodging," said Peter. "I only was asking a preliminary question. If you will get up, before breakfast, and ride with me, I will tell you everything that actually occurred at that dinner. You will be the only person, I think, who wasn't there, who knows." It was shameful and open bribery, but bosses are shameful and open in their doings, so Peter was only living up to his rôle.

The temptation was too strong to be resisted. Leonore said, "Of course I will," and the corners of her mouth reversed their position. But she said to herself: "I shall have to snub you in something else to make up for it." Peter was in for a bad quarter of an hour somewhere.

Leonore had decided just how she was going to treat Peter. To begin with, she intended to accentuate that "five years" in various ways. Then she would be very frank and friendly, just as long as he, too, would keep within those limits, but if Peter even verged on anything more, she intended to leave him to himself, just long enough to show him that such remarks as his "not caring to be friends," brought instant and dire punishment. "And I shan't let him speak," Leonore decided, "no matter if he wants to. For if he does, I'll have to say 'no,' and then he'll go back to New York and sulk, and perhaps never come near me again, since he's so obstinate, while I want to stay friends." Many such campaigns have been planned by the party of the first part. But the trouble is that, usually, the party of the second part also has a plan, which entirely disconcerts the first. As the darkey remarked: "Yissah. My dog he wud a beat, if it hadn't bin foh de udder dog."

Peter found as much contrast in his evening, as compared with his morning, as there was in his own years. After dinner, Leonore said:

"I always play billiards with papa. Will you play too?"

"I don't know how," said Peter.

"Then it's time you learned. I'll take you on my side, because papa always beats me. I'll teach you."

So there was the jolliest of hours spent in this way, all of them laughing at Peter's shots, and at Leonore's attemps to show him how. "Every woman ought to play billiards," Peter thought, when it was ended. "It's the most graceful sight I've seen in years."

Leonore said, "You get the ideas very nicely, but you hit much too hard. You can't hit a ball too softly. You pound it as if you were trying to smash it."

"It's something I really must learn," said Peter, who had refused over and over again in the past.

"I'll teach you, while you are here," said Leonore.

Peter did not refuse this time.

Nor did he refuse another lesson. When they had drifted into the drawing-room, Leonore asked: "Have you been learning how to valse?"

Peter smiled at so good an American using so European a word, but said seriously, "No. I've been too busy."

"That's a shame," said Leonore, "because there are to be two dances this week, and mamma has written to get you cards."

"Is it very hard?" asked Peter.

"No," said Leonore. "It's as easy as breathing, and much nicer."

"Couldn't you teach me that, also?"

"Easily. Mamma, will you play a valse? Now see." Leonore drew her skirts back with one hand, so as to show the little feet, and said: "One, two, three, so. One, two, three, so. Now do that."

Peter had hoped that the way to learn dancing was to take the girl in one's arms. But he recognized that this would follow. So he set to work manfully to imitate that dainty little glide. It seemed easy as she did it. But it was not so easy when he tried it.

"Oh, you clumsy," said Leonore, laughing. "See. One, two, three, so. One, two, three, so."

Peter forgot to notice the step, in his admiration of the little feet and the pretty figure.

"Well," said Leonore, after a pause, "are you going to do that?"

So Peter tried again, and again, and again. Peter would have done it all night, with absolute contentment, so long as Leonore, after every failure, would show him the right way in her own person.

Finally she said, "Now take my hands. No. Way apart, so that I can see your feet. Now. We'll try it together. One, two, change. One, two, change."

Peter thought this much better, and was ready to go on till strength failed. But after a time, Leonore said, "Now. We'll try it the true way. Take my hand so and put your arm so. That's the way. Only never hold a girl too close. We hate it. Yes. That's it. Now, mamma. Again. One, two, three. One, two, three."

This was heavenly, Peter thought, and could have wept over the shortness, as it seemed to him, of this part of the lesson.

But it ended, and Leonore said: "If you'll practice that in your room, with a bolster, you'll get on very fast."

"I always make haste slowly," said Peter, not taking to the bolster idea at all kindly. "Probably you can find time to-morrow for another lesson, and I'll learn much quicker with you."

"I'll see."

"And will you give me some waltzes at the dances?"

"I'll tell you what I'll do," said Leonore. "You shall have the dances the other men don't ask of me. But you don't dance well enough, in case I can get a better partner.

I love valsing too much to waste one with a poor dancer."
A moment before Peter thought waltzing the most exquisite pleasure the world contained. But he suddenly
changed his mind, and concluded it was odious.

"Nevertheless," he decided, "I will learn how."

CHAPTER LI

THE COURSE OF TRUE LOVE

PETER had his ride the next morning, and had a very
interested listener to his account of that dinner. The
listener, speaking from vast political knowledge, told him
at the end, "You did just right. I thoroughly approve of
you."

"That takes a great worry off my mind," said Peter
soberly. "I was afraid, since we were to be such friends,
and you wanted my help in the whirligig this winter, that
you might not like my possibly having to live in Albany."

"Can't you live in New York?" said Leonore, looking
horrified.

"No."

"Then I don't like it at all," said Leonore. "It's no
good having friends if they don't live near one."

"That's what I think," said Peter. "I suppose I
couldn't tempt you to come and keep house for me?"

"Now I must snub him," thought Leonore. "No,"
she said, "it will be bad enough to do that five years from
now, for the man I love." She looked out from under her
eyelashes to see if her blow had been fatal, and concluded
from the glumness in Peter's face, that she really had been
too cruel. So she added: "But you may give me a ball,
and we'll all come up and stay a week with you."

Peter relaxed a little, but he said dolefully, "I don't
know what I shall do. I shall be in such need of your
advice in politics and housekeeping."

"Well," said Leonore, "if you really find that you can't
get on without help, we'll make it two weeks. But you
must get up toboggan parties, and other nice things."

"I wonder what the papers will say," thought Peter, "if a governor gives toboggan parties?"

After the late breakfast, Peter was taken down to see the tournament. He thought he would not mind it, since he was allowed to sit next Leonore. But he did. First he wished that she wouldn't pay so much attention to the score. Then that the men who fluttered round her would have had the good taste to keep away. It enraged Peter to see how perfectly willing she was to talk and chat about things of which he knew nothing, and how more than willing the men were. And then she laughed at what they said!

"That's fifteen-love, isn't it?" Leonore asked him presently.

"He doesn't look over fifteen," actually growled Peter. "I don't know whether he's in love or not. I suppose he thinks he is. Boys fifteen years old always do."

Leonore forgot the score, even, in her surprise. "Why," she said, "you growl just like Bêtise (the mastiff). Now I know what the papers mean when they say you roar."

"Well," said Peter, "it makes me cross to see a lot of boys doing nothing but hit a small ball, and a lot more looking at them and thinking that it's worth doing." Which was a misstatement. It was not that which made Peter mad.

"Haven't you ever played tennis?"

"Never. I don't even know how to score."

"Dear me," said Leonore. "You're dreadfully illiterate."

"I know it," growled Peter, "I don't belong here, and have no business to come. I'm a ward boss, and my place is in saloons. Don't hesitate to say it."

All this was very foolish, but it was real to Peter for the moment, and he looked straight ahead with lines on his face which Leonore had never seen before. He ought to have been ordered to go off by himself till he should be in better mood.

Instead Leonore turned from the tennis, and said: "Please don't talk that way, Peter. You know I don't think that." Leonore had understood the misery which lay back of the growl. "Poor fellow," she thought, "I must cheer him up." So she stopped looking at the tennis. "See," she said, "there are Miss Winthrop and Mr. Pell. Do take me over to them and let me spring my surprise. You talk to Miss Winthrop."

"Why, Peter!" said Pell. "When did you come?"

"Last night. How do you do, Miss Winthrop?" Then for two minutes Peter talked, or rather listened, to that young lady, though sighing internally. Then, *Laus Deol* up came the poor little chap, whom Peter had libelled in age and affections, only ten minutes before, and set Peter free. He turned to see how Leonore's petard was progressing, to find her and Pell deep in tennis. But just as he was going to expose his ignorance on that game, Leonore said:

"Mr. Pell, what do you think of the political outlook?"

Pell sighed internally. "You can read it in the papers," he said.

"No. I want your opinion. Especially about the great departure the Democratic Convention is going to make."

"You mean in endorsing Maguire?"

Leonore began to visibly swell in importance. "Of course not," she said, contemptuously. "Every one knows that that was decided against at the Manhattan dinner. I mean the unusual resolution about the next senator."

Pell ceased to sigh. "I don't know what you mean," he said.

"Not really?" said Leonore incredulously, her nose cocking a little more airily. "I thought of course you would know about it. I'm so surprised!"

Pell looked at her half quizzically, and half questioningly. "What is the resolution?"

"Naming a candidate for the vacancy for the Senate."

"Nonsense," said Pell, laughing. "The Convention has nothing to do with the senators. The Legislature elects them." He thought, "Why can't women, if they will talk politics, at least learn the A B C."

"Yes," said Leonore, "but this is a new idea. The Senate has behaved so badly, that the party leaders think it will be better to make it a more popular body by having the New York convention nominate a man, and then they intend to make the legislature elect him. If the other states will only follow New York's lead, it may make the Senate respectable and open to public opinion."

Pell sniffed obviously. "In what fool paper did you read that?"

"I didn't read it," said Leonore, her eyes dancing with delight. "The papers are always behind the times. But I didn't think that you would be, since you are to be named in the resolution."

Pell looked at her blankly. "What do you mean?"

"Didn't you know that the Convention will pass a resolution, naming you for next Senator?" said Leonore, with both wonder and pity in her face and voice.

"Who told you that?" said Pell, with an amount of interest blended with doubt that was a decided contrast to a moment ago.

"That's telling," said Leonore. "You know, Mr. Pell, that one mustn't tell people who are outside the party councils everything."

"I believe you are trying to stuff me," said Pell. "If it is so, or anything like it, you wouldn't know."

"Oh," said Leonore, tantalizingly, "I could tell you a great deal more than that. But of course you don't care to talk politics with a girl."

Pell weakened. "Tell me who told you about it?"

"I think we must go home to lunch," said Leonore, turning to Peter, who had enjoyed Leonore's triumph almost as much as she had.

"Peter," said Pell, "have you heard what Miss D'Alloi has been saying?"

"Part of it."

"Where can she have picked it up?"

"I met Miss D'Alloi at a lunch at the White House, last June," said Peter seriously, "and she, and the President, and I, talked politics. Politically, Miss D'Alloi is rather a knowing person. I hope you haven't been saying anything indiscreet, Miss D'Alloi?"

"I'm afraid I have," laughed Leonore, triumphantly adding, "but I won't tell anything more."

Pell looked after them as they went towards the carriage. "How extraordinary!" he said. "She couldn't have it from Peter. He tells nothing. Where the deuce did she get it, and is it so?" Then he said: "Senator Van Brunt Pell," with a roll on all the r's. "That sounds well. I wonder if there's anything in it?"

"I think," said Leonore to Peter, triumphantly, "that he would like to have talked politics. But he'll get nothing but torture from me if he tries."

It began to dawn on Peter that Leonore did not, despite her frank manner, mean all she said. He turned to her, and asked:

"Are you really in earnest in saying that you'll refuse every man who asks you to marry him within five years?"

Leonore's triumph scattered to the four winds. "What an awfully impudent question," she thought, "after my saying it so often. What shall I answer?" She looked Peter in the eye with severity. "I shan't refuse," she said, "because I shan't even let him speak. If any man dares to attempt it, I'll tell him frankly I don't care to listen."

"She really means it," sighed Peter internally. "Why is it, that the best girls don't care to marry?" Peter became very cross, and, what is worse, looked it.

Nor was Leonore much better. "There," she said, "I knew just how it would be. He's getting sulky already. He isn't nice any more. The best thing will be to let him speak, for then he'll go back to New York, and won't bother me." The corners of her mouth drew away down, and life became very gray.

So "the best of friends" rode home from the Casino, without so much as looking at each other, much less speaking. Clearly Peter was right. There was no good in trying to be friends any longer.

Precedent or habit, however, was too strong to sustain this condition long. First Leonore had to be helped out of the carriage. This was rather pleasant, for she had to give Peter her hand, and so life became less unworth living to Peter. Then the footman at the door gave Peter two telegraphic envelopes of the bulkiest kind, and Leonore too began to take an interest in life again.

"What are they about?" she asked.

"The Convention. I came off so suddenly that some details were left unarranged."

"Read them out loud," she said calmly, as Peter broke the first open.

Peter smiled at her, and said: "If I do, will you give me another waltzing lesson after lunch?"

"Don't bargain," said Leonore, disapprovingly.

"Very well," said Peter, putting the telegrams in his pocket, and turning towards the stairs.

Leonore let him go up to the first landing. But as soon as she became convinced that he was really going to his room, she said, "Peter."

Peter turned and looked down at the pretty figure at the foot of the stairs. He came down again. When he had reached the bottom he said, "Well?"

Leonore was half angry, and half laughing. "You ought to want to read them to me," she said, "since we are such friends."

"I do," said Peter. "And you ought to want to teach me to waltz, since we are such friends."

"But I don't like the spirit," said Leonore.

Peter laughed. "Nor I," he said. "Still, I'll prove I'm the better, by reading them to you."

"Now I will teach him," said Leonore to herself.

Peter unfolded the many sheets. "This is very secret, of course," he said.

"Yes." Leonore looked round the hall as if she was a conspirator. "Come to the window-seat upstairs," she whispered, and led the way. When they had ensconced themselves there, and drawn the curtains, she said, "Now."

"You had better sit nearer me," said Peter, "so that I can whisper it."

"No," said Leonore. "No one can hear us." She thought, "I'd snub you for that, if I wasn't afraid you wouldn't read it."

"You understand that you are not to repeat this to any one." Peter was smiling over something.

Leonore said, "Yes," half crossly and half eagerly.

So Peter read:

"Use Hudson knowledge counties part not belief local twenty imbecility certified of yet till yesterday noon whose Malta could accurately it at seventeen. Potomac give throw Haymarket estimated Moselle thirty-three to into fortify through jurist arrived down right—"

"I won't be treated so!" interrupted Leonore, indignantly.

"What do you mean?" said Peter, still smiling. "I'm reading it to you, as you asked."

"No, you are not. You are just making up."

"No," said Peter. "It's all here."

"Let me see it." Leonore shifted her seat so as to overlook Peter.

"That's only two pages," said Peter, holding them so that Leonore had to sit very close to him to see. "There are eighteen more."

Leonore looked at them. "Was it written by a lunatic?" she asked.

"No." Peter looked at the end. "It's from Green. Remember. You are not to repeat it to any one."

"Luncheon is served, Miss D'Alloi," said a footman.

"Bother luncheon," thought Peter.

"Please tell me what it means?" said Leonore, rising.

"I can't do that, till I get the key and decipher it."

"Oh!" cried Leonore, clapping her hands in delight. "It's a cipher. How tremendously interesting! We'll go at it right after lunch and decipher it together, won't we?"

"After the dancing lesson, you mean, don't you?" suggested Peter.

"How did you know I was going to do it?" asked Leonore.

"You told me."

"Never! I didn't say a word."

"You looked several," said Peter.

Leonore regarded him very seriously. "You are not 'Peter Simple' a bit," she said. "I don't like deep men." She turned and went to her room. "I really must be careful," she told the enviable sponge as it passed over her face, "he's a man who needs very special treatment. I ought to send him right back to New York. But I do so want to know about the politics. No. I'll keep friends till the campaign's finished. Then he'll have to live in Albany, and that will make it all right. Let me see. He said the governor served three years. That isn't five, but perhaps he'll have become sensible before then."

As for Peter, he actually whistled during his ablutions, which was something he had not done for many years.

He could not quite say why, but it represented his mood better than did his earlier growl.

CHAPTER LII

A GUARDIAN ANGEL

PETER had as glorious an afternoon as he had had a bad morning. First he danced a little. Then the two sat at the big desk in the deserted library and worked together over those very complex dispatches till they had them translated. Then they had to discuss their import. Finally they had to draft answers and translate them into cipher. All this with their heads very close together, and an utter forgetfulness on the part of a certain personage that snubbing rather than politics was her "plan of campaign." But Leonore began to feel that she was a political power herself, and so forgot her other schemes. When they had the answering dispatches fairly transcribed, she looked up at Peter and said:

"I think we've done that very well," in the most approving voice. "Do you think they'll do as we tell them?"

Peter looked down into that dearest of faces, gazing at him so frankly and with such interest, so very near his, and wondered what deed was noble or great enough to win a kiss from those lips. Several times that afternoon, it had seemed to him that he could not keep himself from leaning over and taking one. He even went so far now as to speculate on exactly what Leonore would do if he did. Fortunately his face was not given to expressing his thoughts. Leonore never dreamed how narrow an escape she had. "If only she wouldn't be so friendly and confiding," groaned Peter, even while absolutely happy in her mood. "I can't do it, when she trusts me so."

"Well," said Leonore, "perhaps when you've done staring at me, you'll answer my question."

"I think they'll do as we tell them," smiled Peter. "But we'll get word to-morrow about Dutchess and Steuben.

Then we shall know better how the land lies, and can talk plainer."

"Will there be more ciphers, to-morrow?"

"Yes." To himself Peter said, "I must write Green and the rest to telegraph me every day."

"Now we'll have a cup of tea," said Leonore. "I like politics."

"Then you would like Albany," said Peter, putting a chair for her by the little tea-table.

"I wouldn't live in Albany for the whole world," said Leonore, resuming her old self with horrible rapidity. But just then she burnt her finger with the match with which she was lighting the lamp, and her cruelty vanished in a wail. "Oh!" she cried. "How it hurts."

"Let me see," said Peter, sympathetically.

The little hand was held up. "It does hurt," said Leonore, who saw that there was a painful absence of all signs of injury, and feared Peter would laugh at such a burn after those he had suffered.

But Peter treated it very seriously. "I'm sure it does," he said, taking possession of the hand. "And I know how it hurts." He leaned over and kissed the little thumb. Then he didn't care a scrap whether Leonore liked Albany or not.

"I won't snub you this time," said Leonore to herself, "because you didn't laugh at me for it."

Peter's evening was not so happy. Leonore told him as they rose from dinner that she was going to a dance. "We have permission to take you. Do you care to go?"

"Yes. If you'll give me some dances."

"I've told you once that I'll only give you the ones not taken by better dancers. If you choose to stay round I'll take you for those."

"Do you ever have a dance over?" asked Peter, marvelling at such a possibility.

"I've only been to one dance. I didn't have at that."

"Well," said Peter, growling a little, "I'll go."

"Oh," said Leonore, calmly, "don't put yourself out on my account."

"I'm not," growled Peter. "I'm doing it to please myself." Then he laughed, so Leonore laughed too.

After a game of billiards they all went to the dance. As they entered the hall, Peter heard his name called in a peculiar voice behind. He turned and saw Dorothy.

Dorothy merely said, "Peter!" again. But Peter understood that explanations were in order. He made no attempt to dodge.

"Dorothy," he said softly, giving a glance at Leonore, to see that she was out of hearing, "when you spent that summer with Miss De Voe, did Ray come down every week?"

"Yes."

"Would he have come if you had been travelling out west?"

"Oh, Peter," cried Dorothy, below her breath, "I'm so glad it's come at last!"

We hope our readers can grasp the continuity of Dorothy's mental processes, for her verbal ones were rather inconsequent.

"She's lovely," continued the verbal process. "And I'm sure I can help you."

"I need it," groaned Peter. "She doesn't care in the least for me, and I can't get her to. And she says she isn't going to marry for——"

"Nonsense!" interrupted Dorothy, contemptuously, and sailed into the ladies' dressing-room.

Peter gazed after her. "I wonder what's nonsense?" he thought.

Dorothy set about her self-imposed task with all the ardor for matchmaking, possessed by a perfectly happy married woman. But Dorothy evidently intended that Leonore should not marry Peter, if one can judge from the tenor of her remarks to Leonore in the dressing-room. Peter liked Dorothy, and would probably not have believed her capable of treachery, but it is left to masculine mind to draw any other inference from the dialogue which took place between the two, as they prinked before a cheval glass.

"I'm so glad to have Peter here for this particular evening," said Dorothy.

"Why?" asked Leonore, calmly, in the most uninterested of tones.

"Because Miss Biddle is to be here. For two years I've been trying to bring those two together, so that they might make a match of it. They are made for each other."

Leonore tucked a rebellious curl in behind the drawn-back lock. Then she said, "What a pretty pin you have."

"Isn't it? Ray gave it to me," said Dorothy, giving Leonore all the line she wanted.

"I've never met Miss Biddle," said Leonore.

"She's a great beauty, and rich. And then she has that nice Philadelphia manner. Peter can't abide the young-girl manner. He hates giggling and talking girls. It's funny, too, because, though he doesn't dance or talk, they like him. But Miss Biddle is an older girl, and can talk on subjects which please him. She is very much interested in politics and philanthropy."

"I thought," said Leonore, fluffing the lace on her gown, "that Peter never talked politics."

"He doesn't," said Dorothy. "But she has studied political economy. He's willing to talk abstract subjects. She's just the girl for a statesman's wife. Beauty, tact, very clever, and yet very discreet. I'm doubly glad they'll meet here, for she has given up dancing, so she can entertain Peter, who would otherwise have a dull time of it."

"If she wants to," said Leonore.

"Oh," said Dorothy, "I'm not a bit afraid about that. Peter's the kind of man with whom every woman's ready to fall in love. Why, my dear, he's had chance after chance, if he had only cared to try. But, of course, he doesn't care for such women as you and me, who can't enter into his thoughts or sympathize with his ambitions. To him we are nothing but dancing, dressing, prattling flutter-birds." Then Dorothy put her head on one side, and seemed far more interested in the effect of her own frock than in Peter's fate.

"He talks politics to me," Leonore could not help saying. Leonore did not like Dorothy's last speech.

"Oh, Peter's such a gentleman that he always talks seriously even to us; but it's only his politeness. I've seen him talk to girls like you, and he is delightfully courteous, and one would think he liked it. But, from little things Ray has told me, I know he looks down on society girls."

"Are you ready, Leonore?" inquired Mrs. D'Alloi.

Leonore was very ready. Watts and Peter were ready also; had been ready during the whole of this dialogue. Watts was cross; Peter wasn't. Peter would willingly have waited an hour longer, impatient only for the moment of meeting, not to get downstairs. That is the difference between a husband and a lover.

"Peter," said Leonore, the moment they were on the stairs, "do you ever tell other girls political secrets?"

Dorothy was coming just behind, and she poked Peter in the back with her fan. Then, when Peter turned, she said with her lips as plainly as one can without speaking: "Say yes."

Peter looked surprised. Then he turned to Leonore and said, "No. You are the only person, man or woman, with whom I like to talk politics."

"Oh!" shrieked Dorothy to herself. "You great, big foolish old stupid! Just as I had fixed it so nicely!" What Dorothy meant is quite inscrutable. Peter had told the truth.

But, after the greetings were over, Dorothy helped Peter greatly. She said to him, "Give me your arm, Peter. There is a girl here whom I want you to meet."

"Peter's going to dance this valse with me," said Leonore. And Peter had two minutes of bliss, amateur though he was. Then Leonore said cruelly, "That's enough; you do it very badly!"

When Peter had seated her by her mother, he said: "Excuse me for a moment. I want to speak to Dorothy."

"I knew you would be philandering after the young married women. Men of your age always do," said Leonore, with an absolutely incomprehensible cruelty.

So Peter did not speak to Dorothy. He sat down by Leonore and talked, till a scoundrelly, wretched, villainous, dastardly, low-born, but very good-looking fellow carried off his treasure. Then he wended his way to Dorothy.

"Why did you tell me to say 'yes'?" he asked.

Dorothy sighed. "I thought you couldn't have understood me," she said; "but you are even worse than I supposed. Never mind, it's done now. Peter, will you do me a great favor?"

"I should like to," said Peter.

"Miss Biddle, of Philadelphia, is here. She doesn't know many of the men, and she doesn't dance. Now, if I introduce you, won't you try to make her have a good time?"

"Certainly," said Peter, gloomily.

"And don't go and desert her, just because another man comes up. It makes a girl think you are in a hurry to get away, and Miss Biddle is very sensitive. I know you don't want to hurt her feelings." All this had been said as they crossed the room. Then "Miss Biddle, let me introduce Mr. Stirling."

Peter sat down to his duty. "I mustn't look at Leonore," he thought, "or I shan't be attentive." So he turned his face away from the room heroically. As for Dorothy, she walked away with a smile of contentment. "There, miss," she remarked, "we'll see if you can trample on dear old Peter!"

"Who's that girl to whom Mr. Stirling is talking?" asked Leonore of her partner.

"Ah, that's the rich Miss Biddle, of Philadelphia," replied the scoundrel, in very gentleman-like accents of one of his class. "They say she's never been able to find a man good enough for her, and so she's keeping herself on ice till she dies, in hopes that she'll find one in heaven. She's a great catch."

"She's decidedly good-looking," said Leonore.

"Think so? Some people do. I don't. I don't like blondes."

When Leonore had progressed as far as her fourth partner, she asked: "What sort of a girl is that Miss Biddle?"

"She's really stunning," she was told. "Fellows are all wild about her. But she has an awfully snubbing way."

"Is she clever?"

"Is she? That's the trouble. She won't have anything to do with a man unless he's clever. Look at her to-night! She got her big fish right off, and she's driven away every man who's come near her ever since. She's the kind of a girl that, if she decides on anything, she does it."

"Who's her big fish?" said Leonore, as if she had not noticed.

"That big fellow, who is so awfully exclusive—Stirling. He doesn't think any people good enough for him but the Pells, and Miss De Voe, and the Ogdens. What they can see in him I can't imagine. I sat opposite him once at dinner, this spring, at the William Pells, and he only said three things in the whole meal. And he was sitting next that clever Miss Winthrop."

After the fifth dance, Dorothy came up to Leonore. "It's going beautifully," she said; "do you see how Peter has turned his back to the room? And I heard a man say that Miss Biddle was freezing to every man who tried to interrupt them. I must arrange some affairs this week so that they shall have chances to see each other. You will help me?"

"I'm very much engaged for this week," said Leonore.

"What a pity! Never mind; I'll get Peter. Let me see. She rides beautifully. Did Peter bring his horses?"

"One," said Leonore, with a suggestion of reluctance in stating the fact.

"I'll go and arrange it at once," said Dorothy, thinking that Peter might be getting desperate.

"Mamma," said Leonore, "how old Mrs. Rivington has grown!"

"I haven't noticed it, dear," said her mother.

Dorothy went up to the pair and said: "Peter, won't you show Miss Biddle the conservatories! You know," she explained, "they are very beautiful."

Peter rose dutifully, but with a very passive look on his face.

"And, Peter," said Dorothy, dolefully, "will you take me in to supper? I haven't found a man who's had the grace to ask me."

"Yes."

"We'll sit at the same table," said Dorothy to Miss Biddle.

When Peter got into the carriage that evening he was very blue. "I had only one waltz," he told himself, "and did not really see anything else of her the whole evening."

"Is that Miss Biddle as clever as people say she is?" asked Mrs. D'Alloi.

"She is a very unusual woman," said Peter. "I rarely have known a better informed one." Peter's tone of voice carried the inference that he hated unusual and informed women, and as this is the case with most men, his voice presumably reflected his true thoughts.

"I should say so," said Watts. "At our little table she said the brightest things, and told the best stories. That's a girl as is a girl. I tried to see her afterwards, but found that Peter was taking an Italian lesson of her."

"What do you mean?" asked Mrs. D'Alloi.

"I have a chap who breakfasts with me three times a week, to talk Italian, which I am trying to learn," said Peter, "and Dorothy told Miss Biddle, so she offered to talk in it. She has a beautiful accent, and it was very good of her to offer, for I know very little as yet, and don't think she could have enjoyed it."

"What do you want with Italian?" asked Mrs. D'Alloi.

"To catch the Italian vote," said Peter.

"Oh, you sly-boots," said Watts. Then he turned. "What makes my Dot so silent?" he asked.

"Oh," said Leonore in weary tones, "I've danced too much and I'm very, very tired."

"Well," said Watts, "see that you sleep late."

"I shall be all right to-morrow," said Leonore, "and I'm going to have an early horseback ride."

"Peter and I will go too," said Watts.

"I'm sorry," said Peter. "I'm to ride with Dorothy and Miss Biddle."

"Ha, ha," said Watts. "More Italian lessons, eh?"

Two people looked very cross that evening when they got to their rooms.

Leonore sighed to her maid: "Oh, Marie, I am so tired! Don't let me be disturbed till it's nearly lunch."

And Peter groaned to nobody in particular, "An evening and a ride gone! I tried to make Dorothy understand. It's too bad of her to be so dense."

So clearly Dorothy was to blame. Yet the cause of all this trouble fell asleep peacefully, remarking to herself, just before she drifted into dreamland, "Every man in love ought to have a guardian, and I'll be Peter's."

CHAPTER LIII

INTERFERENCE

WHEN Peter returned from his ride the next day, he found Leonore reading the papers in the big hall. She gave him a very frigid "good-morning," yet instantly relaxed a little in telling him there was another long telegram for him on the mantel. She said nothing of his reading the despatch to her, but opened a new sheet of paper, and began to read its columns with much apparent interest. That particular page was devoted to the current prices of "Cotton;" "Coffee;" "Flour;" "Molasses;" "Beans;" "Butter;" "Hogs;" "Naval Stores;" "Ocean Freights," and a large number of equally kindred and interesting subjects.

Peter took the telegram, but did not read it. Instead he looked down at all of his pretty "friend" not sedulously hidden by the paper. He recognized that his friend had a distinctly "not-at-home" look, but after a moment's hesitation he remarked, "You don't expect me to read this alone?"

Silence.

"Because," continued Peter, "it's an answer to those we wrote and sent yesterday, and I shan't dare reply it without your advice."

Silence.

Peter coolly put his hand on the paper and pushed it down till he could see Leonore's face. When he had done that he found her fairly beaming. She tried to put on a serious look quickly, and looked up at him with it on.

But Peter said, "I caught you," and laughed. Then Leonore laughed. Then they filled in the space before lunch by translating and answering the telegram.

As soon as that meal was over, Peter said, "Now will you teach me waltzing again?"

"No."

"Why not?"

"I'm not going to spend time teaching a man to dance, who doesn't dance."

"I was nearly wild to dance last night," said Peter.

"Then why didn't you?"

"Dorothy asked me to do something."

"I don't think much of men who let women control them."

"I wanted to please Dorothy," said Peter. "I was as well off talking to one girl as to another. Since you don't like my dancing, I supposed you would hardly choose to dance again with me, or ropes wouldn't have held me."

"I can talk Italian too," said Leonore, with no apparent connnection.

"Will you talk it with me?" said Peter eagerly. "You see, there are a good many Italians in the district now, who, by their ignorance and their not speaking English, are getting into trouble all the time. I want to learn, so as to help them, without calling in an interpreter." Peter was learning to put his requests on grounds other than his own wishes.

"Yes," said Leonore, very sweetly, "and I'll give you another lesson in dancing. How did you enjoy your ride?"

"I like Dorothy," said Peter, "and I like Miss Biddle. But I didn't get the ride I wanted."

He got a very nice look from those slate-colored eyes.

They set a music-box going, and Peter's instruction began. When it was over, Leonore said:

"You've improved wonderfully."

"Well enough to dance with you?"

"Yes," said Leonore. "I'll take pity on you unless you'd rather talk to some other girl."

Peter only smiled quietly.

"Peter," said Leonore, later, as he was sipping his tea, "do you think I'm nothing but a foolish society flutterbird?"

"Do you want to know what I think of you?" asked Peter, eagerly.

"No," said Leonore hastily. "But do you think of me as nothing but a society girl?"

"Yes," said Peter, truth speaking in voice and face.

The corners of Leonore's mouth descended to a woeful degree.

"I think you are a society girl," continued Peter, "because you are the nicest kind of society."

Leonore fairly filled the room with her smile. Then she said, "Peter, will you do me a favor?"

"Yes."

"Will you tell Dorothy that I have helped you translate cipher telegrams and write the replies?"

Peter was rather astonished, but said, "Yes."

But he did it very badly, Leonore thought, for meeting Dorothy the next day at a lawn party, after the mere greetings, he said:

"Dorothy, Miss D'Alloi has been helping me translate and write cipher telegrams."

Dorothy looked startled at the announcement for a moment. Then she gave a glance at Leonore, who was standing by Peter, visibly holding herself in a very triumphant attitude. Then she burst out into the merriest of laughs, and kept laughing.

"What is it?" asked Peter.

"Such a joke," gasped Dorothy, "but I can't tell you."

As for Leonore, her triumphant manner had fled, and her cheeks were very red. And when some one spoke to Dorothy, and took her attention, Leonore said to Peter very crossly:

"You are so clumsy! Of course I didn't mean that way."

Peter sighed internally. "I am stupid, I suppose," he said to himself. "I tried to do just what she asked, but she's displeased, and I suppose she won't be nice for the rest of the day. If it was only law or politics! But women!"

But Leonore didn't abuse him. She was very kind to him, despite her displeasure. "If Dorothy would only let me alone," thought Peter, "I should have a glorious time. Why can't she let me stay with her when she's in such a nice mood? And why does she insist on my being attentive to her? I don't care for her. It seems as if she was determined to break up my enjoyment, just as I get her to myself." Peter mixed his "hers" and "shes" too thoroughly in this sentence to make its import clear. His thoughts are merely reported verbatim, as the easiest way. It certainly indicates that, as with most troubles, there was a woman in it.

Peter said much this same thing to himself quite often during the following week, and always with a groan. Dorothy was continually putting her finger in. Yet it was in the main a happy time to Peter. His friend treated him very nicely for the most part, if very variably. Peter never knew in what mood he should find her. Sometimes he felt that Leonore considered him as the dirt under her little feet. Then again, she could not be too sweet to him. There was an evening—a dinner—at which he sat between Miss Biddle and Leonore, when, it seemed to Peter, Leonore said and looked such nice things, that the millennium had come. Yet the next morning, she told him that: "It was a very dull dinner. I talked to no-body but you."

Fortunately for Peter, the D'Allois were almost as new an advent in Newport, so Leonore was not yet in the running. But by the time Peter's first week had sped, he found that men were putting their fingers in, as well as Dorothy. Morning, noon, and night they gathered. Then lunches, teas, drives, yachts, and innumerable other affairs also plunged their fingers in. Peter did not yield to the superior numbers. He went wherever Leonore went. But the other men went also, and understood the ropes far better. He fought on, but a sickening feeling began to creep over him of impending failure. It was soon not merely how Leonore treated him; it was the impossibility of getting her to treat him at all. Even though he was in the same house, it seemed as if there was always some one else calling, or mealing, or taking tea, or playing tennis, or playing billiards, or merely drop-ping in. And then Leonore took fewer and fewer meals at home, and spent fewer and fewer hours there. One day Peter had to translate those dispatches all by himself! When he had a cup of tea now, even with three or four men about, he considered himself lucky. He understood at last what Miss De Voe had meant when she had spoken of the difficulty of seeing enough of a popular girl either to love her or to tell her of it. They prayed for rain in church on Sunday, on account of the drought, and Peter said "Amen" with fervor. Anything to end such fluttering.

At the end of two weeks, Peter said sadly that he must be going.

"Rubbish," said Watts. "You are to stay for a month."

"I hope you'll stay," said Mrs. D'Alloi.

Peter waited a moment for some one else to speak. Some one else didn't.

"I think I must," he said. "It isn't a matter of my own wishes, but I'm needed in Syracuse." Peter spoke as if Syracuse was the ultimate of human misery.

"Is it necessary for you to be there?" asked Leonore.

"Not absolutely, but I had better go."

Later in the day Leonore said, "I've decided you are not to go to Syracuse. I shall want you here to explain what they do to me."

And that cool, insulting speech filled Peter with happiness.

"I've decided to stay another week," he told Mrs. D'Alloi.

Nor could all the appeals over the telegraph move him, though that day and the next the wires to Newport from New York and Syracuse were kept hot, the despatches came so continuously.

Two days after this decision, Peter and Leonore went to a cotillion. Leonore informed him that: "Mamma makes me leave after supper, because she doesn't like me to stay late, so I miss the nice part."

"How many waltzes are you going to give me?" asked Peter, with an eye to his one ball-room accomplishment.

"I'll give you the first," said Leonore, "and then if you'll sit near me, I'll give you a look every time I see a man coming whom I don't like, and if you are quick and ask me first, I'll give it to you."

Peter became absolutely happy. "How glad I am," he thought, "that I didn't go to Syracuse! What a shame it is there are other dances than walzes."

But after Peter had had two waltzes, he overheard his aged friend of fifteen years say something to a girl that raised him many degrees in his mind. "That's a very brainy fellow," said Peter admiringly. "That never occurred to me!"

So he waited till he saw Leonore seated, and then joined her. "Won't you sit out this dance with me?" he asked.

Leonore looked surprised. "He's getting very clever," she thought, never dreaming that Peter's cleverness, like so many other people's nowadays, consisted in a pertinent use of quotations. Parrot cleverness, we might term it. Leonore listened to the air which the musicians were beginning, and finding it the Lancers, or dreariest of dances, she made Peter happy by assenting.

"Suppose we go out on the veranda," said Peter, still quoting.

"Now of what are you going to talk?" said Leonore, when they were ensconced on a big wicker divan, in the soft half light of the Chinese lanterns.

"I want to tell you of something that seems to me about a hundred years ago," said Peter. "But it concerns myself, and I don't want to bore you."

"Try, and if I don't like it I'll stop you," said Leonore, opening up a line of retreat worthy of a German army.

"I don't know what you'll think about it," said Peter. faltering a little. "I suppose I can hardly make you understand it, as it is to me. But I want you to know, because—well—it's only fair."

Leonore looked at Peter with a very tender look in her eyes. He could not see it, because Leonore sat so that her face was in shadow. But she could see his expression, and when he hesitated, with that drawn look on his face, Leonore said softly:

"You mean—about—mamma?"

Peter started. "Yes! You know?"

"Yes," said Leonore gently. "And that was why I trusted you, without ever having met you, and why I wanted to be friends."

Peter sighed a sigh of relief. "I've been so afraid of it," he said. "She told you?"

"Yes. That is, Miss De Voe told me first of your having been disappointed, so I asked mamma if she knew the girl, and then mamma told me. I'm glad you spoke of it, for I've wanted to ask you something."

"What?"

"If that was why you wouldn't call at first on us?"

"No."

"Then why did mamma say you wouldn't call?" When Peter made no reply, Leonore continued, "I knew—that is I felt, there was something wrong. What was it?"

"I can't tell you."

"Yes," said Leonore, very positively.

Peter hesitated. "She thought badly of me about something, till I apologized to her."

"And now?"

"Now she invites me to Grey-Court."

"Then it wasn't anything?"

"She had misjudged me."

"Now, tell me what it was."

"Miss D'Alloi, I know you do not mean it," said Peter, "but you are paining me greatly. There is nothing in my whole life so bitter to me as what you ask me to tell."

"Oh, Peter," said Leonore, "I beg your pardon. I was very thoughtless!"

"And you don't think the worse of me, because I loved your mother, and because I can't tell you?" said Peter, in a dangerous tone.

"No," said Leonore, but she rose. "Now we'll go back to the dancing."

"One moment," begged Peter.

But Leonore was already in the full light blazing from the room. "Are you coming?" she said.

"May I have this waltz?" said Peter, trying to get half a loaf.

"No," said Leonore, "it's promised to Mr. Rutgers."

Just then mine host came up and said: "I congratulate you, Mr. Stirling."

Peter wanted to kick him, but he didn't.

"I congratulate you," said another man.

"On what?" Peter saw no cause for congratulation, only for sorrow.

"Oh, Peter," said Dorothy, sailing up at this junction, "how nice! And such a surprise!"

"Why, haven't you heard?" said mine host.

"Oh," cried Leonore, "is it about the Convention?"

"Yes," said a man. "Manners is in from the club and tells us that a despatch says your name was sprung on the Convention at nine, and that you were chosen by acclamation without a single ballot being taken. Every one's thunderstruck."

"Oh, no," said a small voice, fairly bristling with importance, "I knew all about it."

Every one laughed at this, except Dorothy. Dorothy had a suspicion that it was true. But she didn't say so. She sniffed visibly, and said, "Nonsense. As if Peter would tell you secrets. Come, Peter, I want to take you over and let Miss Biddle congratulate you."

"Peter has just asked me for this waltz," said Leonore. "Oh, Mr. Rutgers, I'm so sorry. I'm going to dance this with Mr. Stirling."

And then Peter felt he was to be congratulated.

"I shan't marry him myself," thought Leonore, "but I won't have my friends married off right under my nose, and you can try all you want, Mrs. Rivington."

So Peter's guardianship was apparently bearing fruit. Yet man to this day holds woman to be the weaker vessel!

CHAPTER LIV

OBSTINACY

THE next morning Peter found that his prayer for a rainy day had been answered, and came down to breakfast in the pleasantest of humors.

"See how joyful his future Excellency looks already," said Watts, promptly recalling Peter to the serious part of life. And fortunately too, for from that moment, the time which he had hoped to have alone (if *two* ever can be alone), began to be pilfered from him. Hardly were they seated at breakfast when Pell dropped in to congratulate him, and from that moment, despite the rain, every friend in Newport seemed to feel it a bounden duty to do the same, and to stay the longer because of the rain. Peter wished he had set the time for the Convention two days earlier or two days later.

"I hope you won't ask any of these people to luncheon," Peter said in an aside to Mrs. D'Alloi.

"Why?" he was asked.

Peter looked puzzled, and finally said weakly, "I—I have a good deal to do."

And then as proper punishment for his misdemeanor the footman announced Dorothy and Miss Biddle, Ray and Ogden. Dorothy sailed into the room with the announcement:

"We've all come to luncheon if we are asked."

"Oh, Peter," said Ray, when they were seated at the table. "Have you seen this morning's 'Voice of Labor?' No? Good gracious, they've raked up that old verse in Watts's class-song and print it as proof that you were a drunkard in your college days. Here it is. Set to music and headed 'Saloon Pete.' "

"Look here, Ray, we must write to the 'Voice' and tell them the truth," said Watts.

"Never write to the paper that tells the lie," said Peter, laughing. "Always write to the one that doesn't. Then it will go for the other paper. But I wouldn't take the trouble in this case. The opposition would merely say that: 'Of course Mr. Stirling's intimate friends are bound to give such a construction to the song, and the attempt does them credit.' "

"But why don't you deny it, Peter?" asked Leonore anxiously. "It's awful to think of people saying you are a drunkard!"

"If I denied the untruths told of me I should have my hands full. Nobody believes such things, except the people who are ready to believe them. They wouldn't believe otherwise, no matter what I said. If you think a man is a scoundrel, you are not going to believe his word."

"But, Peter," said Mrs. D'Alloi, "you ought to deny them for the future. After you and your friends are dead, people will go back to the newspapers, and see what they said about you, and then will misjudge you."

"I am not afraid of that. I shall hardly be of enough account to figure in history, or if I become so, such attacks will not hurt me. Why, Washington was charged by the papers of his day, with being a murderer, a traitor, and a tyrant. And Lincoln was vilified to an extent which seems impossible now. The greater the man, the greater the abuse."

"Why do the papers call you 'Pete'?" asked Leonore anxiously. "I rather like Peter, but Pete is dreadful!"

"To prove that I am unfit to be governor."

"Are you serious?" asked Miss Biddle.

"Yes. From their point of view, the dropping of the 'r' ought to convince voters that I am nothing but a tough and heeler."

"But it won't!" declared Leonore, speaking from vast experience.

"I don't think it will. Though if they keep at it, and really convince the voters who can be convinced by such arguments, that I am what they call me, they'll elect me."

"How?" asked Mrs. D'Alloi.

"Because intelligent people are not led astray but outraged by such arguments, and ignorant people, who can be made to believe all that is said of me, by such means, will think I am just the man for whom they want to vote."

"How is it possible that the papers can treat you so?" said Watts. "The editors know you?"

"Oh, yes. I have met nearly every man connected with the New York press."

"They must know better?"

"Yes. But for partisan purposes they must say what they do."

"Then they are deliberately lying to deceive the people?" asked Miss Biddle.

"It's rather a puzzling matter in ethics," said Peter. "I don't think that the newspaper fraternity have any lower standard of morals, than men in other professions. In the main they stand for everything that is admirable, so long as it's non-partisan, and some of the men who to-day are now writing me down, have aided me in the past more than I can say, and are at this moment my personal friends."

"How dishonest!"

"I cannot quite call it that. When the greatest and most honorable statesmen of Europe and America will lie and cheat each other to their utmost extent, under cover of the term 'diplomacy,' and get rewarded and praised by their respective countries for their knavery, provided it is successful, I think 'dishonest' is a strong word for a merely partisan press. Certain it is, that the partisan press would end to-morrow, but for the narrowness and meanness of readers."

"Which they cause," said Ogden.

"Just as much," said Peter, "as the saloon makes a drunkard, food causes hunger, and books make readers."

"But, at least, you must acknowledge they've got you, when they say you are the saloon-keepers' friend," laughed Watts.

"Yes. I am that—but only for votes, you understand."

"Mr. Stirling, why do you like saloons?" asked Miss Biddle.

"I don't like saloons. My wish is to see the day come, when such a gross form of physical enjoyment as tippling shall cease entirely. But till that day comes, till humanity has taught itself and raised itself, I want to see fair play."

"What do you mean?"

"The rich man can lay in a stock of wine, or go to a hotel or club, and get what he wants at any time and all times. It is not fair, because a man's pockets are filled with nickels instead of eagles, that he shall not have the same right. For that reason, I have always spoken for the saloon, and even for Sunday openings. You know what I think myself of that day. You know what I think of wine. But if I claim the right to spend Sunday in my way and not to drink, I must concede an equal right to others to do as they please. If a man wants to drink at any time, what right have I to say he shall not?"

"But the poor man goes and makes a beast of himself," said Watts.

"There is as much champagne drunkenness as whisky drunkenness, in proportion to the number of drinkers of each. But a man who drinks champagne, is sent home in a cab, and is put to bed, while the man who can't afford that kind of drink, and is made mad by poisoned and doctored whisky, doctored and poisoned because of our heavy tax on it, must take his chance of arrest. That is the shameful thing about all our so-called temperance legislation. It's based on an unfair interference with personal liberty, and always discriminates in favor of the man with money. If the rich man has his club, let the poor man have his saloon."

"How much better, though," said Mrs. D'Alloi, "to stop the sale of wine everywhere."

"That is neither possible nor right. You can't strengthen humanity by tying its hands. It must be left free to become strong. I have thought much about the problem, and I see only one fair and practical means of bettering our present condition. But boss as the papers say I am, I am not strong enough to force it."

"What is that, Peter?" asked Dorothy.

"So long as a man drinks in such a way as not to interfere with another person's liberty we have no right to check him. But the moment he does, the public has a right to protect itself and his family, by restraining him, as it does thieves, or murderers, or wife-beaters. My idea is, that a license, something perhaps like our dog-license, shall be given to every one who applies for it. That before a man can have a drink, this license must be shown. Then if a man is before the police court a second time, for drunkenness, or if his family petition for it, his license shall be cancelled, and a heavy fine incurred by any one who gives or sells that man a drink hereafter."

"Oh," laughed Watts, "you are heavenly! Just imagine a host saying to his dinner-party, 'Friends, before this wine is passed, will you please show me your drink licenses."

"You may laugh, Watts," said Peter, "but such a request would have saved many a young fellow from ruin, and society from an occasional terrible occurrence which even my little social experience has shown me. And it would soon be so much a matter of course, that it would be no more than showing your ticket, to prove yourself entitled to a ride. It solves the problem of drunkenness. And that is all we can hope to do, till humanity is——" Then Peter, who had been looking at Leonore, smiled.

"Is what?" asked Leonore.

"The rest is in cipher," said Peter, but if he had finished his sentence, it would have been, "half as perfect as you are."

After this last relay of callers had departed, it began to pour so nobly that Peter became hopeful once more. He wandered about, making a room-to-room canvass, in search of happiness, and to his surprise saw happiness descending the broad stair incased in an English shooting-cap, and a mackintosh.

"You are not going out in such weather?" demanded Peter.

"Yes. I've had no exercise to-day, and I'm going for a walk."

"It's pouring torrents," expostulated Peter.

"I know it."

"But you'll get wet through."

"I hope so. I like to walk in the rain."

Peter put his hand on the front door-handle, to which this conversation had carried them. "You mustn't go out," he said.

"I'm going," said Leonore, made all the more eager now that it was forbidden.

"Please don't," said Peter weakening.

"Let me pass," said Leonore decisively.

"Does your father know?"

"Of course not."

"Then you should ask him. It's no weather for you to walk in."

"I shan't ask him."

"Then I shall," and Peter went hurriedly to the library.

"Watts," he said, "it's raining torrents and Leonore insists on going to walk. Please say she is not to go."

"All right," said Watts, not looking up from his book.

That was enough. Peter sped back to the hall. It was

empty. He put his head into the two rooms. Empty. He looked out of the front door. There in the distance, was that prettiest of figures, distinguishable even when buried in a mackintosh. Peter caught up a cap from the hall rack, and set out in pursuit. Leonore was walking rapidly, but it did not take Peter many seconds to come up with her.

"Your father says you are not to go out."

"I can't help it, since I am out," said Leonore, sensibly.

"But you should come back at once."

"I don't care to," said Leonore.

"Aren't you going to obey him?"

"He never would have cared if you hadn't interfered. It's your orders, not his. So I intend to have my walk."

"You are to come back," said Peter.

Leonore stopped and faced him. "This is getting interesting," she thought. "We'll see who can be the most obstinate." Aloud she said, "Who says so?"

"I do."

"And I say I shan't."

Peter felt his helplessness. "Please come back."

Leonore laughed internally. "I don't choose to."

"Then I shall have to make you."

"How?" asked Leonore.

That was a conundrum, indeed. If it had been a knotty law point, Peter would have been less nonplussed by it.

Leonore felt her advantage, and used it shamefully. She knew that Peter was helpless, and she said, "How?" again, laughing at him.

Peter groped blindly. "I shall make you," he said again, for lack of anything better.

"Perhaps," said Leonore, helping him out, though with a most insulting laugh in her voice and face, "you will get a string and lead me?"

Peter looked the picture of helplessness.

"Or you might run over to the Goelets', and borrow their baby's perambulator," continued that segment of the Spanish Inquisition. If ever an irritating, aggravating, crazing, exasperating, provoking, fretting, enraging, "I dare you," was uttered, it was in Leonore's manner as she said this.

Peter looked about hopelessly.

"Please hurry up and say how," Leonore continued, "for I want to get down to the cliff walk. It's very wet here on the grass. Perhaps you will carry me back? You evidently think me a baby in arms." "He's such fun to tease," was her thought, "and you can say just what you please without being afraid of his doing anything ungentlemanly." Many a woman dares to torture a man for just the same reason.

She was quite right as to Peter. He had recognized that he was powerless; that he could not use force. He looked the picture of utter indecision. But as Leonore spoke, a sudden change came over his face and figure. "Leonore had said it was wet on the grass! Leonore would wet her feet! Leonore would take cold! Leonore would have pneumonia! Leonore would die!" It was a shameful chain of argument for a light of the bar, logic unworthy of a school-boy. But it was fearfully real to Peter for the moment, and he said to himself: "I must do it, even if she never forgives me." Then the indecision left his face, and he took a step forward.

Leonore caught her breath with a gasp. The "dare-you" look, suddenly changed to a very frightened one, and turning, she sped across the lawn, at her utmost speed. She had read something in Peter's face, and felt that she must fly, however ignominious such retreat might be.

Peter followed, but though he could have caught her in ten seconds, he did not. As on a former occasion, he thought: "I'll let her get out of breath. Then she will not be so angry. At least she won't be able to talk. How gracefully she runs!"

Presently, as soon as Leonore became convinced that Peter did not intend to catch her, she slowed down to a walk. Peter at once joined her.

"Now," he said, "will you come back?"

Leonore was trying to conceal her panting. She was not going to acknowledge that she was out of breath since Peter wasn't. So she made no reply.

"You are walking in the wrong direction," said Peter, laying his hand on her arm. Then, since she made no reply, his hand encircled the arm, and he stopped. Leonore took two more steps. Then she too, curiously enough, halted.

"Stop holding me," she said, not entirely without betraying her breathlessness.

"You are to come back," said Peter.

He got an awful look from those eyes. They were perfectly blazing with indignation.

"Stop holding me," she repeated.

It was a fearful moment to Peter. But he said, with an appeal in his voice, "You know I suffer in offending you. I did not believe that I could touch you without your consent. But your health is dearer to me than your anger is terrible. You must come home."

So Leonore, realizing that helplessness in a man exists only by his own volition, turned, and began walking towards the now distant house. Peter at once released her arm, and walked beside her. Not a glimpse did he get of those dear eyes. Leonore was looking directly before her, and a grenadier could not have held himself straighter. If insulted dignity was to be acted in pantomime, the actor could have obtained some valuable points from that walk.

Peter walked along, feeling semi-criminal, yet semi-happy. He had saved Leonore from an early grave, and that was worth while doing. Then, too, he could look at her, and that was worth while doing. The run had made Leonore's cheeks blaze, as Peter's touch had made her eyes. The rain had condensed in little diamonds on her stray curls, and on those long lashes. It seemed to Peter that he had never seen her lovelier. The longing to take her in his arms was so strong, that he almost wished she had refused to return. But then Peter knew that she was deeply offended, and that unless he could make his peace, he was out of favor for a day at least. That meant a very terrible thing to him. A whole day of neglect; a whole day with no glimpse of those eyes; a whole day without a smile from those lips!

Peter had too much sense to say anything at once. He did not speak till they were back in the hall. Leonore had planned to go straight to her room, but Peter was rather clever, since she preceded him, in getting to the foot of the staircase so rapidly that he was there first.

This secured him his moment for speech. He said simply: "Miss D'Alloi, I ask your forgiveness for offending you."

Leonore had her choice of standing silent, of pushing past Peter, or of speaking. If she had done the first, or the second, her position was absolutely impregnable. But a woman's instinct is to seek defence or attack in words rather than actions. So she said: "You had no right, and you were very rude." She did not look at Peter.

"It pained me far more than it could pain you."

Leonore liked Peter's tone of voice, but she saw that her position was weakening. She said, "Let me by, please."

Peter with reluctance gave her just room to pass. He felt that he had not said half of what he wished, but he did not dare to offend again.

As it turned out, it was the best thing he could do, for the moment Leonore had passed him, she exclaimed, "Why! Your coat's wringing wet."

"That's nothing," said Peter, turning to the voice.

He found those big dark eyes at last looking at him, and looking at him without anger. Leonore had stopped on the step above him.

"That shows how foolish you were to go out in the rain," said Leonore.

"Yes," said Peter, venturing on the smallest of smiles.

Leonore promptly explained the charge in Peter's "yes." "It's very different," he was told. "I put on tips and a mackintosh. You didn't put on anything. And it was pouring torrents."

"But I'm tough," said Peter. "A wetting won't hurt me."

"So am I," said Leonore. "I've tramped for hours in the Orkneys, and Sweden and Norway, when it was raining. But then I was dressed for it. Go and put on dry clothes at once."

That was what Peter had intended to do, but he saw his advantage. "It isn't worth while," he said.

"I never heard of such obstinacy," said Leonore. "I pity your wife, if you ever get one. She'll have an awful time of it."

Peter did not like that view at all. But he did not forego at once his hope of getting some compensation out of Leonore's wish. So he said: "It's too much trouble to change my clothes, but a cup of your tea may keep me from taking cold." It was nearly five o'clock, and Peter was longing for that customary half-hour at the tea-table.

Leonore said in the kindness of her heart, "When you've changed your clothes, I'll make you a cup." Then she went upstairs. When she had reached the second floor, she turned, and leaning over the balustrade of the gallery, said, "Peter."

"Yes," said Peter, surveying her from below, and thinking how lovely she was.

Leonore was smiling saucily. She said in triumph: "I had my way. I did get my walk." Then she went to her room, her head having a very victorious carriage.

Peter went to his room, smiling. "It's a good lawyer," he told his mirror, "who compromises just enough to make both sides think they've won." Peter changed his clothes with the utmost despatch, and hurried downstairs to the tea-table. She was not there! Peter waited nearly five minutes quietly, with a patience almost colossal. Then he began to get restless. He wandered about the room for another two minutes. Then he became woe-begone. "I thought she had forgiven me," he remarked.

"What?" said the loveliest of visions from the doorway. Most women would have told one that the beauty lay in the Parisian tea-gown. Peter knew better. Still, he was almost willing to forgive Leonore the delay caused by the donning of it, the result was so eminently satisfactory. "And it will take her as long to make tea as usual, anyway," he thought.

"Hadn't I better put some rum into it to-day?" he was asked, presently.

"You may put anything in it, except the sugar tongs," said Peter, taking possession of that article.

"But then I can't put any sugar in."

"Fingers were made before forks," suggested Peter. "You don't want to give me anything bitter, do you?"

"You deserve it," said Leonore, but she took the lumps in her fingers, and dropped them in the cup.

"I can't wait five years!" thought Peter. "I can't wait five months—weeks—days—hours—minutes—sec——"

Watts saved Peter from himself by coming in here. "Hello! Here you are. How cosy you look. I tried to find you both a few minutes ago, but thought you must have gone to walk after all. Here, Peter. Here's a special delivery letter, for which I receipted a while ago. Give me a cup, Dot."

Peter said, "Excuse me," and, after a glance at the envelope, opened the letter with a sinking sensation. He read it quickly, and then reached over and rang the bell. When the footman came, Peter rose and said something in a low voice to him. Then he came back to his tea.

"Nothing wrong, I hope," asked Watts.

"Yes. At least I am called back to New York," said Peter gloomily.

"Bother," said Watts. "When?"

"I shall leave by the night express."

"Nonsense. If it was so important as that, they'd have wired you."

"It isn't a matter which could be telegraphed."

"What is it, Peter?" said Leonore, putting her finger in.

"It's confidential."

So Leonore did not ask again. But when the tea was finished, and all had started upstairs, Leonore said, "Peter," on the landing. When Peter stopped, she whispered, "Why are you going to New York?"

"I can't tell you," said Peter.

"Yes, you can, now that papa isn't here."

"No."

"Yes. I know it's politics, and you are to tell me."

"It isn't politics."

"Then what is it?"

"You really want to know?"

"Of course."

"It's something really confidential."

Leonore gave Peter one look of insulted dignity, and went upstairs to her room. "He's different," she said.

"He isn't a bit afraid of displeasing me any more. I don't know what to do with him."

Peter found Jenifer waiting. "Only pack the grip," he said. "I hope to come back in a few days." But he looked very glum, and the glumness stuck to him even after he had dressed and had descended to dinner.

"I am leaving my traps," he told Mrs. D'Alloi. "For I hope to be back next week."

"Next week!" cried Watts. "What has been sprung on you that will take you that long?"

"It doesn't depend on me, unfortunately," said Peter, "or I wouldn't go."

When the carriage was announced later, Peter shook hands with Watts and Mrs. D'Alloi, and then held out his hand to Leonore. "Good-bye," he said.

"Are you going to tell me why you are going?" said that young lady, with her hands behind her, in the prettiest of poses.

"No."

"Then I shan't say good-bye."

"I cannot tell you," said Peter, quietly; "please say good-bye."

"No."

That refusal caused Peter gloom all the way to the station. But if Leonore could have looked into the future she would have seen in her refusal the bitterest sorrow she had ever known.

CHAPTER LV

OATHS

As soon as Peter was on the express he went into the smoking cabin of the sleeping-car, and lighting a cigar, took out a letter and read it over again. While he was still reading it, a voice exclaimed:

"Good! Here's Peter. So you are in it too?" Ogden continued, as Ray and he took seats by Peter.

"I always did despise Anarchists and Nihilists," sighed

Ray, "since I was trapped into reading some of those maudlin Russian novels, with their eighth-century ideas grafted on nineteenth-century conditions. Baby brains stimulated with whisky."

Ogden turned to Peter. "How serious is it likely to be, Colonel?"

"I haven't any idea," replied Peter. "The staff is of the opposite party now, and I only have a formal notification to hold my regiment in readiness. If it's nothing but this Socialist and Anarchist talk, there is no real danger in it."

"Why not?"

"This country can never be in danger from discontent with our government, for it's what the majority want it to be, or if not, it is made so at the next election. That is the beauty of a Democracy. The majority always supports the government. We fight our revolutions with ballots, not with bullets."

"Yet Most says that blood must be shed."

"I suppose," said Peter, "that he has just reached the stage of intelligence which doctors had attained when they bled people to make them strong."

"What can you do with such a fellow's talk? You can't argue with him," said Ogden.

"Talk!" muttered Ray. "Don't dignify it with that word. Gibberish!"

"No," said Peter. "It's too earnest to deserve that name. The man can't express himself, but way down underneath all the absurd talk of 'natural monopolies,' and of 'the oppression of the money-power,' there lies a germ of truth, without which none of their theories would have a corporal's guard of honest believers. We have been working towards that truth in an unsystematic way for centuries, but we are a long way from it, and till we solve how to realize it, we shall have ineffectual discontent."

"But that makes the whole thing only the more arrant nonsense," grumbled Ray. "It's foolish enough in all conscience sake, if they had a chance of success, but when they haven't any, why the deuce do they want to drag us poor beggars back from Newport?"

"Why did Rome insist on burning while Nero fiddled?" queried Peter smiling. "We should hear nothing of socialism and anarchy if Newport and the like had no existence."

"I believe at heart you're a Socialist yourself," cried Ray.

"No danger," laughed Ogden; "his bank account is too large. No man with Peter's money is ever a Socialist."

"You forget," said Ray, "that Peter is always an exception to the rule."

"No," said Peter. "I disagree with Socialists entirely both in aims and methods, but I sympathize with them, for I see the fearful problems which they think their theories will solve, and though I know how mistaken they are, I cannot blame them, when I see how seriously and honestly they believe in, and how unselfishly they work for, their ideas. Don't blame the Socialists, for they are quite as conscientious as were the Abolitionists. Blame it to the lack of scientific education, which leaves these people to believe that theories containing a half truth are so wholly true that they mean the regeneration and salvation of society."

"I suppose you are right," sighed Ray, "for you've thought of it, and I haven't. I don't want to, either. I thank the Lord I'm not as serious as you, Graveyard. But if you want to air your theory, I'll lend you my ears, for friendship's sake. I don't promise to remember."

Peter puffed his cigar for a moment. "I sometimes conclude," he said, "that the people who are most in need of education, are the college-bred men. They seem to think they've done all the work and study of their life in their four years, and so can dissipate mentally ever after." But Peter smiled as he said this and continued, more seriously: "Society and personal freedom are only possible in conjunction, when law or public opinion interferes to the degree of repressing all individual acts that interfere with the freedom of others; thus securing the greatest individual freedom to all. So far as physical force is concerned, we have pretty well realized this condition. Because a man is strong he can no longer take advantage of the weak. But strength is not limited to muscle. To pro-

tect the weak mind from the strong mind is an equal duty,
and a far more difficult task. So far we have only partially
succeeded. In this difficulty lies the whole problem. Socialism, so far as it attempts to repress individualism, and
reduce mankind to an evenness opposed to all natural laws,
is suicidal of the best in favor of mediocrity. But so far
as it attempts to protect that mediocrity and weakness
from the superior minds of the best, it is only in line with
the laws which protect us from murder and robbery. You
can't expect men of the Most variety, however, to draw
such distinctions."

"I do wish they would settle it, without troubling me,"
groaned Ray. "Lispenard's right. A man's a fool who
votes, or serves on a jury, or joins a regiment. What's
the good of being a good citizen, when the other fellow
won't be? I'm sick of being good for nothing."

"Have you just discovered that?" laughed Ogden.
"You're progressing."

"No," said Ray. "I am good for one thing. Like a
good many other men I furnish the raw material on which
the dearest of women may lavish her affection. Heigh-ho!
I wish I was before the fire with her now. It's rather
rough to have visits to one's wife cut short in this way."

Peter rose. "I am going to get some sleep, for we
don't know what's before us, and may not have much
after to-night. But, Ray, there's a harder thing than leaving one's wife at such a time."

"What's that, Peter?" asked Ray, looking at Peter with
surprise.

"To know that there is no one to whom your going or
return really matters." Peter passed out of the cabin.

"By George!" said Ray, "if it wasn't Peter, I'd have
sworn there was salt water in his eyes."

"Anneke has always insisted that he was lonely. I
wonder if she's right?" Ogden queried.

"If he is, why the deuce does he get off in those solitary
quarters of his?"

"Ray," said Ogden, "I have a sovereign contempt for
a man who answers one question with another."

Peter reached the city at six the next morning, and, despite the hour, began his work at once. He made a num-

ber of calls in the district, holding whispered dialogues with men; who, as soon as Peter was gone, hurried about and held similar conversations with other men; who promptly went and did the same to still others. While they were doing this, Peter drove uptown, and went into Dickel's riding academy. As he passed through the office, a man came out.

"Ah, Mr. Stirling. Good-morning."

"Good-morning, Mr. Byrnes," said Peter. "How serious is it likely to be?"

"We can't say yet. But the force has all it can do now to handle the Anarchists and unemployed, and if this strike takes place we shall need you."

Peter passed into another room where were eight men.

"Good-morning, Colonel," said one. "You are prompt."

"What is the trouble?"

"The Central has decided to make a general reduction. They put it in force at noon to-day, and are so certain that the men will go out, that they've six hundred new hands ready somewhere to put right in."

"Byrnes tells me he has all he can do."

"Yes. We've obtained the Governor's consent to embody eight regiments. It isn't only the strike that's serious, but this parade of the unemployed to-morrow, and the meeting which the Anarchists have called in the City Hall. Byrnes reports a very ugly feeling, and buying of arms."

"It's rather rough on you, Stirling," spoke up a man, "to have it come while you are a nominee."

Peter smiled, and passed into the room beyond. "Good-morning, General Canfield," he said. "I have taken the necessary steps to embody my regiment. Are there any further orders?"

"If we need you, we shall put you at the Central Station," the officer replied; "so, if you do not know the lay of the land, you had better familiarize yourself at once."

"General Canfield," said Peter, "my regiment has probably more sympathizers with the strikers than has any other in the city. It could not be put in a worse place."

"Are you objecting to orders?" said the man, in a sharp decisive voice.

"No," replied Peter. "I am stating a fact, in hopes that it may prevent trouble."

The man and Peter looked each other in the eye.

"You have your orders," said the man, but he didn't look pleased or proud.

Peter turned and left the room, looking very grave. He took his cab and went to his quarters. He ate a hurried breakfast, and then went down into the streets. They seemed peaceably active as he walked through them. A small boy was calling an extra, but it was in reference to the arrival of a much-expected racing-yacht. There was nothing to show that a great business depression rested with crushing weight on the city, and especially on the poor; that anarchy was lifting its head, and from hungering for bread was coming to hunger for blood and blaze; that capital and labor were preparing to lock arms in a struggle which perhaps meant death and destruction.

The armory door was opened only wide enough to let a man squeeze through, and was guarded by a keeper. Peter passed in, however, without question, and heard a hum of voices which showed that if anarchy was gathering, so too was order. Peter called his officers together, and gave a few orders. Then he turned and whispered for a moment with Dennis.

"They don't put us there, sir!" exclaimed Dennis.

"Yes."

"Are they mad?"

"They've given us the worst job, not merely as a job, but especially for the regiment. Perhaps they won't mind if things do go wrong."

"Yez mean?"

"What will people say of me on November fourth, if my regiment flunks on September thirtieth?"

"Arrah musha dillah!" cried Dennis. "An' is that it?"

"I'm afraid so. Will the men stand by me?"

"Oi'll make them. Yez see," shouted Dennis, "Oi'll tell the b'ys they are tryin' to put yez in a hole, an' they'll stan' by yez, no matter what yez are told to do."

As quickly as possible Peter put on his fatigue uniform.

When he came out, it was to find that the rank and file had done the same, and were now standing in groups about the floor. A moment later they were lined up.

Peter stepped forward and said in a clear, ringing voice: "Before the roll is called I wish to say a word. We may receive orders any moment to take possession of the buildings and switches at the Central Station, to protect the property and operators of that road. This will be hard to some of you, who believe the strikers are right. But we have nothing to do with that. We have taken our oath to preserve order and law, and we are interested in having it done, far more than is the capitalist, for he can buy protection, whether laws are enforced or not, while the laboring man cannot. But if any man here is not prepared to support the State in its duty to protect the life and property of all, by an enforcement of the laws, I wish to know it now."

Peter stood a moment waiting, and then said, "Thank you, men."

The roll-call was made, and Peter sent off a line to headquarters, stating that his regiment, with only eighteen reported "missing" was mustered and ready for further orders. Then the regiment broke ranks, and waited.

Just as two o'clock struck a despatch was handed Peter. A moment later came the rap of the drum, and the men rose from the floor and fell in. A few sharp, quick words were passed from mouth to mouth. Guns rose to the shoulders with a click and a movement almost mechanical. The regiment swung from a long straight line into companies, the door rolled open, and without a sound, except the monotonous pound of the regular tread, the regiment passed into the street. At the corner they turned sharply, and marched up a side street, so narrow that the ranks had to break their lines to get within the curbs. So without sound of drum or music they passed through street after street. A regiment is thrilling when it parades to music: it is more so when it marches in silence.

Presently it passed into a long tunnel, where the footfalls echoed in a startling way. But as it neared the other end, a more startling sound could be heard. It was a low murmur, as of many voices, and of voices that were not pleasant. Peter's wisdom in availing himself of the protection and secrecy of the tunnel as an approach became obvious.

A moment later, as the regiment debouched from the tunnel's mouth, the scene broke upon them. A vast crowd filled Fourth Avenue and Forty-second Street. Filled even the cut of the entrance to the tunnel. An angry crowd, judging from the sounds.

A sharp order passed down the ranks, and the many broad lines melted into a long thin one again, even as the regiment went forward. It was greeted with yells, and bottles and bricks were hurled from above it, but the appearance of the regiment had taken the men too much by surprise for them to do more. The head entered the mob, and seemed to disappear. More and more of the regiment was swallowed up. Finally, except to those who could trace the bright glint of the rifle-barrels, it seemed to have been submerged. Then even the rifles disappeared. The regiment had passed through the crowd, and was within the station. Peter breathed a sigh of relief. To march up Fifth Avenue, with empty guns, in a parade, between ten thousand admiring spectators is one thing. To march between ten thousand angry strikers and their sympathizers, with ball cartridges in the rifles, is quite another. It is all the difference between smoking a cigar after dinner, and smoking one in a powder magazine.

The regiment's task had only just begun, however. Peter had orders to clear the streets about the station. After a consultation with the police captain, the companies were told off, and filing out of the various doors, they began work. Peter had planned his debouchments so as to split the mob into sections, knowing that each fragment pushed back rendered the remainder less formidable. First a sally was made from the terminal station, and after two lines of troops had been thrown across Forty-second Street, the second was ordered to advance. Thus a great tongue of the mob, which stretched towards Third Avenue, was pressed back, almost to that street, and held there, without a quarter of the mob knowing that anything was being done. Then a similar operation was repeated on Forty-third Street and Forty-fourth Street, and possession was taken of Madison Avenue. Another wedge was driven into the mob and a section pushed along Forty-second, nearly to Fifth Avenue. Then what was left of the mob was pushed back from the front of the building down Park Avenue. Again Peter breathed more freely.

"I think the worst is done," he told his officers. "Fortunately the crowd did not expect us, and was not prepared to resist. If you can once split a mob, so that it has no centre, and can't get together again, except by going round the block, you've taken the heart out of it."

As he said this a soldier came up, and saluting, said: "Captain Moriarty orders me to inform you that a committee of the strikers ask to see you, Colonel."

Peter followed the messenger. He found a couple of sentries marking a line. On one side of this line sat or reclined Company D and eight policemen. On the other stood a group of a dozen men, and back of them, the crowd.

Peter passed the sentry line, and went up to the group. Three were the committee. The rest were the ubiquitous reporters. From the newspaper report of one of the latter we quote the rest:

> "You wish to see me?" asked Colonel Stirling.
>
> "Yes, Colonel," said Chief Potter. "We are here to remonstrate with you."
>
> "We've done nothing yet," said Doggett, "and till we had, the troops oughtn't to have been called in."
>
> "And now people say that the scabs are to be given a regimental escort to the depot, and will go to work at eight."
>
> "We've been quiet till now," growled a man in the crowd surlily, "but we won't stand the militia protecting the scabs and rats."
>
> "Are you going to fight for the capitalist?" ask Kurfeldt, when Colonel Stirling stood silent.
>
> "I am fighting no man's battle, Kurfeldt," replied Colonel Stirling. "I am obeying orders."
>
> The committee began to look anxious.
>
> "You're no friend of the poor man, and

you needn't pose anymore," shouted one of the crowd.

"Shut your mouth," said Kurfeldt to the crowd. "Colonel Stirling," he continued, "we know you're our friend. But you can't stay so if you fight labor. Take your choice. Be the rich man's servant, or our friend."

"I know neither rich man nor poor man in this," Colonel Stirling said. "I know only the law."

"You'll let the scabs go on?"

"I know no such class. If I find any man doing what the law allows him to do, I shall not interfere. But I shall preserve order."

"Will you order your men to fire on us?"

"If you break the laws."

"Do it at your peril," cried Potter angrily. "For every shot your regiment fires, you'll lose a thousand votes on election day."

Colonel Stirling turned on him, his face blazing with scorn. "Votes," he cried. "Do you think I would weigh votes at such a time? There is no sacrifice I would not make, rather than give the order that ends a human life; and you think that paper ballots can influence my action? Votes compared to men's lives!"

"Oh," cried Doggett, "don't come the heavy nobility racket on us. We are here for business. Votes is votes, and you needn't pretend you don't think so."

Colonel Stirling was silent for a moment. Then he said calmly: "I am here to do my duty, not to win votes. There are not votes enough in this country to make me do more or less."

"Hear him talk," jeered one of the crowd, "and he touting round the saloons to get votes."

The crowd jeered and hissed unpleasantly.

"Come, Colonel," said Kurfeldt, "we know you're after votes this year, and know too much to drive them away. You ain't goin' to lose fifty thousand votes, helpin' scabs to take the bread away from us, only to see you and your party licked."

"No," shouted a man in the crowd. "You don't dare monkey with votes!"

Colonel Stirling turned and faced the crowd. "Do you want to know how much I care for votes," he called, his head reared in the air.

"Speak up loud, sonny," shouted a man far back in the mass, "we all want to hear."

Colonel Stirling's voice rang quite clear enough, "Votes be damned!" he said, and turning on his heel, strode back past the sentries. And the strikers knew the fate of their attempt to keep out the scabs. Colonel Stirling's "damn" had damned the strike as well as the votes.

Dead silence fell on the committee and crowd. Even Company D looked astounded. Finally, however, one of the committee said, "There's no good wasting time here." Then a reporter said to a confrère, "What a stunning headline that will make?" Then the Captain of Company D got his mouth closed enough to exclaim, "Oi always thought he could swear if he tried hard. Begobs, b'ys, it's proud av him we should be this day. Didn't he swear strong an' fine like? Howly hivens! it's a delight to hear damn said like that."

For some reason that "swear-word" pleased New York and the country generally, showing that even an oath has its purpose in this world, so long as it is properly used. Dean Swift said a lie "was too good to be lavished about." So it is of profanity. The crowd understood Peter's remark as they would have understood nothing else. They understood that besides those rifles and bayonets there was something else not to be trifled with. So in this case, it was not wasted.

And Mr. Bohlmann, Christian though he was, as he read his paper that evening cried, "Och! Dod Beder Stirling he always does say chust der righd ding!"

CHAPTER LVI

CUI BONO?

OF the further doings of that day it seems hardly necessary to write, for the papers recorded it with a fulness impossible here. The gathering crowds. The reinforcement of the militia. The clearing and holding of Forty-second Street to the river. The arrival of the three barge-loads of "scabs." Their march through that street to the station safely, though at every cross street greeted with a storm of stones and other missiles. The struggle of the mob at the station to force back the troops so as to get at the "rats." The impact of the "thin line" and that dense seething mass of enraged, crazed men. The yielding of the troops from mere pressure. The order to the second rank to fix bayonets. The pushing back of the crowd once more. The crack of a revolver. Then the dozen shots fired almost simultaneously. The great surge of the mob forward. The quick order, and the rattle of guns, as they rose to the shoulder. Another order, and the sheet of flame. The great surge of the mob backwards. Then silence. Silence in the ranks. Silence in the mob. Silence in those who lay on the ground between the two.

Capital and Labor were disagreed as to a ten per cent. reduction of wages, and were trying to settle it. At first blush capital had the best of it. "Only a few strikers and militia-men killed," was the apparent result of that struggle. The scabs were in safety inside the station, and trains were already making up, preparatory to a resumption of traffic. But capital did not go scot-free. "Firing in the streets of New York," was the word sent out all over the world, and on every exchange in the country, stocks fell. Capital paid twenty-five million dollars that day, for those few ounces of lead. Such a method of settlement seems rather crude and costly, for the last decade of the nineteenth century.

"Boys all over the city were quickly crying extras of the "Labor-party" organ, the first column of which was headed:

BUTCHER STIRLING

THE NOMINEE OF THE DEMOCRATIC PARTY

SHOOTS DOWN UNARMED MEN

IN

COLD BLOOD

This was supplemented by inflammatory broadsides. Men stood up on fences, lamp-posts, or barrels, wherever they could get an audience, and shrieked out invectives against police, troops, government, and property; and waved red flags. Orders went out to embody more regiments. Timid people retired indoors, and bolted their shutters. The streets became deserted, except where they were filled by groups of angry men listening to angrier speakers. It was not a calm night in New York.

Yet in reality, the condition was less serious, for representatives of Capital, Labor, and Government were in consultation. Inside the station, in the Directors' room of the railroad, its officials, a committee of the strikers, and an officer in fatigue uniform, with a face to match, were seated in great leather-covered chairs, around a large table. When they had first gathered, there had been dark brows, and every sentence had been like the blow of flint on steel. At one moment all but the officer had risen from their seats, and the meeting had seemed ended. But the officer had said something quietly, and once more they had seated themselves. Far into the night they sat, while mobs yelled, and sentries marched their beats. When the gathering ended, the scowls were gone. Civil partings were exchanged, and the committee and the officer passed out together.

"That Stirling is a gritty bull-dog for holding on, isn't he?" said one of the railroad officials. "It's a regular surrender for us."

"Yes, but we couldn't afford to be too obstinate with him, for he may be the next governor."

One of the committee said to the officer as they passed into the street, "Well, we've given up everything to the road, to please you. I hope you'll remember it when you're governor and we want things done."

"Gentlemen," said Peter, "for every surrender of opinion you and the railroad officials have made to-night, I thank you. But you should have compromised twelve hours sooner."

"So as you should not have had to make yourself unpopular?" asked Kurfeldt. "You needn't be afraid.

You've done your best for us. Now we'll do our best for you."

"I was not thinking of myself. I was thinking of the dead," said Peter.

Peter sent a despatch to headquarters and went the rounds to see if all was as it should be. Then spreading his blanket in the passenger waiting-room, he fell asleep, not with a very happy look on the grave face.

But the morning-papers announced that the strike was ended by a compromise, and New York and the country breathed easier.

Peter did not get much sleep, for he was barely dreaming of—of a striker, who had destroyed his peace, by striking him in the heart with a pair of slate-colored eyes —when a hand was placed on his shoulder. He was on his feet before the disturber of his dreams could speak.

"A despatch from headquarters," said the man.

Peter broke it open. It said:

"Take possession of Printing-House Square, and await further orders." In ten minutes the regiment was tramping through the dark, silent streets, on its way to the new position.

"I think we deserve a rest," growled the Lieutenant-Colonel to Peter.

"We shan't get it," said Peter. "If there's anything hard to be done, we shall have it." Then he smiled. "You'll have to have an understanding hereafter, before you make a man colonel, that he shan't run for office."

"What are we in for now?"

"I can't say. To-day's the time of the parade and meeting in City Hall Park."

It was sunrise when the regiment drew up in the square facing the Park. It was a lovely morning, with no sign of trouble in sight, unless the bulletin boards of the newspapers, which were chiefly devoted to the doings about the Central Station, could be taken as such. Except for this, the regiment was the only indication that the universal peace had not come, and even this looked peaceful, as soon as it had settled down to hot coffee, bread and raw ham.

In the Park, however, was a suggestive sight. For not merely were all the benches filled with sleeping men, but the steps of the City Hall, the grass, and even the hard asphalt pavement were besprinkled with a dirty, ragged, hungry-looking lot of men, unlike those usually seen in the streets of New York. When the regiment marched into the square, a few of the stragglers rose from their recumbent attitudes, and looked at it, without much love in their faces. As the regiment breakfasted, more and more rose from their hard beds to their harder lives. They moved about restlessly, as if waiting for something. Some gathered in little groups and listened to men who talked and shrieked far louder than was necessary in order that their listeners should hear. Some came to the edge of the street and cursed and vituperated the breakfasting regiment. Some sat on the ground and ate food which they produced from their pockets or from paper bundles. It was not very tempting-looking food. Yet there were men in the crowd who looked longingly at it, and a few scuffles occurred in attempts to get some. That crowd represented the slag and scum of the boiling pot of nine-teenth-century conditions. And as the flotsam on a river always centres at its eddies, so these had drifted, from the country, and from the slums, to the centre of the whirl-pool of American life. Here they were waiting. Waiting for what? The future only would show. But each moment is a future, till it becomes the present.

While the regiment still breakfasted it became conscious of a monotonous sound, growing steadily in volume. Then came the tap of a drum, and the regiment rose from a half-eaten meal, and lined up as if on parade. Several of the members remarked crossly: "Why couldn't they wait ten minutes?"

The next moment the head of another regiment swung from Chambers Street into the square. It was greeted by hisses and groans from the denizens of the park, but this lack of politeness was more than atoned for, by the order: "Present arms," passed down the immovable line awaiting it. After a return salute the commanding officers advanced and once more saluted.

"In obedience to orders from headquarters, I have the

honor to report my regiment to you, Colonel Stirling, and await your orders," said the officer of the "visiting" regiment, evidently trying not to laugh.

"Let your men break ranks, and breakfast, Major Rivington," said Peter. In two minutes dandy and Mick were mingled, exchanging experiences, as they sliced meat off the same ham-bones and emptied the same cracker boxes. What was more, each was respecting and liking the other. One touch of danger is almost as efficacious as one touch of nature. It is not the differences in men which make ill-feeling or want of sympathy, it is differences in conditions.

In the meantime, Peter, Ray and Ogden had come together over their grub, much as if it was a legal rather than an illegal trouble to be dealt with.

"Where were you?" asked Peter.

"At the Sixty-third Street terminals," said Ray. "We didn't have any fun at all. As quiet as a cow. You always were lucky! Excuse me, Peter, I oughtn't to have said it," Ray continued, seeing Peter's face. "It's this wretched American trick of joking at everything."

Ogden, to change the subject, asked: "Did you really say 'damn'?"

"Yes."

"But I thought you disapproved of cuss words."

"I do. But the crowd wouldn't believe that I was honest in my intention to protect the substitutes. They thought I was too much of a politician to dare to do it. So I swore, thinking they would understand that as they would not anything else. I hoped it might save actual firing. But they became so enraged that they didn't care if we did shoot."

Just then one of the crowd shrieked, "Down with the blood-suckers. On to freedom. Freedom of life, of property, of food, of water, of air, of land. Destroy the money power!"

"If we ever get to the freedom he wants," said Ray, "we'll utilize that chap for supplying free gas."

"Splendid raw material for free soap," said Ogden.

"He's not the only one," said Ray. "I haven't had a wash in nine hours, and salt meats are beginning to pall."

"There are plenty of fellows out there will eat it for you, Ray," said Peter, "and plenty more who have not washed in weeks."

"It's their own fault."

"Yes. But if you burn or cut yourself, through ignorance, that doesn't make the pain any the less."

"They don't look like a crowd which could give us trouble."

"They are just the kind who can. They are men lifted off their common sense, and therefore capable of thinking they can do anything, just as John Brown expected to conquer Virginia with forty men."

"But there's no danger of their getting the upper hand."

"No. Yet I wish we had orders to clear the Park now, while there are comparatively few here, or else to go back to our armories, and let them have their meeting in peace. Our being here will only excite them."

"Hear that," said Ray, as the crowd gave a great roar as another regiment came up Park Place, across the Park and spread out so as to cover Broadway.

As they sat, New Yorkers began to rise and begin business. But many seemed to have none, and drifted into the Park. Some idlers came from curiosity, but most seemed to have some purpose other than the mere spectacle. From six till ten they silted in imperceptibly from twenty streets. As fast as the crowd grew, regiments appeared, and taking up positions, lay at ease. There was something terrible about the quiet way in which both crowd and troops increased. The mercury was not high, but it promised to be a hot morning in New York. All the car lines took off their cars. Trucks disappeared from the streets. The exchanges and the banks closed their doors, and many hundred shops followed their example. New York almost came to a standstill as order and anarchy faced each other.

While these antagonistic forces still gathered, a man who had been yelling to his own coterie of listeners in that dense crowd, extracted himself, and limped towards Peter.

"Mr. Stirling," he shouted, "come out from those murderers. I want to tell you something."

Peter went forward. "What is it, Podds?" he asked.

Podds dropped his voice. "We're out for blood to-day. But I don't want yours, if you do murder my fellow-men. Get away from here, quick. Hide yourself before the people rise in their might."

Peter smiled sadly. "How are Mrs. Podds and the children?" he asked kindly.

"What is a family at such a moment?" shrieked Podds. "The world is my family. I love the whole world, and I'm going to revolutionize it. I'm going to give every man his rights. The gutters shall reek with blood, and every plutocrat's castle shall be levelled to the soil. But I'll spare you, for though you are one of the classes, it's your ignorance, not your disposition, that makes you one. Get away from here. Get away before it's too late."

Just then the sound of a horse's feet was heard, and a staff officer came cantering from a side street into the square. He saluted Peter and said, "Colonel Stirling, the governor has issued a proclamation forbidding the meeting and parade. General Canfield orders you to clear the Park, by pushing the mob towards Broadway. The regiments have been drawn in so as to leave a free passage down the side streets."

"Don't try to move us a foot," screamed Podds, "or there'll be blood. We claim the right of free meeting and free speech."

Even as he spoke, the two regiments formed, stiffened, fixed bayonets, and moved forward, as if they were machines rather than two thousand men.

"Brethren," yelled Podds, "the foot of the tyrant is on us. Rise. Rise in your might." Then Podds turned to find the rigid line of bayonets close upon him. He gave a spring, and grappled with Peter, throwing his arms about Peter's neck. Peter caught him by the throat with his free arm.

"Don't push me off," shrieked Podds in his ear, "it's coming," and he clung with desperate energy to Peter.

Peter gave a twist with his arm. He felt the tight clasp relax, and the whole figure shudder. He braced his arm for a push, intending to send Podds flying across the street.

But suddenly there was a flash, as of lightning. Then a crash. Then the earth shook, cobble-stones, railroad tracks, anarchists, and soldiers, rose in the air, leaving a great chasm in crowd and street. Into that chasm a moment later, stones, rails, anarchists, and soldiers fell, leaving nothing but a thick cloud of overhanging dust. Underneath that great dun pall lay soldier and anarchist, side by side, at last at peace. The one died for his duty, the other died for his idea. The world was none the better, but went on unchanged.

CHAPTER LVII

HAPPINESS

THE evening on which Peter had left Grey-Court, Leonore had been moved "for sundry reasons" to go to her piano and sing an English ballad entitled "Happiness." She had sung it several times, and with gusto.

The next morning she read the political part of the papers. "I don't see anything to have taken him back," she said, "but I am really glad, for he was getting hard to manage. I couldn't send him away, but now I hope he'll stay there." Then Leonore fluttered all day, in the true Newport style, with no apparent thought of her "friend."

But something at a dinner that evening interested her.

"I'm ashamed," said the hostess, "of my shortage of men. Marlow was summoned back to New York last night, by business, quite unexpectedly, and Mr. Dupont telegraphed me this afternoon that he was detained there."

"It's curious," said Dorothy. "Mr. Rivington and my brother came on Tuesday expecting to stay for a week, but they had special delivery letters yesterday, and both started for New York. They would not tell me what it was."

"Mr. Stirling received a special delivery, too," said Leonore, "and started at once. And he wouldn't tell."

"How extraordinary!" said the hostess. "There must be something very good at the roof-gardens."

"It has something to do with headwears," said Leonore, not hiding her light under a bushel.

"Headwear?" said a man.

"Yes," said Leonore. "I only had a glimpse of the heading, but I saw 'Headwears N. G. S. N. Y.'"

A sudden silence fell, no one laughing at the mistake.

"What's the matter?" asked Leonore.

"We are wondering what will happen," said the host, "if men go in for headwear too."

"They do that already," said a man, "but unlike women, they do it on the inside, not the outside of the head."

But nobody laughed, and the dinner seemed to drag from that moment.

Leonore and Dorothy had come together, and as soon as they were in their carriage, Leonore said, "What a dull dinner it was."

"Oh, Leonore," cried Dorothy, "don't talk about dinners. I've kept up till now, bu——" and Dorothy's sentence melted into a sob.

"Is it home, Mrs. Rivington?" asked the tiger, sublimely unconscious, as a good servant should be, of this dialogue, and of his mistress's tears.

"No, Portman, the Club," sobbed Dorothy.

"Dorothy," begged Leonore, "what is it?"

"Don't you understand?" sobbed Dorothy. "All this fearful anarchist talk and discontent? And my poor, poor darling! Oh, don't talk to me." Dorothy became inarticulate once more.

"How foolish married women are!" thought Leonore, even while putting her arm around Dorothy, and trying blindly to comfort her.

"Is it a message, Mrs. Rivington?" asked the man, opening the carriage-door.

"Ask for Mr. Melton, or Mr. Duer, and say Mrs. Rivington wishes to see one of them." Dorothy dried her eyes, and braced up. Before Leonore had time to demand an explanation, Peter's gentlemanly scoundrel was at the door.

"What is it, Mrs. Rivington?" he asked.

"Mr. Duer, is there any bad news from New York?"

"Yes. A great strike on the Central is on, and the troops have been called in to keep order."

"Is that all the news?" asked Dorothy.

"Yes."

"Thank you," said Dorothy. "Home, Portman."

The two women were absolutely silent during the drive. But they kissed each other in parting, not with the peck which women so often give each other, but with a true kiss. And when Leonore, in crossing the porch, encountered the mastiff which Peter had given her, she stopped and kissed him too, very tenderly. What is more, she brought him inside, which was against the rules, and put him down before the fire. Then she told the footman to bring her the evening-papers, and sitting down on the rug by Bêtise, proceeded to search them, not now for the political outlook, but for the labor troubles. Leonore suddenly awoke to the fact that there were such things as commercial depressions and unemployed. She read it all with the utmost care. She read the outpourings of the Anarchists, in a combination of indignation, amazement and fear. "I never dreamed there could be such fearful wretches!" she said. There was one man—a fellow named Podds—whom the paper reported as shrieking in Union Square to a select audience:

"Rise! Wipe from the face of the earth the money power! Kill! Kill! Only by blood atonement can we lead the way to better things. To a universal brotherhood of love. Down with rich men! Down with their paid hirelings, the troops! Blow them in pieces!"

"Oh!" cried Leonore shuddering. "It's fearful. I wish some one would blow you in pieces!" Thereby was she proving herself not unlike Podds. All humanity have something of the Anarchist in them. Then Leonore turned to the mastiff and told him some things. Of how bad the strikers were, and how terrible were the Anarchists. "Yes, dear," she said, "I wish we had them here, and then you would treat them as they deserve, wouldn't you, Bêtise? I'm so glad he has my luck-piece!"

A moment later her father and another man came into the hall from the street, compelling Leonore to assume a more proper attitude.

"Hello, Dot!" said Watts. "Still up? Vaughan and I are going to have a game of billiards. Won't you score for us?"

"Yes," said Leonore.

"Bad news from New York, isn't it?" said Vaughan, nonchalantly, as he stood back after his first play.

Leonore saw her father make a grimace at Vaughan, which Vaughan did not see. She said, "What?"

"I missed," said Watts. "Your turn, Will."

"Tell me the news before you shoot?" said Leonore.

"The collision of the strikers and the troops."

"Was any one hurt?" asked Leonore, calmly scoring two to her father's credit.

"Yes. Eleven soldiers and twenty-two strikers."

"What regiment was it?" asked Leonore.

"Colonel Stirling's," said Vaughan, making a brilliant *massé*. "Fortunately it's a Mick regiment, so we needn't worry over who was killed."

Leonore thought to herself: "You are as bad every bit as Podds!" Aloud she said, "Did it say who were killed?"

"No. The dispatch only said fourteen dead."

"That was a beautiful shot," said Leonore. "You ought to run the game out with that position. I think, papa, that I'll go to bed. I find I'm a little tired. Good-night, Mr. Vaughan." Leonore went upstairs, slowly, deep in thought. She did not ring for her maid. On the contrary she lay down on her bed in her dinner-gown, to its everlasting detriment. "I know he isn't hurt," she said, "because I should feel it. But I wish the telegram had said." She hardly believed herself, apparently, for she buried her head in the pillow, and began to sob quietly. "If I only had said good-bye," she moaned.

Early the next morning Watts found Leonore in the hall.

"How pale my Dot is!" he exclaimed.

"I didn't sleep well," said Leonore.

"Aren't you going to ride with me?"

"No. I don't feel like it this morning," said Leonore.
As Watts left the hall, a servant entered it.

"I had to wait, Miss D'Alloi," he said. "No papers are
for sale till eight o'clock."

Leonore took the newspaper silently and went to the
library. Then she opened it and looked at the first column.
She read it hurriedly.

"I knew he wasn't hurt," she said, "because I would
have felt it, and because he had my luck piece." Then
she stepped out of one of the windows, called Bêtise to
her, and putting her arms about his neck, kissed him.

When the New York papers came things were even
better, for they recorded the end of the strike. Leonore
even laughed over that big, big D. "I can't imagine
him getting so angry," she said. "He must have a temper, after all." She sang a little, as she fixed the flowers
in the vases, and one of the songs was "Happiness."
Nor did she snub a man who hinted at afternoon tea, as
she had a poor unfortunate who suggested tennis earlier
in the day.

While they were sipping their tea, however, Watts came
in from the club.

"Helen," he said, going to the bay window farthest
from the tea-table, "come here. I want to say something."

They whispered for a moment, and then Mrs. D'Alloi
came back to her tea.

"Won't you have a cup, papa?" asked Leonore.

"Not to-day, dear," said Watts, with an unusual tenderness in his voice.

Leonore was raising a spoon to her mouth, but suddenly
her hand trembled a little. After a glance at her father
and mother, she pushed her tea-cup into the centre of the
table as if she had finished it, though it had just been
poured. Then she turned and began to talk and laugh
with the caller.

But the moment the visitor was out of the room, Leonore said:

"What is it, papa?"

Watts was standing by the fire. He hesitated. Then
he groaned. Then he went to the door. "Ask your
mother," he said, and went out of the room.

"Mamma?" said Leonore.

"Don't excite yourself, dear," said her mother. "I'll tell you to-morrow."

Leonore was on her feet. "No," she said huskily, "tell me now."

"Wait till we've had dinner."

"Mamma," cried Leonore, appealingly, "don't you see that—that—that I suffer more by not knowing it? Tell me."

"Oh, Leonore," cried her mother, "don't look that way. I'll tell you; but don't look that way!"

"What?"

Mrs. D'Alloi put her arms about Leonore. "The Anarchists have exploded a bomb."

"Yes?" said Leonore.

"And it killed a great many of the soldiers."

"Not——?"

"Yes."

"Thank you, mamma," said Leonore. She unclasped her mother's arms, and went towards the door.

"Leonore," cried her mother, "stay here with me, dear."

"I'd rather be alone," said Leonore, quietly. She went upstairs to her room and sank down by an ottoman which stood in the middle of the floor. She sat silent and motionless, for over an hour, looking straight before her at nothing, as Peter had so often done. Is it harder to lose out of life the man or woman whom one loves, or to see him or her happy in the love of another? Is the hopelessness of the impossible less or greater than the hopelessness of the unattainable?

Finally Leonore rose, and touched her bell. When her maid came she said, "Get me my travelling dress." Ten minutes later she came into the library, saying to Watts.

"Papa, I want you to take me to New York, by the first train."

"Are you crazy, my darling?" cried Watts. "With riots and Anarchists all over the city."

"I must go to New York," said Leonore. "If you won't take me, I'll go with madame."

"Not for a moment——" began Watts.

"Papa," cried Leonore, "don't you see it's killing me! I can't bear it——" and Leonore stopped.

"Yes, Watts, we must," said Mrs. D'Alloi.

Two hours later they were all three rolling towards New York. It was a five hours' ride, but Leonore sat the whole distance without speaking, or showing any consciousness of her surroundings. For every turn of those wheels seemed to fall into a rhythmic repetition of: "If I had only said 'good-bye.'"

The train was late in arriving, and Watts tried to induce Leonore to go to a hotel for the night. She only said "No. Take me to him," but it was in a voice which Watts could not disregard. So after a few questions at the terminal, which produced no satisfactory information, Watts told the cabman to drive to the City Hall Park.

They did not reach it, however, for at the corner of Centre Street and Chambers, there came a cry of "halt," and the cab had to stop.

"You can't pass this line," said the sentry. "You must go round by Broadway."

"Why?" asked Watts.

"The street is impassable."

Watts got out, and held a whispered dialogue with the sentry. This resulted in the summoning of the officer of the watch. In the meantime Leonore descended and joined them. Watts turned and said to her: "The sentry says he's here."

Presently an officer came up.

"An' what do the likes av yez want at this time av night?" he inquired crossly. "Go away wid yez."

"Oh, Captain Moriarty," said Leonore, "won't you let me see him? I'm Miss D'Alloi."

"Shure," said Dennis, "yez oughtn't to be afther disturbin' him. It's two nights he's had no sleep."

Leonore suddenly put her hand on Dennis' arm. "He's not killed?" she whispered, as if she could not breathe, and the figure swayed a little.

"Divil a bit! They got it wrong entirely. It was that dirty spalpeen av a Podds."

"Are you sure?" said Leonore, pleadingly. "You are not deceiving me?"

"Begobs," said Dennis, "do yez think Oi could stand here wid a dry eye if he was dead?"

Leonore put her head on Dennis's shoulder, and began to sob softly. For a moment Dennis looked aghast at the results of his speech, but suddenly his face changed. "Shure," he whispered, "we all love him just like that, an' that's why the Blessed Virgin saved him for us."

Then Leonore, with tears in her eyes, said, "I felt it," in the most joyful of voices. A voice that had a whole *Te Deum* in it.

"Won't you let me see him?" she begged. "I won't wake him, I promise you."

"That yez shall," said Dennis. "Will yez take my arm?" The four passed within the lines. "Step careful," he continued. "There's pavin' stones, and rails, and plate-glass everywheres. It looks like there'd been a primary itself."

All thought that was the best of jokes and laughed. They passed round a great chasm in the street and sidewalk. Then they came to long rows of bodies stretched on the grass, or rather what was left of the grass, in the Park. Leonore shuddered. "Are they all dead?" she whispered. "Dead! Shurely not. It's the regiment sleepin'," she was told. They passed between these rows for a little distance. "This is him," said Dennis, "sleepin' like a babby." Dennis turned his back and began to describe the explosion to Mrs. D'Alloi and Watts.

There, half covered with a blanket, wrapped in a regulation great coat, his head pillowed on a roll of newspapers, lay Peter. Leonore knelt down on the ground beside him, regardless of the proprieties or the damp. She listened to hear if he was breathing, and when she found that he actually was, her face had on it a little thanksgiving proclamation of its own. Then with the prettiest of motherly manners, she softly pulled the blanket up and tucked it in about his arms. Then she looked to see if there was something else to do. But there was nothing. So she made more. "The poor dear oughtn't to sleep without something on his head. He'll take cold." She took her handkerchief and tried to fix it so that it should protect Peter's head. She tried four different ways, any one of which would have served; but each time she thought of a better way, and had to try once more. She probably would have thought of a fifth, if Peter had not suddenly opened his eyes.

"Oh!" said Leonore, "what a shame. I've waked you up. And just as I had fixed it right."

Peter studied the situation calmly, without moving a muscle. He looked at the kneeling figure for some time. Then he looked up at the arc light a little distance away. Then he looked at the City Hall clock. Then his eyes came back to Leonore. "Peter," he said finally, "this is getting to be a monomania. You must stop it."

"What?" said Leonore, laughing at his manner as if it was intended as a joke.

Peter put out his hand and touched Leonore's dress. Then he rose quickly to his feet. "What is the matter?" he asked.

"Hello," cried Watts. "Have you come to? Well. Here we are, you see. All the way from Newport to see you in fragments, only to be disappointed. Shake!"

Peter said nothing for a moment. But after he had shaken hands, he said, "It's very good of you to have thought of me."

"Oh," explained Leonore promptly, "I'm always anxious about my friends. Mamma will tell you I am."

Peter turned to Leonore, who had retired behind her mother. "Such friends are worth having," he said, with a strong emphasis on "friends."

Then Leonore came out from behind her mother. "How nice he's stupid," she thought. "He is Peter Simple, after all."

"Well," said Watts, "your friends are nearly dying with hunger and want of sleep, so the best thing we can do, since we needn't hunt for you in scraps, is to go to the nearest hotel. Where is that?"

"You'll have to go uptown," said Peter. "Nothing down here is open at this time."

"I'm not sleepy," said Leonore, "but I am so hungry!"

"Serves you right for eating no din——" Watts started to say, but Leonore interjected, in an unusually loud voice. "Can't you get us something?"

"Nothing that will do for you, I'm afraid," said Peter. "I had Dennett send up one of his coffee-boilers so that the men should have hot coffee through the night, and there's a sausage-roll man close to him who's doing a big business. But they'll hardly serve your purpose."

"The very thing," cried Watts. "What a lark!"

"I can eat anything," said Leonore.

So they went over to the stands. Peter's blanket was spread on the sidewalk, and three Newport swells, and the Democratic nominee for governor sat upon it, with their feet in the gutter, and drank half-bean coffee and ate hot sausage rolls, made all the hotter by the undue amount of mustard which the cook would put in. What is worse, they enjoyed it as much as if it was the finest of dinners. Would not society have been scandalized had it known of their doings?

How true it is that happiness is in a mood rather than in a moment. How eagerly we prepare for and pursue the fickle sprite, only to find our preparations and chase giving nothing but dullness, fatigue, and ennui. But then how often without exertion or warning, the sprite is upon us, and tinges the whole atmosphere. So it was at this moment, with two of the four. The coffee might have been all beans, and yet it would have been better than the best served in Viennese cafés. The rolls might have had even a more weepy amount of mustard, and yet the burning and the tears would only have been the more of a joke. The sun came up, as they ate, talked and laughed, touching everything about them with gold, but it might have poured torrents, and the two would have been as happy.

For Leonore was singing to herself: "He isn't dead. He isn't dead."

And Peter was thinking: "She loves me. She must love me."

CHAPTER LVIII

GIFTS

AFTER the rolls and coffee had been finished, Peter walked with his friends to their cab. It had all been arranged that they were to go to Peter's quarters, and get some sleep. These were less than eight blocks away, but the parting was very terrific! However, it had to be done, and so it was gone through with. Hard as it was, Peter had presence of mind enough to say, through the carriage window.

"You had better take my room, Miss D'Alloi, for the spare room is the largest. I give you the absolute freedom of it, minus the gold-box. Use anything you find."

Then Peter went back to the chaotic street and the now breakfasting regiment, feeling that strikes, anarchists, and dynamite were only minor circumstances in life.

About noon Leonore came back to life, and succeeded in making a very bewitching toilet despite the absence of her maid. Whether she peeped into any drawers or other places, is left to feminine readers to decide. If she did, she certainly had ample authority from Peter.

This done she went into the study, and, after sticking her nose into some of the window flowers, she started to go to the bookshelves. As she walked her foot struck something which rang with a metallic sound, as it moved on the wood floor. The next moment, a man started out of a deep chair.

"Oh!" was all Leonore said.

"I hope I didn't startle you. You must have kicked my sword."

"I—I didn't know you were here!" Leonore eyed the door leading to the hall, as if she were planning for a sudden flight.

"The regiment was relieved by another from Albany this morning. So I came up here for a little sleep."

"What a shame that I should have kept you out of your room," said Leonore, still eyeing the door. From Leonore's appearance, one would have supposed that she had purloined something of value from his quarters, and was meditating a sudden dash of escape with it.

"I don't look at it in that light," said Peter. "But since you've finished with the room for the moment, I'll borrow the use temporarily. Strikers and anarchists care so little for soap and water themselves, that they show no consideration to other people for those articles." Peter passed through the doorway towards which Leonore had glanced. Then Leonore's anxious look left her, and she no longer looked at the door. One would almost have inferred that Leonore was afraid of Peter, but that is absurd, since they were such good friends, since Leonore had come all the way from Newport to see him, and since Leonore had decided that Peter must do as she pleased.

Yet, curiously enough, when Peter returned in about twenty minutes, the same look came into Leonore's face.

"We shall have something to eat in ten minutes," Peter said, "for I hear your father and mother moving."

Leonore looked towards the door. She did not intend that Peter should see her do it, but he did.

"Now what shall we do or talk about?" he said. "You know I am host and mustn't do anything my guests don't wish."

Peter said this in the most matter-of-fact way, but Leonore, after a look from under her eyelashes at him, stopped thinking about the door. She went over to one of the window-seats.

"Come and sit here by me," she said, "and tell me everything about it."

So Peter described "the war, and what they fought each other for," as well as he was able, for, despite his intentions, his mind would wander as those eyes looked into his.

"I am glad that Podds was blown to pieces!" said Leonore.

"Don't say that."

"Why?"

"Because it's one of those cases of a man of really good intentions, merely gone wrong. He was a horse-car driver, who got inflammatory rheumatism by the exposure, and was discharged. He suffered fearful pain, and saw his family suffer for bread. He grew bitter, and took up with these wild theories, not having enough original brain force, or decision, to see their folly. He believed firmly in them. So firmly, that when I' tried to reason him out of them many years ago he came to despise me and ordered me out of his rooms. I had once done him a service, and felt angered at what I thought ungrateful conduct, so I made no attempt to keep up the friendliness. He knew yesterday that dynamite was in the hands of some of those men, and tried to warn me away. When I refused to go, he threw himself upon me, to protect me from the explosion. Nothing else saved my life."

"Peter, will your regiment have to do anything more?"

"I don't think so. The dynamite has caused a reaction, and has driven off the soberer part of the mob. The pendulum, when it swings too far, always swings correspondingly far the other way. I must stay here for a couple of days, but then if I'm asked, I'll go back to Newport."

"Papa and mamma want you, I'm sure," said Leonore, glancing at the door again, after an entire forgetfulness.

"Then I shall go," said Peter, though longing to say something else.

Leonore looked at him and said in the frankest way: "And I want you too." That was the way she paid Peter for his forbearance.

Then they all went up on the roof, where in one corner there were pots of flowers about a little table, over which was spread an awning. Over that table, too, Jenifer had spread himself. How good that breakfast was! What a glorious September day it was! How beautiful the view of the city and the bay was! It was all so thoroughly satisfactory that the three nearly missed the "limited." Of course Peter went to the station with them, and, short as was the time, he succeeded in obtaining for one of the party, "all the comic papers," "the latest novel," a small basket of fruit, and a bunch of flowers, not one of which, with the exception of the latter, the real object of these attentions wanted in the least.

Just here it is of value to record an interesting scientific discovery of Leonore's, because women so rarely have made them. It was, that the distance from New York to Newport is very much less than the distance from Newport to New York.

Curiously enough, two days later, his journey seemed to Peter the longest railroad ride he had ever taken. "His friend" did not meet him this time. His friend felt that her trip to New York must be offset before she could resume her proper self-respect. "He was very nice," she had said, in monologue, "about putting the trip down to friendship. And he was very nice that morning in his study. But I think his very niceness is suspicious, and so I must be hard on him!" A woman's reasoning is apt to seem defective, yet sometimes it solves problems not otherwise answerable.

Leonore found her "hard" policy harder than she thought for. She told Peter the first evening that she was going to a card-party. "I can't take you," she said.

"I shall be all the better for a long night's sleep," said Peter, calmly.

This was bad enough, but the next morning, as she was arranging the flowers, she remarked to some one who stood and watched her, "Miss Winthrop is engaged. How foolish of a girl in her first season! Before she's had any fun, to settle down to dull married life."

She had a rose in her hand, prepared to revive Peter with it, in case her speech was too much for one dose, but when she glanced at him, he was smiling happily.

"What is it?" asked Leonore, disapprovingly.

"I beg your pardon," said Peter. "I wasn't listening. Did you say Miss Winthrop was married?"

"What were you smiling over?" said Leonore, in the same voice.

"I was thinking of—of——" Then Peter hesitated and laughed.

"Of what?" asked Leonore.

"You really mustn't ask me," laughed Peter.

"Of what were you thinking?"

"Of eyelashes," confessed Peter.

"It's terrible!" cogitated Leonore, "I can't snub him any more, try as I may."

In truth, Peter was not worrying any longer over what

Leonore said or did to him. He was merely enjoying her
companionship. He was at once absolutely happy, and
absolutely miserable. Happy in his hope. Miserable in
its non-certainty. To make a paradox, he was confident
that she loved him, yet he was not sure. A man will be
absolutely confident that a certain horse will win a race,
or he will be certain that a profit will accrue from a given
business transaction. Yet, until the horse has won, or the
profit is actually made, he is not assured. So it was with
Peter. He thought that he had but to speak, yet dared
not do it. The present was so certain, and the future
might have such agonies. So for two days, he merely
followed Leonore about, enjoying her pretty ways and
hardly heeding her snubs and petulance. He was very
silent, and often abstracted, but his silence and abstraction brought no relief to Leonore, and only frightened her
the more, for he hardly let her out of his sight, and the
silent devotion and tenderness were so obvious that Leonore felt how absolutely absurd was her pretence of unconsciousness. In his very "Miss D'Alloi" now, there
was a tone in his voice and a look in his face which really
said the words: "My darling." Leonore thought this was
a mean trick, of apparently sustaining the conventions of
society, while in reality outraging them horribly, but she
was helpless to better his conduct. Twice unwittingly he
even called her "Leonore" (as he had to himself for two
months), thereby terribly disconcerting the owner of that
name. She wanted to catch him up and snub him each
time, but she was losing her courage. She knew that
she was walking on a mine, and could not tell what chance
word or deed of hers would bring an explosion. "And
then what can I say to him?" she asked.

What she said was this:

Peter came downstairs the third evening of his stay
"armed and equipped as the law directs" for a cotillion.
In the large hallway, he found Leonore, likewise in gala
dress, resting her hand on the tall mantel of the hall, and
looking down at the fire. Peter stopped on the landing to
enjoy that pose. He went over every detail with delibera-
tion. But girl, gown, and things in general, were much
too tempting to make this distant glimpse over lengthy.
So he descended to get a closer view. The pose said noth-

ing, and Peter strolled to the fire, and did likewise. But if he did not speak he more than made up for his silence with his eyes.

Finally the pose said, "I suppose it's time we started?" "Some one's got to speak," the pose had decided. Evidently the pose felt uneasy under that silent gaze.

"It's only a little past ten," said Peter, who was quite satisfied with the *status quo*.

Then silence came again. After this had held for a few moments, the pose said: "Do say something!"

"Something," said Peter. "Anything else I can do for you?"

"Unless you can be more entertaining, we might as well be sitting in the Purdies' dressing-rooms, as standing here. Suppose we go to the library and sit with mamma and papa?" Clearly the pose felt nervous.

Peter did not like this idea. So he said, "I'll try to amuse you. Let me tell you something very interesting to me. It's my birthday to-morrow."

"Oh!" said Leonore. "Why didn't you tell me sooner? Then I would have had a gift for you."

"That's what I was afraid of."

"Don't you want me to give you something?"

"Yes." Then Peter's hand trembled, and he seemed to have hard work in adding, "I want you to give me— a kiss."

"Peter!" said Leonore, drawing back grieved and indignant. "I didn't think you would speak to me so. Of all men!"

"You mustn't think," said Peter, "that I meant to pain you."

"You have," said Leonore, almost ready to cry.

"Because," said Peter, "that isn't what I meant." Peter obviously struggled to find words to say what he did mean as he had never struggled over the knottiest of legal points, or the hardest of wrestling matches. "If I thought you were a girl who would kiss a man for the asking, I should not care for a kiss from you." Peter strayed away from the fire uneasily. "But I know you are not." Peter gazed wildly round, as if the furnishings of the hall might suggest the words for which he was blindly groping. But they didn't, and after one or two half-begun sentences, he continued: "I haven't watched you, and dreamed about you, and loved you, for all this time, without learning what you are." Peter roamed about the great hall restlessly. "I know that your lips will never give what your heart doesn't." Then his face took a despairing look, and he continued quite rapidly: "I ask without much hope. You are so lovely, while I—well I'm not a man women care for. I've tried to please you. Tried to please you so hard, that I may have deceived you. I probably am what women say of me. But if I've been otherwise with you it is because you are different from any other woman in the world." Here the sudden flow of words ended, and Peter paced up and down, trying to find what to say. If any one had seen Peter as he paced, without his present environment, he would have thought him a man meditating suicide. Suddenly his voice and face became less wild, and he said tenderly: "There is no use in my telling you how I love you. You know it now, or will never learn it from anything I can say." Peter strode back to the fire. "It is my love which asks for a kiss. And I want it for the love you will give with it, if you can give it."

Leonore had apparently kept her eyes on the blazing logs during the whole of this monologue. But she must have seen something of Peter's uneasy wanderings about the room, for she said to herself: "Poor dear! He must be fearfully in earnest. I never knew him so restless. He prowls just like a wild animal."

A moment's silence came after Peter's return to the fire. Then he said: "Will you give it to me, Miss D'Alloi?" But his voice in truth, made the words, "Give me what I ask, my darling."

"Yes," said Leonore softly. "On your birthday." Then Leonore shrank back a little, as if afraid that her gift would be sought sooner. No young girl, however much she loves a man, is quite ready for that first kiss. A man's lips upon her own are too contrary to her instinct and previous training to make them an unalloyed pleasure. The girl who is over-ready for her lover's first kiss, has tasted the forbidden fruit already, or has waited over-long for it.

Peter saw the little shrinking and understood it. What was more, he heeded it as many men would not have done. Perhaps there was something selfish in his self-denial, for the purity and girlishness which it indicated were very dear to him, and he hated to lessen them by anything he did. He stood quietly by her, and merely said, "I needn't tell you how happy I am!"

Leonore looked up into Peter's face. If Leonore had seen there any lack of desire to take her in his arms and kiss her, she would never have forgiven him. But since his face showed beyond doubt that he was longing to do it, Leonore loved him all the better for his repression of self, out of regard for her. She slipped her little hand into Peter's confidingly, and said, "So am I." It means a good deal when a girl does not wish to run away from her lover the moment after she has confessed her love.

So they stood for some time, Leonore looking down into the fire, and Peter looking down at Leonore.

Finally Peter said, "Will you do me a great favor?"

"No," said Leonore, "I've done enough for one night. But you can tell me what it is."

"Will you look up at me?"

"What for?" said Leonore, promptly looking up.

"I want to see your eyes," said Peter.

"Why?" asked Leonore, promptly looking down again.

"Well," said Peter, "I've been dreaming all my life about some eyes, and I want to see what my dream is like in reality."

"That's a very funny request," said Leonore perversely. "You ought to have found out about them long ago. The idea of any one falling in love, without knowing about the eyes!"

"But you show your eyes so little," said Peter. "I've never had a thoroughly satisfying look at them."

"You look at them every time I look at you," said Leonore. "Sometimes it was very embarrassing. Just supposing that I showed them to you now, and that you find they aren't what you like?"

"I never waste time discussing impossibilities," said Peter. "Are you going to let me see them?"

"How long will it take?"

"I can tell better after I've seen them," said Peter, astutely.

"I don't think I have time this evening," said Leonore, still perversely, though smiling a look of contentment down into the fire.

Peter said nothing for a moment, wishing to give Leonore's conscience a chance to begin to prick. Then he ended the silence by saying: "If I had anything that would give you pleasure, I wouldn't make you ask for it twice."

"That's—different," said Leonore. "Still, I'll—well, look at them," and Leonore lifted her eyes to Peter's half laughingly and half timidly.

Peter studied those eyes in silence—studied them till Leonore, who did not find that steady look altogether easy to bear, and yet was not willing to confess herself stared out of countenance, asked: "Do you like them?"

"Yes," said Peter.

"Is that all you can say? Other people have said very complimentary things!" said Leonore, pretending to be grieved over the monosyllable, yet in reality delighting in its expressiveness as Peter said it.

"I think," said Peter, "that before I can tell you what I think of your eyes, we shall have to invent some new words."

Leonore looked down again into the fire, smiling a satisfied smile. Peter looked down at that down-turned head, also with a satisfied smile. Then there was another long silence. Incidentally it is to be noted that Peter still held the hand given him some time before. To use a poker term, Peter was standing "pat," and wished no change. Once or twice the little hand had hinted that it had been held long enough, but Peter did not think so, and the hand had concluded that it was safest to let well alone. If it was too cruel it might rouse the sleeping lion which the owner of that hand knew to exist behind that firm, quiet face.

Presently Peter put his unoccupied hand in his breast-pocket, and produced a small sachet. "I did something twice," he said, "that I have felt very meanly about at times. Perhaps you'll forgive me now?" He took from the sachet, a glove, and a small pocket-handkerchief, and without a word showed them to Leonore.

Leonore looked at them. "That's the glove I lost at Mrs. Costell's, isn't it?" she asked gravely.

Peter nodded his head.

"And is that the handkerchief which disappeared in your rooms, at your second dinner?"

Peter nodded his head.

"And both times you helped me hunt for them?"

Peter nodded his head. He at last knew how prisoners felt when he was cross-examining them.

"I knew you had them all the time," said Leonore laughing. "It was dreadfully funny to see you pretend to hunt, when the guilty look on your own face was enough to show you had them. That's why I was so determined to find them."

Peter knew how prisoners felt when the jury says, "Not guilty."

"But how did the holes come in them?" said Leonore. "Do you have mice in your room?" Leonore suddenly looked as worried as had Peter the moment before.

Peter put his hand in the sachet, and produced a bent coin. "Look at that," he said.

"Why, it's my luck-piece!" exclaimed Leonore. "And you've spoiled that too. What a careless boy!"

"No," said Peter. "They are not spoiled to me. Do you know what cut these holes and bent this coin?"

"What?"

"A bullet."

"Peter!"

"Yes. Your luck-piece stopped it, or I shouldn't be here."

"There," said Leonore triumphantly, "I said you weren't hurt, when the news of the shooting came, because I knew you had it. I was so glad you had taken it!"

"I am going to give it back to you by and by," said Peter.

"I had rather that you should have it," said Leonore. "I want you to have my luck."

"I shall have it just the same even after I've given it to you," said Peter.

"How?"

"I'm going to have it made into a plain gold ring," replied Peter, "and when I give it to you, I shall have all your luck."

Then came a silence.

Finally Peter said, "Will you please tell me what you meant by talking about five years!"

"Oh! Really, Peter," Leonore hastened to explain, in an anxious way, as if Peter had charged her with murder or some other heinous crime. "I did think so. I didn't find it out till—till that night. Really! Won't you believe me?"

Peter smiled. He could have believed anything. "Now," he said, "I know at last what Anarchists are for."

His ready acceptance of her statement made Leonore feel a slight prick of conscience. She said: "Well—Peter —I mean—that is—at least, I did sometimes think before then—that when I married, I'd marry you—but I didn't think it would come so soon. Did you? I thought we'd wait. It would have been so much more sensible!"

"I've waited a long time," said Peter.

"Poor dear!" said Leonore, putting her other hand over Peter's, which held hers.

Peter enjoyed this exquisite pleasure in silence for a time, but the enjoyment was too great not to be expressed. So he said:

"I like your hands almost as much as your eyes."

"That's very nice," said Leonore.

"And I like the way you say 'dear,'" said Peter. "Don't you want to say it again?"

"No, I hate people who say the same thing twice."

Then there was a long pause.

"What poor things words are," said Peter, at the end of it.

"I know just what you mean," said Leonore.

Clearly they both meant what they said, for there came another absence of words. How long the absence would have continued is a debatable point. Much too soon a door opened.

"Hello!" said a voice. "Back already? What kind of an evening had you?"

"A very pleasant one," said Peter, calmly, yet expressively.

"Let go my hand, Peter, please," a voice whispered imploringly. "Oh, please! I can't to-night. Oh, please!"

"Say 'dear,'" whispered Peter, meanly.

"Please, dear," said Leonore. Then Leonore went towards the stairs hurriedly.

"Not off already, Dot, surely?"

"Yes. I'm going to bed."

"Come and have a cigar, Peter," said Watts, walking towards the library.

"In a moment," said Peter. He went to the foot of the stairs and said, "Please, dear," to the figure going up.

"Well?" said the figure.

Peter went up five steps. "Please," he begged.

"No," said the figure, "but there is my hand."

So Peter turned the little soft palm uppermost and kissed it. Then he forgot the cigar and Watts. He went to his room, and thought of—of his birthday gift.

CHAPTER LIX

"GATHER YE ROSEBUDS WHILE YE MAY"

IF Peter had roamed about the hall that evening, he was still more restless the next morning. He was down early, though for no apparent reason, and did nothing but pass from hall to room, and room to hall, spending most of his time in the latter, however.

How Leonore could have got from her room into the garden without Peter seeing her was a question which puzzled him not a little, when, by a chance glance out of the window, he saw that personage clipping roses off the bushes. He did not have time to spare, however, to reason out an explanation. He merely stopped roaming, and went out to—to the roses.

"Good-morning," said Leonore pleasantly, though not looking at Peter, as she continued her clipping.

Peter did not say anything for a moment. Then he asked, "Is that all?"

"I don't know what you mean," said Leonore, innocently. "Besides, some one might be looking out of a window."

Peter calmly took hold of the basket to help Leonore sustain its enormous weight. "Let me help you carry it," he said.

"Very well," said Leonore. "But there's no occasion to carry my hand too. I'm not decrepit."

"I hoped I was helping you," said Peter.

"You are not. But you may carry the basket, since you want to hold something."

"Very well," said Peter meekly.

"Do you know," said Leonore, as she snipped, and dropped roses into the basket, "you are not as obstinate as people say you are."

"Don't deceive yourself on that score," said Peter.

"Well! I mean you are not absolutely determined to have your own way."

"I never give up my own views," said Peter, "unless I can see more to be gained by so doing. To that extent I am not at all obstinate."

"Suppose," said Leonore, "that you go and cut the roses on those furthest bushes while I go in and arrange these?"

"Suppose," said Peter calmly, and with an evident lack of enthusiasm.

"Well. Will you?"

"No."

"Why not?"

"The motion to adjourn," said Peter, "is never debatable."

"Do you know," said Leonore, "that you are beginning very badly?"

"That is what I have thought ever since I joined you."

"Then why don't you go away?"

"Why make bad, worse?"

"There," said Leonore. "Your talking has made me cut my finger, almost."

"Let me see," said Peter, reaching out for her hand.

"I'm too busy," said Leonore.

"Do you know," said Peter, "that if you cut many more buds, you won't have any more roses for a week. You've cut twice as many roses as you usually do."

"Then I'll go in and arrange them. I wish you would give Bêtise a run across the lawn."

"I never run before breakfast," said Peter. "Doctors say it's very bad."

So he followed her in. Leonore became tremendously occupied in arranging the flowers. Peter became tremendously occupied in watching her.

"You want to save one of those for me," he said, presently.

"Take one," said Leonore.

"My legal rule has been that I never take what I can get given me. You can't do less than pin it in my button-hole, considering that it is my birthday."

"If I have a duty to do, I always get through with it at once," said Leonore. She picked out a rose, arranged the leaves as only womankind can, and, turning to Peter, pinned it in his button-hole. But when she went to take her hands away, she found them held against the spot so firmly that she could feel the heart-beats underneath.

"Oh, please," was all she said, appealingly, while Peter's rose seemed to reflect some of its color on her cheeks.

"I don't want you to give it to me if you don't wish," said Peter, simply. "But last night I sat up late thinking about it. All night I dreamed about it. When I waked up this morning, I was thinking about it. And I've thought about it ever since. I can wait, but I've waited so long!"

Then Leonore, with very red cheeks, and a very timid manner, held her lips up to Peter.

"Still," Leonore said presently, when again arranging of the roses, "since you've waited so long, you needn't have been so slow about it when you did get it."

"I'm sorry I did it so badly," said Peter, contritely. "I always was slow! Let me try again?"

"No."

"Then show me how."

"No."

"Now who's obstinate?" inquired Peter.

"You," said Leonore, promptly. "And I don't like it."

"Oh, Leonore," said Peter. "If you only knew how happy I am!"

Leonore forgot all about her charge of obstinacy. "So am I," she said. "And I won't be obstinate any more."

"Was that better?" Peter asked, presently.

"No," said Leonore. "That wouldn't have been possible. But you do take so long! I shan't be able to give you more than one a day. It takes so much time."

"But then I shall have to be much slower about it."

"Then I'll only give you one every other day."

"Then I shall be so much the longer."

"Yes," sighed Leonore. "You are obstinate, after all!"

So they went on till breakfast was announced. Perhaps it was foolish. But they were happy in their foolishness, if such it was. It is not profitable to write what they said. It is idle to write of the week that followed. To all others what they said and did could only be the sayings and doings of two very intolerable people. But to them it was what can never be told in words—and to them we will leave it.

It was Leonore who put an end to this week. Each day that Peter lingered brought letter and telegraphic appeals to him from the party-leaders, over which Peter only laughed, and which he not infrequently failed even to answer. But Mr. Pell told Leonore something one day which made her say to Peter later:

"Is it true that you promised to speak in New York on the fifteenth?"

"Yes. But I wrote Green last night saying I shan't."

"And were you to have made a week of speeches through the State?"

"Yes. But I can't spare the time."

"Yes, you can. You must leave to-morrow and make them."

"I can't," groaned Peter.

"You must."

"Who says so?"

"I do. Please, Peter? I so want to see you win. I shall never forgive myself if I defeat you."

"But a whole week," groaned Peter.

"We shall break up here on the eighteenth, and of course you would have to leave a day sooner. So you'll not be any better off."

"Well," sighed Peter, "if I do as you want, will you give me the seven I shall lose before I go?"

"Dear me, Peter," sighed Leonore, "you oughtn't to ask them, since it's for your own sake. I can't keep you contented. You do nothing but encroach."

"I should get them if I was here," said Peter. "And one a day is little enough! I think, if I oblige you by going away, I shouldn't be made to suffer more than is necessary."

"I'm going to call you Growley," said Leonore, patting him on the cheek. Then she put her own against it. "Thank you, dear," she said. "It's just as hard for me."

So Peter buckled on his armor and descended into the arena. Whether he spoke well or ill, we leave it to those to say who care to turn back to the files of the papers of that campaign. Perhaps, however, it may be well to add that an entirely unbiassed person, after reading his opening speeches, delivered in the Cooper Union and the Metropolitan Opera House, in New York City, wrote him: "It is libel to call you Taciturnity. They are splendid! How I wish I could hear you—and see you, dear. I'm very lonely, and so are Bêtise and Tawny-eye. We do nothing but wander round the house all day, waiting for your letter, and the papers." Three thousand people in the Brooklyn Rink were kept waiting for nearly ten minutes by Peter's perusal of that letter. But when he had finished it, and had reached the Rink, he out-Stirlinged Stirling. A speaker nowadays speaks far more to the people absent than to the people present. Peter did this that evening. He spoke, it is true, to only one person that night, but it was the best speech of the campaign.

A week later, Peter rang the bell of the Fifty-seventh

Street house. He was in riding costume, although he had not been riding.

"Mr. and Mrs. D'Alloi are at breakfast," he was informed.

Peter rather hurriedly laid his hat and crop on the hall-table, and went through the hall, but his hurry suddenly came to an end, when a young lady, carrying her napkin, added herself to the vista. "I knew it must be you," she said, offering her hand very properly—(on what grounds Leonore surmised that a ring at the door-bell at nine o'clock meant Peter, history does not state—"I wondered if you knew enough to come to breakfast. Mamma sent me out to say that you are to come right in."

Peter was rather longer over the handshake than convention demands, but he asked very politely, "How are your father and——?" But just then the footman closed a door behind him, and Peter's interest in parents suddenly ceased.

"How could you be so late?" said some one presently. "I watched out of the window for nearly an hour."

"My train was late. The time-table on that road is simply a satire!" said Peter. "Yet it is the best managed road in the country, and this particular train was only seven minutes overdue."

"You have been to ride, though," said Leonore.

"No. I have an engagement to ride with a disagreeable girl after breakfast, so I dressed for it."

"Suppose the disagreeable girl should break her engagement—or declare there never was one?"

"She won't," said Peter. "It may not have been put in the contract, but the common law settles it beyond question."

Leonore laughed a happy laugh. Then she asked: "For whom are those violets?"

"I had to go to four places before I could get any at this season," said Peter. "Ugly girls are just troublesome enough to have preferences. What will you give me for them?"

"Some of them," said Leonore, and obtained the bunch. Who dares to say after that that women have no business ability nor shrewdness? It is true that she kissed the fraction returned before putting it in Peter's button-hole, which raises the question which had the best of the bargain.

"I'm behind the curtain, so I can't see anything," said a voice from a doorway, "and therefore you needn't jump; but I wish to inquire if you two want any breakfast?"

A few days later Peter again went up the steps of the Fifty-seventh Street house. This practice was becoming habitual with Peter; in fact, so habitual that his cabby had said to him this very day, "The old place, sir?" Where Peter got the time it is difficult to understand, considering that his law practice was said to be large, and his political occupations just at present not small. But that is immaterial. The simple fact that Peter went up the steps is the essential truth.

From the steps, he passed into a door; from the door he passed into a hall; from a hall he passed into a room; from a room he passed into a pair of arms.

"Thank the Lord, you've come," Watts remarked. "Leonore has up and down refused to make the tea till you arrived."

"I was at headquarters, and they would talk, talk, talk," said Peter. "I get out of patience with them. One would think the destinies of the human race depended on this campaign!"

"So the Growley should have his tea," said a vision, now seated on the lounge at the tea-table. "Then Growley will feel better."

"I'm doing that already," said Growley, sitting down on the delightfully short lounge—now such a fashionable and deservedly popular drawing-room article. "May I tell you how you can make me absolutely contented?"

"I suppose that will mean some favor from me," said Leonore. "I don't like children who want to be bribed out of their bad temper. Nice little boys are never bad-tempered."

"I was only bad-tempered," whispered Peter, "because I was kept from being with you. That's cause enough to make the best-tempered man in the universe murderous."

"Well?" said Leonore, mollifying, "what is it this time?"

"I want you all to come down to my quarters this evening after dinner. I've received warning that I'm to be serenaded about nine o'clock, and I thought you would like to hear it."

"What fun," cried Leonore. "Of course we'll go. Shall you speak?"

"No. We'll sit in my window-seats merely, and listen."

"How many will there be?"

"It depends on the paper you read. The 'World' will probably say ten thousand, the 'Tribune' three thousand, and the 'Voice of Labor' a handful. Oh! by the way, I brought you a 'Voice'." He handed Leonore a paper, which he took from his pocket.

Now this was simply shameful of him! Peter had found, whenever the papers really abused him, that Leonore was doubly tender to him, the more, if he pretended that the attacks and abuse pained him. So he brought her regularly now that organ of the Labor party which was most vituperative of him, and looked sad over it just as long as was possible, considering that Leonore was trying to comfort him.

"Oh, dear!" said Leonore. "That dreadful paper. I can't bear to read it. Is it very bad to-day?"

"I haven't read it," said Peter, smiling. "I never read" —then Peter coughed, suddenly looked sad, and continued—"the parts that do not speak of me." "That isn't a lie," he told himself, "I don't read them." But he felt guilty. Clearly Peter was losing his old-time straightforwardness.

"After its saying that you had deceived your clients into settling those suits against Mr. Bohlmann, upon his promise to help you in politics, I don't believe they can say anything worse," said Leonore, putting two lumps of sugar (with her fingers) into a cup of tea. Then she stirred the tea, and tasted it. Then the touched the edge of the cup with her lips. "Is that right? " she asked, as she passed it to Peter.

"Absolutely," said Peter, looking the picture of bliss. But then he remembered that this wasn't his rôle, so he looked sad and said: "That hurt me, I confess. It is so unkind."

"Poor dear," whispered a voice. "You shall have an extra one to-day, and you shall take just as long as you want!"

Now, how could mortal man looked grieved, even over an American newspaper, with that prospect in view? It is true that "one" is a very indefinite thing. Perhaps Leonore merely meant another cup of tea. Whatever she meant, Peter never learned, for, barely had he tasted his tea when the girl on the lounge beside him gave a cry. She rose, and as she did so, some of the tea-things fell to the floor with a crash.

"Leonore!" cried Peter. "What——"

"Peter!" cried Leonore. "Say it isn't so?" It was terrible to see the suffering in her face and to hear the appeal in her voice.

"My darling," cried the mother, "what is the matter?"

"It can't be," cried Leonore. "Mamma! Papa! Say it isn't so?"

"What, my darling?" said Peter, supporting the swaying figure.

"This," said Leonore, huskily, holding out the newspaper.

Mrs. D'Alloi snatched it. Once glance she gave it. "Oh, my poor darling!" she cried. "I ought not to have allowed it. Peter! Peter! Was not the stain great enough, but you must make my poor child suffer for it?" She shoved Peter away, and clasped Leonore wildly in her arms.

"Mamma!" cried Leonore. "Don't talk so! Don't! I know he didn't! He couldn't!"

Peter caught up the paper. There in big head-lines was:

SPEAK UP, STIRLING!

WHO IS THIS BOY?

DETECTIVE PELTER FINDS A WARD UNKNOWN
TO THE COURTS, AND EXPLANATIONS ARE
IN ORDER FROM

PURITY STIRLING

The rest of the article it is needless to quote. What it said was so worded as to convey everything vile by innuendo and inference, yet in truth saying nothing.

"Oh, my darling!" continued Mrs. D'Alloi. "You have a right to kill me for letting him come here after he had confessed it to me. But I—oh, don't tremble so. Oh, Watts! We have killed her."

Peter held the paper for a moment. Then he handed it to Watts. He only said "Watts?" but it was a cry for help and mercy as terrible as Leonore's had been the moment before.

"Of course, chum," cried Watts. "Leonore, dear, it's all right. You mustn't mind. Peter's a good man. Better than most of us. You mustn't mind."

"Don't," cried Leonore. "Let me speak. Mamma, did Peter tell you it was so?"

All were silent.

"Mamma! Say something. Papa! Peter! Will nobody speak?"

"Leonore," said Peter, "do not doubt me. Trust me and I will——"

"Tell me," cried Leonore interrupting, "was this why you didn't come to see us? Oh! I see it all! This is what mamma knew. This is what pained you. And I thought it was your love for——!" Leonore screamed.

"My darling," cried Peter wildly, "don't look so. Don't speak——"

"Don't touch me," cried Leonore. "Don't. Only go away." Leonore threw herself upon the rug weeping. It was fearful the way those sobs shook her.

"It can't be," said Peter. "Watts! She is killing herself."

But Watts had disappeared from the room.

"Only go away," cried Leonore. "That's all you can do now. There's nothing to be done."

Peter leaned over and picked up the prostrate figure, and laid it tenderly on the sofa. Then he kissed the edge of her skirt. "Yes. That's all I can do," he said quietly. "Good-bye, sweetheart. I'll go away." He looked about as if bewildered, then passed from the room to the hall, from the hall to the door, from the door to the steps.

He went down them, staggering a little as if dizzy, and tried to walk towards the Avenue. Presently he ran into something. "Clumsy," said a lady's voice. "I beg your pardon," said Peter mechanically. A moment later he ran into something again. "I beg your pardon," said Peter, and two well-dressed girls laughed to see a bare-headed man apologize to a lamp-post. He walked on once more, but had not gone ten paces, when a hand was rested on his shoulder.

"Now then, my beauty," said a voice. "You want to get a cab, or I shall have to run you in. Where do you want to go?"

"I beg your pardon," said Peter.

"Come," said the policeman shaking him, "where do you belong? My God! It's Mr. Stirling. Why, sir. What's the matter?"

"I think I've killed her," said Peter.

"He's awfully screwed," ejaculated the policeman. "And him of all men! Nobody shall know." He hailed a passing cab, and put Peter into it. Then he gave Peter's office address, and also got in. He was fined the next day for being off his beat "without adequate reasons," but he never told where he had been. When they reached the building, he helped Peter into the elevator. From there he helped him to his door. He rang the bell, but no answer came. It was past office-hours, and Jenifer having been told that Peter would dine up-town, had departed on his own leave of absence. The policeman had already gone through Peter's pockets to get money for cabby, and now he repeated the operation, taking possession of Peter's keys. He opened the door and, putting him into a deep chair in the study, laid the purse and keys on Peter's desk, writing on a scrap of paper with much difficulty: "mr. stirling $2.50 I took to pay the carriage. John Motty policeman 22 precinct," he laid it beside the keys and purse. Then he went back to his beat.

And what was Peter doing all this time? Just what he now did. He tried to think, though each eye felt as if a red hot needle was burning in it. Presently he rose, and began to pace the floor, but he kept stumbling over the desk and chairs. As he stumbled he thought, sometimes to himself, sometimes aloud: "If I could only think! I can't see. What was it Dr. Pilcere said about her eyes? Or was it my eyes? Did he give me some medicine? I can't remember. And it wouldn't help her. Why can't I think? What is this pain in her head and eyes? Why does everything look so dark, except when those pains go through her head? They feel like flashes of lightning, and then I can see. Why can't I think? Her eyes get in the way. He gave me something to put on them. But I can't give it to her. She told me to go away. To stop this agony! How she suffers. It's getting worse every moment. I can't remember about the medicine. There it comes again. Now I know. It's not lightning. It's the petroleum! Be quick, boys. Can't you hear my darling scream? It's terrible. If I could only think. What was it the French doctor said to do, if it came back? No. We want to get some rails." Peter dashed himself against a window. "Once more, men, together. Can't you hear her scream? Break down the door!" Peter caught up and hurled a pot of flowers at the window, and the glass shattered and fell to the floor and street. "If I could see. But it's all dark. Are those lights? No. It's too late. I can't save her from it."

So he wandered physically and mentally. Wandered till sounds of martial music came up through the broken window. "Fall in," cried Peter. "The Anarchists are after her. It's dynamite, not lightning. Podds, don't let them hurt her. Save her. Oh! save her! Why can't I get to her? Don't try to hold me," he cried, as he came in contact with a chair. He caught it up and hurled it across the room, so that it crashed into the picture-frames, smashing chair and frames into fragments. "I can't be the one to throw it," he cried, in an agonized voice. "She's all I have. For years I've been so lonely. Don't. I can't throw it. It kills me to see her suffer. It wouldn't be so horrible if I hadn't done it myself. If I didn't love her so. But to blow her up myself. I can't. Men, will you stand by me, and help me to save her?"

The band of music stopped. A moment's silence fell and then up from the street, came the air of: "Marching through Georgia," five thousand voices singing:

"Rally round our party, boys;
Rally to the blue,
And battle for our candidate,
So sterling and true.
Fight for honest government, boys,
And down the vicious crew;
Voting for freedom and Stirling.

"Hurrah, hurrah, for Stirling, brave and strong.
Hurrah, hurrah, for Stirling, never wrong.
And roll the voters up in line,
Two hundred thousand strong;
Voting for freedom and Stirling."

"I can't fight so many. Two hundred thousand! I have no sword. I didn't shoot them. No! I only gave the order. It hurt me, but I didn't mean to hurt her. She's all I have. Do you think I intended to kill her? No! No sacrifice would be too great. And you can talk to me of votes! Two hundred thousand votes! I did my best for her. I didn't mean to hurt her. And I went to see the families. I went to see them all. If I only could think. But she is suffering too much. I can't think as long as she lies on the rug, and trembles so. See the flashes of lightning pass through her head. Don't bury your face in the rug. No wonder it's all dark. Try to think, and then it will be all right."

Up from the street came the air of: "There were three crows," and the words:

"Steven Maguire has schemed to be elected November fourth,
Steven Maguire has schemed to be elected November fourth,
Steven Maguire has schemed and schemed,
    But all his schemes will end in froth!
And the people will all shout, Hurrah, rah, rah, rah.
And the people will all shout, Hurrah, rah, rah, rah.

For Peter Stirling elected will be upon November fourth,
For Peter Stirling elected will be upon November fourth,
For Peter Stirling elected will be
    And Steven Maguire will be in broth,
And the people will all shout, Hurrah, rah, rah, rah,
And the people will all shout, Hurrah, rah, rah, rah."

"It's Steven Maguire. He never could be honest. If I had him here!" Peter came in contact with a chair. "Who's that? Ah! It's you. You've killed her. Now!"

And another chair went flying across the room with such force, that the door to the hall flew off its hinges, and fell with a crash. "I've killed him," screamed Peter. "I've— No, I've killed my darling. All I have in the world!"

And so he raved, and roamed, and stumbled, and fell; and rose, and roamed, and raved, and stumbled, and fell, while the great torchlight procession sang and cheered him from below.

He was wildly fighting his pain still when two persons, who, after ringing and ringing, had finally been let in by Jenifer's key, stood where the door had been.

"My God," cried one, in terror. "He's crazy! Come away!"

But the other, without a word or sign of fear, went up to that wild-looking figure, and put her hand in his.

Peter stopped his crazed stride.

"I can't think, I tell you. I can't think as long as you lie there on the rug. And your eyes blaze so. They feel just like balls of fire."

"Please sit down, Peter. Please? For my sake. Here. Here is the chair. Please sit down."

Peter sank back in the chair. "I tell you I can't think. They do nothing but burn. It's the petroleum!" He started forward, but a slender arm arrested his attempt to rise, and he sank back again as if it had some power over him.

"Hyah, miss. Foh de lub ub heaben, put some ub dis yar on he eyes," said Jenifer, who had appeared with a bottle, and was blubbering enough to supply a whole whaling fleet. "De doctor he done give dis yar foh de Aspic nerve." Which is a dish that Jenifer must have invented himself, for it is not discoverable even on the fullest of menus.

Leonore knelt in front of Peter, and, drenching her fingers with the wash, began rubbing it softly over his eyes. It has always been a problem whether it was the remedy or the ends of those fingers which took those lines of suffering out of Peter's face and made him sit quietly in that chair. Those having little faith in medicines, and much faith in a woman's hands, will opine the latter. Doctors will not.

Sufficeth it to say, after ten minutes of this treatment, during which Peter's face had slowly changed, first to a look of rest, and then to one which denoted eagerness, doubt and anxiety, but not pain, that he finally put out his hands and took Leonore's.

"You have come to me," he said. "Has he told you?"

"Who? What?" asked Leonore.

"You still think I could?" cried Peter. "Then why are you here?" He opened his eyes wildly and would have risen, only Leonore was kneeling in front of the chair still.

"Don't excite yourself, Peter," begged Leonore. "We'll not talk of that now. Not till you are better."

"What are you here for?" cried Peter. "Why did you come——?"

"Oh, please, Peter, be quiet."

"Tell me, I will have it." Peter was exciting himself, more from Leonore's look than by what she said.

"Oh, Peter. I made papa bring me—because—oh! I wanted to ask you to do something. For my sake!"

"What is it?"

"I wanted to ask you," sobbed Leonore, "to marry her. Then I shall always think you were what I—I—have been loving, and not——" Leonore laid her head down on his knee, and sobbed bitterly.

Peter raised Leonore in his arms, and laid the little head on his shoulder.

"Dear one," he said, "do you love me?"

"Yes," sobbed Leonore.

"And do you think I love you?"

"Yes."

"Now look into your heart. Could you tell me a lie?"

"No."

"Nor can I you. I am not the father of that boy, and I never wronged his mother."

"But you told——" sobbed Leonore.

"I lied to your mother, dear."

"For what?" Leonore had lifted her head, and there was a look of hope in her eyes, as well as of doubt.

"Because it was better at that time than the truth. But Watts will tell you that I lied."

"Papa."

"Yes, Dot. Dear old Peter speaks the truth."

"But if you lied to her, why not to me?"

"I can't lie to you, Leonore. I am telling you the truth. Won't you believe me?"

"I do," cried Leonore. "I know you speak the truth. It's in your face and voice." And the next moment her arms were about Peter's neck, and her lips were on his.

Just then some one in the "torchlight" shouted: "What's the matter wid Stirling?"

And a thousand voices joyfully yelled:

"He's all right."

And so was the crowd.

CHAPTER LX

A CONUNDRUM

MR. PIERCE was preparing to talk. Usually Mr. Pierce was talking. Mr. Pierce had been talking already, but it had been to single listeners only, and for quite a time in the last three hours Mr. Pierce had been compelled to be silent. But at last Mr. Pierce believed his moment had come. Mr. Pierce thought he had an audience, and a plastic audience at that. And these three circumstances in combination made Mr. Pierce fairly bubbling with words. No longer would he have to waste his precious wit and wisdom, *tête-à-tête,* or on himself.

At first blush Mr. Pierce seemed right in his conjecture. Seated—in truth, collapsed, on chairs and lounges, in a disarranged and untidy-looking drawing-room, were nearly twenty very tired-looking people. The room looked as if there had just been a free fight there, and the people looked as if they had been the participants. But the multitude of flowers and the gay dresses proved beyond question that something else had made the disorder of the room and had put that exhausted look upon the faces.

Experienced observers would have understood it at a glimpse. From the work and fatigues of this world, people had gathered for a little enjoyment of what we call society. It is true that both the room and its occupants did not indicate that there had been much recreation. But, then, one can lay it down as an axiom that the people who work for pleasure are the hardest-working people in the world; and, as it is that for which society labors, this scene is but another proof that they get very much fatigued over their pursuit of happiness and enjoyment, considering that they hunt for it in packs, and entirely exclude the most delicious intoxicant known—usually called oxygen—from their list of supplies from the caterer. Certainly this particular group did look exhausted far beyond the speech-making point. But this, too, was a deception. These limp-looking individuals had only remained in this drawing-room for the sole purpose of "talking it over," and Mr. Pierce had no walk-over before him.

Mr. Pierce cleared his throat and remarked: "The development of marriage customs and ceremonies from primeval days is one of the most curious and——"

"What a lovely wedding it has been!" said Dorothy, heaving a sigh of fatigue and pleasure combined.

"Wasn't it!" went up a chorus from the whole party, except Mr. Pierce, who looked eminently disgusted.

"As I was remarking——" began Mr. Pierce again.

"But the best part," said Watts, who was lolling on one of the lounges, "was those 'sixt' ward presents. As Mr. Moriarty said: 'Begobs, it's hard it would be to find the equal av that tureen!' He was right! Its equal for ugliness is inconceivable."

"Yet the poor beggars spent eight hundred dollars on it," sighed Lispenard, wearily.

"Relative to the subject——" said Mr. Pierce.

"And Leonore told me," said a charmingly-dressed girl, "that she liked it better than any other present she had received."

"Oh, she was more enthusiastic," laughed Watts, "over all the 'sixt' ward and political presents than she was over what we gave her. We weren't in it at all with the Micks. She has come out as much a worshipper of hoi-polloi as Peter."

"I don't believe she cares a particle for them," said

our old friend, the gentlemanly scoundrel; "but she worships them because they worship him."

"Well," sighed Lispenard, "that's the way things go in life. There's that fellow gets worshipped by every one, from the Irish saloon-keeper up to Leonore. While look at me! I'm a clever, sweet-tempered, friendly sort of a chap, but nobody worships me. There isn't any one who gives a second thought for yours truly. I seem good for nothing, except being best man to much luckier chaps. While look at Peter! He's won the love of a lovely girl, who worships him to a degree simply inconceivable. I never saw such idealization."

"Then you haven't been watching Peter," said Mrs. D'Alloi, who, as a mother, had no intention of having it supposed that Leonore was not more loved than loving.

"Taking modern marriage as a basis——" said Mr. Pierce.

"Oh," laughed Dorothy, "there's no doubt they are a pair, and I'm very proud of it, because I did it."

"Cock-a-doodle-doo!" crowed Ray.

"I did," said Dorothy, "and my own husband is not the one to cast reflection on my statement."

"He's the only one who dares," said Ogden.

"Well, I did. Leonore would never have cared for such a silent, serious man if I hadn't shown her that other women did, and——"

"Nonsense," laughed Ogden. "It was Podds did it. Dynamite is famous for the uncertainty of the direction in which it will expend its force, and in this case it blew in a circle, and carried Leonore's heart clear from Newport to Peter."

"Or, to put it scientifically," said Lispenard, "along the line of least resistance."

"It seems to me that Peter was the one who did it," said Le Grand. "But of course, as a bachelor, I can't expect my opinion to be accepted."

"No," said Dorothy. "He nearly spoiled it by cheapening himself. No girl will think a man is worth much who lets her tramp on him."

"Still," said Lispenard, "few girls can resist the flattery of being treated by a man as if she is the only woman worth considering in the world, and Peter did that to an extent which was simply disgraceful. It was laughable to see the old hermit become social the moment she appeared, and to see how his eyes and attention followed her. And his learning to dance! That showed how things were."

"He began long before any of you dreamed," said Mrs. D'Alloi. "Didn't he, Watts?"

"Undoubtedly," laughed Watts. "And so did she. I really think Leonore did quite as much in her way, as Peter did. I never saw her treat any one quite as she behaved to Peter from the very first. I remember her coming in after her runaway, wild with enthusiasm over him, and saying to me 'Oh, I'm so happy. I've got a new friend, and we are going to be such friends always!'"

"That raises the same question," laughed Ogden, "that the Irishman did about the street-fight, when he asked 'Who throwed that last brick first?'"

"Really, if it didn't seem too absurd," said Watts, "I should say they began it the moment they met."

"I don't think that at all absurd," said a gray-haired, refined looking woman who was the least collapsed of the group, or was perhaps so well bred as to conceal her feelings. "I myself think it began before they even met. Leonore was half in love with Peter when she was in Europe, and Peter, though he knew nothing of her, was the kind of a man who imagines an ideal and loves that. She happened to be his ideal."

"Really, Miss De Voe," said Mr. Pierce, "you must have misjudged him. Though Peter is now my grandson, I am still able to know what he is. He is not at all the kind of man who allows himself to be controlled by an ideal."

"I do not feel that I have ever known Peter. He does not let people perceive what is underneath," said Miss De Voe. "But of one thing I am sure. Nearly everything he does is done from sentiment. At heart he is an idealist."

"Oh!" cried several.

"That is a most singular statement," said Mr. Pierce. "There is not a man I know who has less of the sentimental and ideal in him. An idealist is a man of dreams and romance. Peter is far too sensible a fellow to be that. There is nothing heroic or romantic in him."

"Nonsense, *Paternus*," said Watts. "You don't know anything about the old chap. You've only seen him as a cool clever lawyer. If your old definition of romance is right: that it is 'Love, and the battle between good and evil,' Peter has had more true romance than all the rest of us put together."

"No," said Mr. Pierce. "You have merely seen Peter in love, and so you all think he is romantic. He isn't. He is a cool man, who never acts without weighing his actions, and therein has lain the secret of his success. He calmly marks out his line of life, and, regardless of everything else, pursues it. He disregards everything not to his purpose, and utilizes everything that serves. I predicted great success for him many years ago when he was fresh from college, simply from a study of his mental characteristics and I have proved myself a prophet. He has never made a slip, legally, politically, or socially. To use a yachting expression, he has 'made everything draw.' An idealist, or a man of romance and fire and impulse could never succeed as he has done. It is his entire lack of feeling which has led to his success. Indeed——"

"I can't agree with you," interrupted Dorothy, sitting up from her collapse as if galvanized into life and speech by Mr. Pierce's monologue. "You don't understand Peter. He is a man of great feeling. Think of that speech of his about those children! Think of his conduct to his mother as long as she lived! Think of the goodness and kindness he showed to the poor! Why, Ray says he has refused case after case for want of time in recent years, while doing work for people in his ward which was worth nothing. If——"

"They were worth votes," interjected Mr. Pierce.

"Look at his buying the Costell place in Westchester when Mr. Costell died so poor, and giving it to Mrs. Costell," continued Dorothy, warming with her subject. "Look at his going to those strikers' families, and arranging to help them. Were those things done for votes? If I could only tell you of something he once did for me, you would not say that he was a man without feeling."

"I have no doubt," said Mr. Pierce blandly, "that he did many things which, on their face, seemed admirable and to indicate feeling. But if carefully examined, they would be found to have been advantageous to him. Any service he could have done to Mrs. Rivington surely did not harm him. His purchase of Costell's place pleased the political friends of the dead leader. His aiding the strikers' families placated the men, and gained him praise from the press. I dislike greatly to oppose this rose-colored view of Peter, but, from my own knowledge of the man, I must. He is without feeling, and necessarily makes no mistakes, nor is he led off from his own ambitions by sentiment of any kind. When we had that meeting with the strikers, he sat there, while all New York was seething, with mobs and dead just outside the walls, as cool and impassive as a machine. He was simply determined that we should compromise, because his own interests demanded it, and he carried his point merely because he was the one cool man at that meeting. If he had had feeling he could not have been cool. That one incident shows the key-note of his success."

"And I say his strong sympathies and feeling were the key-note," reiterated Dorothy.

"I think," said Pell, "that Peter's great success lay in his ability to make friends. It was simply marvellous. I've seen it, over and over again, both in politics and society. He never seemed to excite envy or bitterness. He had a way of doing things which made people like him. Every one he meets trusts him. Yet nobody understands him. So he interests people, without exciting hostility. I've heard person after person say that he was an uninteresting, ordinary man, and yet nobody ever seemed to forget him. Every one of us feels, I am sure, that, as Miss De Voe says, he had within something he never showed people. I have never been able to see why he did or did not do hundreds of things. Yet it always turned out that what he did was right. He makes me think of the Frenchwoman who said to her sister, 'I don't know why it is, sister, but I never meet any one who's always right but myself.'"

"You have hit it," said Ogden Ogden, "and I can prove

that you have by Peter's own explanation of his success. I spoke to him once of a rather curious line of argument, as it seemed to me, which he was taking in a case, and he said: "Ogden, I take that course because it is the way Judge Potter's mind acts. If you want to convince yourself, take the arguments which do that best, but when you have to deal with judges or juries, take the lines which fit their capacities. People talk about my unusual success in winning cases. It's simply because I am not certain that my way and my argument are the only way and the only argument. I've studied the judges closely, so that I know what lines to take, and I always notice what seems to interest the jury most, in each case. But, more important than this study, is the fact that I can comprehend about how the average man will look at a certain thing. You see I am the son of plain people. Then I am meeting all grades of mankind, and hearing what they say, and getting their points of view. I have never sat in a closet out of touch with the world and decided what is right for others, and then spent time trying to prove it to them. In other words, I have succeeded, because I am merely the normal or average man, and therefore am understood by normal or average people, or by majorities, to put it in another way.'"

"But Mr. Stirling isn't a commonplace man," said another of the charmingly dressed girls. "He is very silent, and what he says isn't at all clever, but he's very unusual and interesting."

"Nevertheless," said Ogden, "I believe he was right. He has a way of knowing what the majority of people think or feel about things. And that is the secret of his success, and not his possession or lack of feeling."

"You none of you have got at the true secret of Peter's success," said Ray. "It was his wonderful capacity for work. To a lazy beggar like myself it is marvellous. I've known that man to work from nine in the morning till one at night, merely stopping for meals."

"Yet he did not seem an ambitious man," said Le Grand. "He cared nothing for social success, he never has accepted office till now, and he has refused over and over again law work which meant big money."

"No," said Ray. "Peter worked hard in law and politics. Yet he didn't want office or money. He could more than once have been a judge, and Costell wanted him governor six years ago. He took the nomination this year against his own wishes. He cared as little for money or reputation in law, as he cared for society, and would compromise cases which would have added greatly to his reputation if he had let them go to trial. He might have been worth double what he is to-day, if he had merely invested his money, instead of letting it lie in savings banks or trust companies. I've spoken about it repeatedly to him, but he only said that he wasn't going to spend time taking care of money, for money ceased to be valuable when it had to be taken care of; its sole use to him being to have it take care of him. I think he worked for the sake of working."

"That explains Peter, certainly. His one wish was to help others," said Miss De Voe. "He had no desire for reputation or money, and so did not care to increase either."

"And mark my words," said Lispenard. "From this day, he'll set no limit to his endeavors to obtain both."

"He can't work harder than he has to get political power," said an usher. "Think of how anxious he must have been to get it, when he would spend so much time in the slums and saloons! He couldn't have liked the men he met there."

"I've taken him to task about that, and told him he had no business to waste his time so," said Ogden; "but he said that he was not taking care of other people's money or trying to build up a great business, and that if he chose to curtail his practice, so as to have some time to work in politics, it was a matter of personal judgment."

"I once asked Peter," said Miss De Voe, "how he could bear, with his tastes and feelings, to go into saloons, and spend so much time with politicians, and with the low, uneducated people of his district. He said, 'That is my way of trying to do good, and it is made enjoyable to me by helping men over rough spots, or by preventing political wrong. I have taken the world and humanity as it is, and have done what I could, without stopping to criti-

cise or weep over shortcomings and sins. I admire men
who stand for noble impossibilities. But I have given
my own life to the doing of small possibilities. I don't
say the way is the best. But it is my way, for I am a
worker, not a preacher. And just because I have been
willing to do things as the world is willing to have them
done, power and success have come to me to do more.'
I believe it was because Peter had no wish for worldly
success, that it came to him."

"You are all wrong," groaned Lispenard. "I love
Peter as much as I love my own kin, with due apology to
those of it who are present, but I must say that his whole
career has been the worst case of sheer, downright luck
of which I ever saw or heard."

"Luck!" exclaimed Dorothy.

"Yes, luck!" said Lispenard. "Look at it. He starts
in like all the rest of us. And Miss Luck calls him in to
look at a sick kitten die. Very ordinary occurrence that!
Health-board report several hundred every week. But
Miss Luck knew what she was about and called him in to
just the right kind of a kitten to make a big speech about.
Thereupon he makes it, blackguarding and wiping the
floor up with a millionaire brewer. Does the brewer wait
for his turn to get even with him? Not a bit. Miss Luck
takes a hand in and the brewer falls on Peter's breast-bone,
and loves him ever afterwards. My cousin writes him,
and he snubs her. Does she annihilate him as she would
have other men? No. Miss Luck has arranged all that,
and they become the best of friends."

"Lispenard—" Miss De Voe started to interrupt indignantly, but Lispenard continued, "Hold on till I finish.
One at a time. Well. Miss Luck gets him chosen to a
convention by a fluke and Peter votes against Costell's
wishes. What happens? Costell promptly takes him up
and pushes him for all he's worth. He snubs society,
and society concludes that a man who is more snubby
and exclusive than itself must be a man to cultivate. He
refuses to talk, and every one promptly says: 'How
interesting he is!' He gets in the way of a dynamite
bomb. Does it kill him? Certainly not. Miss Luck
has put an old fool there, to protect him. He swears a

bad word. Does it shock respectable people? No! Every one breathes easier, and likes him the better. He enrages and shoots the strikers. Does he lose votes? Not one. Miss Luck arranges that the directors shall yield things which they had sworn not to yield; and the strikers are reconciled and print a card in praise of him. He runs for office. Do the other parties make a good fight of it? No. They promptly nominate a scoundrelly demagogue and a nonentity who thinks votes are won by going about in shirtsleeves. So he is elected by the biggest plurality the State has ever given. Has Miss Luck done enough? No. She at once sets every one predicting that he'll get the presidential nomination two years from now, if he cares for it. Be it friend or enemy, intentional or unintentional, every one with whom he comes in contact gives him a boost. While look at me! There isn't a soul who ever gave me help. It's been pure, fire-with-your-eyes-shut luck."

"Was this morning luck too?" asked a bridesmaid.

"Absolutely," sighed Lispenard. "And what luck! I always said that Peter would never marry, because he would insist on taking women seriously, and because at heart he was afraid of them to a woeful degree, and showed it in such a way, as simply to make women think he didn't like them individually. But Miss Luck wouldn't allow that. Oh, no! Miss Luck isn't content even that Peter shall take his chance of getting a wife, with the rest of us. She's not going to have any accidents for him. So she takes the loveliest of girls, and trots her all over Europe, so that she shan't have friends, or even know men well. She arranges, too, that the young girl shall have her head filled with Peter by a lot of admiring women, who are determined to make him into a sad, unfortunate hero, instead of the successful man he is. A regular conspiracy to delude a young girl. Then before the girl has seen anything of the world, she trots her over here. Does she introduce them at a dance, so that Peter shall be awkward and silent? Not she! She puts him where he looks his best—on a horse. She starts the thing off romantically, so that he begins on the most intimate footing, before another man has left his pasteboard. So he's way ahead of the pack when they open cry. Is that enough? No! At the critical moment he is called to the aid of his country. Gets lauded for his pluck. Gets blown up. Gets everything to make a young girl worship him. Pure luck! It doesn't matter what Peter says or does. Miss Luck always arranges that it turn up the winning card."

"There is no luck in it," cried Mr. Pierce. "It was all due to his foresight and shrewdness. He plans things beforehand, and merely presses the button. Why, look at his marriage alone. Does he fall in love early in life, and hamper himself with a Miss Nobody? Not he! He waits till he has achieved a position where he can pick from the best, and then he does exactly that, if you'll pardon a doting grandfather's saying it."

"Well," said Watts, "we have all known Peter long enough to have found out what he is, yet there seems to be a slight divergence of opinion. Are we fools, or is Peter a gay deceiver?"

"He is the most outspoken man I ever knew," said Miss De Voe.

"But he tells nothing," said an usher.

"Yes. He is absolutely silent," said a bridesmaid.

"Except when he's speechifying," said Ray.

"And Leonore says he talks and jokes a great deal," said Watts.

"I never knew any one who is deceiving herself so about a man," said Dorothy. "It's terrible. What do you think she had the face to say to me to-day?"

"What?"

"She was speaking of their plans after returning from the wedding journey, and she said: 'I am going to have Peter keep up his bachelor quarters.' 'Does he say he'll do it?' I asked. 'I haven't spoken to him,' she replied, 'but of course he will.' I said: 'Leonore, all women think they rule their husbands, but they don't in reality, and Peter will be less ruled than any man I know.' Then what do you think she said?"

"Don't keep us in suspense."

"She said: 'None of you ever understood Peter. But I do.' Think of it! From that little chit, who's known

Peter half the number of months that I've known him years!"

"I don't know," sighed Lispenard. "I'm not prepared to say it isn't so. Indeed, after seeing Peter, who never seemed able to understand women till this one appeared on the scene, develop into a regulation lover, I am quite prepared to believe that every one knows more than I do. At the same time, I can't afford to risk my reputation for discrimination and insight over such a simple thing as Peter's character. You've all tried to say what Peter is. Now I'll tell you in two words and you'll all find you are right, and you'll all find you are wrong."

"You are bad as Leonore," cried Dorothy.

"Well," said Watts, "we are all listening. What is Peter?"

"He is an extreme type of a man far from uncommon in this country, yet who has never been understood by foreigners, and by few Americans."

"Well?"

"Peter is a practical idealist."

CHAPTER LXI

LEONORE'S THEORY

AND how well had that "talk-it-over" group at the end of Peter's wedding-day grasped his character? How clearly do we ever gain an insight into the feelings and motives which induce conduct even in those whom we best know and love? Each had found something in Peter that no other had discovered. We speak of rose-colored glasses, and Shakespeare wrote, "All things are yellow to a jaundiced eye." When we take a bit of blue glass, and place it with yellow, it becomes green. When we put it with red, it becomes purple. Yet blue it is all the time. Is not each person responsible for the tint he seems to produce in others? Can we ever learn that the thing is blue, and that the green or purple aspect is only the tinge which we ourselves help to give? Can we ever learn that we love and are loved entirely as we give ourselves colors which may harmonize with those about us? That love, wins love; kindness, kindness; hate, hate? That just such elements as we give to the individual, the individual gives back to us? That the sides we show are the sides seen by the world? There were people who could truly believe that Peter was a ward boss; a frequenter of saloons; a drunkard; a liar; a swearer; a murderer, in intention, if not in act; a profligate; and a compromiser of many of his own strongest principles. Yet there were people who could say other things of him.

But more important than the opinion of Peter's friends, and of the world, was the opinion of Peter's wife. Was she right in her theory that she was the only one who understood him? Or had she, as he had once done, reared an ideal, and given that ideal the love which she supposed she was giving Peter? It is always a problem in love to say whether we love people most for the qualities they actually possess, or for those with which our own love endows them. Here was a young girl, inexperienced in world and men, joyfully sinking her own life in that of a man whom, but a few months before, had been only a matter of hearsay to her. Yet she had apparently taken him, as women will, for better, for worse, till death, as trustfully as if he and men generally were as knowable as A B C, instead of as unknown as the algebraic X. Only once had she faltered in her trust of him, and then but for a moment. How far had her love, and the sight of Peter's misery, led her blindly to renew that trust? And would it hold? She had seen how little people thought of that scurrilous article, and how the decent papers had passed it over without a word. But she had also seen the scandal harped upon by partisans and noted that Peter failed to vindicate himself publicly, or vouchsafe an explanation to her. Had she taken Peter with trust or doubt, knowledge or blindness?

Perhaps a conversation between the two, a week later, will answer these questions. It occurred on the deck of a vessel. Yet this parting glimpse of Peter is very different from that which introduced him. The vessel is not drifting helplessly, but its great screw is whirling it towards the island of Martinique, as if itself anxious to reach that fairy land of fairy lands. Though the middle of November, the soft warmth of the tropics is in the air. Nor are the sea and sky now leaden. The first is turned into liquid gold by the phosphorescence, and the full moon silvers everything else. Neither is Peter pacing the deck with lines of pain and endurance on his face. He is up in the bow, where the vessel's forefoot throws up the white foam in silver drops in the moonlight. And he does not look miserable. Anything but that. He is sitting on an anchor stock, with his back comfortably braced against the rail. Another person is not far distant. What that person sits upon and leans against is immaterial to the narrative.

"Why don't you smoke?" asked that person.

"I'm too happy," said Peter, in a voice evidencing the truth of his words.

"Will you if I bite off the end?" asked Eve, Jr., placing temptation most temptingly.

"I like the idea exceedingly," said Peter. "But my right arm is so very pleasantly placed that it objects to moving."

"Don't move it. I know where they are. I even know about the matches." And Peter sat calmly while his pockets were picked. He even seemed to enjoy the sensation of that small hand rummaging in his waistcoat pockets. "You see, dear, that I am learning your ways," Leonore continued, in a tone of voice which suggested that that was the chief end of woman. Perhaps it is. The Westminster catechism only tells us the chief end of man.

"There. Now are you really happy?"

"I don't know anybody more so."

"Then, dear, I want to talk with you."

"The wish is reciprocal. But what have we been doing for six days?"

"We've been telling each other everything, just as we ought. But now I want to ask two favors, dear."

"I don't think that's necessary. Just tell me what they are."

"Yes. These favors are. Though I know you'll say 'yes.'"

"Well?"

"First. I want you always to keep your rooms just as they are."

"Dear-heart, after our six weeks' trip, we must be in Albany for three years, and when we come back to New York, we'll have a house of course."

"Yes. But I want you to keep the rooms just as they are, because I love them. I don't think I shall ever feel the same for any other place. It will be very convenient to have them whenever we want to run down from Albany. And of course you must keep up with the ward."

"But you don't suppose, after we are back in New York, that I'll stay down there, with you uptown?"

"Oh, no! Of course not. Peter! How absurd you are! But I shall go down very often. Sometimes we'll give little dinners to real friends. And sometimes, when we want to get away from people, we'll dine by ourselves and spend the night there. Then whenever you want to be at the saloons or primaries we'll dine together there and I'll wait for you. And then I think I'll go down sometimes, when I'm shopping, and lunch with you. I'll promise not to bother you. You shall go back to your work, and I'll amuse myself with your flowers, and books, till you are ready to go uptown. Then we'll ride together."

"Lispenard frightened me the other day, but you frighten me worse."

"How?"

"He said you would be a much lovelier woman at thirty than you are now."

"And that frightened you?" laughed Leonore.

"Terribly. If you are that I shall have to give up law and politics entirely, so as to see enough of you."

"But what has that to do with my lunching with you?"

"Do you think I could work at law with you in the next room?"

"Don't you want me? I thought it was such a nice plan."

"It is. If your other favor is like that I shan't know what to say. I shall merely long for you to ask favors."

"This is very different. Will you try to understand me?"

"I shan't misunderstand you, at all events." Which was a crazy speech for any man to make any woman.

"Then, dear, I want to speak of that terrible time— only for a moment, dear. You mustn't think I don't believe what you said. I do! I do! Every word of it, and to prove it to you I shall never speak of it again. But when I've shown you that I trust you entirely, some stormy evening, when we've had the nicest little dinner together at your rooms, and I've given you some coffee, and bitten your cigar for you, I shall put you down before the fire, and sit down in your lap, as I am doing now, and put my arms about your neck so, and put my cheek so. And then I want you, without my asking, to tell me why you told mamma that lie, and all about it."

"Dear-heart," said Peter, "I cannot tell. I promised."

"Oh, but that didn't include your wife, dear, of course. Besides, Peter, friends should tell each other everything. And we are the best of friends, aren't we?"

"And if I don't tell my dearest friend?"

"I shall never speak of it, Peter, but I know sometimes when I am by myself I shall cry over it. Not because I doubt you, dear, but because you won't give me your confidence."

"Do you know, Dear-heart, that I can't bear the thought of your doing that!"

"Of course not, dear. That's the reason I tell you. I knew you couldn't bear it."

"How did you know?"

"Because I understand you, dear. I know just what you are. I'm the only person who does."

"Tell me what I am."

"I think, dear, that something once came into your life that made you very miserable, and took away all your hope and ambition. So, instead of trying to make a great position or fortune, you tried to do the most good to others. You found that you could do the most good among the poor people, so you worked among them. Then you found that you needed money, so you worked hard to get that. Then you found that you could help most by working in politics, so you did that. And you have tried to gain power so as to increase your power for good. I know you haven't liked a great deal you have had to do. I know that you much prefer to sit before your study-fire and read than sit in saloons. I know that you would rather keep away from tricky people than to ask or take their help. But you have sacrificed your own feelings and principles because you felt that they were not to be considered if you could help others. And, because people have laughed at you or misunderstood, you have become silent and unsocial, except as you have believed your mixing with the world to be necessary to accomplish good."

"What a little idealist we are!"

"Well, dear, that isn't all the little idealist has found out. She knows something else. She knows that all his life her ideal has been waiting and longing for some one who did understand him, so that he can tell her all his hopes and feelings, and that at last he has found her, and she will try to make up for all the misery and sacrifice he has endured. She knows, too, that he wants to tell her everything. You mustn't think, dear, that it was only prying which made me ask you so many questions. I— I really wasn't curious except to see if you would answer, for I felt that you didn't tell other people your real thoughts and feelings, and so, whenever you told me, it was really getting you to say that you loved me. You wanted me to know what you really are. And that was why I knew that you told me the truth that night. And that is the reason why I know that some day you will tell me about that lie."

Peter, whatever he might think, did not deny the correctness of Leonore's theories concerning his motives in the past or his conduct in the future. He kissed the soft cheek so near him, tenderly, and said:

"I like your thoughts about me, dear one."

"Of course you do," said Leonore. "You said once that when you had a fine subject it was always easy to make a fine speech. It's true, too, of thoughts, dear."

THE END

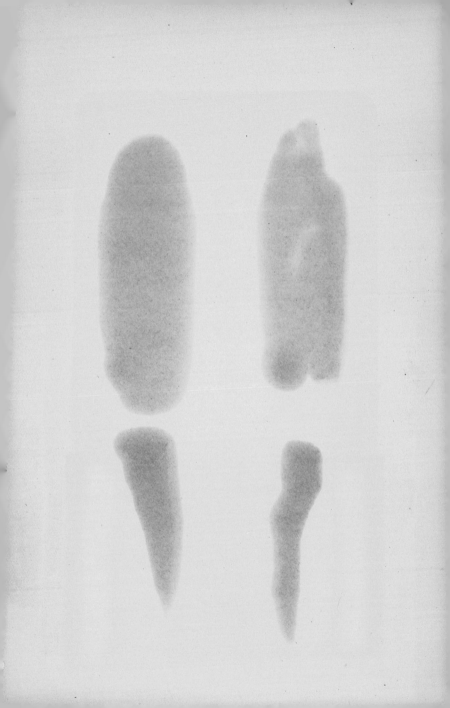

DATE DUE

GAYLORD   PRINTED IN U.S.A.